THE VIENNE/E DRE//MAKER

A Haunting Story
of Wartime Vienna

KATHRYN GAUCI

First published in 2022 by Ebony Publishing

ISBN: 9798408275670

"Deprive the average human being of his illusion in life and you rob him of his happiness."

The Wild Ducks — Henrik Ibsen

CONTENTS

CHAPTER 1

The Night of Broken Glass.

LEOPOLDSTADT, VIENNA. NOVEMBER 9, 1938

MIRKA ROSEN WAS adding the last touches of beading to the neckline of Fräulein Christina Lehmann's blue silk dress when she heard what sounded like a loud explosion coming from the direction of the synagogue. All night there had been strange noises of one sort or another, often interspersed by screams which sent shivers down her spine. This one was different. She looked anxiously at Hannah, her sixteen-year-old daughter, and then at her watch. It was 11:00 p.m. Against her wishes, her son, Nathan, had gone out earlier that evening and had not returned. She was worried about him.

'Mutti,' Hannah said, her voice bearing more than a hint of fear. 'What was that noise?'

Mirka drew back the curtains and looked out of the window. Their apartment was on the third floor of a tenement block in Zirkusgasse. They weren't rich enough to have a view of the street. Instead they overlooked a pokey yard and other narrow and oblique apartments in the rat-infested hovel that passed for their home. As a rule, the view at night-time was of softly lit rooms, their inhabitants moving around like shadows in a space barely large enough to swing a cat around, let alone house an entire family. On a full moon, this scene widened, taking in the uneven tiled roofs and distant spire of a church. Tonight was one such night. Unfettered by clouds, a beautiful, silver gibbous moon hung over Vienna, a great luminous pearl highlighting the rooftops of Leopoldstadt like an expressionist theatrical backdrop. To her horror, the velvet black sky started to change colour, steadily taking on an eerie red glow.

Hannah threw aside her sewing and ran to her mother's side. 'What's happening? Are there fireworks?'

Mirka held her daughter tightly. In a matter of minutes, the moon was veiled in clouds of billowing smoke and the sky was a glow of orange and red streaks.

'No, my darling,' she replied, fighting back tears. 'Those are not fireworks. The synagogue is on fire.'

Hannah's eyes widened with panic. 'Nathan,' she screamed. 'He's still out. We must find him.'

Before her mother could reply, they heard someone banging loudly on a door downstairs.

'God in heaven!' Mirka grabbed her shawl and ran to the door. 'Stay here. Whatever you do, don't come out. Look after your sister.' She gestured towards the small child lying asleep on a makeshift bed. 'Take Malka upstairs and stay there.'

'Mutti!' Hannah shouted, but it was too late. Mirka Rosen was already running down the stairs.

Hannah grabbed her little sister, quickly carried her up a narrow flight of steps to the attic and laid her on her bed. Sleepily, the child rubbed her eyes. After coaxing her back to sleep and placing her beloved doll, Pipina, on the pillow next to her, Hannah covered her with thick blankets and left the attic, locking the door behind her. She ran outside the apartment to the landing and peered down the narrow flights of stairs. In the dimly lit hallway below, she could see her mother trying to soothe a hysterical Frau Weber, their landlady and owner of the hat store that occupied the ground floor. She lived on the first floor above the premises. In the street, someone banged on the outside door, shouting for the occupants to open up.

The loud sound of shattering glass told Hannah that someone had smashed the window to the hat shop. Frau Weber let out a piercing scream and ran to unlock the door. Mirka tried desperately to stop her, but it was no use. As soon as she pulled back the latch, the door flew open, knocking Frau Weber to the ground. Two men carrying sticks burst into the hallway and made their way up the stairs. Mirka turned on her heels and fled back to her apartment with one of the men running after her.

'Quickly,' Mirka said to her daughter. 'Hide!'

'Hide where?' said a terrified Hannah.

With only seconds to spare before the man barged into the room, Mirka pushed her daughter underneath the cutting table and pulled down its long protective felt cover to hide her. From her dark hideout, Hannah could just see her mother's ankles and her beautiful dark brown leather shoes with the gold trim. With her eyes fixed on the shoes, she watched her mother run to the far side of the table. The door burst open and Hannah's eyes now focused on a pair of men's heavy brown combat boots.

'Saujud,' the man said, his voice full of hatred. 'Jewish pig!'

'Get out,' Mirka screamed. She hurled something at him – a heavy wooden box filled with sewing tools. It missed and hit the wall, showering the floor with thimbles, small scissors, tape-measures, and a tin of pins.

'Saujud,' he said again. 'You will be sorry you did that.'

Her mother threw something else at him. This time it was the heavy tailor's ham filled with sawdust. It hit him with a thud which only served to anger him more. Crouching in absolute terror, her heart beating so loudly she thought it would burst, Hannah watched on helplessly as the man strode across the room towards her mother. Mirka tried to run but the man was too quick and grabbed her. She started to fight. There was a dull thud and the man let out a loud cry. Hannah saw him take a few steps backwards. An iron dropped to the floor.

'You bitch! You'll pay for that.'

The man lashed out, smacking Mirka across the face. A scuffle ensued, in which the mannequin with Fräulein Lehmann's dress crashed to the ground, ending up only inches away from the edge of the cutting table. Hannah listened helplessly to her mother's screams, all the while focusing on their feet which moved about like a devilish Mephisto Waltz dance scene. The man lashed out again. In a desperate attempt to beat off her attacker, Mirka grabbed a pair of cutting scissors and stabbed the man in the lower neck. He screamed out in pain, momentarily releasing his grip.

Mirka went to strike again, but the man was too quick. He wrenched the scissors out of her hand and aimed his gun at her. In her dark hideout, Hannah heard a loud bang and clasped her trembling hands over her mouth to stop herself from screaming. She saw her mother totter and take a few steps backwards. Her legs started to buckle and in an attempt to stop herself collapsing onto the floor, she grabbed the cloth covering the cutting table. A mound of fabric and a tin of sewing needles slid off the table onto the floor. Horrified, Hannah realised that if the cloth was pulled away, she would be discovered. With her eyes still fixed on her mother's shoes, now splattered with droplets of blood, she clutched the far side of the cloth to prevent it from sliding off.

Mirka slid to the ground, turning her face to the wall. Through her tears, Hannah watched her mother's chest rise and fall slowly until she finally took her last breath. Silent screams pounded in her head so hard she thought it would burst. She dared not reach out to touch her mother: so close and yet so far.

A man's voice called from the stairwell. 'Heinz. Where are you? Are you all right?'

Another pair of feet entered the room. This man wore smart civilian shoes. 'Good God! You look in a bad way,' he said. 'Is she dead?'

Mirka's attacker leaned over the body and pressed his hand to the side of her neck, feeling her pulse.

'Let's get out of here and get that wound seen to,' the second man said.

The first man wasn't listening. His eyes fell on the watch Mirka was wearing. 'Look at this,' he exclaimed excitedly. 'What's a dirty Jew doing wearing a watch like this? I bet she stole it. I wouldn't put anything past these pariahs.'

It was Mirka's prize possession – a sleek, platinum and diamond half-bracelet watch in the Arts décoratifs style, given to her in appreciation of her work by Fräulein Lehmann.

Hannah instinctively began to reach out a hand to stop him, but fear prevented her from revealing herself. Mirka was a delicate woman, her wrists narrow and elegant, and the man's thick hands pulled at the watch roughly. To Hannah, she looked like a rag-doll being mishandled.

'She's not going to need this anymore,' the attacker said, finally succeeding in removing it and greedily stuffing it in his pocket. 'If she's got this, she's probably got other valuables hidden somewhere.'

The second man said, 'Come on, Heinz. I'm leaving. You know we've been warned not to steal, only to teach them a lesson.' He started to walk out of the room.

The attacker took one more look at Mirka, spat on her body and the men left. Hannah listened to their heavy footsteps pounding down the stairs. Minutes later she heard the outside door slam shut.

Traumatized, Hannah spent the rest of the night curled up in a ball, staring at her mother's body and listening to the terrifying screams and loud noises that now echoed from the street. In the early morning, the noises subsided. When she was sure her mother's attacker would not return, she crawled out from under the table and sat by her mother's body, sobbing uncontrollably. Then she unlocked the attic door and went to check on her sister. Mercifully, Malka had slept through it all. Hannah locked the attic door, climbed into bed by her sister's side and cried herself to sleep.

She was woken by the sound of men's voices followed by a loud banging on the attic door.

'Hannah! Malka!' a man's voice shouted. 'Are you in there? It's Max Hauser. Open up.'

The hammering grew louder and she realised that if she didn't open the door, it would be broken down. Daylight streamed through the small window. She had no idea what time it was or how long she'd been asleep. All she knew was that the nightmare she thought she'd had was real. She rubbed her eyes. Malka, her eyes wide with fear, was still in bed with her, clutching her doll.

'Where's Mutti?' Malka asked. 'Why are those people banging on the door? Why are your eyes red?'

Malka's questions went unanswered. Hannah got up to open the door. She was still fully dressed. It was then that she noticed blood on her clothes. Malka saw it too, and started to cry.

'It's all right, sweetheart,' Hannah said, kissing her sister on the forehead. 'It's nothing. I had a small accident. Now I want you to promise me you'll be a good girl and stay here for a while.'

Malka looked confused. 'I want Mutti.'

Hannah pulled the covers back over her again. 'Mutti went out for a while. Now, be a good girl and stay put. Promise?'

Malka nodded.

Hannah unlocked the door. There was a second man with Herr Hauser that Hannah didn't know.

'Thank God you're alright,' Herr Hauser said. 'Where's Malka?' He made a move to step inside the attic, but she blocked his way.

'Please don't,' Hannah replied in a whisper. 'She has no idea what took place.'

He looked into her terrified eyes.

'I saw it all, Herr Hauser. I saw what they did to Mutti.' The tears started to stream down her cheeks again.

Forgoing propriety, Max Hauser pulled her into his arms and held her tenderly. Hannah's tears soaked into his cotton shirt. Words were not enough to comfort the young girl and he allowed her to cry her heart out. After a few minutes, she pulled away and followed him back downstairs into Frau Rosen's living room that had also served as her sewing room since the time they'd moved in. Two men were carrying

Frau Rosen's body away on a stretcher. Hannah ran to the door but Max pulled her back.

'Mutti, Mutti,' she cried out in anguish, struggling to get past him. 'Please don't leave us.'

At that moment, her eyes fell on the pool of blood where her mother had lain, and she screamed out in anguish and pain.

A voice from above broke her cries and a terrified Malka was standing in the attic doorway with her doll. 'Mutti! I want Mutti.'

'Pack a few things, Hannah,' Max Hauser said. 'You can't stay here. I'm taking you both away now.'

Hannah looked at him, wide-eyed. 'We can't leave. Nathan will wonder where we are.'

Hauser threw a worried look at his friend. 'Where is he?' he asked her.

'I don't know. He went out last night even though Mutti begged him not to.'

Hauser put a firm hand on her shoulder. 'Look, Hannah, we cannot stay here a moment longer. When Nathan returns, he will probably try and contact the police station or even Fräulein Lehmann. I promise you we will find him.'

Hannah wiped her eyes. 'Where are you taking us?'

'Somewhere safe. Now quickly, go and pack.'

Hannah ran to her sister and pulled her back into the attic. 'Get dressed, Malka – we are going with Herr Hauser.' She gave her a warm skirt and knitted jumper while she threw a few belongings into a bag.

Malka was so confused she started to cry. 'Why isn't Mutti here?'

'She had to go out.' Hannah helped her sister into her pale blue coat. She sat on the bed and, as she buttoned it up for her, she told her she had to be strong; that everything would work out fine. They were going away for a while.

A voice called out from below. 'Hannah, are you ready?'

Hannah put a knitted hat on Malka's head and wrapped a scarf around her neck.

'Can I bring Pipina?' Malka asked.

Hannah handed Malka her doll. 'Of course, *Bubala*.' As soon as she said the word, Hannah realised she'd stepped into her mother's shoes. It was a term of endearment her mother used all the time, especially when she comforted them. At the thought of it, Hannah fought back the tears. 'Come now. We must leave.'

Max Hauser was pacing the room when the two girls came downstairs. He picked Malka up and hurriedly carried her down the three flights of stairs with Hannah behind him. The stench of smoke permeated the building, forcing them to cover their mouths and noses. When they reached the first floor they could see that Frau Weber's apartment had been ransacked. He tried to turn Malka's head away but it was impossible to hide it from her. On the ground floor it was even worse. Frau Weber was screaming hysterically and no amount of soothing from her neighbours could quieten her. The door to the street was wide open and had been daubed with the yellow Star of David. Out in the street the sight was even worse, even though, with the first light of day, attempts had been made to clean up the mess.

Frau Weber's hat shop, which had been in the family since the end of the Great War, had been completely looted. The windows were smashed and the sign over the window – *Weber: Hutmanifactur Seit 1919* – had been torn down and lay in two pieces across the pavement, daubed in the same yellow paint as the door. The accoutrements of the shop she had been so proud of also lay scattered on the pavement: hat stands, and mannequins with their rosy cheeks, cupid lips and painted eyes, rolled onto the road, mingling with an assortment of broken feathers and metres of coloured felt. Everything was so badly destroyed it was no longer of use to anyone, even looters and opportunistic thieves. Worst of all, everywhere, as far as the eye could see, there were shards of glass, glistening and sparkling like diamonds in the cold morning frost.

The four hurried along the street to where Max had parked his car. To their dismay, there was not one shop that had not been vandalized, set on fire, or daubed with the yellow Star of David or the word "*Juden*". The Nazi paramilitary presence – the SS, the S.A, and the Hitler Youth, who Max and his friend knew were responsible for wreaking the havoc, had more or less dissipated, although a few were still out and about, making sure the Viennese police and firefighters were slow to act, particularly when it was a Jewish home or business alight.

As they neared the car, they came across a group of elderly Jewish men and women who had been forced to kneel and clean up the street. There was even a small boy among them who was ordered to write "*Juden*" on his father's storefront. He was covered in yellow paint. At that moment two trucks arrived and a large group of men, who had been rounded up earlier, were forced at gunpoint to get in.

Max Hauser pushed the girls into the back of the car, along with their bag, and got into the driver's seat with his friend next to him. A voice called out to them. 'Halt!'

Two burly middle-aged men came over dressed in the uniform of the S.A. and demanded to know what they were doing. 'Your papers,' one of them said.

Max was about to show them when another vehicle arrived and parked next to them. A smartly dressed plainclothes official got out. Max recognized him immediately. It was Dieter Klein, eldest son of the Kleins, family friends of Christina Lehmann's family.

'Hauser,' the man said with a smirk. 'What are you doing here? It's not the sort of place I'd expected to find you.'

Max was about to say the same to him but thought better of it. Klein dismissed the two stormtroopers and leaned closer to take a look at the other occupants. 'Who is this man?' he asked.

The man handed him his papers. 'Stephen Pembroke. I'm an American.' Max noticed that Stephen omitted to say that he was a freelance journalist.

Klein narrowed his eyes and checked his papers carefully. 'I hope you keep your mouth shut about what's happened here. We wouldn't like foreigners thinking we were to blame for this mess the Jews created.' He jerked his head in the direction of the devastation. 'You know what I mean.' Pembroke didn't answer. 'And who have we here?' Klein continued eyeing the two girls in the back seat.

A trembling Malka hid her face behind her doll and Hannah pulled her coat collar up, trying her best to shrink into her coat to avoid looking at the man.

'Ask Fräulein Christina,' Max replied curtly. 'They belong to one of her seamstresses.'

At the mention of Christina, Klein threw Hauser a dirty look. 'What she sees in someone like you, I will never know. Now get out of here before you join those men over there.' He indicated the men being herded onto the trucks.

Max didn't need to be told twice, and he drove away as fast as he could.

'What was all that about?' Pembroke asked.

Max scoffed. 'He's got a soft spot for Christina. It's the only reason he let me go.'

The car skirted past more streets filled with broken glass and devastation, until they were safely out of the Jewish area and into the Ringstrasse. Max dropped his friend off near the opera house and thanked him for helping him.

'Stay out of trouble, my friend,' Pembroke said. 'After what I've just witnessed, no Jew is safe in Vienna any longer.'

CHAPTER 2

THE CAR PULLED up outside the entrance of a stylish salon in Mariahilferstrasse. This was a bustling thoroughfare of Baroque buildings, lined with shops that sold all manner of fine goods to the aristocratic and wealthy of Viennese society, from oriental carpets, furniture, to porcelain, jewellery and crystal. Alongside them were beauticians, and several Viennese fashion houses and milliners. Above the well-appointed shops with their wide awnings, were fine apartments, all of which were filled with expensive antiques and artworks.

The sign over the door, executed in bold gold lettering on black in the *Wiener-Werkstätte-Stil* – the Modernist Vienna Workshop style, read:

CHRISTINA LEHMANN
HAUTE COUTURE
MARIAHILFERSTRASSE, WIEN

In the window stood a single mannequin wearing an amber-coloured, satin opera coat with a fur trim on the collar and cuffs. Max opened the car door and gestured for the two girls to get out. They followed him into the salon where an anxious woman with loose blonde hair, wearing a black silk kaftan decorated with a single red and gold sweeping floral motif, awaited them in the reception room. The look in her eyes was one of dread when she saw the two girls.

'Max...' She couldn't bring herself to say Frau Rosen's name.

Max glanced at the children and then back at her and shook his head.

Christina clasped the two girls to her and held them tight. 'Lock the door,' she said to him, 'and put the CLOSED sign in the window.' She ushered the two girls into her office, where her sister was sitting at a large desk, poring over the accounts.

'Karin, leave that for now and be a darling and get the girls something to eat and drink. They must be starving.' Christina turned to the girls. 'Why don't you go with Frau Krassner and she'll get you a nice slice of cake.'

Karin understood the situation only too well and refrained from asking questions. Accommodating her sister's request, she took them upstairs where Christina had her own apartment. As soon as the door closed, Christina asked what had happened to Frau Rosen. They spoke quietly.

'We were too late,' Max said. 'When we got there, Frau Rosen was already dead. From the look of her body, I'd say she was killed sometime in the early hours of the morning. The place was in a terrible mess. It looked like she tried to put up a fight. We managed to get her body taken away before the young one saw her, but it seems that Hannah was in the room when her mother was killed. She hid under the table and heard it all.'

Christina put her hand to her mouth. 'Oh God, the poor child! Did she say who did it?'

'She was hiding under the cutting table, so couldn't see their faces. If you ask me, she's lucky to be alive. Whoever killed Frau Rosen would surely have killed her if they'd seen her. The little one doesn't know her mother is dead.'

Christina gave a heavy sigh. 'They can't go back. That much is clear. They can stay in the apartment until I find them something more permanent.' She paused for a moment's thought. 'Nathan! What happened to him?'

'By all accounts he went out before the troubles started and didn't return. Are you aware they are rounding up Jewish men as we speak?' Max's earlier calm, due more to shock than anything else, was now turning to anger. 'Do you know who turned up as we were leaving?'

'Who?'

'That bastard, Dieter Klein.'

'Dieter! What on earth was he doing there?'

'Trying to ingratiate himself with his German counterparts I suppose. He's ambitious, that one. I wouldn't trust him as far as I could throw him – and he hates me.'

Christina listened without saying a word, but she knew Max was right. Klein was a lawyer and a member of the SS, who now worked for Gauleiter Odilo Globočnik, a fervent Nazi who adhered to National Socialist ideals. It was also no secret that the Klein family had hoped Dieter and she would marry one day. They had dropped hints to her family for several years now and Dieter himself had declared he was in love with her. When she politely declined, he took it hard and told her he would wait. At the time she begged him to find someone else, but he refused. 'One day, you will change your mind,' he said. 'And when you do, I will be waiting.' She never forgot the way he'd said it. It had a menacing tone about it.

For Christina, there was only one man she wanted, and that was Max. But Max was half-Jewish and, as much as he loved her, he refused to marry her, saying that her life and career would be ruined if they married. It was the only time they argued, but both were too much in love with each other to part, and so their affair was conducted in private. For those in the know, it wasn't hard to see what they meant to each other. As for Dieter, he suspected that Max was a rival, but then, Christina Lehmann was a stunning beauty and belonged to Vienna's social elite. She had many admirers.

'Kiki, my love,' Max said. 'I fear my own life is in danger.' He looked past her, as if his mind was elsewhere. 'It's strange, but for some reason, I thought we'd get through it, that the Nazis would just try and teach us a lesson. Now I realise I've been fooling myself.'

Christina moved closer, clasping his hands tightly. 'Don't say that. You're a famous artist. They wouldn't dare touch you.'

He ran his hand through her silken hair and looked at her with his large, sad eyes. 'I no longer believe that. Every Jew is in danger, not just the lower classes that live in Leopoldstadt.' He kissed her tenderly.

'Max…'

He covered her lips with his mouth in a long, lingering kiss to stop her questioning him more. Then he drew back and said they must make the best of their time together – just in case. The last thing Christina wanted was to argue with him at a time like this. After a while, Karin returned, saying the girls had eaten and were sleeping. Max told her what had taken place in Leopoldstadt. Like her sister, she too found it hard to comprehend.

'Hannah is as white as a sheet, poor girl,' she said. 'It's evident she's traumatized. And as for the little one – sweetness herself – she's clutching her doll for dear life and asking when she will see her Mutti again.' She threw her hands in the air. 'Someone has to tell her.'

'I will,' Christina replied. 'I feel responsible for them.'

'You are not responsible for what those thugs did,' Karin replied sharply. 'No one is immune from such behaviour. And the authorities allow it, so what can you do?'

Max nodded. 'Listen to your sister, Kiki. You do your best, but sometimes that's not enough.'

Karin served them all a tray of food and placed it on the desk. 'Eat something, Max. It will do you good. You too, Christina.' She poured them a cup of coffee and handed each of them a plate.

Christina pushed her plate away. 'How can I eat after what has just taken place?'

Karin, the elder, and always the more practical one of the two sisters, chastised her. 'You need to keep up your energy and be strong. We will face harsher things than this.' She glanced at Max, hoping he would agree with her.

He took the plate from her and helped himself to a slice of chocolate cake. 'She's right, Kiki.'

Christina looked at him despondently. 'We'll keep the salon closed today – as a mark of respect. Anyway, I'm in no mood to fit clients out in beautiful clothes after this.'

When he'd finished eating, she suggested she and Max get some fresh air and go for a walk to the Volksgarten. It would give them time to think. He agreed.

CHAPTER 3

THE WEATHER HAD turned bitterly cold and the winter sky was a sheet of pale gun-metal grey, casting a dull light over the grand buildings. Somehow it reflected their mood – sombre and tinged with melancholy; their beloved Vienna with its Strauss music, imperial grandeur and easy charm, seemed to be disappearing before their eyes. Despite this, the Volksgarten was filled with people out for a leisurely stroll. Several sat on the park benches, reading newspapers or books as if they didn't have a care in the world. On closer observation, it was clear the gloomy air was not only due to the weather; no one could ignore the stench of smoke in the air that signified something terrible had taken place. Clothed in a warm ankle-length woollen coat with a large collar, Christina walked arm-in-arm with Max, feeling secure in his closeness. They found a seat near the neoclassical Theseus Temple. A newly erected sign on the bench stated in large letters, "For Aryans Only".

'Ignore it,' Christina said, seeing the look on Max's face.

They sat down and she cuddled closer to him, whispering in his ear how much she loved him. Her words would normally have set his heart racing, but after what he'd seen he was overwhelmed by a sense of melancholia. It clung to him like the cold weather, suffocating his joy of being with the woman he loved, and he felt powerless to fight it. 'Emotions are vital to who we are,' he used to tell Christina. Now he wanted to freeze them out. He thought back to the time when he met her nine years ago. How life had changed in that time.

'What are you thinking?' Christina asked. 'You're far away. If it's about the Rosen children, I will make sure they are safe.'

'Actually, I was thinking of the time I had my first exhibition.' Max smiled at the memory. 'It was a couple of years before we met. I'd just arrived back from Paris and was filled with enthusiasm. Little did I know then or imagine I would be successful. It wasn't an easy period. The economic crisis was deepening and people told me I should just concentrate on portraits. They said that's where the money was, but until I went to Paris, I wasn't interested in the classic style; the new avant-garde was what inspired me the most. After exhibiting my first works publicly – drawings, tempera and engravings – along with several other artists, I was offered a teaching post at the Academy. That's when things took off and I had my first solo exhibition. Then I started to get commissions – good ones that paid well. The first was from a member of the Esterhazy family, another from the wife of Count von Alters, and through them I received more.'

Christina smiled. 'That's when you met Fannie, isn't it?'

Max's eyes shone at the thought of his former lover. Fannie had not only been his first love, she was his first real muse. Until then, few women had held his attention. Tall and handsome with a swarthy complexion, large, expressive amber eyes, and a mop of unruly dark curls that gave him a rakish, bohemian look, the girls were attracted to him like bees to a honey pot. At thirty-two, he was older than some of his contemporaries, but the women fell for his quiet charm and inquiring mind. They all revelled in the soirees he held in his studio, where everything was discussed, from the arts, psychoanalysis, politics, and – since the rise of Nazism – eugenics. There was hardly a topic with which Max Hauser was not familiar.

The only son of a Hungarian Jewish mother, who died while giving birth to him, and an Austrian shopkeeper from a village near the city of Graz, his childhood had been a happy one. When Max was a year old, his father remarried, and his new wife bore him two more children, Anita and Friedrich. His stepmother was a kindly woman and brought Max up as her own, caring for him along with her own two children. The fact that his own mother was a Jew was never mentioned as she'd converted to Catholicism when she married. Max only found out himself when he left to live in Vienna. Fearing the rise in anti-Semitism, his father warned him to be careful. 'Keep your Jewishness in your heart,' he said, tapping his chest. 'It's better that way.' Fannie and Christina, and a handful of close friends, were the few he discussed his "Jewishness" with, but it was always on his mind, especially given the political upheavals. Several of his fellow artists' work had been derided as degenerate art, and, within a matter of weeks, they had found themselves without any commissions. Max was afraid that could happen to him too.

As an artist herself, Christina was deeply sensitive to the worsening anti-Semitism. She had many Jewish customers and her family cautioned her to be careful. She was a successful couturier now, but they warned her it wouldn't last if she got on the wrong side of the new regime.

Christina couldn't fail to notice the way Max's eyes lit up at the thought of Fannie. She wasn't jealous in the slightest. It was because of her that he'd changed his subject matter and started to paint nudes. In the early years, he became a close friend of Oskar Kokoschka and was influenced by expressionism and a colour palette similar to those featured in the works of the German *Die Brücke* artists, but, after spending a year in Paris, he decided against the use of shrill, harsh colours that made his subjects appear as the rotting corpses of a decomposing age, and found himself drawing on the works of the old masters – Titian, Rubens, Goya, Jules Josef Lefebre, Cabarel, and Henri Gervex. In Paris, he painted "behind the curtains" – in the brothels where there was never a shortage of models.

He met Fannie shortly after he returned to Vienna. She was a dark beauty with a tempestuous personality and a love of life that equalled his own. He never talked much about her to Christina, but as she grew to know him better, she could tell from his painting and sketches what she'd meant to him. He once told her that only a lover could reveal his subject's inner beauty. Fannie died of tuberculosis a year before Christina met him. He was drinking so heavily at that time, his friends feared he might kill himself. Max's personality was sensitive and volatile and she feared that, if the political situation deteriorated even more and started to affect, not only his career, but their life together, he would slip back into that dark place and seek solace in drink again.

Talking about his early days as an artist filled him with happiness, but that feeling of despondency quickly returned. 'I'm afraid of what the future holds if they find out I'm Jewish,' he said.

'My darling, your mother was Jewish, that's all, and she converted when she married your father. You were baptized a Catholic, and you're not even religious, so please stop worrying. Besides, only your closest friends know you are part Jewish.'

'Dieter Klein knows I'm a Jew.'

Christina gave him an anxious look. 'He knows little about you except that you are a renowned artist. Why do you say that?'

'It was the way he spoke to me. I'm sure he would have made it his business to find out everything he can about me. He loathes me because of you.'

Christina told him not to lose heart; that everything would work out, but after what had just taken place, she knew in her heart things would get worse before they got better. Their thoughts returned to the urgent problems in hand, what to do with the Rosen girls, and finding Nathan.

'You can't keep those girls in the apartment, Kiki,' Max said. 'You know that.'

'I will take them to Hietzing. My mother will look after them until things calm down.'

'Are you sure that's wise? What will her friends say?'

'The villa is large and they'll have a garden to play in. Leave it with me and stop worrying, I'll find them a safe home. Now, please cheer up. It could be worse.'

Max sighed. 'I suppose it could.' At that moment a line of tarpaulin-covered army trucks filled with male civilians passed along the Burgring. Passers-by stopped to look, wondering what was going on.

'Yes, you are quite right. It could be much worse,' he repeated with a hint of sarcasm. 'I could be one of the people in those trucks.'

Christina suggested they go to Café Landtmann for a coffee to cheer themselves up. As they made their way out of the park, there was a heated argument taking place between an elderly couple and the park attendant. The attendant pointed to a newly erected sign stating "Jews are not wanted here". 'Can't you read?' he shouted. 'Aryans only. Go away before I call the police.'

The elderly man looked indignant and ushered his distressed wife away. Two women out walking their dogs arrived and asked the attendant what was going on.

'Jews!' he said, watching to make sure they didn't return. 'They started arguing with me.' He shrugged. 'I don't make the laws. I just carry out my duties and my duty now is not to allow any Jews into the Volksgarten.'

The two women looked at each other and tutted. 'They didn't look like Jews,' one of them said. 'Still, these days you never can tell, can you. I mean, some of them look just like us.'

Max glanced back over his shoulder as they walked away. 'Do *I* look like a Jew?' he asked Christina.

She hooked her arm through his. 'Max, please stop this nonsense? I've got too much on my mind as it is.'

Max hated himself for making her unhappy. 'I'm sorry. You're right. Let's go and get that coffee.'

Enveloped in the aroma of freshly brewed coffee and the ever-present cigarette smoke in the air, Café Landtmann was filled with customers, many of whom were either poring over the morning newspapers hoping to find out what had taken place the night before, or playing bridge. The manager knew them both well, and guided them to a plush upholstered seat for two. An ornate mirror next to the table reflected the dimmed light from a chandelier that hung from the beautifully carved ceiling. They ordered coffee, topped with a thick layer of whipped cream.

'Can I get you anything to eat?' the waiter asked, taking Christina's coat and hanging it on a nearby brass peg. 'We have a wonderful hazelnut cream torte.'

The pair declined, promising to try it next time. When he'd gone, Max looked around at the people reading. 'The press will be muzzled so I don't expect they'll learn anything,' he said. 'Let's hope the foreign press reports the truth. I know Stephen Pembroke sent a dispatch to the New York Times, and, from what I gather, other journalists sent dispatches too. The question is, will the foreign politicians take notice?'

After a few minutes of silence, Christina reached across the table and took Max's hand. 'Do you realise, this is where I was sitting when I first saw you?' The thought made them both smile. 'I was with Karin and she pointed you out. "There's the painter they're all talking about," she said to me. You were with your friends, getting into a heated argument, if I recall.'

Max laughed. 'I forget what we were discussing at the time.'

'That's because you'd drunk too much. It's a wonder you could paint at all with the amount of drink you consumed in those days. When Karin suggested going to the opening of one of your exhibitions, I confess I was intrigued. "How could a drunk like that paint anything of importance?" I said to her. Then your friend, Otto, noticed us looking and asked if we'd like to join you. Of course we politely declined, and that's when he invited us to the opening on your behalf.'

'Well, Kiki, my darling, I'm glad he did. Otherwise we wouldn't be here now, would we?' He leaned closer. 'It was *you* who made me forget Fannie; *you* who made me stop drinking; *you* who saved me from going the same way so many other artists end up.'

'You're probably right, although neither of us knew it would turn into a love affair at the time.'

'Do you regret it? After all, nine years is a long time to be in love with a person without getting married. I've taken the best years of your life.'

Christina leaned back in her seat. 'I never knew what life was about until I met you, so no, I don't regret one minute of it. I would do it all again.' She flashed him a coquettish smile. 'What about you?'

He picked up her hand and kissed it. The look in his eyes said it all.

CHAPTER 4

After walking Christina back to the salon, Max returned to his own apartment to work on his paintings and the illustrations for Christina's upcoming Spring Collection, saying he would see her the following evening. When Karin told her there was still no word from Nathan, she made a telephone call to Frau Weber's hat shop to see if she had any news of him, but the line was dead.

'I must go over there myself and find out. Maybe he's returned,' she said. Karin looked alarmed. 'I have no other option. If I don't find him, I'll make inquires at the police station.'

She called her chauffeur, and told him to get the car ready.

'Where to, Fräulein Christina?' Kurt Beck asked.

'Leopoldstadt – Zirkusgasse.'

The chauffeur threw her an anxious glance as he started the engine. 'I believe certain roads are blocked off.'

'Then go to the nearest street and I will walk.'

Christina was in no mood to be put off. Seeing the trucks pass by the Volksgarten, taking men away, told her she had no time to spare. She hadn't been sure what to expect, but, when she arrived in Leopold-stadt the horrifying scene sickened her. The Brownshirts were congregating again, forcing more Jews to clean up the previous night's mess. Others were being tormented by having their beards and locks cut off by hoodlums who thought it all a great joke. One elderly Jew had been made to wear a sign over his chest saying "I am a Jewish swine". Christina told Beck to wait at the end of the street where Max had parked earlier. Two policemen standing nearby looked at each other when they saw the gleaming red and black Steyr 220 park next to a ransacked clothes shop. They were even more shocked when a beautiful, elegant blonde lady stepped out. Unable to contain their curiosity, they came over and asked what she was doing there.

'I'm looking for a teenage boy,' Christina replied. 'He lives in the apartment above the hat shop.'

One of the men smirked. 'Are you sure you're in the right street?' He eyed her expensive clothes with curiosity.

Standing by the passenger door, Beck took a step closer in case she needed protection, but Christina calmly put out a gloved hand, saying she was fine. She turned to face the two policemen and gave them a dressing down.

'If you would do your civic duty for our beloved city, and stop these hoodlums disgracing the good name of Viennese citizens, then you wouldn't be here asking me such a ridiculous question.'

The second policeman's jaw dropped. 'You're Fräulein Christina Lehmann – the couturier? I thought I recognised your face.' He stammered when he mentioned her name. Christina acknowledged him with a nod.

'I am very sorry. We didn't mean to be so rude. It's just that...' His face was reddening by the second, and he apologised, saying they had been told not to interfere.

'Who told you that?' she asked, sternly.

'The orders came from above. We are only doing our job.'

'Then you will allow me to do my job too, and look for the boy.'

'Can we escort you?' the policeman asked. 'These men,' he nodded in the direction of the stormtroopers, 'are, as you rightly said, hoodlums, and we can't be held responsible for their actions.'

'Fine, one of you can escort me. The other will stay here and make sure no one bothers my chauffeur.' Both men bowed graciously and the one who'd recognised her walked with her to Frau Weber's hat shop.

'Wait outside,' she said to him. 'I won't be long.'

The shop still had a gaping hole in the window. No one had made an attempt to board it up. There was nothing of value left to take, anyway.

She pushed open the side door, with the yellow Star of David still on it, and made her way up the staircase. The sound of her shoes on the wooden stairs alerted a middle-aged woman who popped her head out of Frau Weber's apartment.

'It's all right, I'm a friend of Frau Rosen,' Christina said.

Frau Weber recognised her voice and limped out of her apartment. Christina was appalled when she saw the state the hat designer was in. Her eyes were red and swollen from constant crying, and she had a large bruise on the side of her cheek. 'Did those thugs do that to you?' she asked. 'You should get it seen to as soon as possible.'

Frau Weber said she was too afraid to step out into the street in case the men started on her again. 'Fräulein Lehmann, I'm sorry to tell you this, but Frau Rosen was killed last night and the girls are not here. Two men took them away this morning and I have no idea where they are.'

Christina thought it better not to tell her she already knew about Frau Rosen and the girls. She asked about Nathan.

'I don't know where he is.' Frau Weber was struggling to stand, and propped herself against the banister. 'I heard raised voices last night. His mother was pleading with him not to go out, but he's headstrong, that one. The next minute, the outside door slammed shut and I knew he'd gone. He hasn't been back and, after the round-ups, I hope for his sake he doesn't return.'

'Do you know where the men who were rounded up were taken?' Christina asked.

'I wish I did. They were herded away like cattle. No explanation. No nothing!'

Christina felt for them. 'Can I take a look in Frau Rosen's apartment? She was working on something for me.'

'Of course. The door is unlocked, but I warn you, it's not a pretty sight.'

Christina made her way to the apartment and, with great trepidation, stepped inside. After Max's description she expected a shocking scene, but she still wasn't prepared for what she saw. She put a gloved hand to her mouth to stop herself crying out. God in heaven, she said to herself. She moved through the apartment cautiously, examining the mess like a detective examining a crime scene, picking up bits and pieces and placing them on the cutting table. Even though someone had attempted to clean up the blood where the body had lain, it was evident that what took place had been violent. She picked up the mannequin with her dress still on it. The dress was torn, and there was a stain where the blood had seeped into it.

She recalled that Hannah had hidden under the cutting table and took a peek, yet, as hard as she tried, it was impossible to imagine the terror the poor girl had experienced. Near the door was a single shoe of dark brown leather with a gold trim. Christina's eyes filled with tears when she thought of the pride Frau Rosen took in her appearance, always making sure she wore good clothes, even though she could barely afford to raise three children.

Pulling herself together, she continued up the narrow flight of stairs to the attic. Malka's dolls were scattered around the room. It was a pokey place with very little light and she chastised herself for not doing more to get her best seamstress away from such a hovel. Yet, try as she did, Mirka had refused to leave, saying that she felt at home near her people – Galician Jews who never truly assimilated with the cosmopolitan Jews of the old empire.

It crossed her mind to take a few of Malka and Hannah's belongings, but she thought better of it as she didn't want to draw attention to herself. Like Max, neither would she leave a note in case Nathan returned. One never knew where that note would end up.

Back outside, she saw the policeman talking to a stormtrooper. When they spotted her, they stood to attention with a look of embarrassment on their faces. 'Did you find what you were looking for?' the policeman asked.

She ignored them and headed back to the car. The policeman ran beside her, trying to ingratiate himself with her. 'My wife is a fervent admirer of yours. She follows your collections in the magazines, but I am afraid we are not wealthy enough to purchase your fine clothes.'

Christina stopped in her tracks and looked at him. 'What's your name?'

'Fischer – Joseph Fischer.'

'Well Herr Fischer, would you like to do something for me? In exchange I will give your wife a thank-you present.'

The man's eyes widened. He couldn't believe what he was hearing. 'What would you like me to do, *gnädige* Fräulein?'

'Find out where the men who live around here have been taken to. In particular, I want all the names of those who lived in this street.'

The man looked aghast. 'I can't do that! I have no idea – and besides, we've been told to keep our mouths closed. I could be shot – my family could end up on the streets!'

'That's a pity.' Christina continued toward the car.

The man caught up with her again. 'Wait! I will do my best. That's all I can promise.'

Christina smiled at him. 'That's better. Now, if you do what I ask, and bring me this information, your wife will have a gift as a gesture of my appreciation.' The man was so shocked, he couldn't stop thanking her. 'Bring me this information by tomorrow evening. That should give you enough time.'

'Tomorrow evening!' He took his cap off and wiped his brow with a handkerchief.

'Let's say, nine o'clock at Café Landtmann.' The man said he never went there, that it was too expensive and not for his class of people. Christina put her hand out to quieten him. 'Tell the manager I sent you. He will look after you.'

'Will you be there?'

'No, but don't worry, you will be looked after.' She flashed him one of her beguiling smiles and leaned closer. 'Just think how Frau Fischer will adore you, *mein Herr*.' She watched his face. 'Put the information in an envelope inside a newspaper. That's all you have to do.' Her face bore a look of seriousness. 'A word of caution: be discreet and don't tell a soul. It wouldn't be good for you. These are challenging times and we have to know who our friends are.'

'And the gift for my Frau?' The man could barely look her in the eyes.

'Leave a telephone number or an address where I can contact you. Don't say a word to her about what you are doing, either. Understand?'

The man nodded. 'I give you my word I will do my best.'

As they neared the car, Christina shook the man's hand. 'Thank you, Herr Fischer. You have been most kind.'

He was joined by his friend and they watched the chauffeur open the car door for Christina to step inside. The door slammed shut. She wound down the window, gave him a smile, and waved.

'Everything all right, Fräulein Christina?' the chauffeur asked, when he got into the car.

'Everything's fine, but I want you to take a good look at the man who accompanied me. Remember his face.'

The chauffeur did as he was asked. When he was sure he'd committed the man's face to memory, they drove away.

CHAPTER 5

'THE GIRLS HAVE been fretting all morning,' Karin said. 'Especially Hannah. She's fearful something bad has happened to her brother. As for the little one, I've given her a box of your crayons and she seems to be fine for the moment. Did you find out anything at Zirkusgasse?'

Christina slumped in a chair and kicked off her shoes. 'They've taken most of the men away. Only a few are left to clean up the mess.'

Karin poured her a glass of water. 'Was it that bad?'

She gave a heavy sigh. 'No doubt what Max saw was much worse. Even so, seeing the mess in the apartment was… well, I don't have words to describe it. I saw where Hannah hid when her mother was killed.' She ran a hand through her hair. 'I simply cannot take it all in. We have become uncivilized.'

Karin informed her that she'd had a word with their mother, and that it was fine to take the girls there until a longer-term solution was found.

'She seemed quite nervous about it, so we cannot call on Mama's kindness for too long,' Karin said. 'I even thought about taking them in myself, but it wouldn't be safe. Walter has friends and work colleagues to the apartment and it would be difficult for us.'

'That's fine. We don't want to put Walter's job in jeopardy.'

Karin had been married for four years. Her husband was a music teacher at the Academy for Music and the Performing Arts, but immediately after the Anschluss an SS-intelligence unit was housed in the Academy and no classes were held until March 23. Because of the Nazi alliance, approximately one hundred pupils were not able to continue their studies and many instructors had been fired. Walter was not a Jew, but he had Jewish friends. After the sackings, a notice had gone around telling the non-Jews they would lose their jobs if they associated with Jews.

When Christina told her about the policeman, Karin raised her eyebrows. 'Is that wise, involving someone you don't know? You could have asked Dieter Klein. He would be only too happy to tell you anything you wanted to know. He is a family friend, after all.'

'I loathe the man, and you know why. How can you suggest such a thing?'

'My dear, he may be loathsome, but he *is* in a position to know what's going on.'

Christina changed the subject. 'How are we going for fittings?'

Karin showed her the diary. When many of Vienna's richest Jews fled, soon after the Anschluss, their clientele had dropped dramatically. 'I managed to change today's appointments but we still have quite a few more on the books waiting to come and see you. I am afraid that business is not as good as it was, so you'll have ample time to prepare the Spring Collection.'

A wave of despondency swept over them when they thought of their Jewish customers. Not only were some of them their close friends, they were among the Viennese Avant Garde who had used their money to further the arts. With these women, Christina could be creative; they understood modern art and were willing to try out new designs. They were trendsetters in every way, and her design house flourished under their patronage. Through them, Max's painting flourished too, his portraits gracing the salons of their Viennese homes and country residences. When Austria became part of the Greater Reich, life as they knew it changed overnight. Many of those who left were forced to leave their priceless belonging behind in the hope that Hitler and his cronies would lose power sometime soon, and there would be a return to normality. Try as they might to be optimistic, the Lehmanns feared the worst. To make matters worse, several seamstresses left Vienna for Paris at the same time.

'I've lost some of my best seamstresses,' Christina lamented. 'And now Mirka. It will be impossible to replace her.'

She settled down at her desk and began checking samples for the Spring Collection. One of them Mirka had dropped off only a week ago. She fought back the tears when she thought of her; a soft, fragile woman who was far stronger than she looked. She distinctly recalled the day she hired her. It was in 1934, a year after Hitler took power in Germany. Mirka was a Galician Jew who met her husband, Moses, a German Jew, through a matchmaker. He was a lot older than her, and not in good health, but she accepted, and they married soon after. When the Nazis came to power, the family fled to Vienna. Malka was one, Hannah twelve, and Nathan thirteen. At the time, Christina's couture house was expanding, and she needed more seamstresses. Most worked in the workroom on the third floor above her apartment, a light and airy space big enough to accommodate up to twelve seamstresses, along with the cutting tables and sewing machines.

Mirka saw Christina's advertisement in the newspaper and promptly applied. She arrived for the interview in a smart, dark brown coat, a felt hat ringed with a ribbon, and matching bag and gloves. She also wore a beautiful pair of leather shoes with a gold buckle. Christina was impressed. During the interview, Mirka showed her samples of her work. She had worked for German ladies in a private capacity and was familiar with all the latest trends. Christina asked her to take a look at a few designs she had been working on. Did she like them? If not, what would she do to improve them? Mirka was observant and made a few pertinent points, which Christina took on board.

'Excellent, Frau Rosen.' Christina then handed her a box of ribbons, embroideries, and lace. 'Now tell me what you would do with these, and which colour you think suits them best.' She was given a pile of swatches with various textures, from knobbly wools and heavy jacquards, to printed velvet, silk and organza. In no time at all, she matched the fabrics together beautifully.

Christina offered her a one month trial period. She was to work alongside the other seamstresses and was paid two hundred schilling. She proved an excellent worker and was hired on a permanent basis with an extra fifty schilling a month and the promise of bonuses. Mirka was overwhelmed. It was a good wage that would help to keep a roof over their heads and feed her family. Moses made very little money, and the family had been forced to move into a two-roomed tenement in Leopoldstadt, an area where most of the people conversed in Yiddish. She used her money wisely, and managed to save a little. But then tragedy struck. Moses' health deteriorated, and he died after a short illness. Because of the children, Christina allowed her to work from home, setting her up with all the sewing equipment she would need. They might have been from different social classes, but the two women formed a close bond. Mirka was a hard worker, a person of great integrity. She never discussed her work or Christina's clients with anyone outside the salon. Because of this, together with the fact that they had no relatives in Vienna, Christina felt it was her duty to look after the Rosen children.

At five o'clock, the telephone rang. It was Max, informing her he would meet her in the auditorium at the Burgtheater. They had agreed to go with friends to a performance of Ibsen's *The Wild Ducks*, which many considered his finest work.

Christina luxuriated in a warm bath, scented with lavender oil, before preparing to dress. It helped sooth her nerves. But it wasn't the play that was on her mind; she wondered whether the policeman would show up. She'd taken a risk asking him to get the information, and he might change his mind and tell his superior what took place. That would be a disaster, as the Gestapo was already known to be monitoring the population and hauling people up for the slightest misdemeanour. In her position, she couldn't afford that. They might even close her fashion house down. That had already happened to quite a few, either because they were Jewish, or for something trivial, like not hanging a Nazi flag outside the premises. The idea of hanging a Nazi flag up appalled her, but after heeding the advice of others, she reluctantly agreed. In fact, all the businesses in Vienna displayed the swastika, fearing closure if they didn't comply. Now, every time she stepped outside a wave of sorrow swept through her; the whole of Mariahilferstrasse, especially the shopping area, was a sea of red and black flags.

An hour later, dressed in a halter-neck evening gown of cream chiffon, she felt like a new woman. Her gown was spectacular. It had a close-fitted bodice, embroidered with silk and metallic thread with highlights of rhinestones and glass cabochons. She normally preferred to wear her hair loose when alone, but this evening she wore it swept up in an elegant French twist into which she placed an onyx comb. The dress was one of Max's favourites, not least because of the way the fabric was cut on the bias and draped in soft folds from the bodice, but because the halter-neck exposed her flawless back. With her hair up, it looked even more elegant. *This will lighten his mood*, she said to herself, happy at the choice she'd made.

A gold bracelet in the shape of a coiled snake added an extra touch of glamour and sensuality. It was the first gift Max had given her after completing a commission for a client who appreciated his work, and paid accordingly. When she was satisfied with her looks, she put on her silk copper-coloured opera coat edged with sable, picked up her bag, and went outside into the icy-cold night. Beck was patiently waiting with the car. After the stream of trucks and army vehicles on the roads earlier in the day, the streets were much quieter. She wondered if it was due to people fearful of coming across mob violence, or simply that winter was setting in. Beck dropped Christina off at the Burgtheater, where Max was waiting for her with their friends. Before entering the foyer, she whispered something to Beck. He nodded, and the car drove away.

As expected, Max's face lit up when he saw what she was wearing. He brought her hand to his lips and brushed it lightly with a lingering kiss, and complimented her on being the most beautiful woman in the theatre. After drinks in the bar with friends, they took their seats in the dress circle in the auditorium. Under the glittering chandeliers, they couldn't help noticing how many Nazi officials were there, including Gauleiter Globočnik. Max whispered to her that he'd heard a rumour that Gustav Klimt's friezes decorating the theatre were to be replaced with something more in keeping with National Socialist ideals.

'What they would have thought of my earlier work doesn't bear thinking about,' he added, contemptuously.

Christina gave him a playful smack on his thigh. 'Don't spoil the evening, darling. Let's forget all about politics and enjoy ourselves, shall we?'

The lights dimmed and the curtains drew back, revealing a stage decked out for the dinner party hosted by Håkon Werle, the wealthy merchant and industrialist in the play. Christina picked up her opera glasses and leaned forward a little to get a better view.

The play, a tragic comedy, was performed brilliantly by talented actors and she was pleased to have seen it, despite the presence of Nazis. When it finished, they joined their friends in the bar again to discuss the merits of the performance. In the play, the revelation of the truth is not a happy event, because it tears apart the foundation of the Ekdal family, the skeletons are brought out of the closet, and their dream world collapses. The weak husband believes it is his duty to leave his wife, and their little girl, after trying to sacrifice her precious duck, shoots herself, overhearing the fatal words from Hjalmar, "*Would she lay down her life for me?*"

Max leaned closer to Christina. 'Would you lay down your life for me, my sweetness?'

'How can you ask such a question? Yes. And you, would you lay down your life for me?'

'I would fight a duel for you.' He gave her a warm smile and squeezed her hand. The earlier gloom had gone and his eyes shone with love.

The group then started to discuss another famous quote in the play, this time from Doctor Relling. "*Deprive the average human being of his illusion in life and you rob him of his happiness.''* The group considered this quote apt, given the times they were living through.

'Soon we all will be robbed of happiness,' Max's friend, Otto, declared. They changed the conversation to something lighter, after that.

Christina whispered to Max that she hoped she would learn of the whereabouts of Nathan that night. When he asked how, she simply said she would tell him tomorrow.

'Then I will not be holding you in my arms tonight, caressing you in the way that drives you wild.' His voice was soft and gentle.

Christina rubbed her thigh against his. 'Tomorrow night, my darling. I promise.'

Their friends couldn't help noticing their affectionate glances and whispers. 'It's obvious that the presence of Nazi uniforms hasn't dampened your ardour, my dear Max,' Otto joked, light-heartedly. 'But then, who can blame you when you are in the company of such a ravishing beauty.'

Christina's cheeks reddened and the women playfully chastised him. Their good company was just the tonic she needed at that moment, yet all evening she'd kept her eye on the time, thinking about the rendezvous with the policeman. At five minutes to nine, she excused herself, saying she needed to get home. Max walked her outside where Beck was waiting with the car.

'Are you sure you will be all right, my darling,' Max said, pulling her fur collar up around her neck so that she wouldn't get cold.

'Quite sure, now go back to our friends. I will see you tomorrow.'

As soon as they drove away, Christina asked Beck how the meeting went.

'Like clockwork.' He handed her an envelope. 'I think you'll find what you're looking for in there.'

'Good man. I knew I could rely on you.'

In the quiet of her bedroom, Christina poured herself a cognac and lay on the bed, propped up by a mound of pillows, and began reading the information Joseph Fischer had given her. In all, there were six pages filled with a list of names, ages, addresses and occupations. Alongside each name was a separate column with a typed "J" denoting whether the person was a Jew or not. She carefully went through each name, running her finger down the page as she read them out – Moser Apfelbaum, Aaron Bacher, Bruno Erdheim, Samuel Krauskopf... When she came to the letter "R" her finger shook. Rashkin, Riez, Roitman – and the next – Rosen. Her heart raced as she scanned her eyes across the page – *Nathan Rosen, 96 Zirkusgasse, Leopoldstadt. Age: 17, Occupation...* There was no occupation listed. Apart from odd jobs, Nathan hadn't had a permanent job since he left school. He eked a few schilling a day from hawking goods around Vienna. What was listed, however, was a typed "J".

Christina's emotions vacillated between joy and despair. Joy because she'd finally located him, and despair because the comments at the bottom of the page were signed and stamped *"To be interned in Dachau"*.

Dachau! She'd already heard of the concentration camp in Southern Germany which had recently become a training centre for SS guards. Word had reached her a while ago that prisoners were forced to do hard manual work under terrible conditions, and were regularly beaten. She let out a deep sigh. *Was she too late to save him?*

She returned to the papers and saw a barely legible scribbled comment, written by Fischer himself. It said the men would be transported from the Vienna Criminal Court with the next transport. It was too late to do anything now, but she would go there herself first thing in the morning. Fischer had not left a contact telephone number or address, but he did attach a small sepia photograph of his wife, Gretel, to the last page. On the back was written "Gretel – the blue carousel – Prater – Friday at 11:00 a.m." She realised he wanted to meet her there in two days' time and had sent the photo for her to see what his wife was like, rather than risk exposing himself or Gretel to unwelcome gossip. Everyone was on guard these days.

Christina found it hard to sleep that evening. She tossed and turned, hoping she wasn't too late to save Nathan. It was bad enough for the girls to lose their mother, but Nathan – that would break their hearts.

In the morning, she was up bright and early and had Beck take her to the Criminal Court in Landesgerichtesstrasse before Karin arrived. She knew full well there would be a crowd of people in the same position as her, all searching for their loved ones, but she wasn't prepared for just how busy it was. Either side of the main entrance of the large and imposing building, hung two enormous Nazi banners emblazoned with the *Hakenkreuz*, and lines of prisoners were being escorted into the back of a row of army trucks. Most were men, their ages ranged from teenagers to the very old. Armed soldiers, some with dogs who strained on their leashes and snapped viciously at the prisoners, hurried the men along, shouting abuse if they stumbled or were too slow – *Schnell, Schnell!* Two long lines of distraught people stretched in both directions, craning their necks to see if any of their loved ones were part of the convoy. One line was for Jews, and the shorter one for Aryans. They had all been waiting for hours, some all night. Occasionally someone yelled out when they recognized a brother, a father, a husband, being escorted to the trucks, but they were soon pushed back into line by more soldiers and dogs. It was mayhem. Beck advised her to be careful. As always, he waited nearby as she left the car.

She walked confidently past a line of people and up the stairs, where two armed guards stopped her and asked for her papers.

'What is your business here, Fräulein Lehmann?' the man said.

'I have an appointment with Judge von Nauckhoff. He's expecting me.'

It was a ruse she'd thought about during the night. The judge was an old family friend, but he had retired a week after the Anschluss because he disagreed with the National Socialist ideology. He resigned rather than wait for the inevitable: the new regime would sack all those they deemed traitors. All Christina wanted was to get into the building. Once she was in, she would use her charm and position to get what she wanted. It was a gamble to mention von Nauckoff's name, but the guards let her pass. She breathed a sigh of relief and looked over her shoulder towards Beck as she entered the building. He was standing by the car smoking a cigarette and watching her.

Inside, the place was a hive of activity and the atmosphere was thick with a combination of fear, mistrust, and hope. More people queued up in front of desks while plainclothes officials carried out their business, proud of the way they held power over distraught and vulnerable people. 'I can do nothing,' she overheard one official say, oblivious to the woman's pleas. He shooed her away like a dog, calling out, 'Next please.' The woman collapsed on the floor in tears and two guards were called to escort her out of the building.

While this was taking place, Christina grabbed her chance and went to the man's desk.

'Good morning, *mein Herr*. I was wondering if you could help me. I am an acquaintance of Judge von Nauckhoff and I would like to see him, please.'

Again, she was taking a chance mentioning the name.

'I am sorry, Herr Richter von Nauckhoff is no longer with us.' The man eyed her up and down, noting her refined Viennese accent and elegant clothing. 'Can I help you?'

At that moment there were more distressed screams coming from the lady at the next desk. Christina tried to block the screams out and leaned a little closer. '*Mein Herr*, it's rather a delicate matter. You see I have reason to believe you are holding a young man by the name of Nathan Rosen. He lives in Leopoldstadt.' The man opened a ledger and searched for all names under Rosen, Leopoldstadt. There were quite a few. 'His address is number 96 Zirkusgasse,' she added.

'Yes, his name is here,' the man replied. 'Why do you ask?' He could see Christina and Nathan were from different echelons of society, and was intrigued. 'He's a Jew.'

'Yes, I am aware of that. The thing is, his mother was a seamstress of mine and she was...' Christina did not want to use the word "murdered". 'She died suddenly, and the boy was doing some work for me. I'd hired him as a painter as I was having my salon redecorated. Until the work is finished, I cannot open and I have clients who are waiting to see me.'

The man cocked his head to one side. 'It says here that he is to be deported to Germany on the next convoy. Can't you hire someone else?'

Christina felt her throat tighten. 'You are quite right, I could. The thing is, he is very good. If I hired someone else I would have to pay double.' She noticed the man's eyes rest on her jewellery, in particular, a large diamond ring set in gold. She recognized the look in his eyes – one of greed and envy. 'Is there anywhere we could go to discuss this matter privately?' She twisted her ring with her fingers.

The man picked up the ledger. 'Follow me.'

They walked down a long corridor to a room divided into booths with glass partitions. In each booth a bureaucrat talked privately to others. She guessed why they were there. Probably for the same reason as her – to offer bribes to corrupt officials.

The man wasted no time in getting down to business. 'What exactly it is you want me to do for you, Fräulein Lehmann?'

'Free him immediately – if, of course, you have the power to do so.' By deliberately adding the last part of the sentence, she played to his ego. She was sure he would want to prove to her he was more than a minor bureaucrat.

The man's mouth curled in a smirk. '*Meine gnädige* Fräulein, if only I could.' He was enjoying stringing her along. Christina took off her ring and, after a quick glance to check that no one was looking, placed it on the open ledger.

The man hastily covered it with a sheet of paper. After a few minutes' silence, he stood up, slid his hand under the paper and in the blink of an eye, slipped the ring into his pocket.

'Wait here and I will see what I can do for you.'

When he left the booth, Christina started to feel anxious. *What if he reports me?* All manner of terrible thoughts entered her head. He had been gone for almost half an hour, and she was thinking about leaving, when he walked back into the room.

'Follow me, please.' He picked up his ledger and took her to another room, where pools of typists were kept busy typing out documents for half a dozen officials. They headed to one typist, a middle-aged woman with short wavy dark hair and spectacles, just as she was finishing typing a document. She pulled it out of the typewriter and handed it to the man along with a pen.

'Sign here, please.' The man stood back a little and watched Christina while she read it. It was a release form for Nathan. She quickly scribbled her signature, and thanked him.

He escorted her back to the main reception, and told her that "the Jew" would be released soon, possibly within the next hour.

Christina shook his hand. 'You have been most kind, *mein Herr*. Thank you.'

He asked her to wait outside for him, clicked his heels together and saluted. 'Heil Hitler.'

Once outside the building, Christina was overcome by a wave of nausea. She hurried down the steps as the trucks, jam-packed with prisoners, started to drive away, Five minutes later, another half a dozen trucks arrived.

'How did it go?' Beck asked.

'We found him just in time and they're going to release him. The situation in there is awful –desperate people and vultures on the take.'

Christina waited inside the car with her eyes peeled, watching the entrance, hoping Nathan would appear. Almost two hours later, he walked out. She was elated.

'There he is,' she said to Beck, relieved that the man had kept his word.

Beck told Christina to stay in the car while he went over to collect him. Nathan looked dazed, but when he saw Beck's familiar face heading towards him, he was relieved. Christina's elation quickly dissipated when she saw the condition he was in. He had been badly beaten and exuded a foul odour. She pushed the car door open for him to get in.

'Come on,' she said to him, 'let's get you out of here quickly.'

CHAPTER 6

DURING THE DRIVE back to Mariahilferstrasse, Christina learnt that Nathan had been rounded up on the morning of November 10, as he was heading home, a few hours before Max and Stephen Pembroke got there. When she broke the news to him about his mother, his face showed no emotion. He simply stared ahead. His reaction disturbed her and she put her hand on his, telling him she was sorry and that she would help sort things out for them. But nothing could bring back his mother. They both knew that.

The car drew up outside the salon. Beck checked to see who was around before letting Nathan out of the car. Vienna was fast becoming a place of mistrust and it wouldn't look good if a bruised and dishevelled young man was seen entering Fräulein Christina Lehmann's fashion house. Beck even offered to take him to his own home, but Christina wouldn't hear of it. Nathan needed to be with his sisters. The two girls were relieved to see him, and the desperate way they clung to him brought tears to Christina's eyes.

'Have you seen Mutti?' Malka asked. She started to sob.

Christina had asked him not to discuss his mother's untimely death with Malka.

'Mutti has gone away for awhile,' he replied. Somehow he mustered up a smile. 'She's gone to find us another home. When she's ready, she'll let us know and we'll go to her. Isn't that right, Hannah?'

Hannah bit her lip, fighting back the tears and trying hard to stay strong.

Karin was shocked when she saw the state Nathan was in. 'Oh my goodness, what have they done to you, poor boy? Come on, let's get you cleaned up. When did you last eat?'

Christina answered for him. 'He hasn't eaten since he left home.'

'In that case, I will prepare you one of my special dishes while you bathe,' Karin replied. 'Follow me. Let's get you sorted out.'

She took Nathan upstairs to the apartment and the girls went with them. They were so relieved at seeing their brother safe and sound that they didn't want to let him out of their sight. Karin ran a bath and laid out a set of towels. 'Go on,' she said to him. 'Take a long soak. You'll feel much better.' As she was leaving the bathroom, she told him to leave his clothes outside the door. 'I'll find something else for you to wear.'

Christina told Karin to give him some of Max's spare clothes. Karin left them outside the bathroom door and picked up the ones he'd been wearing. They stank of grime – a mixture of smoke, blood, and urine. *Mother of God*, she muttered aloud to herself, covering her nose with her handkerchief. As she was about to walk away, she heard a strange sound in the bathroom and put her ear against the door to listen. Nathan was sobbing. It crossed her mind to knock and see if he was all right, but she thought better of it and left him in peace to grieve. She took the clothes to the basement where the washing and ironing were done, opened the *Kachelofen* and tossed them onto the burning logs. She scrubbed her hands in warm soapy water but the foul smell still lingered. With the girls in the drawing room in the apartment and Nathan in the bathroom, Karin joined Christina in the office. She was handing Beck some money.

'God in heaven,' Karin blurted out. 'The boy is close to a breakdown. I had to burn his clothes, they were torn and stank.'

'I know. I was just giving Kurt money to buy him new clothes. Max's are far too big.'

Karin slumped in the chair, rubbing her temples. 'My dear sister, we have taken on more than we should. You do realise, don't you, that we're putting ourselves in jeopardy...'

'Taking care of Jews, you mean.' Christina quickly apologized. 'I'm

47

sorry. I know that's not what you meant. It's just that my nerves are frayed at the moment.'

Beck looked embarrassed at their outburst and left, saying he would return in the evening with a set of new clothes.

'What does Max have to say about all this?' Karin asked.

'He doesn't know we've found Nathan. He'll be here this evening. He knows Mama has said she will take the two girls for a while, but maybe it's asking too much of her to take Nathan as well.'

'We'll discuss it when he arrives. For the moment you'd better get ready. You have two appointments this afternoon. Don't worry about the children. I'll make sure they're occupied. I can do the bookkeeping with them upstairs in the drawing room.' She got up to prepare the food she'd promised Nathan.

'What are you going to cook?' Christina asked.

'*Paprikahendl* – Paprika chicken with plenty of *Spätzle*. They will enjoy that.'

Christina went into the salon to prepare for her clients. The winter sun was streaming through the large window, highlighting the clothes on the mannequin and a large portrait of her that Max had given her when she opened her fashion house in 1932. That was a year before Hitler took power in Germany. She was twenty and had just completed a dress-making course when they met. With a combination of design flair, passion and dedication, it wasn't long before she established herself as a successful businesswoman and the owner of the esteemed haute couture fashion salon – "Christina Lehmann: Haute Couture".

Max's life-sized portrait of Christina hung in a prominent position in the salon, in front of several red-velvet couches and chairs. Her mass of golden hair contrasted beautifully with the Japanese black silk kimono she wore, which was embroidered with exquisite white and silver cranes. Her eyes radiated the love she had for him. Max considered it to be one of his finest works.

Interspersed among the couches was a collection of ebonized oak and boxwood inlay side tables on which were kept all the latest fashion magazines. It was where models would give a private showing for her clientele. The décor, designed in the modernist style of the earlier Wiener Werkstätte, was simple and elegant. Black and white chequered rugs covered the parquetry floor. The red velvet couches created a burst of colour next to the black gloss walls. Light came from the large window and twelve bell-shaped, hand-blown glass lamps hanging from the high ceiling. There were large wall mirrors and an exquisite 18th-century six-panelled Japanese screen, depicting scenes from *The Tale of Genj*, a gift from her parents on the opening of the salon. The screen, painted on silk in gold ink and gold leaf on paper, and the portrait, were Christina's pride and joy.

She flicked through the client book and noted just how many good clients she'd lost in a matter of a few months. Where they were, she had no idea; America, England, France, Palestine? Only a few said goodbye in person. As for the rest, she learnt of their departures from others. Hanging on the rack behind her were several half-finished clothes from their last fittings. *Did they know then they were going away and thought it better to keep it a secret?* She would never know.

The first client to arrive was a long-standing customer, Baroness Elisabeth von Fürstenberg, a beautiful dark-haired opera singer in her mid-thirties. During her fitting, they spoke about the events of what had now become known as *Kristallnacht*. The Baroness was appalled at what took place, but, unlike Christina, had not witnessed the humiliations suffered by the Jews. She had been at a rehearsal at the opera house. When she left she had wondered why there was so much activity on the streets. Angry mobs were pouring into the inner part of the city carrying placards and torches. Fearing trouble, she urged her chauffeur to drive back to her villa in Döbling as quickly as possible. From there, she saw the night sky lit up in a fiery red glow. The next day, she learnt what had taken place, and, despising the National Socialists as much as Christina did, met with her friends to see what could be done about it. She too had Jewish friends who were now vulnerable. When her fitting ended, Christina confided in her about

Mirka's murder and the plight of the Rosen children. The Baroness offered to help in any way she could.

'Of course, we all hope sanity will prevail and those responsible will be punished, but I am afraid, if Germany is anything to go by, it's already too late for that.'

Sadly, Christina agreed with her.

The last client, Frau Adler, a Jewish banker's wife did not show up at all, and, probably fearing the telephone lines would be tapped, did not call to cancel the meeting. Tired and exhausted, Christina shut her appointment book and closed the salon.

☾

Kurt Beck was outside polishing the car when Max arrived.

'She's in rather a fragile state,' Beck told him. 'I fear she's taking on more than she ought to. Look after her, won't you?'

Kurt Beck had been Christina's chauffeur ever since the couture house opened. He was in his mid-fifties and had worked as a chauffeur since he was a young man. His CV included chauffeuring for the Rothschilds and members of the Habsburg family. His own family knew Christina's from the time she and Karin were children, and when offered the well-paid job of her chauffeur, including the use of the car for himself, he jumped at the chance. It meant he could take his grandchildren for the occasional ride into the countryside. A solid-built man with a wide, thick moustache with the ends turned sharply upwards in the old "Kaiser" style, he was loyal and steadfast. He was also fiercely anti-Fascist, and despised Adolf Hitler.

Max made his way upstairs to Christina's apartment. The three Rosen children were in bed. Christina was sitting alone in the drawing room by the *Kachelofen*, reading a copy of *Wiener Damenmode*. She got up and threw her arms around his neck, giving him an affectionate kiss.

'I'm so relieved to see you,' she said.

'What's happened? I saw Kurt as he was leaving. He's concerned about you.'

'I've had a hell of a day, but in the end we achieved something – Nathan is safe and sound.'

Max warmed his hands next to the stove while Christina poured him a cognac. When she told him what had transpired, he was both delighted and concerned.

'Excellent sleuth work, my darling – but highly dangerous.'

'I thought you would be happy. If we'd waited any longer, he would have ended up in Dachau.'

Max put his glass down, clasped her shoulders firmly, and looked her in the eyes. 'Of course I'm happy, but the fact remains, you put yourself in danger by going to Landesgerichtesstrasse in the first place. Did you offer a bribe to get such a result?'

Christina shook herself free from his grasp and looked away.

'You did, didn't you – how much?' She held the back of her hand towards him. He was aghast when he saw she no longer wore the diamond ring. 'Good God, Kiki – are you mad! That ring cost a small fortune.'

She gave him an angry look. 'And Nathan's life is worth less than a diamond ring?'

'I'm not saying that. Don't twist things. Did anyone see you?'

'Of course not! We were alone.'

He sat down on the couch and wiped his brow with his handkerchief. 'You have no idea whether that man will rat on you. How will he explain what he did to his superiors?'

Christina laughed. 'Now who's being naïve? They're all on the take.'

'What about the policeman –Joseph Fischer?'

'He won't talk. I promised to look after his wife. Goodness knows when he last gave her a gift. It was obvious he didn't want me to go to his house as he left a message for me to meet him in the Prater on Friday. That alone told me he was being cautious. I intend to keep my promise and meet him.' She took Max's hand. 'I am sure he won't breathe a word or he will be in trouble too. He's compromised. If he was found out, I doubt he would even make it as far as Dachau.'

'All the same,' he replied after giving it some thought, 'let me check him out, keep an eye on him.'

'How are you going to do that? We don't know where he lives.' Christina slumped back into the gold pillows that adorned the couch. 'Max, you're beginning to make me angry. Don't treat me like a child.'

'Kiki, you are headstrong and your actions are putting us all at risk. Think of your sister and your mother. Think of me.' He tapped his finger on his chest, angrily. 'I helped you out after *Kristallnacht*, but you are becoming impossible. Dammit! I am a Jew. Jews disappear these days – even well-connected ones – in case you hadn't noticed.'

At that point Christina was conscious of someone standing in the doorway. It was Hannah. She jumped up and went over to her. 'I'm so sorry. Did we wake you up?' She invited her to come in and sit with them.

'I can't sleep.' Hannah said. 'I'm frightened.'

Christina drew her into her arms and hugged her affectionately, telling her everything would be fine. After several minutes, she took her back to the bedroom and tucked her in bed. Nathan and Malka were fast asleep.

'Were you arguing because of us?' Hannah asked.

'No. It has nothing to do with you. It's the situation we're in. Rest assured you are safe with us. Now go to sleep.' She gave her a kiss on the forehead. 'Sweet dreams.'

When she returned to the drawing room, Max apologized for raising his voice, pulled her into his arms and kissed her hard on the mouth. Within seconds, the tension subsided and they devoured each other in a passionate embrace.

Max gestured toward the window. Look, there's a full moon tonight so let's sleep here in front of this lovely warm fire.' He lay her down on the rug and started to unbutton her blouse. 'And then I can watch the moonlight dance on your naked flesh.'

She slipped off her blouse exposing her firm breasts, and put his

52

hands on them. 'Tonight I am all yours.' She gave him one of her seductive smiles and pulled him to her.

In the early hours of the morning, the fire had gone out and the room was cold. They tiptoed into bed and after making love again, fell asleep. When Christina woke up, Max was standing in front of the mirror getting dressed.

'You're up early,' she said, propping herself up on her elbow.

'I have to go. There's something urgent I need to attend to.'

'Now who's being mysterious? Won't you even have breakfast before you leave?'

He looked at his watch. 'Sorry, I would love to, but I'm late already.' He sat on the side of the bed. 'I've given it some thought. I will take Nathan until we get something sorted out. There's a spare room in my apartment.' Christina was about to speak, but he put his finger on her lips. 'Not another word. Your mother has offered to take the girls, but Nathan is another matter. It's for the best.'

'When will I see you again?' she asked.

'You're taking the girls to Hietzing today. No doubt you'll be there a while. And tomorrow you're meeting Fischer, so let's say tomorrow evening. I'll leave it with you to tell Nathan he'll be staying with me for a while. We don't want to spring it on to him at the last moment.'

'I love you, my darling.' Christina's voice was soft and warm. 'Thank you for your understanding and for always being there for me. I don't know what I'd do without you.'

He blew her a kiss as he left the room. 'Just be careful.'

Christina lay back on the bed, listening to his footsteps descending the stairs. *Why did this have to happen? If only those children had a family. And Max – he wasn't himself at all these days. It didn't take much for him to become melancholic or lose his temper.* She resolved to sort the Rosen children out as soon as possible. At least that would be one less headache for him.

CHAPTER 7

AT EXACTLY TEN minutes to eleven, Christina left Beck at the entrance to the Prater, tucked the package under her arm, and made her way along the tree-lined pathway to the blue carousel in the amusement park, as arranged. There was a damp, icy chill in the air but it didn't stop people going for a stroll, enjoying themselves at the many sideshows, or drinking beer and eating *Wiener Würstchen* at the many sausage stands and beer tents.

She sat on the bench under a horse chestnut tree and waited, listening to the lively mechanical organ music while watching the children riding on the theatrically ornate carousels with their gilded caryatids, mermaids and mirrors. To the children, the gaudily-painted wooden figures, moving up and down, round and round, were amusing, but Christina thought them grotesque; their wide mouths and large eyes seemed cold and mocking. Added to the cacophony of sounds were the shouts of showmen enticing passers-by to step inside an illuminated booth to experience a death-defying show of sword-swallowing and fire-eating, or to try their luck and test their ability at games of chance like the Crossbow Shoot game or the Balloon and Darts. Elsewhere, a boxing match was being performed. A man wearing a large placard advertising a freak show walked by with a megaphone – *Standing room only! Don't miss out! Johannes the Giant and Lela, the smallest woman in the world. Direct from Budapest.* Christina hated the freak shows more than anything else and, thankfully, she had read that the National Socialists had started to ban them. In most places in Austria, these shows had already closed. She couldn't understand why they were still allowing them here in the Prater. Maybe they didn't want to appear

54

heavy-handed, but then, the National Socialists never had a problem with that before.

She looked at her watch. It was fifteen minutes past eleven, but there was no sign of Fischer. In polite Viennese society, being late was frowned upon, and she started to worry. *What if he had been caught? Maybe she should leave before it was too late.* To make matters worse, several women passers-by seemed to recognize her, which made her feel even more uncomfortable. She thought of Max, about how protective he was of her, and felt a surge of love. With him, she would get through these trying times. Minutes later, Fischer appeared from the opposite direction. Christina couldn't help noticing how shabby he appeared, dressed in an old woollen coat and hat instead of his smart police uniform.

He shook her hand. 'Good day, Fräulein Lehmann. Please forgive me for being late. It is most impolite, but unfortunately I was held up.' His eyes fell on the package tied neatly with a red ribbon. 'Not here,' he whispered. 'Let's go somewhere where we won't be interrupted.'

Christina followed him. They headed to the Ferris wheel and joined the queue.

'Two tickets, please,' Fischer said to a heavily rouged plump lady in the box office.

The door to the cabin in front of them slammed shut and the large iron wheel moved a little, bringing the next empty one to a standstill. As they stepped inside, Christina glanced over her shoulder to check that no one was following them. When each cabin was full, the giant wheel started to move, gently rocking in the soft breeze. The higher they got, the colder it became and Christina pulled her coat tighter with her gloved hand. With the other, she passed the package to Fischer.

'My gift for Frau Fischer. I hope she likes it. I made her a cream silk blouse. I'm sure it will fit. The photograph you gave me was good enough for me to guess her size. I thought the cream would look good against her dark hair. She's a beautiful lady.' His face reddened and

Christina could tell he was embarrassed. 'It's the least I could do. A promise is a promise.'

Fischer looked down at the beautifully wrapped package with tears in his eyes. 'Thank you. It saddens me to say that I have not been able to give my dear Frau a gift in years, yet she doesn't complain. A policeman's pay doesn't go far these days, you know. Still at least I have a job with prospects, so I suppose I am fortunate.' He pulled himself together and asked her if his list had served its purpose.

She assured him it had. 'I cannot thank you enough, although I *was* worried I'd asked too much of you. As you implied at the time, what you did was dangerous. Do you mind if I ask how you achieved it?'

Fischer hesitated a few seconds before answering, 'My uncle is an official at Leopoldstadt police precinct. I knew he would have access to the files. At first he refused to help me, especially as I said I couldn't tell him why I wanted them. In the end I said it was for a trusted friend and he relented, but told me to watch my step or we'd both be done for.' Fischer gave a nervous laugh, his eyes revealing his conflicting emotions. 'Where is the list now?'

'I burnt it,' Christina replied, 'as soon as I found what I was looking for.'

Fischer looked relieved.

By now, the Ferris wheel had completed half a turn and they were at the top, looking over the city with the Danube snaking its way through the suburbs on one side and the Vienna Woods on the other. From where she stood, precariously looking down below at the people, moving like dots among the carousels, amusement tents, restaurants, and coffee houses, Christina felt a surge of pride in her city. The great wheel had earned a place in the people's hearts, perhaps even more than the opera house and Burgtheater. The Prater was for everyone, rich and poor alike.

'Tell me,' Christina asked, 'why did you feel the need to bring me here to talk? Surely we could have conversed in the park?'

Fischer's reply was that it didn't seem right that he, a poor man, should be seen in the company of such an elegant and beautiful woman, who, he added, was well-known in Vienna. He saw people looking at her as he approached and became nervous. 'I don't want to attract attention to myself – or to your good self for that matter. The list contained the names of Jews, and I know it's none of my business, but I thought you should know that the authorities are going to clamp down on them.'

Christina didn't seem surprised. Everyone in Austria knew this by now. 'Why are you telling me this?'

'I might be a simple, uneducated man, but I have it on good authority that the Jews are going to be made to pay for the destruction of the night of November 9 – 10 and already 30,000 Jewish men have been sent to concentration camps in Dachau, Buchenwald, and Sachsenhausen, so who will be able to pay? Those who can't will be thrown onto the streets.'

Christina had already heard a rumour about this, but refused to believe it. Was it just another tactic to rob the Jews? A law had been implemented on April 26, a few weeks after the Anschluss – the "Decree for the Reporting of Jewish-Owned Property", as it was called, which was issued by Hitler's government. Under this new law, all Jews in both Germany and Austria were required to register any property or assets valued at more than 5,000 Reichsmark. From furniture and paintings to life insurance and stocks, nothing was immune from the registry. By July 31, Austrian and German finance officials had collected paperwork from some 700,000 Jewish citizens. She recalled her Jewish friends' reactions, including Max. 'Another step in the "Aryanization" of the Jewish people,' he said at the time. It caused him great distress as he had not registered himself as a Jew.

'I hope you're wrong,' she said to Fischer.

'I have it on good authority, Fräulein Lehmann, so if you are protecting any Jews, you put yourself in grave danger.' He was thinking of her friends in Leopoldstadt. 'This government will stop at nothing to rid Austria of its Jews.' Fischer momentarily looked away, embarrassed. 'I can see you have a good heart, and I know you are a woman of influence, but these people don't care about any of that.' His eyebrows knitted together in a frown. 'I loathe what is happening to my country. My father and uncle fought in the Great War and want nothing but peace, but I fear we are heading the wrong way. I only have my job because I joined the National Socialist Party – my Uncle too. In fact, everyone who doesn't join will lose their job. It doesn't make us National Socialists, though.'

Christina thanked him for sharing his thoughts, promising that their conversation would go no further.

'Was it your uncle who told you this?' she asked.

'Yes. He gets it from higher up. I'm sorry, I can't say from whom.'

'That's all right. I won't pry.'

When the ride was over, they stepped out of the cabin and shook hands.

'Herr Fischer, I cannot tell you how much I appreciate our conversation. I consider you a friend and if ever you need anything from me, please let me know; anything at all. If you feel uncomfortable to come to my salon, you can always leave a message for me at Café Landtmann. And by the way, I put the photo of Frau Fischer in the package with the blouse.'

Fischer bowed slightly, lifting his hat, 'Good luck, kind lady. It was a pleasure to meet you, and an honour to know you.'

They parted ways and she watched him pass a group of *Heuriger* singers performing their melodies for a group of children with balloons. When he'd gone, she made her way back to the car outside the main entrance, making sure she was not being followed.

'Everything all right, Fräulein Christina?' Beck asked. 'Did the meeting go well?'

'Under the circumstances, yes,' she replied.

CHAPTER 8

BECK DROVE THROUGH the black iron gates and along the curved driveway, bordered by thick hedges, to the villa. He dropped Christina off at the main entrance, parked the car at the side of the house, and entered by the servants' door, where he would have afternoon tea with Frau Julia Lehmann's cook, Irma, and the rest of the staff. Beck was a likeable, friendly man and Irma had a soft spot for him. Knowing that he was bringing Christina over, she baked him one of her special cakes – a chocolate cake which he devoured with relish, complimenting her by saying it was comparable to anything the Hotel Sacher served. From the kitchen, he caught a glimpse of Malka and Hannah playing with the Lehmann's hunting dog on the lawn.

Irma, a buxom woman with neat greying hair swept back into a thick bun, wiped her hands on her apron and threw him a knowing glance as she poured out his coffee, but neither mentioned their presence. It was as if it was off-limits. Instead they spoke about light-hearted things such as what she was cooking, his family, and in particular, his grandchildren. In fact they spoke about anything that didn't concern politics, especially the National Socialists and their rallies which were taking place all over the city.

Upstairs in the drawing room, Christina greeted her mother with a kiss. Gitta, her mother's maid, a young woman in her mid-twenties, laid out a platter of *belegte Brote*, open sandwiches made from fresh, dark rye bread, cut into small rectangles and smothered in various spreads, along with a variety of cakes. In the Viennese Kaffeehaus, these tasty sandwiches were accompanied by a *Pfiff* – small quantity – of beer, but today the ladies decided on hot chocolate instead. After

Gitta left the room to join Irma and Beck, Christina turned her attention to Hannah and Malka.

She spoke in a low voice. 'How are they settling in?'

'Malka frets terribly, and she carries her doll everywhere. Hannah puts on a brave face but I can tell her heart is broken. I've tried to make them comfortable, but they must have a more permanent home. My house maybe large, but it's not suitable for them. I have too many guests and I can't keep them hidden for too long. Irma and Gitta have been told not to mention their presence to anyone and to keep an eye on them when I have visitors. You can't trust anyone these days.' Julia Lehmann paused to take a small bite of sandwich topped with egg mayonnaise with a sprinkle of paprika. 'What's happening with the boy?'

'Max will take him this evening.'

Julia Lehmann wiped the corner of her mouth with a serviette and began to pour out the hot chocolate. 'How has he taken it?'

'He didn't say a word, but I'm sure he's not too happy. It's better he's with a man than with me.'

'Have you thought about asking any of the seamstresses if they can take them? After all, some are Jewish.'

'When they heard what happened in Leopoldstadt, they were appalled. Now they're frightened for their own safety, and as none offered to take the children, I never mentioned it again. Maybe one girl would have been easier, but two – that's too much to ask. Nathan is another matter. He's a young man.'

Christina turned her head to take in the view of the garden and the rooftops of the nearby villas. Growing up in this part of Vienna, with its close proximity to Schönbrunn Palace and the Vienna Woods, had been an idyllic childhood. Every week was filled with walks and picnics through the woods with her sister and parents, and when she wasn't studying, there were always friends to visit. Johann Strauss II, the "Waltz King", and Katharina Schratt, the confidante of the Emperor, had also lived here. On March 12, 1938, when Austria became part of

Greater Germany, the official removal of Jewish citizens commenced. The Lehmanns couldn't believe it. Several of their friends' properties and villas were Aryanised. In a matter of a few weeks, they had lost friends, some of whom Christina had known all her life, and many had been her best clients. Nazi reforms were swift and by rezoning areas of Vienna, thousands of its citizens were uprooted and left vulnerable to ever-worsening Nazi plans to eliminate them.

Politically, Christina's family had supported the Christian Democrats, but Austria had been going through political turmoil during the thirties and when Chancellor Engelbert Dollfuss was shot, after a series of riots, Christina's father, Heinrich, who disliked Dollfuss immensely, warned that Fascism was on the rise everywhere, and that the Austrian Nazis' affiliation with Hitler and Germany would only get stronger. Heinrich Lehmann died from an accidental gunshot wound while hunting in the woods at their family hunting lodge, Schloss Steinbrunnhof, shortly after Dollfuss was assassinated. His body was taken back to Hietzing and, ironically, was buried close to Dollfuss' grave in the nearby cemetery.

It was in this same drawing room, with the blue and gold brocaded couch and high-backed chairs in which Christina and her mother now sat, that Max had first spoken with Heinrich Lehmann about his love for Christina and revealed why he was reluctant to marry her. The old man had taken a liking to him, but he confessed to his wife after the meeting that Max being a Jew worried him. Heinrich Lehmann was professor of psychology at Vienna University and a friend of another important Viennese Jew, Sigmund Freud, so he was well aware of rising anti-Semitic elements in Austria. After a long discussion with Julia, they agreed that Max was doing the right thing in postponing the marriage. It was better for them to wait until things died down. Julia Lehmann knew her daughter well; she was headstrong and would fight their decision, but Max persuaded her that even though they were not married, he would never look at another woman. In his eyes, he was already wedded to his beautiful Kiki. In the end, love won over, and as she had her fashion house to think of, she reluctantly agreed. True to his word, Max, who had always had an eye for beautiful and talented women, never looked at another woman from that moment on. Christina accepted the status quo.

'Guess who I had a visit from this morning?' Julia Lehmann said. 'Frau Klein. She said she'd received good news and wanted to share it with me.'

At the mention of the Kleins, Christina frowned. 'What did she want?'

'To tell me Dieter has a promotion. He now works with Ernst Kaltenbrunner who has been appointed SS and Police leader.'

Christina felt her chest tighten. This was the last thing she wanted to hear. It was long suspected that Kaltenbrunner, acting on orders from Hermann Göring, had assisted in the Anschluss with Germany in March, and for his loyalty, was awarded the role as the state secretary for public security in the Seyss-Inquart cabinet. Kaltenbrunner's new position meant he now had direct access to Himmler, and Christina knew what that meant. Dieter Klein would now be in a position to oversee the Nazification of all aspects of Austrian society.

She got up and walked over to look out of the window in an effort to hide her distress, but she could not fool her mother who knew exactly what was going through her mind.

'Thank God, Papa didn't live long enough to see this day,' Christina said. 'He would not have tolerated the Kleins in the house.'

'I know, my darling. To think we were once all so close and how good life used to be before Hitler rose to power in Germany.' Julia Lehmann sighed. 'I have such fond memories of both you and Karin playing with the Klein children when you were young. It's hard to believe how we could have grown apart. We had our disagreements, but, after your father died, I took his advice and never voice my political opinions in their company. Better to keep our thoughts to ourselves, don't you think?'

Christina turned to face her mother. 'Oh Mama, I fear for Max.

Frau Klein adores her son, but she doesn't seem to realise how ambitious he is.'

'That's true, but he *is* good to her. That's all she sees: a son who spoils her with fine gifts. Of the three children, he was always her favourite and she spoilt him. Who am I to tell her how to bring up her own family – or that the SS he now works for is feared. She will turn against me, and that will mean she'll turn against you too. We must try to live with it.'

The Kleins had three children. Dieter was the eldest and the same age as Karin. Sigmund, a quiet man who lived in the constant shadow of his older brother, was a year younger than Christina and a doctor at the Am Steinhof Hospital in Vienna. And then there was Gudrun, the "unexpected" child born later in life when Frau Klein was going through an early and painful menopause. She had tried to rid herself of the unborn child with herbal potions and medicines, but it was no use. The child was born a month early and there were problems. The girl was backward and rather awkward. As she grew older, she was kept away from social gatherings and grew progressively worse. When she was eleven, the Kleins admitted her to the Lower Austrian Provincial Institution for the Care and Cure of the Mentally Ill and for Nervous Disorders Am Steinhof, which opened in 1907. She was there, intermittently, for a few years. The treatment, a series of electric shocks intended to make her more manageable and easier to care for, only made things worse. In the end, the family decided to keep her at home and a full-time nurse was hired to look after her. Frau Klein always blamed herself for her daughter's plight.

'How is Gudrun?' Christina asked.

'Whenever I ask about her, the question is brushed off with a simple "she's fine". I don't ask anymore.'

Christina broke off a luscious dark grape from a large bunch that had hung from a decorative Viennese enamelled *tazza*. 'How old would she be now?'

'I believe about sixteen. The same age as Hannah. And speaking of

Hannah, are you aware just how good a seamstress she is?'

'Her mother did tell me she was teaching her. She wanted her to follow in her footsteps. Why do you ask?'

'Because the girl has talent. When I looked for clothes for her to wear, she told me what she did with her mother. Mirka taught her all about fabrics, how to drape them on mannequins to get the desired cut, how to use a sewing machine, and how to sew sequins and embroider. She reminds me of you at that age. Why don't you take her under your wing? That way everyone wins. You will have another pair of hands, she will have a wage, and we can find them somewhere affordable to rent.'

'I've been too caught up in what took place to even think about it, but now that you mention it, it's a good idea. I'll certainly keep it in mind, but there's still the problem of Malka and Nathan. Jewish children have been banned from schools, and Nathan – well – that's a difficult one. Who will employ him these days?'

Julia Lehmann couldn't answer, and changed the conversation to lighter topics. After a couple of hours, Christina said she'd better return to Mariahilferstrasse. She was looking forward to seeing Max again and hoped he would be in brighter spirits.

'What about coming away with me for a few days?' Julia Lehmann said as Christina prepared to leave. 'I've enjoyed our afternoon together and these days I don't see enough of you.'

Christina knew she was right. Her fashion house, Max, and the events taking place in Vienna, had consumed her more than she wanted to admit. Even Karin had mentioned that their mother was disappointed not to see her as often as she used to.

'What did you have in mind? Do you want to go to Salzburg, maybe a concert, or perhaps go to a guesthouse by Lake Neusiedl?'

'Neither. I was thinking we could go to the old hunting lodge.'

Christina's eyes widened. 'Schloss Steinbrunnhof! We haven't been there since Papa died.'

'That's right. At the time I couldn't bear to see the place again; too many painful memories. Maybe now is the time to put that behind us and start going again. What do you say? We can ask Karin and Walter – and Max, of course.' Julia Lehmann wouldn't take no for an answer. 'Let's say in a fortnight. I will go ahead and make sure the place is nice and clean, and you can all follow later.'

Christina wrapped her arms around her mother. After the initial surprise, she thought it a splendid idea. 'I agree. It may be just the tonic we all need, but what about the girls?'

'I'll take them with me. It will do them good to get away too, and I'll find something to occupy them. Hopefully by then you will have decided what to do with them.' She rang the bell and asked Gitta to bring the girls to see her.

Malka gave Christina the first smile in days.

Christina turned her attention to Hannah. 'Mama tells me you've been talking about your work with your mother. Would you like to make something while you're here?'

Hannah gave a shy smile. 'Thank you, Fräulein Lehmann. Mutti taught me many things. I want to be like her.' The smile faded. 'What did you want me to do?'

'Well, let's see. How about you make a nice dress for yourself and Malka? Mama has a sewing room here. I'm sure she won't mind you using it.' Christina looked across at her mother.

'Christina used to work there when she was a sewing student,' Julia Lehmann added. 'It would please me to see it used again.'

Hannah thanked them for their kindness and said she would be delighted.

'Excellent,' said Christina. 'Now let's see. Tell me what your favourite colour is and I'll send over some fabric.'

'Rose,' Hannah replied. 'It was Mutti's favourite colour too.'

Christina gave her mother another fleeting glance. Any mention of Frau Rosen caused great unease. 'Wonderful. And you, Malka, what colour would you like?'

Malka's eyes shone with delight. 'Blue,' she answered quickly. 'Like the sky. Fräulein Lehmann, can Pipina have a new blue dress too?'

Christina took one look at the doll Malka carried everywhere and saw how dirty and scruffy her clothes were, no doubt made worse by the constant tears she had shed on it.

'What a good idea.'

'Fräulein Lehmann,' Hannah said, 'does this mean we will be staying here?'

'Well...'

Julia Lehmann came to her daughter's rescue. 'For a couple of weeks – until we find you a nice apartment of your own.'

Malka asked if her mother would be back by then. Hannah looked at the ground, afraid of giving herself away. No one knew what to say.

'I have some more good news for you both,' Julia Lehmann said, quickly avoiding the awkward question. 'We're going on a little holiday – to the country. How would you like that?'

This time there was a smile on both the girls' faces and Julia Lehmann winked at Christina. 'There,' she said to them. 'I knew you'd like that.'

When the girls left the room, Christina thanked her mother for her kindness. 'It certainly made me feel a lot better to see them smile again.'

'I will do what I can, my darling, but one way or another, you must resolve this problem by the time we return from Schloss Steinbrunnhof.'

CHAPTER 9

AFTER THE TRAUMATIC events of *Kristallnacht*, the following week passed by quietly for Christina. Max took Nathan to live with him for a while and found him work with a wine producer in Grinzing. A quaint suburb of Vienna, Grinzing was filled with wine taverns, cobblestoned streets, and old trams winding their way up to the Vienna Woods foothills. Finding work for him had not been easy, as most people were wary of employing Jews, regardless of how young and desperate they were. Christina's couture house was still busy, but with at least half of her most important Jewish customers leaving the country, both she and Karin felt that spark of optimism they'd once had when preparing for new collections, was fading.

One unforeseen aspect of Nazi power in 1933 was Hitler's attempt to control every aspect of women's lives, including what they wore, and the new German Fashion Institute, the *Deutsches Modeamt*, oversaw the uniform for the *Bund Deutsche Mädel*. Following the Anschluss, Christina was sure it wouldn't be long before they, too, were affected. Hitler loved attractive women, claiming, *"What I like best of all is to dine with a pretty woman"*, but he hated make-up, disapproved of hair dye, and perfume disgusted him. He preferred dresses to trousers, as he considered them unfeminine, and fur was distasteful because it involved killing animals. Added to the growing list of things he disapproved of, was Parisian fashion. He wanted to make Berlin women the best dressed in Europe – and now Viennese women too. Christina already thought German and Austrian women were beautifully dressed, but she still looked toward Paris for inspiration. 'Inspiration comes from everywhere', Max remarked to her. 'It doesn't observe borders.'

Thankfully, no one had yet banned the international fashion magazines. Taking advantage of the political situation, the Association of Aryan Clothing Manufacturers also sprung up, making its own label to be sewn into garments, guaranteeing that they had only been touched by Aryan hands. Christina vowed she would rather close the salon than add these to her garments beside her name.

'It's only a matter of time before we are asked to make dirndls, bodices, and Tyrolean jackets,' Karin said sarcastically to Christina. 'Very soon our books will be full of women wanting to wear *Tracht* rather than stylish gowns.'

'Most women already have these outfits,' Christina replied. '*Tracht* has its place, but it's not couture, so hopefully this crazy idea will fade. From what I hear, Magda Goebbels was made honorary president of the Fashion Institute, but was sacked because her idea of being stylish doesn't conform to their ideology. On top of that, her favourite designers are Paul Kuhnen, Fritz Grünfeld, and Richard Goetz – all Jewish. Annelies von Ribbentrop has similar taste. If the wives of the Nazi hierarchy are not in favour of it, it's doomed to fail.'

'Let's hope you're right,' Karin replied. 'All the same, it may help if we put a mannequin wearing *Tracht* in the window every now and again.'

That idea brought a laugh to an otherwise sombre situation and lightened the atmosphere for a while, but it didn't last long. Beck arrived to say that one of the largest department stores in Mariahilferstrasse – Weiss & Wertheimer – which sold quality clothing, footwear, bedding, furniture, jewellery, beauty products, and housewares, had been Aryanized and was now about to be called Schneider & Sohn. He was in the Kaffeehaus with his son when he saw the Treuhänder, the governmental trustee, step out of the building with Herr Weiss and his wife.

'They shook hands as if all was well,' Beck said, 'more as a show for the public I would say, because a crowd of people, including journalists, were gathering outside. It was evident that Frau Weiss was distressed, but she carried herself with dignity. As they got into their car and drove away, some in the crowd started cheering.'

Christina and Karin looked at each other. They knew the Weiss family well. Rumours about a takeover had circulated for a while, but this store was a well-known and respected institution in Vienna, and many thought it would escape Aryanization, particularly if they paid money to someone in the know. Frau Weiss had picked up a coat a month or so earlier and said nothing to them about their predicament, so this came as quite a shock.

'What a disgrace!' Karin said. 'That store has been there since before 1900. The family lost relatives in the Great War.'

Beck handed Christina an envelope. 'Baroness Elisabeth's chauffeur arrived just as I was about to enter. He asked that I give you this personally.'

Karin looked on while Christina opened it. Inside were four tickets to a performance of Johann Strauss's operetta, *Das Spitzentuch der Königin*, The Queen's Lace Handkerchief, on Saturday evening. As a soprano, the Baroness was playing the part of the queen. There was a note with the tickets.

'She says she wants us to join her afterwards in her suite at the Hotel Sacher. It's a matter of urgency.' Christina showed Karin the note. 'I wonder what it's about.'

When Saturday arrived, Christina and Max, accompanied by Karin and her husband, Walter, arrived to a sold-out performance at the *Wiener Staatsoper*, one of the leading opera houses of the world, and took their seats in one of the boxes with close proximity to the stage. This romantic operetta had always been a favourite with the Viennese, and Christina had lost count of the times she'd danced with Max to "Rosen aus dem Süden", one of their favourite waltzes from the operetta. She looked through her opera glasses and scanned the auditorium. It was filled with men in Nazi uniform.

Max nudged her. 'Look who's in the next box,' he whispered. 'Dieter Klein, and by the look of it, he's found himself a glamorous girlfriend – the German actress, Lina Lindner.'

Christina moved forward slightly to take a look. From the way Dieter was paying amorous attention to the woman, it was obvious he was besotted with her. She breathed a sigh of relief hoping he would no longer have ideas of marrying her. Lina was wearing a silver halter-neck dress exposing her beautiful skin which glistened sensually under the soft lights. Dieter leaned over and planted a kiss on her bare shoulder. As he did, he caught sight of Christina looking at him. Embarrassed, he quickly sat back into his seat.

Throughout the performance, she occasionally glanced in the pair's direction. His earlier flirtatious gestures appeared to have stopped. She vowed not to let his presence detract her from a good night out. All the same, the presence of so many National Socialists reminded her that a few weeks after the Anschluss, the Baroness's close friend, the violinist Viktor Robitsek, had received a note from the management of the Vienna Philharmonic Orchestra telling him his services were no longer needed. His crime – he was Jewish. During one of her fittings in the salon, the Baroness confided to Christina that she suspected there was a spy in the orchestra, someone who was producing intelligence and denouncing musicians. Altogether, thirteen members of the prestigious orchestra had been forced to leave. What their fate would be, Christina could not imagine, but she hoped they would get work in other countries.

The operetta was a resounding success and the Baroness received a standing ovation. To rapturous applause, she received the many bouquets of flowers with bows of gratitude, occasionally throwing kisses to the audience. As they made their way from their private box and down the staircase into the foyer, Karin remarked in a low voice how the beautiful Renaissance revival building was marred by so many large flags emblazoned with swastikas. If others were feeling despondent by this, they certainly weren't showing it. Unless you knew someone well, it was getting harder by the day to know people's true feelings. Besides, it took a lot for polite Viennese society to let politics mar their beloved opera. Happily for Christina and Max, Dieter Klein was nowhere to be seen.

Outside, the weather had turned icy, and a flurry of snowflakes swirled softly in the night sky veiled by the yellow cones of light of the streetlamps. The city was shrouded in an ominous silence. Thankfully, the Hotel Sacher was situated behind the opera house and they didn't have far to walk. The place was doing a brusque business as it always did whenever there was a performance at the opera house, and tonight there were a number of high-ranking politicians and members of the National Socialist Party in the hotel. Max made his way to the reception desk and told the receptionist they were guests of the Baroness. They were directed to a suite on the top floor. Making their way past the bar, they spotted Stephen Pembroke sitting at a table near the pianist.

'What are you doing here?' Max asked.

'The same as you,' Pembroke replied. 'I'm a guest of the Baroness. Come on, let's get going. It's getting noisy in here.' He indicated two SS men who were trying to impress their girlfriends.

They all took the elevator in silence, listening to the creaking, grinding noise as it strained against the cables, until it stopped with a shudder on the top floor. The lift operator pulled aside the sliding doors, bid them a good night, and the lift descended again, the sound fading with the lift. Pembroke led the way down the corridor and stopped outside Suite 507. To the rest of the group's surprise, he took out a key and unlocked the door. The room was in darkness, but when he switched on the light, they saw a table in the centre of the room, elaborately laid out with canapés, champagne and wine.

'What's going on?' Max asked. 'We thought this was some kind of party to celebrate the Baroness's success in the operetta.'

'All will be revealed in due time, my good friend. Now, take your coats off and let me pour you all a drink until she arrives.'

An hour passed before the Baroness, carrying armfuls of bouquets, arrived with her lover, the distinguished and handsome actor-tenor, Lucien Lassalle from the Paris Opera House who was with the Vienna Opera for the winter season and who sang the part of Don Sancho d'Avellaneday Villapinquedones in the operetta.

'I'm so sorry to have kept you waiting, but you know what it's like: photographs and autograph signing.' She placed the flowers down and handed her hat and long ermine coat to Lucien, giving him a peck on the cheek while whispering endearments to him in French. She wore one of Christina's creations, a calf-length cream silk dress embroidered in rhinestones that clung to her voluptuous body like a second skin. Stephen Pembroke poured them both glasses of champagne and everyone congratulated her on yet another stellar performance.

'I'm sorry if you expected a party,' the Baroness said. 'I have something I want to discuss with you, and as I said in my note, it's a matter of urgency.'

'Why all the secrecy?' Karin asked.

'Discretion, I'm afraid. Let me explain. As you know, I have family in Czechoslovakia and they informed me that there's an Englishman in Prague who is trying to help Jewish children get to England.'

Christina, Max, Karin and her husband looked at each other in surprise. 'Can you elaborate?' Max asked.

The Baroness took off her shoes and settled into a more comfortable position in her chair. Placing a cigarette in her stylishly long and slender pear wood and ebony cigarette holder, she turned to Lucien for him to light it. She paused for a moment to inhale the perfumed smoke deep into her lungs. 'When the leaders of Britain, France, Italy, and Germany held a conference in Munich on September 29–30, they agreed to the German annexation of the Sudetenland in exchange for a pledge of peace from Hitler. As you are all well aware, this peace is a lie. The Nazis took back the Sudetenland a few days later, protests broke out, and National Socialist supporters and the *Freikorps* unleashed unbridled terror with acts of violence and vandalism against Jews and Czechs. In the wake of the invasion, *Einsatzgruppen* units have followed, helping to enforce Nazi repression. We have it on good authority that according to lists of anti-Nazis maintained by the SD, *Sicherheitsdienst*, the Gestapo offices have already reported over 2,000 arrests. Although Jews were not explicitly targeted as a group, many are arrested as political offenders. My friends, they are in dire straits and have approached this Englishman to help get their children out of the country.'

'What is happening there is no different to here,' Max replied, 'We have been unable to stop the escalating violence and attacks on Jews and dissenters which has been made worse by the Aryanization laws passed in the parliament.' He was clearly upset that another good evening was to be ruined by politics.

Christina put a hand on his thigh in an effort to calm him. 'Please continue, Baroness.'

The Baroness shifted uncomfortably in her chair and handed her glass to Lucien who refilled it, along with everyone else's. With the possible exception of Lucien, everyone in the room was aware that Max was half-Jewish.

'The point is, the day I heard about this, I happened to see Stephen in Café Landtmann and when I told him, he agreed to check it out.' She looked across at Pembroke and asked him to continue.

'We are already aware of the queues that form around the embassies and consulates on a daily basis. It's no secret this has accelerated since the Anschluss. In most cases these people are requesting exit visas and passports for themselves and their families. After checking with a friend in the American consulate, I discovered a few were asking for exit visas only for their children. Clearly they'd heard of what was happening in Prague. The consulate is in a difficult position. They face pressure from the Department of State to enforce restrictive immigration policies. The Consul General works with compassion, but must maintain the letter of the law while providing as many qualified applicants as possible with immigration visas.'

'They are bureaucrats who advance their careers by doing what they're told,' Max said. 'They have an institutional mindset that discourages sensitivity to local conditions. What do you expect them to do?'

Pembroke tactfully ignored Max's sarcasm by saying they do their best. 'My friend, however, knew what was taking place in Prague and suggested we contact the Home Office in Britain, as they are the only ones open to the idea of taking children.'

Karin looked aghast. As a woman who had been trying to get pregnant since she married, the idea appalled her. 'Surely no parent in their right mind will send their children away without them – to a foreign country where goodness knows what will happen to them. A mother in particular! This is a terrible idea.'

The Baroness interjected, 'You are right, Karin, but these are desperate times and people do desperate things. The Jews are being deprived of their work, their assets are being frozen, and many are suffering beatings or being sent to labour camps on trumped up charges. Their children can no longer go to school, and in the rare cases they do, must sit at the back of the class as if they had done something wrong.'

Pembroke continued. 'I sent a telegraph to a fellow journalist in London and he made enquires for us. The British Committee for Refugee Children has been set up and they are actively looking for foster parents for these children.'

This time, Walter Krassner spoke. 'Karin, my dear, I agree wholeheartedly with what has been said. It disgusts me to see my fellow musicians sacked for no reason at all. I don't talk about it with you because I don't want to distress you, but their families are suffering. I, for one, applaud the idea. At least they will have a roof over their heads, food and education. They will be safe and can be re-united with their families when Hitler and his thugs fall from grace.'

'Well spoken, Herr Krassner,' said Lucien, in his deep voice with a lilting French accent. 'In France we have seen thousands flee Austria and Germany, but unless they have family there, it's not easy for them. At least, these children will go to good homes.'

'I've been assured that steps are in place to check out the families,' Pembroke replied. He paused to let the group digest the information.

'Why are you telling us this?' Christina asked.

'Because we trust you and we need your help. Besides, I know you're looking after the Rosen girls. Maybe we can get them out of Austria too.'

Christina bit her lip. Nothing like this had crossed her mind. 'There's Nathan too,' she replied hastily.

'What we are proposing is not going to be easy. Too many people are already coming forward and, to put it bluntly, it's not possible to save everyone. We may have to concentrate only on the very young. They are the most vulnerable.'

'Are you proposing I try to get the girls out without their brother?' asked Christina.

Stephen didn't answer. He turned to Max and said they needed his help.

'What can *I* do?' Max asked.

'We need a photograph of all those children whose names we put forward. Some of them lost their possessions on *Kristallnacht*; others don't have money for this. I know you have a couple of friends who are photographers – Johannes and Anton. They are against the Nazis. Do you think you can ask them to help?'

'You are a journalist. You must have contacts yourself. Why don't you ask them?'

'Because I don't want to put them in jeopardy with the authorities. They could revoke their visas if they were seen to be aiding – undesirables.'

'You mean Jews,' Max answered sharply. 'And where do we get the money from? This will be costly.'

The Baroness interjected that she would be funding much of this. In the end, both she and Pembroke won everyone over to the idea. Max promised to speak with the photographers in the morning, and Christina, Karin and Walter said they'd keep their eyes and ears open for any family who fitted the bill. Knowing France was not interested in taking unaccompanied minors, Lucien said he would use his contacts to help anyone else who was able to go to France. They arranged to meet in Café Central in two days' time. In the meantime, they had a lot to do, as nothing was guaranteed at this point. In a strange way they felt optimistic, despite the difficulties they knew they'd encounter.

When they arrived back at the apartment in Mariahilferstrasse, Max and Christina discussed the meeting over a glass of cognac until the early hours of the morning. Stephen Pembroke had apologized for not telling Max earlier, saying he hadn't wanted to say anything at all until they'd received the go-ahead from the Home Office in London.

'What do you think?' Christina asked. 'About Malka, Hannah, and Nathan, I mean. Do you think they will agree to go – that is if we *can* get them an exit visa?' She stared into her glass, gloomily.

'I doubt they would understand, let alone be agreeable. This is a decision for adults to make in their interests. Karin was right when she questioned how many parents will want to give up their children. Only time will tell.'

He ran his hand through her hair. 'We can only do our best. For the moment, let's get some sleep. There's a lot to do between now and when we go to Steinbrunnhof.'

CHAPTER 10

ON ANY GIVEN day, Café Central on the corner of Ecke Herrengasse and Strauchgasse was packed with customers, many of them reading the daily newspapers or in conversation with friends over coffee and cake. It was one of the Baroness's favourite cafés and a table had been reserved for them. Christina and Max arrived at the same time as Johannes and Anton. Stephen Pembroke was already there, deep in conversation with Walter. Karin had offered to remain in the salon to attend to one of Christina's clients, who'd arranged a fitting earlier in the week. The Baroness arrived soon after, accompanied by the dapper Lucien, attired in a long back cape and carrying a silver-topped cane.

'Well,' she said, as the waiter placed coffee and cakes in front of them. 'Are we all good to go?'

Everyone said yes, and she thanked the two photographers for joining them.

'I put a discreet word out,' Walter said. 'Several families are interested, but they want some sort of assurance first. When I told them it was early days, they backed away. In the end, only one family said they were on board.' He sighed. 'It's not going to be easy.'

The Baroness shrugged him off. 'They will come running to us in droves when they see how successful we are. We must be patient.'

The attention turned to the photographers. 'We can work from my studio,' Anton said. 'It's only a few minutes from here, in Strauchgasse.'

'Perfect. I will pay you ten schilling for every photograph. How does that sound?'

Anton's eyes widened. '*Gnae'* Frau, that's far too much.'

The Baroness wouldn't argue. That was what she would pay and not a schilling less. Stephen Pembroke told them he was waiting on more information from London which he expected to receive any day now, and the Baroness said she'd already contacted Viennese officials at the Central Office for Jewish Emigration, situated in Prinz-Eugen-Strasse. The office had been setup by a man called Eichmann, specifically for the purpose of expediting anything at all to do with Jewish emigration. Would-be emigrants would have to pay an exit fee, of course, which she would sort out. Until then there was little they could do, except wait.

'Once the officials give the go-ahead, how long do you think it will take before we can send the first group of children away?' Christina asked.

'These things take time. Hopefully soon after Christmas: maybe a couple of months if things don't take a turn for the worst.'

Christina's heart sank. *A couple of months! That was an eternity.*

The meeting only lasted an hour and they parted ways outside the café with the Baroness saying she would contact them as soon as she had more news. Christina returned to the salon alone, as she wanted to do some shopping. She needed to buy a few things to take with her to Steinbrunnhof. This suited Max, as he had a commission to finish before they left.

'How did it go?' Karin asked, when Christina returned.

'Fine. Nothing more can be done until we receive word from London. At least that gives me time to work on the collection.'

She spent the rest of the day with the seamstresses in the workroom, choosing colour combinations and draping fabric on mannequins. The radio was tuned to a music station and the atmosphere was calm and uplifting, despite the fact that the women had lost several workmates. They were glad to have steady work, and Christina was a good woman to work for. One by one, she went through Max's sketches with them, checking to see that they understood the drape and what type of seams to use. 'Details,' she always told them, 'it's all about the details.' Her seamstresses were skilled and quick to understand her ideas.

In spring and summer, women gravitated toward saturated pastels such as peach, rose pink, lilac, sunny yellow, sky blue, and sea green. Add to that the year round colours of red, copen blue, emerald green, orange, and ochre. For winter, there was chocolate brown, grey, tan, rust, burgundy, navy blue, and black: warm and rich colours. There was, however, always one colour which was popular – white. White was everywhere – a year-round colour. If a garment was a solid colour, then white would accentuate the dress by means of a belt or a fabric inset. Otherwise white accessories would be worn. Perhaps white gave hope during difficult times – and goodness knows, there had been plenty of that after the Great War.

Christina wanted her clients to be sophisticated, impeccably tailored, and to look and feel like movie stars, adding her own variations of the popular style of broad, padded shoulders, nipped in waists, and shorter A-line skirts which were emerging. At the same time, she strove for a romantic look. Whether they were pleated, straight or flared, or came with tightly fitted jackets and blouses, she purposely made her suits feminine. Formal dresses dramatically displayed the willowy, elegant silhouette, and evening gowns in fluid fabrics were cut on the bias to create flowing, figure-hugging lines that reached the floor in chiffon, satin, and rayon.

Max had been a great help to her during the past few years. Besides being an acclaimed artist, he was a superb illustrator who understood what she wanted to achieve. At the end of each launch, Christina framed the best of his sketches and hung them in the salon where they could be admired as works of art in themselves. After going over one of the sketches with a seamstress, discussing where the embroidered embellishments should be placed, she retired to her apartment on the floor below to pack for the long weekend at Steinbrunnhof.

C

The car took a sharp right-hand turn off the Vienna-Budapest road and headed through the undulating, snow-covered farmland of Lower

Austria, passing through several picturesque hamlets and villages until it finally reached Schloss Steinbrunnhof, not far from the village of Seibersdorf. The pleasant drive took less than an hour, and Max and Christina were there in time for morning tea. The car swerved through a wrought-iron gate flanked by two stone obelisks, made its way through an allée of beech trees and over a stone bridge to the three-storey hunting lodge, surrounded by a former moat. As Max parked in the courtyard, one of the servants came out of the building to take their suitcases. Julia Lehmann was waiting for them in the drawing room with Karin and Walter.

'Walter has been telling me all about your plans with Baroness Elisabeth,' she said. 'It sounds like an excellent idea and I applaud the man in Prague who first thought of it.'

'Mama also has news for us,' Karin said. 'She's found out what's been happening here and in Burgenland, especially with the Jews. It's not good.' She turned to her mother. 'Tell them what Albrecht and Hildegard told you.'

Christina helped herself to a slice of apple strudel and sat in her favourite chair near the window where she had a good view of the surrounding parkland. The winter sun streamed into the room, highlighting the intense colours of the oriental silk carpet.

'What do you mean?' she asked. 'What's happened?'

'The Jews have been driven from their homes. It's as simple as that! Their houses were taken from them under the Aryanization laws and they were rounded up. It started almost immediately after the Anschluss. On April 23, a new council was appointed and a policy of expulsion and dispossession was aggressively implemented. Ten locations, including Eisenstadt, have been declared *Judenrein*. Almost two thousand were expelled and the others, numbering well over a thousand, left for Vienna, where I am told they are entirely destitute.'

Christina's face paled. She put her fork down on the plate alongside the unfinished strudel and placed it on a side table. 'Eisenstadt is less than half an hour's drive from here.' She knew there had been problems concerning the Jews in the area, but had no idea of the scale. 'What else did you find out, Mama?'

'I've also been told that the expulsion of Jews from the region was discussed at a meeting chaired by Göring in Berlin on November 12 as part of a discussion about the "Jewish question" after *Kristallnacht*. Apparently Göring said that the Gestapo is operating in Burgenland in conjunction with the local leaders. Albrecht and his wife have been filling me in with all this.'

Albrecht and Hildegard Bauer had been in the employ of the Lehmann family for as long as Christina could remember; certainly since she was a young girl. They lived in a nearby cottage on the estate, and worked as caretakers. Albrecht was also the gamekeeper. When the family were not in residence they kept an eye on things for them. On hearing that Frau Julia Lehmann would be returning, they'd helped get the castle back into a liveable condition again. It was an enormous job to get the place clean and tidy. The curtains and rugs all had to be cleaned, the furniture dusted and polished, and the whole place needed airing.

'Albrecht told me about the violent riots that swept across Burgenland soon after he returned home from the mass demonstration in Eisenstadt during the first week of the Anschluss. He has relatives near there. Stones were thrown at the Jews' houses, mobs were shouting for them to drop dead, and the Nazi anthem was sung – "*When Jewish blood drips from the knife, it's twice as good for us!*" A new provincial administration, appointed on March 15, ordered the confiscation of all Jews' bank deposits, the closure of Jewish businesses, the prohibition of the sale of foodstuffs to Jews, and the absolution of debts owed to Jews. A few days later, the administration issued another order for all Jews to fill out questionnaires giving a detailed account of all their property: real estate, businesses, bank accounts in Austria and abroad –including insurance policies, jewellery, and other valuables – which were forwarded to the police stations. They were warned not to provide incorrect details.

'As if this wasn't bad enough, they had to cede all their property in

Austria and abroad to a fund meant to finance the emigration of poor Jews, and had to undertake to leave the country within a specified period of time. In Frauenkirchen, they were especially brutal. Men, women, children, and the elderly, all were interned. After surrendering all their personal possessions, they were placed under guard for an entire day without food and water, enduring beatings and torture.'

Walter shook his head. 'A similar edict was handed down to the Jews in Vienna in late April. The Jews of Burgenland are doomed.' He looked across at Max whose face revealed little. 'This raises several questions. Do we know which officials are behind the expulsion of the Jews and how deeply involved are the various echelons of the Nazi hierarchy? Why have the Jews of Burgenland been driven out, and not the rest of the Austrian Jewry?'

'It's simple,' Max replied. 'They want to see how the locals react. If they can get away with it in Burgenland – and they have – they will implement this everywhere else in Austria.'

An air of despondency filled the room.

'Papa always said the people of this area were conservative,' Christina said, looking at the large portrait of her father hanging on the wall. His eyes seemed to be looking at them as if saying, What are you going to do about all this? 'He used to say that, after 1919, the people around here did not believe that Austria could remain viable after losing its Slavic and Hungarian provinces; that we can only survive as part of a Greater Germany. Many of Burgenland's civil service and police force are from the non-German areas of the old Habsburg Empire, driven from their homes because they had been raised on German culture. This is why the idea of a Greater Germany has fervent supporters here. In 1927, to mark the eightieth birthday of the German president, Paul von Hindenburg, the legislature sent its congratulations while adding its desire to annex its state to Germany. After this, leading German and Burgenland government officials have exchanged visits. Can we really be surprised that the National-Socialist party has roots there?'

Julia Lehmann agreed, 'Sadly, your Papa understood the

implications all too well. He saw how the Nazi cells made use of anti-Semitic propaganda from the very beginning. The focal point of a party rally in Eisenstadt in 1930 was the "Jewish question," and the Social Democratic newspaper *Burgenländische Freiheit*, urged the Jews to emigrate to Palestine, asserting that the National Socialists would not acquiesce in the equalization of the rights of Jews in Austria with those of Aryans. The newspaper also proudly stated that signs were waved at the rally calling for a boycott of Jewish-owned shops. *"Stay away from the Jews' shops! Aryans, do your shopping at Aryan shops!"* and *"Let no Jewish book be found in your home."* In1936, around the time of your papa's death, all local officials received a memorandum instructing them to draw up lists of Jews in the vicinity, to note the names of community activists, and to attach their photographs.'

Max now realised that Christina's father knew more than he let on, and why he agreed so readily when Max said he wouldn't marry her at this time. Herr Lehmann could see what the future held for the Jews. Christina said she'd heard enough for the moment. She had looked forward to getting away for a few days, and now it seemed that escaping politics was impossible.

'Come on,' she said to Max. 'Let's go for a long walk before lunch. I need some air.'

Clad in boots and warm clothes, they headed into the courtyard and through the vegetable garden toward a fringe of woodland that overlooked an expanse of farmland. The winter sun pierced the steely grey sky, melting the frozen earth that scrunched underfoot. The landscape, with its leafless trees, looked serene and peaceful, belying the traumatic events they were being swept up in. Christina looped her arm through Max's and they walked in silence for a while.

'I had a wonderful childhood here,' she said to him. 'Every season is beautiful. In the autumn, Mama and Papa used to take us to pick mushrooms and we'd have them for breakfast, lunch, and dinner until Papa declared he was sick of them. They were one of his favourite foods, especially when eaten with venison and wild berries.'

Max smiled. 'You were lucky. I was a starving artist.'

'*Was.*' Christina laughed. 'You're successful now. Anyway, most artists are supposed to be starving at some point in their lives, aren't they?' She rubbed herself closer to him. 'What was life really like then? I mean, was it really as difficult as you make out?'

'Worse, my darling. I didn't change my clothes for days, I often went without food and occasionally stole a sausage or loaf of rye bread to fend off hunger, and I kept warm by making love to the women who modelled for me. So you see, it wasn't a bad life at all, my sweet love.' He winked at her, his amber eyes filled with adoration.

'Teaser. You're impossible!'

He scooped her in his arms and swung her around. 'Is that why you find me irresistible?'

'One of the reasons.' She looked at him in a playful, coy manner.

'And what would the other reasons be, my angel?'

She slapped him, light-heartedly. 'Because you are unpredictable.' He agreed. 'Because you are a good lover.' He agreed again. 'And because you love me unconditionally.'

'Hmm, how can I help myself?' He gave her a long and passionate kiss. 'Unconditionally – till death do us part.'

'Till death do us part.'

They heard a rustle in the nearby bushes and a stag sauntered out. He stood in front of them for a moment, proud and confident, staring at them with his large dark eyes, fearless, even without the canopy of foliage. His massive body, covered in thick red/brown fur, glistened in the tree-filtered light. He made a loud roar, shook his enormous antlers and, to their relief, turned and walked away back into the bushes.

'What a magnificent creature,' Max said. 'How I would love to paint him, just as he was at that moment – looking at us in that elegant and majestic manner.'

'Thank God it isn't the rutting season. I hate to think what he would have done if it was. Those antlers were enormous. I've seen them fight to the death.'

'They will fight to the death for their territory and the hind. It's nature.'

They walked on further. Surrounded by the beauty and tranquillity of the landscape, they put aside their worries for a while, neither mentioning politics. Instead, he asked her about the Spring Collection and she asked him about his paintings.

Christina looked at her watch. 'I think we'd better return to the house. Lunch will be served and Mama abhors lateness. We can take another walk later.'

Lunch was prepared by Irma and served in the dining room by Gitta. Like the rest of the family, the servants enjoyed going to Steinbrunnhof. It made a change as they rarely went anywhere outside of Vienna. Lunch consisted of fish mousse served with a salad topped with dill, gherkins and mayonnaise, followed by Sachertorte, which Christina had brought with her. Afterwards they retired for coffee, followed by a light afternoon nap.

Being winter, the days were short and, by the time Christina awoke, the sun had disappeared and the sky was a bleak and gloomy darkened sheet of blue-grey with violet undertones. Max was still fast asleep and she went downstairs alone. Her mother was in the drawing room reading in front of a log fire. It was the only room in the building with an enormous open fire that had been in use since the building was renovated in the 19th century. Almost every other room was heated with a *Kachelofen*.

'How are the girls?' Christina asked.

'Fine. They're looking forward to seeing you this evening. Albrecht took them into the village today on his cart and then to play with his grandchildren. I expect them back soon.'

'Is that wise? I mean after our discussion about Jews today.'

Julia Lehmann closed her book. 'I don't know if you are aware, but Hildegard's sister married a Jew. They lived in a village somewhere in Burgenland.'

'No, I didn't know. Is she safe?'

'They haven't heard from them and I don't like to pry. They'll tell me in good time. The point is they hate the Nazis, so the girls are safe with him.'

'I hope you're right.'

'Your father knew Albrecht since he was a boy. He always trusted him. That's good enough for me. Anyway, just to be on the safe side, I had a word with Hannah before we came here. She understands all too well how much most people despise Jews. We spoke about keeping that quiet and if anyone asked questions, they were not to say anything at all about being Jewish. Of course, Malka doesn't understand so we decided to make it a game. I told Hannah to let me know if anyone asked awkward questions. Do you know, they even say grace at meal-times now – before the meal. I told her it's quite all right for them to say their own prayers quietly in the privacy of their own room. ' She paused for a moment. 'Have you thought any more about their future?'

'Yes. I think I will try and get them to England on the Kindertransport. I can't see what other option there is. They don't have family here and no one will rent rooms to Jews. None of the seamstresses will take them on, either. They have their own problems.'

'How is Nathan?'

'Max found him work and, from what I gather, he works long hours, poor boy. Sometimes he sleeps in the outbuildings where the wine-presses are. At other times, he stays with Max. The tavern owner does what he can, but he has other people to look after too. What sort of life will he have?' Christina put another log on the fire. It spluttered and crackled, throwing out a wave of heat. 'Do you know who I saw at the opera the other evening? – Dieter Klein. He was with the German actress, Lina Lindner.'

Julia Lehmann gave a little smile. 'His mother will be most pleased. I can imagine how she will brag about it to her friends.' She broached the subject of Max. 'My darling, I know I am probably speaking out of turn, but after what I've heard these last few days, I believe I have sharpened my perceptions. It might be better if Max left Austria for a while.' Christina threw her mother a sharp glance. 'If he stays here he will be in danger. Sooner or later, someone will poke about and find out about his background. Perhaps he could go to Paris, or even London, as you are working with the Baroness and Herr Pembroke.'

'Mama! How can you say such a thing? You know I couldn't bear to be without him. Anyway, Stephen has everything in hand in London. He has contacts there already.'

Julia Lehmann could see this discussion was not going to bear fruit. She would have to speak with Max himself. She turned the conversation to Schloss Steinbrunnhof and the work she'd been doing since she got back. Thankfully, Albrecht and his wife had kept an eye on everything for her, but the only room she told them not to touch was her husband's study. The stale smell of cigars lingered and his papers lay on his desk, just as they had on the day he died.

'I miss him very much,' she said. 'But I've learnt to carry on. I have you and Karin, and who knows, one day I may even have grandchildren.' She looked around the large drawing room, lined with bookshelves and filled with antique furniture and oriental carpets. 'That's what this place needs to bring it alive again – the sound of small children. What a gift that would be.'

Christina gave a heavy sigh. She would never have children while Max refused to marry her. That "gift" would be left to Karin, and she was finding it hard to conceive.

Dinner that night was a formal affair in the main dining room. The family dressed in their finery and dined by candlelight as they had done so many times before. Irma cooked venison, killed and prepared by Albrecht, accompanied by winter vegetables. To complement the food, it was served with several bottles of one of their best wines – a classic *Blaufrankisch* intensely coloured, medium-bodied Burgenland red wine. Dessert was accompanied by another favourite wine. This time a sweet Hungarian Tokaj, paired with caramelized apples. It was delicious and everyone complimented Irma on excelling herself once again. Hanna and Malka were allowed to dine with them too, and they wore the pretty new dresses which Hannah had made, with a little help from Julia Lehmann.

Christina was happy to see smiles on their faces. The change of scenery had done wonders for them. After the meal, she spent time alone with them, chatting about the animals they'd seen on their walks and the things she used to do there when she was a child. They asked about Nathan and she told them he was working hard and sent his love, but the one thing she didn't talk about was whether or not they wanted to go to England. Now was not the right time. She needed them to be strong, first.

On Sunday, the family went to church as they always did when they were in residence. For as long as anyone could remember, this was a ritual the family never missed. Indeed, the small church in the square had been the scene for many a Lehmann baptism, and at least one marriage. After the service, they paid their respects to the village priest, Father Moller, who was more than delighted to see Frau Lehmann again.

'It's been too long,' he said to her. 'We've missed you. Will you be joining us for Christmas this year?'

Julia Lehmann was not sure what to say and, seeing her falter, Christina answered for her. 'The whole family is looking forward to it. You're right. It has been too long.'

Later in the afternoon, Max and Christina returned to Vienna. Karin and Walter left shortly afterwards. Their mother and the girls would stay on for another week. The car drove slowly down the allée and stopped at the gates to let a convoy of armoured trucks pass by. The soldiers sounded their horn and acknowledged them with cheerful shouts and waving flags. Max and Christina glanced at each other in dismay.

CHAPTER 11

The Baroness looked happy with herself. 'I've finally received confirmation that the children will be allowed exit visas.' She asked the waiter to pour everyone a glass of champagne. '*Servus,*' she said, raising her glass to them all. 'This has to be the best Christmas present in a while.'

Everyone congratulated her. She'd used her fame, influence, and money, to pull strings in Vienna to achieve this outcome, but no one was in doubt about how much it was going to cost, and although some parents would have the money, unless they could start up a relief fund, the Baroness would still have to fund much of it herself.

'And what about you, Stephen?' Max asked. 'How are things going in London?'

Stephen Pembroke was also in a good mood. 'I received a telegraph. It's all been approved by the Home Office. They're setting up a separate department called the British Committee for Refugee Children from Austria. Each country has its own committee, but ultimately, it's all under the same banner.'

'This certainly is good news,' Christina said. 'It gives us something solid to work with. What happens next?'

'The newspapers and various charities and societies in Britain are putting out notices asking for families interested in sponsoring a child to contact them. What we have to do now is draw up a list of those we want to send.' Pembroke looked at Anton and Johannes. 'That's where you two come in. Not everyone will have a photograph, so every time we have someone who needs one, they will be directed to your studio.'

'When do we start?' Max asked. 'Walter already has one family interested.'

'We need to get the exit visa forms first,' the Baroness replied. 'As soon as we have those, we'll start with the photographs. Believe me, we all want to act as soon as possible. Things are getting worse by the day for the Jews. There is one important thing, though. We have been advised that the visas will not be given to anyone over sixteen.'

Christina gave a deep sigh.

'Are you thinking of the Rosen children?' the Baroness asked.

Christina nodded. 'Yes. I want the girls to remain together. Hannah is sixteen, but what about Nathan? What can we do about him? He's seventeen.'

Max put his hand on hers. 'We'll work something out. Don't get ahead of yourself. It's still early days.'

'I'm sorry,' the Baroness added. 'The authorities were adamant on that. If we flaunt the rules, they'll cancel the whole thing.'

The meeting lasted barely an hour. There was little more they could do until after Christmas when they had the official Austrian documents and the go ahead from London as to how many families had signed up to take children.

'We'll meet again in the New Year,' the Baroness informed them. 'In the meantime, I will be spending Christmas in Paris with Lucien.'

'And I'm leaving for London tomorrow,' Pembroke added. 'If I have any news, I'll telegraph you.'

Vienna at Christmas was always a wonderful sight. The city was filled with Christmas decorations and carollers singing old favourites like *O Tannenbaum* and *Stille Nacht*, an expression of reflection and spiritual longing for peace, which, given the events of the past year, struck Max and Christina as particularly poignant. In the parks and along the Ringstrasse, musicians with their violins, accordions, and zithers, played everything from Strauss to classical music, and vendors stood on street corners selling hot chestnuts. For all the festive cheer, one barely needed to scratch the surface to see that this Christmas was different. The swastika was everywhere, and the faces of ordinary people going about their business appeared like masks behind which they hid their anxiety and uncertainty. Only a few streets away from the city centre, restaurants and shop windows displayed signs warning Jews not to enter. "No Jews or Dogs" signs were now commonplace – distasteful to some, not to others. Max and Christina passed several Brownshirts with their collection tins. Most people gave them a coin or two for fear of harassment. Max refused and one of them called after them.

'Won't you give for the homeless, *mein Herr?*' His tone was menacing.

Christina took a coin out of her purse and dropped it in the tin, but the man gave Max a look of disdain.

'I refuse to put money into the coffers of these Jew-haters,' he said, indignantly.

'Don't give them a reason to make trouble,' she urged him as they walked away.

Two days before Christmas, Christina and Karin closed the salon and held a small Christmas party for the seamstresses. It was something they'd done every year since they opened, a token of their appreciation for their loyalty and excellent work. During the party, the women were always given a bottle of wine and a gift. This year, they each received a beautiful leather handbag, a different colour for each seamstress. She also gave them an extra month's pay. Inflation had sky-rocketed and even though she paid them well, times were hard. Since Austria was now officially part of the Greater Reich and referred to as "Ostmark" in official circles, the pay was in Reichsmark. It had been a difficult year and one none of them would forget in a hurry. The void left by their fellow seamstresses – especially Mirka – was hard to disguise. The women left early that day. The atelier would re-open in two weeks' time. As an added farewell treat, they would all be chauffeured home. One by one, they piled into her car with their gifts and Beck drove them home. While Christina and Karin stood on the pavement and waved them off, the women's happy faces peered back at them through the rear window of the car. As the car disappeared down Mariahilferstrasse, Karin caught her arm.

'You see that black car over there with the two men in it? It was there a couple of days ago.' Christina looked, but it was too far away to see their faces. 'I don't know why, but I think they're keeping a watch on us.'

'Did you tell Kurt?'

'Yes, and he agreed with me. He thinks they may be Gestapo and up to no good. We decided not to tell you because you already have enough on your mind.' The black car pulled away from the curb, drove away slowly and turned into a side street. 'Well, let's hope that's the last we see of them. My nerves are shattered as it is.'

'You worry too much,' Christina said. 'Tomorrow, we'll be at Steinbrunnhof, away from all this, and then you can relax.'

❦

Christmas at Steinbrunnhof had always been a grand affair, and this year was no exception. Albrecht chopped down a large Christmas tree from the estate and it now stood in the corner of the drawing room, decorated with shiny balls, tinsel, and handmade wooden ornaments, from angels to painted nativity scenes. Hannah and Malka, with a little help from Gitta, also added small white candles that flickered like fireflies. Inside the drawing room, it was warm and cosy in front of the log fire, but outside, the weather had dropped below zero and the countryside lay blanketed in thick snow. The snow, however, had not prevented them all from going to church earlier in the evening. It was a tradition they enjoyed, especially when Herr Lehmann was still alive. On this special evening, all the villagers headed to the church, illuminating the night with torches held high to light their way in the darkness, passing carollers who gathered in the village square to guide them to the Christmas service with their melodies. A nativity scene stood in the corner near the altar, lovingly made by a local woodsman, and here and there someone had placed beautiful wreaths of winter foliage, berries, and pine cones.

It was a custom that the first row of seats were reserved for the Lehmann family in gratitude to Herr Lehmann's grandfather who had been a benefactor of the church, and, now that the family were in residence at Schloss Steinbrunnhof after several years of absence, this year was no exception. Also in the front row, on the opposite side of the church, were three unfamiliar faces, one of them wearing a Nazi uniform with an embroidered insignia of three oak leaves and two diamonds on the collar. After the service, the family mingled with the locals and wished them all a good Christmas and New Year, including the newcomers, introduced by Father Moller. The man wearing the smart black uniform was *Gruppenführer* Wilhelm Kemény, the newly appointed official of the area who reported directly to the Reich Governor for Lower Austria, a man who had been a fervent Nazi since the nineteen-twenties and who was personally appointed by Hitler after the Anschluss.

Kemény, an overweight man who appeared to be in his mid-forties, slightly balding with a clean complexion and wearing round glasses, clicked his heels and kissed Julia Lehmann's gloved hand in a formal and gracious manner. 'It is an honour to meet you, *gnädige* Frau. I have heard much about your family.' He turned to Christina. 'And of course, our most esteemed fashion designer, Fräulein Christina. Your couture house is well-known in Germany. I have even heard Frau Goebbels and others speak of your talents.'

Christina was amused at the way he bolstered his position with a little name-dropping. She thanked him with a polite smile and, noting his wedding ring, said she hoped to have the honour of dressing Frau Kemény in the near future.

Kemény did not leave it at that. He asked if he may be permitted to call by Schloss Steinbrunnhof to pay his respects while the family was in residence. 'It will give us a chance to get to know each other,' he added. He gave a little half-smile, cold and menacing.

Julia Lehmann said it would be an honour. They too, would like to get to know him. By now, the snow had stopped falling, and a sharp, cold wind blew over the flat countryside from the north, making them lift their collars.

'I look forward to it.' Kemény said. He turned towards the men and saluted. 'Heil Hitler.'

'Heil Hitler,' Walter and Max responded. Only Walter gave the salute.

They parted ways, and the family walked home, lamenting their new neighbours, who, by the short conversation that had taken place, left them in no doubt that they would be keeping tabs on them. 'You should have saluted,' Walter said to Max, making sure the women couldn't hear. 'Why provoke them?'

Heiliger Abend – Christmas Eve – was a time everyone looked forward to, especially the children. After eating some of Irma's *Weihnachtsplätzchen*, *Stollengebäck*, and drinking *Glühwein*, the unwrapping began. Julia Lehmann had placed presents under the tree for everyone, including Malka and Hannah, and told them they could now open them. Both girls received a book from Julia herself, a silver brush and comb set from Christina and Karin, and a set of coloured pencils and drawing pads from Max. They were delighted. Julia Lehmann had also prepared something else for the girls and they were asked to keep it in their room and not tell anyone about it, except the immediate family.

'Are you going to show us?' Christina said. 'We're all anxious to know what it is.'

They followed the girls to their room and there on the dressing table was a menorah with eight candles lying in a box nearby. Christina threw her mother a concerned glance.

'Don't worry, its fine. It's for Hanukkah and it's our little secret, isn't it girls?' Malka nodded. 'Hannah has been telling me that Hanukkah is observed for eight nights and days, starting on the 25th day of Kislev according to the Hebrew calendar. This year it coincides with our celebrations. On the first night of Hanukkah, which is tomorrow, a candle is placed in the menorah. On each successive night, another candle is added. By the last night of Hanukkah, eight candles are glowing brightly in celebration of this beautiful festival.'

Seeing the worried look on Christina's face, Hannah said they were grateful to Frau Lehmann because they wanted to pray for their mother and Nathan. Her dark eyes flashed. 'I promise we will tell no one.'

'And now I think it's time for you both to get some sleep, don't you?' Julia Lehmann said. She pulled back the thick eiderdown on the bed. 'We'll see you in the morning.'

'That was a beautiful thing you did for them,' Max said when they returned to the drawing room. 'The day Stephen and I rescued them still haunts me, but through your kindness, they are beginning to smile again.'

'I did what any human being with a heart would do. I am a mother and would hope that if I perished in such a terrible way, some kind soul would look after my children.'

'Sadly, Mama, not everyone is like you,' Christina replied. 'Tell me, where did you get the menorah?'

Julia Lehman flashed her hand through the air. 'Another time.' She changed the subject. 'There's some *Glühwein* left. Let's finish it off before we retire for the evening.'

As 1938 ended and the new year began, the family managed to put their problems aside for a while and enjoy themselves, going for long walks through the snow-covered woods and fields, tobogganing with the two girls, and teaching them how to ice skate on the large frozen pond ringed with willows on the estate. The rest of the time, they read, danced to tango music, or listened to popular music by Ruth Eggeth, Lizzi Waldmüller, Joseph Schmidt, and Gitta Alpár. Gitta Alpár's *Magyar* was a particular favourite of Max's. Gitta was a Hungarian Jew who moved to Germany and starred in several films until 1935 when her marriage to a German actor was deemed illegal under Nazi law and was dissolved. Even though her records were now banned, Max and Christina and their friends still played them in private. He found the haunting gypsy strains moving, once telling Christina that one of the reasons he liked Gitta so much was because she portrayed that deep sadness and melancholia which now swept through every Jew in Europe.

Max used the time at Steinbrunnhof to work on his paintings. The peace and solitude offered by the warmth of the family and the beauty of his surroundings inspired him. While he painted, Christina sat in the chair by the window, working on her Spring Collection. One afternoon, she happened to look up and saw a black Daimler turn into the drive. As it drew closer, she saw the small Nazi flag on the bonnet and recognised the face.

'Mama! We have visitors. It's Herr Kemény.'

Max got up from his easel to take a look. 'What does he want?' he said, wiping his paint brush on a rag.

Julia Lehmann put down her book, calmly ran her hand through her hair, and left the room to greet him. As the car disappeared through the arch and into the courtyard, Christina went to the gramophone player, removed several banned records and slipped them into a drawer. Max returned to his easel. When Julia Lehmann reached the courtyard, she found Kemény and Albrecht engrossed in a conversation. Kemény was waving his hand towards the building and Albrecht's face was red with embarrassment and nervousness.

'Herr Kemény. What a pleasure to see you again. Is everything all right?'

'Good afternoon, Frau Lehmann. I just happened to be passing this way and took it upon myself to pay my respects to your good self and the family. I just happened to mention to Herr...' Kemény glanced at Albrecht.

'Herr Bauer,' Julia Lehmann said.

'I just happened to mention to Herr Bauer that Schloss

Steinbrunnhof does not appear to be flying the Reich flag.' He paused to watch her expression. 'Maybe that is an oversight.'

'You are absolutely right,' Julia Lehmann replied, feigning surprise. 'I am afraid this is my fault. You see we have not been here for a few years – since my husband passed away – and there has been so much to do. It completely slipped my mind.'

She asked Albrecht to get on to it straight away, but Kemény offered to have someone from his office call by with one as soon as possible. Julia Lehmann thanked him and asked him inside to celebrate the New Year with a glass of wine and home-baked *Stollengebäck*. In the drawing room, he found Max still at his easel and Christina working on her fashion sketches.

'Herr Kemény, what a pleasure to see you again,' Christina said. She indicated for him to sit near to the fire, commenting on the particularly harsh winter they were having.

Karin and Walter had gone for a walk and taken the girls with them. Christina prayed Kemény would be gone before they arrived back. No one wanted him asking questions about the girls. They spent the next half-hour talking pleasantries and avoiding politics. Kemény was particularly interested in the large painting Max was working on – the stag in the woods that had captivated him.

'What a magnificence creature,' Kemény said, adjusting his glasses as he held his face closer to the painting. 'You've captured the eyes very well. They appear to be looking into our very soul – as if reading our mind, wouldn't you say?'

'That is what struck me at the time,' Max said. 'Maybe animals can read human beings better than we can.'

'Hmm, you have a point,' Kemény replied.

'I call it instinct,' Max said, adding a few more brush strokes to one of the eyes. 'A survival instinct – they can smell fear.'

Christina glanced at her mother uncomfortably, picked up a plate of buttery, vanilla-infused biscuits and asked Kemény if he would like to try a *Vanillekipferl*.

Happily, Kemény left soon afterwards, thanking them for their hospitality. When the car drove away, Karin and Walter appeared with the two girls. They had returned from their walk not long after Kemény arrived but when Albrecht told them who the visitor was, they decided to keep out of sight.

'Let's hope that's the last we see of him,' Walter said.

When Julia Lehmann told them about the flag, Karin looked distressed and asked if there was any way they could get out of it. 'I'm afraid not, my darling. The last thing we want to do is incur his wrath and have him poking around again. We will have to put up with it.'

The very next day a truck arrived at Steinbrunnhof. 'I have orders to deliver this to you,' the driver said. Two soldiers in the back of the truck were already taking out a large flag. 'We have instructions to hang it for you.' The man waited for a reply but Julia Lehmann was too shocked to answer. Kemény had certainly wasted no time.

'I think over there will be fine,' Christina said, 'Next to the entrance to the courtyard. That way it can be seen from the road.'

She omitted to say that it couldn't be seen from the castle windows. With everyone looking on, in no time at all, the enormous red flag with the black swastika on a white circle hung over the entrance to the castle. It was a black day for the family.

When the time came to return to Vienna, Max had completed his painting of the stag and the family decided to hang it in the drawing room next to the portrait of Herr Lehmann. There it could be enjoyed by all, a reminder that even amid desolate times, one could still find something proud and beautiful in life. Christina reminded her mother that she hadn't told them where she'd got the menorah from.

'A few days before you arrived, Albrecht told me he and Hildegard wanted to try and find her sister. They were frantic as they'd heard nothing from her in months. I decided to go with him. They lived in the village of Mattersburg. I say "lived" because when we arrived, we discovered all the Jews were expelled and dispossessed almost immediately after the Anschluss. What we found filled us with dread. There were no more Jews in Mattersburg. Most of their houses and business-es were now occupied by Austrians, except for a few which lay empty and ransacked. One of them, a smallholding with an orchard and a few hens on the outskirts of the village, belonged to Hildegard's sister and her husband. That too had been ransacked. A neighbour saw us and came over to find out what we were doing. "They've been sent to the border," she told us. When Hildegard said her sister was not Jew-ish, the woman shrugged saying it didn't matter, she was married to a Jew. Hildegard burst into tears. After advising us not to hang around, the woman walked away. However we searched the place first to see if there was anything of value left.'

'And was there?' Christina asked.

'Nothing, but we found the menorah in the chicken shed. Wheth-er it had been thrown there by those who ransacked the place, we couldn't tell. Hildegard wanted to bring it home as a memento. I ad-vised her against it, but she insisted. When we arrived back here, she told me she wanted Malka and Hannah to have it. At first I said no, but after speaking with Hannah, who promised to keep it a secret, I agreed.' Christina looked dismayed. 'Given the uncertain times, we agreed to keep quiet about the fact that her sister married a Jew, so please don't bring it up. It's too upsetting for them both. And you don't have to worry; when we return to Vienna, the menorah will stay here. Albrecht and Hildegard will hide it somewhere safe.'

CHAPTER 12

CHRISTINA WAS IN the workroom with the seamstresses when Karin popped her head around the door and called her out of the room.

'We've got visitors,' she whispered. 'Officials from the Ministry of Employment and Work.'

'What do they want?'

'I think we can guess.'

The two men waited in the salon, one of them flicking through fashion magazines and the other feeling the quality of a dress on a mannequin.

Christina greeted them with a false smile. 'Good day, *meine Herren*. What can we do for you?'

Both men appeared to be in their forties, well-dressed and wearing smart dark overcoats and broad-brimmed hats. The thinner of the two, a man with a hawkish nose, wearing wire-rimmed glasses, showed her an official document and said they would like to have a look around.

Christina took a deep breath to calm herself. 'Whatever for? You won't find anything here, we've done nothing wrong.'

'We have reason to believe you may be employing Jews and that they are working on the premises. We would like to take a look.'

Christina became indignant. 'You have no right to come in here and demand to search the place.'

Beck, who had been taking an afternoon break in the office with Karin, heard the conversation through the partially open door. He'd seen what happened to other people in Mariahilferstrasse who flouted the rules about employing Jews. Many were forced to close their shops, shamed, and lost their businesses overnight. Others were imprisoned or sent to a camp. He listened carefully and quietly went upstairs to the workroom to warn the women.

'I am afraid you cannot stop us, good lady, and unless you would like me to report you, please move aside and let us do our work.'

The two men began searching the premises, starting with Karin's office. One of them asked to see her books. Christina swallowed hard. Karin opened a drawer, took out a ledger and handed it to him. Christina looked on in amazement. *What was she doing?* The man flicked through the book, stopped at a certain page, and indicated to his colleague to make a note of the names. When he'd finished, they asked to see the workroom. Christina felt a bead of sweat trickle down her neck.

'It's on the top floor.'

The man gestured for her to show them. On the first floor, they stopped outside Christina's apartment. 'What's in here?' the man with the hawkish nose asked.

'It's my private apartment.'

The men paused for a moment, considering whether or not to take a look, but decided to move on. By the time they reached the workroom, Christina felt quite ill. Karin gave her a reassuring look but said nothing. Christina announced to the women they had visitors. To her great surprise, she saw not everyone was there.

The nervous women stood up to greet them while the men took a look around the workroom. They asked each woman their name and address and it was ticked off against the names taken from the ledger. Christina noticed the men appeared to take a particular interest in the cups on the women's worktables. *Were they counting them to correspond with the number of women there?* When they were satisfied all was in order, they politely bid them a good day.

Descending the stairs, one of them noticed a narrow door at the end of the corridor.

'Where does that lead?' he asked.

'It's the fire escape,' Karin replied.

The men looked at each other and for a minute, it seemed they might take a look, but they decided they'd seen enough.

The men thanked Christina for their time, but the thinner of the two cautioned her. 'A word of advice, Fräulein Lehmann, you have been lucky this time, but everyone must obey the law.' He took one last look around the salon. 'It would be a pity to see such a fine establishment like this closed down. Heil Hitler.'

Christina and Karin watched the men walk along the street and get into the same black car they'd seen a few weeks earlier.

'You were right,' Christina said. 'They *were* watching us.'

She turned to her sister and asked what was going on. 'Where *are* the other women – and what was that ledger all about? Why have I never seen it before?'

'Kurt must have seen what was taking place and gone to warn the women,' Karin answered. 'Come on, we'll soon find out. As for the ledger, after the law was passed forbidding companies to employ Jews, I kept a separate one for occasions like this. It only lists the Christian women on the payroll. I'm sorry I didn't tell you. I didn't want to alarm you. The truth is, I knew this day would come. I'm only surprised it took so long.'

Christina rubbed her forehead. 'Thank you. What would I do without you?'

'No time for sentimentality. Let's go upstairs and find out what happened to the girls.'

They found the seamstresses still in a state of shock. Christina and Karina apologised, but the women were nervous and agitated.

'Where are the others?' Christina asked.

'Herr Beck took them. They went down the fire escape,' one of the women replied.

Karin looked out the window. The fire escape ran down the side of the building into the courtyard at the back of the salon where Beck sometimes kept the car. There was no sign of the car, or the women.

A year earlier there had been ten seamstresses in Christina's employ, and six of them were Jewish. Two left Vienna soon after the Anschluss and when Mirka was murdered that left only seven. Out of those, four were Catholics. The women all got on well together, but after Mirka's death, there had been a growing anxiety on the part of the Catholic women. Fearing Christina might ask them to leave, they kept their thoughts to themselves, but this untimely visit both alarmed and distressed them. Afraid that they too would be held responsible for not reporting the fact that there were Jews on the premises, they now decided to speak out.

'Fräulein Christina and Frau Krassner,' one of them said, 'we have decided that we cannot work like this. Ruth, Ella, and Frieda are our friends, but what you are doing is...' She stopped short of saying illegal, '...not right. You are putting our lives and the lives of our families at risk. We could be killed, or at best, sent to Dachau.'

Christina was so shocked, she couldn't speak. *How long had they been thinking this? Why didn't she see it coming? Why was she trying to save one group of people, yet at the same time risking the lives of others? What else was she doing wrong?* She pulled out a chair and sat down, trying to come to terms with the gravity of the situation. One of the women saw how pale she was and handed her a glass of water.

'I'm so sorry. I had no idea you felt this way,' Christina replied.

The women looked at each other despondently. In a society where respect for those in authority was paramount, it wasn't easy to talk in such an open manner, but they were not to be deterred and the woman continued, 'You are a woman of integrity – the best employer anyone could wish for – and you have always encouraged us to voice our opinions about our work in an open manner. Now we are voicing our opinions concerning our Jewish sisters. You must choose: us or them.'

One of the women started weeping and Karin put an arm around her. 'Please don't distress yourselves any further. Fräulein Christina and I will give it some thought and we will let you have our answer in the morning. For now, you can take the rest of the day off.'

The women picked up their bags and left.

'What do we do?' Christina asked when they were alone. 'We can't just abandon the others.'

'No. And neither can we afford to abandon our own.'

'You mean Catholics?' Christina replied with a hint of sarcasm.

'You know that's not what I mean. If any of them tell their family about this, we will have more to deal with than two officials wanting to search the place. They are right. We have to let Ruth, Frieda and Ella go.'

'What about the collection?'

'It's almost finished.'

Reluctantly, Christina agreed. An hour later, Beck arrived back and told them that on hearing the conversation, he'd seized the opportunity to get the women out of the workroom via the fire escape to his car. He thought it best to take them home.

'Your quick thinking saved us. I am grateful,' Karin said. 'The problem is, we have to let the women go. It's no longer safe for them to be here.'

'I think they understand that all too well,' Beck replied.

Christina asked if he would give them a moment alone to discuss a financial arrangement for them and then she would personally visit them to give them the bad news. After taking into account the length of time they'd been with her, and the difficulties they faced getting work, she decided to give them a year's salary – an extraordinary amount. But maybe she could persuade them to use the money to go to Paris. Christina wrote each one a glowing reference while Karin took the money from the safe. It was a lot of cash, but there was no other option. Taking such a large amount from a bank would have aroused suspicion.

Christina divided it into three and put it in a large bag. One by one, she visited each seamstress to give them the bad news and a parting gift. None of them held it against her, which made her feel worse. After the last visit, she slumped back in the car, tears streaming down her face.

'Where to now?' Beck asked. 'Back to Mariahilferstrasse?'

'No. I can't face going back there at the moment. Take me to see Max.'

CHAPTER 13

CHRISTINA'S SPRING COLLECTION was launched during the first week of February 1939 and, despite the setbacks with the seamstresses, it was a resounding success. Fashion editors from *Vogue, Harper's Bazaar, Modenschau, Neue Moden, Mode und Heim, Weiner Damenmode,* and many more magazines, all vied with one another to get the best scoop and photographs. Within a week, articles on Christina and her collection appeared in magazines and newspapers throughout Europe.

"*Fräulein Christina Lehmann has excelled herself once again,*" declared the fashion editor of *Modenschau.* "*Whether they are pleated, straight or flared, her suits have become more feminine, often paired with tightly fitted jackets and blouses*".

Harper's Bazaar noted that, "*Vienna's most creative designer, Christina Lehmann, takes her evening dresses to a whole new level with the overall slender and feminine look of one of the most important developments and trends of the decade: the bias cut. Her fluid, body-hugging garments skim over a woman's curves in the most striking and sensuous manner. One of the highlights was her evening collection of low-backed, satin dresses which shimmer under the lights like a mirror.*"

From *Vogue* there was more praise. "*While eveningwear is dominated by the body-skimming silhouette, daywear is romantic and feminine in a variety of patterns, the waists are clearly defined, and the length between the mid-calf and just above the ankle. Her smart suits are crisp and sculptural, the shoulders well defined and exaggerated on suits or dresses, and cleverly created through padding, layers of fabric, and other embellishments, clearly showing the influence of the film on fashion.*"

Christina could not have been more delighted and she and Max decided to go away to Salzburg for a weekend to relax. During the drive, Christina mulled over the showing. It hadn't been easy. Despite her enthusiasm for her work, a dark cloud had settled over Vienna that threw doubts over her future.

When the guest list had been drawn up a few weeks earlier, Christina and Karin were forced to invite some of Vienna's politicians and notables who were now firmly entrenched in the Nazi party. On the advice of Karin, Walter, her mother, and even Max, Dieter Klein was given an invitation, as was his superior, Ernst Kaltenbrunner. Joseph Bürckel, who had only recently succeeded Odilo Globočnik as Nazi Party Gauleiter of *Reichsgau* Vienna, was also invited, along with Franz Joseph Huber, Head of the Gestapo and SD for Vienna. Huber was also the chief of the Central Agency for Jewish Emigration in Vienna, and, although Adolf Eichmann was the de facto leader, it was important to keep on friendly terms, particularly in light of the situation involving the Jewish children being sent to London. It was a distasteful situation, but they understood only too well that to ignore a long-time family friend like Dieter, and his associates, could have negative repercussions.

The collection was shown in the salon in Mariahilferstrasse. On the evening of the showing, the salon was decked out with spectacular pink roses supplied by florists to the opera house. The Hotel Sacher, who were used to creating luxury bespoke experiences for their guests, were hired to do the catering. A long table was set up at the far side of the salon, filled with food served on silver platters and accompanied by an array of fine wines and champagne. Max had even gone to great trouble to hang a life-size portrait of Hitler flanked by two large flags in a prominent position for her. It was an elegant affair and no expense was spared. In a time of extreme financial hardship for so many, it was to be a Black Tie event, essential for such a glamorous occasion. A relaxed moment of escapism was what everyone looked forward to.

Managing to catch a moment alone with Max in her apartment beforehand, Christina remarked how dashing he looked in his black waistcoat, wing collar and boutonniere.

'Kiki, my heart, you will be the toast of Vienna,' he declared. He lifted her chin with his forefinger. 'I love you, always remember that.'

She kissed him tenderly. 'And I love you too. I would not be here now if I hadn't had your support.' She smiled. 'Remember what we said at Steinbrunnhof, till death do us part. Now, go downstairs and let me get changed, or I will be late.'

When he left the room, her smile vanished. She knew that at the back of his mind he was still worried the Nazis would find out he was half-Jewish. Every week the government stepped up their anti-Jewish campaigns. Kaltenbrunner and Bürckel in particular, eager to please the powers that be in Berlin, continued promoting anti-Jewish decrees and seizing Jewish property. Tonight, they would be mixing with them all and she prayed all would go well. She took a deep breath and tried not to think about it.

In the fitting rooms, the models were busily slipping on their garments, while a make-up artist and hairdresser made last minute adjustments. A small orchestra began playing music by Strauss and Lehár. Christina had originally wanted a small jazz trio, but as jazz was now frowned upon, even though there were many in the population, including Nazis, who still enjoyed it, she decided against it. Soon the salon filled with guests and the show was ready to begin.

Christina studied her guests through a small window. Dieter Klein was sitting in the front row with his new lover, Lina Lindner, and three other actresses. Next to them sat Joseph Bürckel and his wife, and Ernst Kaltenbrunner with his long-time mistress, Gisela Gräfin von Westarp. Frau Klein was also there, sitting next to Julia Lehmann. On the opposite side of the walkway, next to Max and Lucien, Baroness Elisabeth sat, fanning herself with a large ostrich-feathered fan. All of Viennese high society was there. The gathering resembled many other showings over the past few years, but with one major difference: this year there were no Jews. Half of her clients had been Jewish, and quite a few of them good friends. No self-respecting Jew remaining in Vienna wanted to socialize in the same circles as the Nazis. Not that she, or they, for that matter, had a choice. It was impossible for Christina to invite them. She would have to visit them alone after the event. A slap in the face and something she felt guilty about, as if she herself was part of this Nazi collusion.

The first model stepped forward wearing a rayon cyclamen-coloured day dress with square-cut shoulders gathered to one side from the bodice. The photographers' cameras flashed, magazine and newspaper editors made copious notes, until finally, almost an hour later, the show finished and Christina stepped into the room to be greeted by resounding applause.

'Bravo, my darling,' Max whispered. 'You've excelled yourself this time.'

Among the many others lining up to congratulate her was Dieter Klein accompanied by Lina Lindner.

'My sincere congratulations: an exquisite collection.' He turned towards the woman looping her arm through his. 'I don't believe you two have been introduced. This is Fräulein Lina Lindner.'

With her flawless Nordic complexion and platinum hair perfectly styled with sleek marcel waves, the German actress was even more beautiful close up. 'It's an honour to meet you, Fräulein Lindner. I am a great admirer of your films.' Christina turned to Max. 'May I introduce Herr Max Hauser.'

Max kissed Lina's hand politely. 'Fräulein Lindner.'

'Ah, so you must be the painter I've heard so much about. Tell me, did you paint that fine portrait of Fräulein Christina?' Lina gestured toward the one that took pride of place in the salon.

'Yes, it was painted for the opening of the salon.'

'Wonderful.' This time she leaned closer to Max and flirtatiously touched his arm. Her deep blue eyes sparkled playfully. 'Maybe I could persuade you to paint my portrait too.'

'It would be a privilege to paint such a beautiful lady.'

Christina tried hard to suppress a smile. Max was being

extraordinarily charming to a woman he had no desire to paint.

Lina returned to the subject of Christina and her work. 'You are highly regarded in Berlin, you know. Magda herself speaks in glowing terms about you and has asked me to choose something from the collection to have sent to Berlin.'

Christina couldn't help thinking she was the second person who'd told her that Magda Goebbels was an admirer and she wondered if it was true. 'That is indeed a great honour. Was there anything in particular that caught your eye?'

'I believe the white silk evening dress with the black edging would suit her perfectly. I particularly love the way the back falls away to the waistline finishing in a large black bow: so simple and yet so clever – and so delightfully seductive.' She moved closer to Dieter who appeared to love the playful, if not cloying affection she showed him. 'I would also like to purchase something for myself. What do you think, darling?'

'Whatever makes you happy. I like to spoil the woman I love.' His steel blue eyes looked straight at Christina as if he was trying to prove a point.

Christina took Lina to browse through the collection, leaving Max and Dieter alone. Lina finally decided on a rose-coloured suit paired with a cream taffeta blouse with ruffles on the bodice and cuffs. 'When can you have it ready?' she asked.

'Let me see. Can you come next week for a fitting?'

'Oh no, that's quite impossible. I'm leaving for Berlin on Thursday. Can you have it ready by Wednesday? I know I'm putting you on the spot, my dear, but maybe if you took the measurements now, it would help.'

Christina could see success had gone to her head. She was adored by everyone, including Hitler and Goebbels, and nothing would stop her getting her way. At that moment, Karin came over to see if she could help.

'Fräulein Lindner needs her outfit by Wednesday... I was just telling her that...'

'I am sure we can measure her now,' Karin replied, a little too hastily for Christina's liking.

Christina felt a pang of guilt at being hesitant and asked Lina to step inside the fitting room. It would take all of five minutes and then she would be free to mingle with her other guests. She grabbed the tape measure and started to note the measurements down. Lina was wearing a long-sleeved silk blouse with billowing sleeves. Christina asked if she could pull it up a little to get a more accurate wrist measurement. As she did so, the sleek, platinum and diamond, half-bracelet watch she had been wearing, previously hidden under the folds of silk, slipped down around her wrist.

Christina's eyes widened, her heart raced, and she felt the urge to vomit.

'Are you all right?' Lina asked.

'This bracelet... Where did you get it?'

Lina laughed. 'Oh this? Dieter gave it to me at Christmas. It's rather unusual isn't it?'

She put her arm out to give Christina a closer look. Christina backed away reaching out for the back of a chair to steady herself.

'Are you sure you're all right?'

'I feel a little faint, that's all,' Christina replied. 'Maybe it's because I haven't eaten today. If you don't mind, I'll ask my sister to finish the measurements.'

Lina looked alarmed. 'Of course.'

Christina stumbled out of the fitting room and stood for a moment against a mannequin. Karin came straight over.

'What on earth's wrong? You look like you've seen a ghost.'

Christina took Karin's half empty glass of champagne from her hand, took a long sip, and gestured towards the fitting room. 'The bracelet – the one I had made for Mirka – she's wearing it. Dieter gave it to her.'

Karin clasped her hand to her mouth in shock. 'Are you sure?'

'Quite sure. Can you finish taking the measurements? I need to compose myself. You can check for yourself.'

Karin moved to step into the fitting room. Christina caught her arm. 'Not a word!'

Inside the fitting room, Christina heard Lina ask if everything was all right.

'She'll be fine,' Karin replied. 'It's been a hectic day. Now, where were we?'

'I quite understand,' Lina replied with a laugh. 'Sometimes nerves get the better of me when it's the opening of my latest film.'

A waiter passed, carrying a tray of wine and champagne. Christina exchanged Karin's empty glass for a full one and joined her guests. Max was still with Dieter, Lina's actress friends, the Baroness, and Lucien. He excused himself to see how she was.

'Hopefully Dieter wasn't making a nuisance of himself,' she said.

'Never mind him. What's happened to you? You're shaking like a leaf.'

'I'll tell you later.'

Max could read her like an open book. He knew something bad had happened but would have to wait until they were alone to find out what. The rest of the evening, Christina tried to put the bracelet to the back of her mind and be the perfect host, attentive and charming. The Spring Collection had gone well and the order book was full.

After the guests left, Christina told Max about the bracelet.

His words echoed Karin's. 'Are you quite sure it was the same one?'

'I saw it myself, Max,' Karin said. 'It's definitely the same one.'

'Maybe whoever took it sold it on the Black Market, and Dieter bought it,' Karin said.

'You don't sell something like that easily on the Black Market without attracting attention – it's worth a small fortune. Whoever took it, knew exactly who to give it to.'

'Kiki, darling, that's a bit of a long shot isn't it?' said Max.

'Is it? So much has been stolen from the Jews since the Anschluss – even more since *Kristallnacht*. Granting favours has become a national pastime for such men as Dieter.'

112

'Well, unless we ask him directly, we won't know, will we?' Karin replied. She saw the look on Christina's face. 'You're not going to ask him are you?' Christina didn't reply. 'You can't. Don't get involved. Think of Max.'

'You're right, but one thing is for sure, sooner or later, I will find out where he got it from – and when I do…'

It was all too much and she burst into tears. Max put his arms around her and for a while no one uttered a word. When Christina calmed down, Karin suggested she and Max go away for a few days.

'I can manage here,' she added.

Christina wiped her eyes. 'We can't keep running away from the Nazis every time something bad happens.'

CHAPTER 14

IN MARCH, CHRISTINA and Max received the message they were all waiting for. Everything was in place and they could start processing the Kindertransport straight away. Everyone was delighted, but they were in no doubt as to the enormity of the task facing them. The group met at Café Central and within minutes of their arrival, families started to trickle in, desperate for their assistance. From the very first moment, it was a heart-breaking sight, and Christina prayed she would have the strength to carry it out.

The first to arrive was Walter's friend who had been sacked from the Academy for Music and the Performing Arts. He had his wife with him and his son, Erich, a shy eight-year-old, clinging to his mother, who kept dabbing her eyes throughout the entire meeting.

The Baroness spoke to them in a calm and dignified manner, assuring them that all would be well. But, in truth, no one knew whether it would all work out.

'How can we be sure Erich will be safe?' the man asked.

Stephen Pembroke explained that sponsors in England had registered their desire to foster a child with the British Committee for Refugees until the troubles were over and that these families had all been vetted.

The Baroness handed them two forms. 'All you have to do now, is register here. Once you've given consent, we will attach Erich's photograph and send it to the authorities. A duplicate copy will be sent to London. Before we do that, you need to go to this address and get a medical check for Erich and have the doctor fill in the second form.'

The couple examined the forms carefully.

'There's one more thing,' the Baroness added. 'The British government is asking for a £50 guarantee covering the children's eventual return. Do you have it? If you don't, we will do our best to raise funds for you.'

The couple looked at each other. 'We took our savings out of the bank last year and have some put aside. It's not a problem.'

'Good, then if you will fill out the details and sign here, we can proceed.'

Christina looked on as the man filled out the form – name, date of birth, place of birth, weight, hair colour, eye colour, distinctive marks. When it came to the address, he said they were living with friends as they'd lost their home.

'Put down Vienna. That will be fine. And where it says "occupation" put "student".'

The man's hand was shaking as he added his signature. 'I am putting my son's life in your hands.'

'And we will look after him,' Stephen Pembroke said.

The Baroness slipped the consent form back in her file. 'Now we need a photograph. Do you have one?'

The man's wife took a couple out of her handbag. 'Will these do?'

Stephen Pembroke took a look and shook his head. 'I'm afraid we need something better than this. For your son to be chosen, we must make sure the photograph...' He wanted to say, a picture that will tug at the heart strings, but stopped short of using those exact words. 'Something more professional. A head and shoulder shot – and a smile.' He turned his attention to the shy boy. 'You can give us a nice big smile, can't you, Erich?'

The boy nodded and Christina had to bite her lip in order not to shed a tear.

Stephen Pembroke turned to Johannes and Anton. 'Are you ready to take Erich's photograph now?'

Anton got up and grabbed his coat. 'If you will please follow me, the studio is not far from here.'

The man and his wife shook hands with everyone and thanked them. 'When can we expect to hear from you?' the man's wife asked.

The Baroness promised that once they had the photographs – one for London, and one for the exit visa – travel pass and the medical certificate, they were all set to go. It was hoped a departure date would be within a week or two.

Over the next two hours, three more couples asked for help. By the end of the week, that number had jumped to over one hundred. The following week there were another hundred applications. As applications grew, Christina realised she had to act quickly with regard to Hannah and Malka. She knew it would be almost impossible to get Nathan out; he was too old. She asked Max to set up a meeting with him in Grinzing.

Nathan still worked in the vineyards and his living conditions were less than desirable. Fearing a visit from the Nazi authorities, the owner of the *Heuriger* employed the Jewish workers on the understanding that they kept a low profile. That often meant sleeping in sheds. They were, however, well fed which was something when so many were starving. The owner was a friend of Max's and he allowed Nathan to meet them in his tavern. He reserved them a table at the back of the restaurant where Nathan would be able to slip away if there were any rowdy Brownshirts around, which happened on a regular basis during the new wine season. Tonight, there were only a few customers.

When Nathan walked into the room, Christina hardly recognized him, he had changed so much. In those few months, he had grown and was as tall as Max. Life had changed him; he was no longer a gawky boy, but a young man.

'Hello Nathan. How are you?' Christina asked.

Nathan shrugged. 'As well as can be expected.' He gestured to the tavern owner sitting with an old man. 'He does what he can, and his wife is a good cook. How are Malka and Hannah?'

'They're fine. In fact they are the reason I am here. I will come straight to the point. I want to get them out of Austria, to send them away to live with a foster family in England, but I wanted your approval first.'

'Max told me they are staying with your mother.'

Christina noted his familiarity with Max. He no longer referred to him as Herr Hauser. 'It's not easy to get rental accommodation for Jews these days and it's difficult for my mother to look after them, so we thought it best if they stayed at Steinbrunnhof for a while. They are living with the caretaker and his wife and have more freedom than here in Vienna. My mother visits regularly to keep an eye on them. They ask after you.'

Nathan gave a half-smile. 'And what do you tell them? That I hide away like a frightened rabbit?'

Christina's cheeks reddened and Max gave him a dressing down. He apologized.

'You know as well as I do,' he continued, 'there's no future here for us. Yes – get them away from this place, as soon as possible.' At that moment the accordionist and guitarist who had been playing for other diners, arrived at their table to serenade them with songs from their repertoire of *Wienerlieder* and *Schrammelmusik*. Max gave them a good tip and they moved on.

'*Gemütlichkeit*,' Nathan scoffed. 'A state or feeling of warmth, friendliness, and good cheer, a sense of belonging and well-being springing from social acceptance – for everyone except Jews.'

'Not everyone is against Jews, Nathan,' Christina said. 'We are all suffering because of the Nazis. I loved your mother. She was a good woman and I took it upon myself to make sure you were all safe. We put our lives in danger to do that.' She realised her words hurt him. 'I'm sorry, I didn't mean to sound so harsh, but it's a fact. I need your blessing for them to leave. Do I have it?'

'Yes, you have it.'

'Unfortunately, you cannot go with them. The authorities will only allow children sixteen and under.'

'Hannah is almost seventeen,' Nathan remarked.

'Yes, we may have to make her appear younger.'

'Have you discussed this with them?'

'No, I wanted your blessing first. Nathan, maybe you should try and leave Vienna. You cannot stay here like this. Perhaps we can get you false documents.'

'I won't leave.' Nathan's voice had a determined, hard edge to it. 'I would rather die.'

'What about Palestine?'

'I told you, I am not leaving.'

Christina looked at him. On the surface he was a young man. Inside, he was a wounded animal.

'Fine. If you change your mind, let us know.'

They got up to leave.

'One more thing, Fräulein Christina, I would like the chance to say goodbye to my sisters before they leave.'

'You have my word.'

CHAPTER 15

MALKA WAS IN the vegetable garden with Albrecht, and Hannah was helping Hildegard in the kitchen when Christina and Max arrived at Steinbrunnhof. Their cheeks were rosy and they had put on weight.

'What a lovely surprise,' Hildegard said, wiping her hands on her apron. 'If you'd let us know you were coming, I would have aired the rooms.'

'No need. We will be returning this evening. It's the girls I've come to see.'

'Are we going back to Vienna?' Hannah asked.

'Not just yet, but something has come up which I'd like to discuss with you.'

'Shall I call Malka?'

'Not at the moment. I want to talk to you first. Let's go outside and sit in the garden.'

Hannah took off her apron and followed Christina outside, while Max stayed behind to keep Hildegard company.

Hildegard watched them through the window as they headed toward the garden seat near the rose arbour. 'Is everything all right?' she asked. Max told her about the Kindertransport. 'What has the world come to when we have to send our little ones away.' It was more of a statement than a question.

Max asked if she'd had news of her sister.

'The last we heard was that they'd been forced across the border and were seen on a boat going down the Danube. I can't bear to think about it.'

In the garden, Christina explained to Hannah about the

119

Kindertransport. 'You will have a new life, free from all this fear and hiding – and it will only be for a while until all this trouble blows over.'

'Will Nathan come too?'

'I'm afraid that will be difficult. He's too old to get the special visa, but he has given his blessings for you and Malka to go.'

Hannah turned her face away, trying to process it all. Since her mother's death, she had grown up fast, yet at heart, she was still the naïve young girl who missed her brother's presence in their lives. On top of that, she knew nothing of England, but, having experienced the racial tension of the last few years, she was also smart enough to grasp that there might be a future somewhere else – away from the Nazis. She trusted Christina and knew she had their best interests at heart.

'I wanted to stay here and become a seamstress like my mother. We don't speak English. Would Malka and I stay together?'

Christina answered as best as she could. She also said it was important that Malka go to school and if her mind was set on being a seamstress, she would write her a glowing reference.

'Your mother would have wanted you all to have the best opportunities in life. I told Nathan that.'

'If you think we will be safe, I agree.'

Now all they had to do was tell Malka. That would not be easy as she was too young to grasp the implications, but with Hannah's help, they managed to achieve the desired outcome. Albrecht was there when Christina and Hannah told her she would be going "on holiday" for a while. Hannah made it sound like fun. Everything was a game these days. Being so vulnerable, it was the way they protected her.

They returned to the kitchen where Max and Hildegard were anxiously awaiting the outcome. They need not have worried. With her big sister looking on, Malka happily told Hildegard they were going on holiday – *across the sea to a place called England*. Fighting back the tears, Hildegard gave her a big hug. 'Oh my little one, be sure to send us a postcard won't you?'

Christina said they needed a couple of photographs. Max had

brought his camera and they decided to take them in the drawing room in the schloss.

'Go and put on your new dresses,' Christina said to them. 'We want you to look your very best.'

Half an hour later, the girls reappeared. Christina tided up their hair and the photographs were taken.

'Beautiful' Max said. He gave a little laugh. 'Hannah, you will have those English boys falling all over you!'

Hannah's cheeks reddened. She understood he was trying his best to put on a happy face.

During the drive back, Max was unusually quiet. Christina knew the thought of what he saw in Leopoldstadt still haunted him.

'I wish we could find the killers,' she said.

Max scoffed. 'The police have no intention of following Mirka's murder up. To them she was just another statistic.'

When they arrived in Vienna, they drove straight to Strauchgasse. Anton was in the darkroom and Johannes was sorting through over two hundred photographs.

'Here's another two for you,' Max said, handing him the film.

Christina looked through the mound of photographs on his desk and at others hanging up throughout the room. 'My God! If we manage to get all these out, it will be a miracle.'

At that moment Anton came out of the darkroom. His hair was dishevelled, he had bags under his eyes, and he looked as though he hadn't had a wink of sleep in a while.

'I thought I heard your voice,' he said to Max. 'What have you got there?'

Christina answered, 'Max took photos of the two Rosen girls. Their mother was my seamstress and she was murdered on *Kristallnacht*. I want them out on the first transport.'

He took the film and, without saying a word, went back into the dark room.

'He needs sleep,' Christina said. 'You both do.'

Johannes picked up a photograph of a three-year-old boy. 'How can we sleep when we see these images? We both have children and if it was one of mine... well, I don't know what I would do.'

They looked through the pictures with great sadness; smiling girls with glossy hair and big ribbons wearing pretty clothes with crisp Peter Pan collars, and smart little boys in neat sweaters and short trousers.

'Baroness Elisabeth told me they are looking for people who are – how can I put it – not too Jewish looking – and that they must be intelligent, healthy children, possessing positive moral qualities. She asked me to capture this in the photographs. We were also told they all have to get medical checks. Is that true?'

'Yes. We cannot send someone who might be a drain on the British government. It saddens us all but we can't dwell on this. We have to stay strong and do what we can.'

After an hour, Anton came out with their photographs. 'You should take up photography.' he said to Max. 'This little one is adorable – just look at those eyes. I like the way she is holding her doll, too.'

Max and Christina took a close look. They were indeed beautiful photographs. Malka and her doll wore identical dresses.

'I think you succeeded in making Hannah look a little younger.'

'How old is she?' Anton asked.

'Sixteen, but she turns seventeen in a couple of weeks. We've been warned that the older a child is, the more difficult it will be to place them.' Max knew he could trust the two photographers. 'I'm afraid we will have to falsify some of the records. I know a fine engraver who's willing to do it for us.'

'Do you want a set of photographs for yourself?' Johannes asked. 'Most of the families requested one for them too. In fact, some even wanted a family portrait – which is why we've been so busy.'

'Yes please, and a set for their brother as he won't be with them.'

Anton looked at the clock. It was almost six. 'Baroness Elisabeth has asked us to take these to her villa this evening. Why don't you come along?'

The Baroness had not only inherited wealth from her family, as a successful opera singer, she had money of her own. As a consequence, she lived in a luxurious and grandiose home in the exclusive suburb of Döbling, overlooking a large park. The rooms were lined with floor to ceiling bookshelves, enormous paintings and mirrors, and the floors were covered in exquisite, priceless oriental carpets. When they arrived, Lucien, attired in a burgundy velvet smoking jacket, was playing a Chopin Nocturne on the grand piano while the Baroness sat at her desk working on a mound of paperwork for the Kindertransport. The place smelt of spices, tobacco, and coffee, the atmosphere, soothing and melancholic.

'Come in, come in. You're just in time for a spot of refreshments,' the Baroness said. She asked the butler to bring a bottle of champagne and prepare a platter of open sandwiches.

Anton gave her the box of photographs.

She took a quick look through them. 'Excellent. Well done. I've had word that it's highly likely the first train will leave at the beginning of April – in a week's time.'

'So soon,' Christina replied. 'Do you have any idea how many we are able to send?'

'I'm hoping about one hundred and fifty. When I've attached these photographs to the forms, I will take them to be processed. The only thing I am waiting on now is the medical certificates. Some have been approved already. I am sorry to say a few were turned down, which made it all the more distressing for the families concerned. How did you get on with the Rosen girls?'

Christina showed her the photographs. The Baroness looked at them carefully, noting the sadness in Christina's eyes. 'I'm so sorry my dear. Sometimes it's better to remain as detached as possible from our work, but in your case I know that's not easy. Believe me, we have all been affected. We would not be human otherwise.'

The Baroness handed them each a glass of champagne. 'Now let's forget our worries and relax for a while.' She went over to Lucien, still seated at the piano, and whispered in his ear. '*Mon amour*, why don't you play us something else? Perhaps "*Adagietto*" from Mahler's 5th Symphony.'

Lucien was almost as good a pianist as he was a tenor and was only too eager to please his lover. Christina lay her head on Max's shoulder, and a feeling of calm flooded over her as she listened to this beautiful arrangement of one of her favourite pieces of music. Being the show-man that Lucien was, when he'd finished, he stood up to take a bow. Next to the piano was a table with a vase of red roses. He reached out, took one, and with a sweeping flourish, kissed it and gave it the Baroness.

She took his hand and returned his gesture with a kiss. 'Thank you for that marvellous and emotional interpretation, my darling.' For a brief moment it was as if their guests were invisible. His appreciative audience clapped heartily.

Both the Baroness and Lucien had an open marriage. Their respective spouses would not grant a divorce, yet they were free to express their love as they saw fit. Seeing this act of devotion to each other, and knowing as he did, that marriage to Christina was even more elusive, Max held Christina a little tighter. The moment was not lost on her. One made the best of one's circumstances.

CHAPTER 16

THE KINDERTRANSPORT. APRIL, 1939

THE SUN STREAMED through the large window into the waiting room at Vienna's Am Steinhof Children's Hospital. The white-tiled room, with its long wooden benches and overpowering smell of antiseptic and disinfectant, had a particularly cold, clinical atmosphere, which only served to make many of those waiting even more anxious. Since the Anschluss, the hospital, like others in Vienna, had sacked all Jewish doctors, and those who had replaced them elevated themselves into prominent positions by adhering to Nazi race hygiene and the science of eugenics. Racial stereotyping was common.

A young, dark-haired nurse sitting behind a desk asked the reason for their visit and, after ticking off their names on the register, told them to take a seat. Ten minutes later she called out Christina's name.

'The doctor will see you now Fräulein Lehmann. Door five just down the corridor.'

Christina whispered to the girls before they entered. 'Remember what I said. I want you to impress the doctor so that he will give us an excellent bill of health, and then I'm going to treat you to an ice cream.'

She knocked on the door and a low voice called out, *Herein!*

The doctor's face and build matched his voice, gentle and kindly, as befitted a children's doctor. He gestured for them to sit down and peered over his glasses at a file. 'I see you are here for the medical examination for the Kindertransport.'

'That's correct, Herr Doctor,' Christina replied.

'I also see here that you are not the mother.'

'No. Their mother…' Christina remembered that Malka still had not been told about her mother's death. 'Their mother is missing and I have taken it upon myself to look after them to the best of my ability, which is why we are here. I think they will be better off in England.'

'And the father?'

'Their father died a while ago. They have no one now, which is why I want them to go to foster parents in England.'

'Yes, yes!'

Christina was becoming anxious. Despite being told to smile, Hannah stared at the doctor with a stony face, and Malka sat on the chair with her doll, swinging her legs.

'All right girls, let me examine you. Which one will go first?' He picked up the file and indicated to Hannah to go behind the screen and take her clothes off. Clad in his white jacket with his stethoscope dangling from his neck, Hannah's eyes widened in fear.

'It's just a routine examination. Nothing to worry about.'

Christina put a reassuring hand on her shoulder. 'It will be fine.'

Hannah disappeared behind the screen, followed by the doctor.

'Excellent,' the doctor said after five minutes. 'You can get dressed now.' He shouted for Malka to go in.

When Hannah reappeared, Christina saw she was fighting back the tears and decided to go with Malka while the doctor conducted his examination. Despite having a kindly voice, the doctor carried out his physical assessment in a cold clinical manner, completely devoid of emotion. Christina watched him as he examined Malka's mouth and moved the stethoscope over the child's naked body as if she were not human – merely a laboratory experiment. After he'd finished the physical examination, he took measurements of their height and head, and asked them a few questions while scribbling notes as they replied. Finally, he issued them a clean bill of health and wished the girls a good trip.

When they'd left his office, Christina gave a sigh of relief.

'Can we have our ice cream now?' Malka asked.

It was then that another man in a white jacket carrying several files appeared from a nearby room. With him were a distraught woman and a boy who appeared to be around ten years old. 'Make another appointment, Frau Schmidt, and we'll see what we can do,' the doctor said to her. 'Don't worry, after a few treatments, he will be fine.' Christina hurried the children away, but when the man saw her he called over. 'Fräulein Christina. Is it really you?'

She spun around. It was Sigmund Klein. It had been a couple of years since she'd last seen him and, judging by the nameplate on his door, his position was an important one – Professor of Psychiatry: Specialist in Nervous and Mental Diseases.

'What are you doing here?' He glanced at Malka and Hannah. 'Are these two girls the reason you're here?'

'Yes. They're leaving for London in a few days' time.'

'I heard you were involved in the Kindertransport.' Christina didn't ask him how he knew. 'I'm just going for a coffee break. Would you care to join me? It's been such a long time since I saw you.'

Christina apologized, saying she would love to but had promised the girls ice creams.

'A pity. Sometimes I could do with a diversion from my work.'

Christina glanced at the woman with the young boy making their way to the reception still in tears.

'What happened?' she asked. 'I mean with the woman – she's in a terrible state.'

Sigmund shook his head. 'She came for the same reason as you – for her son to go to London. Unfortunately he displayed...' He paused for a moment. 'Autistic psychopathic tendencies and although he has intellectual capabilities, above average in some respects, I cannot recommend him for the program – a great pity.'

Given the family situation with Gudrun Klein, Christina had to bite her lip to stop herself from making a comment that may have been deemed inappropriate. Sigmund tapped the files he was holding. 'These are the unsuccessful ones and they have been advised to come back for treatment.'

At a time when Jews were subjected to humiliation and violence in the streets and anti-Semitism had become official policy, that decision seemed questionable to Christina.

Outside, she took a few deep breaths of fresh air. It was as if a crushing weight had been lifted from her. 'Come on girls. We've got what we wanted. Now let's celebrate with an ice cream.'

Over the next few days, Karin took care of Christina's clients while she and Max worked on the final details for the Kindertransport. All the families had been notified about the date of departure and the exit visas given out. As expected, there were last minutes problems. Money had to be found to pay for the visas and not everyone had it. Various charities and Jewish organizations came to the rescue and the Baroness funded the rest. Two days before the departure, Christina received Malka and Hannah's own exit visas. They were staying back in Hietzing with her mother and Christina went to give them the good news.

Julia Lehman took a look at their *Reisepass* stamped with the eagle of the German Reich and the *Hakenkreuz*. Next to their name was a large red "J". Having no fixed abode, their address simply stated "Vienna". Underneath were other particulars: Height, Weight, Colour of Hair, Colour of Eyes, Distinctive Marks, and Profession. Against Profession, Christina had put down "student" for Malka, and "apprentice dressmaker" for Hannah.

Hannah was both surprised and delighted. 'An apprentice dressmaker!'

'I have another little surprise for you,' Christina replied. She handed her a small package. Inside were a few samples Mirka had made when she applied to work for her. With these was a glowing reference written on the company letterhead:

CHRISTINA LEHMANN
HAUTE COUTURE
MARIAHILFERSTRASSE, WIEN

It stated that Hannah had a passion for sewing and a dedication and willingness to learn which would make her a skilled dressmaker.

'This is your chance for a new beginning. Show this to a prospective employer and they will be only too happy to take you on. I know you will make us all proud.'

Hannah threw her arms around her. 'How can I ever thank you?'

Christina knew how difficult it would be for a family to want to foster a sixteen year-old – seventeen in another month's time – and this reference would make it easier for her. Julia Lehmann said they would all look forward to hearing about her work in her letters.

That night, Max brought Nathan to the Lehmann villa in Hietzing for a farewell meeting with his sisters. After a lengthy discussion with Max, Christina thought it best that their last meeting should not be at the train station, for two reasons. Firstly, it would be too traumatic for all concerned, and secondly, the place was likely to be filled with Gestapo and German soldiers who might question Nathan and possibly send him away to a forced labour camp.

It was hard for the siblings to part, and Nathan promised to write once they were settled. Julia Lehmann told the girls that they could write to him at the villa and she would make sure the letters were passed on. This arrangement suited everyone. After a hearty farewell dinner, the Rosen children said their goodbyes. Hannah and Malka could not stop crying and almost had to be wrenched away from their brother. Nathan was stoic. The last few months had hardened him. He was now a man, and men don't cry.

℃

Beck pulled up outside Vienna's Westbahnhof station at ten o'clock at night with the Rosen girls, Christina, and her mother. It was a glorious, warm spring evening. The trees were in blossom, perfuming the night air with a beauty that contrasted greatly with the traumatic scenes taking place inside the station. The train was due to leave just

129

after midnight and already the platform was teaming with distraught parents trying their best to put on a brave face for the sake of their anxious and bewildered children.

The Baroness was moving through the crowd trying her best to put both parents and children at ease. Walter and Max were with her, along with other helpers from the various charities including the Red Cross and members of the Jewish Community Organisation in Vienna, all of whom played a vital role working on the Kindertransport. Documents were checked and rechecked. Nothing could be allowed to go wrong at the last minute.

As expected, the station was filled with soldiers and Gestapo agents waiting to pounce at the slightest indiscretion.

'There you are,' Max said to Hannah and Malka. 'Are you ready for your big adventure?'

Malka nodded. She had been allowed to take her doll, Pipina, and clung to her as dearly as the parents clung to their children. The children were issued with an identification number printed on a large card and told to wear it around their necks until they'd safely arrived in London.

A familiar face made his way through the throng towards them – Stephen Pembroke. With him was a children's nurse from the Red Cross. She was introduced as Mary Wood, the wife of a friend at the British Embassy who was returning home for a few weeks to visit her family. Mary told them the embassy had asked her to keep a check on the children and make sure no harm came to them. An hour before midnight, an announcement was made for the children to board the train. Christina looked around at the sea of faces on the platform and had to force herself from collapsing under the strain of it all. The sight of parents hugging and kissing their children for the last time was more than she could bear; little boys in smart short trousers and woollen jackets, and girls in pretty dresses and warm coats. Without exception, all the children looked tidy and clean, as though their parents had purposely attired them to look their best when they reached

London. It was one of the most distressing sights Christina had ever witnessed.

With pain in their hearts, the women gave the children one last hug, telling them to write as soon as possible. Mary Wood took Malka's suitcase and held her tiny hand tightly as they joined the rest of the children clamouring to board the train. Once on board, she guided them along the corridor to their compartment, where six other children were already settling in. Four girls – one as young as three years old – and two boys, one of whom was a sixteen-year-old orphan who had bravely applied for the refugee program alone after hearing that orphaned boys could be sent to forced labour camps. Mary put the suitcases safely on the overhead rack and gave them a few sweets for the journey. All the children except the orphan, who took out a book and started to read, rushed to the window to look for their parents.

On the platform, parents waited to catch one last glimpse at their children. All along the length of the train, outstretched tiny arms and hands waved from the open windows, and cries of love reverberated through this heart-wrenching scene. Several parents fainted and others were almost hysterical until they laid eyes on their child at the window. And then the moment they dreaded – a loud piercing whistle, the hissing sound of steam being emitted through the stack, and the huffing, rhythmic sound of the locomotive's wheels slowly starting to push back and forth. Within a few minutes the huge train disappeared into the night behind a billowing cloud of steam. The children had gone, and at that moment, only God knew what fate had in store for them.

Max held Christina in his arms, her tears soaking his jacket. Stephen Pembroke assured them they would be fine, yet at that moment, the future was anything but certain.

CHAPTER 17

THE DOWNWARD SPIRAL of events after *Kristallnacht,* combined with the departure of the Kindertransport train, took its toll on Christina's mental health. The salon was thriving and orders from the new collection continued to grow, but as much as she loved her work, she found it hard to concentrate. When she wasn't working on designs or helping the Baroness prepare for the next Kindertransport, she spent time with Max in his studio in Nussdorf in the suburb of Döbling. Knowing as they did, that the future seemed uncertain, Christina clung to the past, trying to relive those happy moments when she first met him. Being in his studio, filled with artist's paraphernalia and the ever-present smell of turpentine and paints, gave her renewed energy. Watching him paint or discussing a multitude of subjects with his like-minded artist friends both fascinated and invigorated her, and she never tired of it. At the moment, Max was fortunate to still have commissions, but like Christina, his best clients had left the country.

His studio was on the ground floor of a two-storey building in a pretty cobblestoned street on a hill. At the bottom of the hill was one of many streams that meandered through the hills to the Danube. With the weather warming, they walked along the tree-lined streets to Grinzing, breathing in the fresh country air, drinking delicious local wine, and eating home-cooked fresh food in a traditional *Heurigen.* Among good company and the beautiful sounds of live *Schrammel* music, Christina began to relax again. More often than not, they would return to the studio, make love, and afterwards he would continue painting, sometimes until the early hours of the morning. While she slept on his bed in the corner of his studio, he would paint her, sometimes moving the sheet away, exposing her curvaceous buttocks or rearranging her golden tresses over her breasts. In the morning, she would find him asleep in the armchair, surrounded by a multitude of charcoal sketches, an empty wineglass, and her likeness on a canvas still wet with fresh paint. When he woke up sometime later, she would be gone, back in the sewing room with the seamstresses, or taking a fitting with a client.

This pattern of events went on for several months. By August, a few more Kindertransport trains had left Vienna and they received word from Stephen Pembroke and their other sources in London that all had gone well with the children. Most of them had been placed in foster homes soon after their arrival, and those that hadn't – mainly the older ones who lacked sponsors – were sent to boarding schools to undergo training, usually of a domestic or agricultural nature created specifically for them to join the British workforce. The best news of all was that Mary Wood returned with a letter from Hannah. The address was a village in Surrey.

Dear Fräulein Christina,
We are very well. Mr and Mrs Hillier are very good to us. Malka goes to school now and we are both learning English. Mrs Hillier helped me find work with a local dressmaker and she is most pleased with my work. I think you and Mutti would be proud.
Please write when you can. Give our love to Nathan.
Hannah Rosen

After so long, this news was a great relief and made everyone happy, including Julia Lehmann, and Albrecht and Hildegard. Unfortunately, Christina's happiness was short-lived. At the end of August, Christina was walking home from Grinzing late one night with Max when she noticed a black car parked at the end of his street. She quickly pulled him off the lamp-lit pavement into the shadows of the nearby trees.

'That car! I'm sure it's the same one that was parked outside the salon before it was searched.'

'Kiki, what's wrong? You're being paranoid. There are often cars around here and most are black.'

'Yes, yes, but that one – have you seen *that* one before?'

Max strained his eyes to look. There was hardly a moon that night and after so much wine, it was hard to see.

'It's too far away. You're being ridiculous. How long do you intend to hide like this – all night?' he asked sarcastically. He stepped back on to the pavement. 'Come on. I'm going home.'

Reluctantly, Christina followed him and they continued on their way. As soon as they came out of the shadows, the car drove away.

'See,' Max said with a laugh. 'You were worrying for nothing.'

Christina wasn't so sure. Just before she got into bed, she peered through the window to double-check the car hadn't returned. Max came over and caressed her. 'My darling, Kiki, what am I going to do with you? Stop worrying and get some sleep.'

He held her in his arms for a while until he was sure she was fast asleep and then went into the kitchen to retrieve a letter from a drawer. He closed the door, careful to make sure the soft light wouldn't wake her, and sat down at the kitchen table to reread it. It was from his father and had arrived a month earlier. The letter told him that the Gestapo had been snooping about and he wanted to warn him.

After this letter, the incident with the black car *did* worry him. Maybe his luck was running out after all, but he reasoned that if the authorities had uncovered his Jewish roots, they would have come looking for him before now. He put the letter back, switched off the light, and returned to bed, taking a peek outside himself, just to make sure the car hadn't returned. Christina stirred slightly when he got back into bed. Her body was warm and the smell of her perfume lingered in the warmth of the night air. He kissed her forehead gently and pulled the sheets over them both. He certainly wasn't going to burden Christina with the letter; she'd been through enough just lately.

Later that week Christina and Karin went for afternoon coffee and cake at Café Landtmann. It had been a while since they'd been out together as work had taken up so much of their time. The Summer Collection had been well received, bringing in a host of new customers, especially from Germany and Czechoslovakia. Much to Christina and Karin's surprise, many were friends of Lina Lindner. Even Magda Goebbels herself ordered more clothes, although she never actually came to visit the salon and preferred placing a personal order over the telephone. However, she did send thank-you notes and flowers. Famed for her love of couture, Christina learned from Lina, that Magda changed several times a day, liberally used Elizabeth Arden cosmetics, chain smoked, and wore handmade Ferragamo shoes, even though the *Führer* hated cosmetics, women smoking, and preferred clothes and shoes to be purchased from German designers. Other senior Nazi wives, especially Annelies von Ribbentrop and Inge Ley, had similar tastes. One day during a fitting, Lina told her the *Führer* also hated women plucking their eyebrows and dying their hair. She looked at herself in the mirror when she made the comment.

'Goodness knows what he must think of me.' Lina laughed as she touched her platinum blonde hair. 'Does he really believe I was born with hair this colour?'

Surprisingly, Christina grew to like Lina. She was a free spirit and light-hearted, and from their few conversations, took her acting career seriously. She never talked about Dieter Klein either, which also surprised her. In fact, she spoke more about her leading men, and in ways which led Christina to think she might not be averse to an amorous liaison with them every now and again. Neither did she wear the bracelet again, but it still continued to puzzle Christina.

The manager of Café Landtmann gave Christina and Karin a warm welcome and showed them to their usual table.

'We'll have the hazelnut torte,' Christina said.

When he returned with the tray of coffee and cakes, he handed her an envelope. 'This came for you a few days ago. The gentleman said I was to give it to you personally.'

'Who's it from?' Karin asked when they were alone.

'It looks like Joseph Fischer's handwriting.' Inside was a scribbled note.

'What's he say?'

'He wants me to meet him at the blue carousel on Sunday – the same time as before.'

Karin looked surprised. 'I wonder what he wants.'

'I have no idea.'

Karin stirred her coffee thoughtfully. 'Maybe he would like you to make something for his wife.'

'Somehow, I don't think so.'

Away from work, Karin and Christina caught up on other things that had been occupying their time. Walter was busy helping the Baroness with the Kindertransport, and their mother had returned to Steinbrunnhof for the summer. There had also been several art exhibitions in Vienna – if the work complied with Reich propaganda which usually meant heroic or romantic themes – and the theatres and opera house played to packed out performances. Apart from that, the groundswell of racial hatred continued. Walter likened it to a dam ready to burst.

On Sunday, Christina went to meet Fischer in the Prater. The weather was warm and sunny, and the park was filled with visitors enjoying themselves. This time Fischer was there before her.

'*Guten Tag*, Fräulein Lehmann. Thank you for coming.'

Christina asked if he would like to sit in an open-air Kaffeehaus, but he declined, suggesting they go for a ride on the Ferris wheel again for absolute privacy. Being a warm day, there was a long queue of people lined up for a ride on the great wheel and they waited in line with neither saying a word. Eventually, they took their tickets and climbed into the carriage.

'I have some information which I think you might like to know about,' Fischer said, when the wheel started to revolve. He paused for a moment and lit a cigarette as if stalling for time. It crossed Christina's mind that maybe he needed money and was about to blackmail her because of the list. She couldn't have been more wrong.

'You remember I told you about my uncle, the official at the Leopoldstadt police station who helped me get that list you asked for, well, he got himself a promotion. Guess where to?'

Christina wasn't in the mood for guessing games. 'I have no idea. Please get to the point.'

'The Hotel Métropole. It's been transformed into the Gestapo Headquarters and they've recruited many policemen, my uncle being one of them.'

Christina already knew that the Gestapo had taken over the hotel, but apart from that she knew very little else. 'Who does he work for?' she asked. 'What does this have to do with me?'

'The man in charge of the whole organisation is a German by the name of Franz Josef Huber. I'm afraid I don't know the name of my uncle's immediate boss. The thing is, part of his job is filing paperwork and preparing documents for his superiors, and as you can imagine, these files are marked Top Secret. I wouldn't be mentioning this if it wasn't for the fact that one day a file appeared on his desk. It had a number on it and when he looked inside, he saw a photograph of Herr Hauser. In fact there were several.'

Christina felt a chill run down her spine. 'I thought you didn't tell your uncle who wanted that file – and how does he know Herr Hauser?'

'I'm sorry, but my uncle pressured me.' Fischer's face reddened. 'Please don't worry, he hasn't told anyone.' He didn't give her time to reply. 'What alerted my uncle was that your photograph was there too – together with Herr Hauser's. One was taken at the theatre, another when you were walking through a park, and several more with you at Café Central with a group of people. There were also several of Herr Hauser alone. My uncle recognised you from photographs in magazines and newspapers and as he knew I'd tried to help you with the list of names. He came over to see me and thought I should warn you.'

Christina was silent for a few minutes, taking it all in. She thought of the black car and was now sure they had been spying on Max. 'What else did this file contain?'

'As I said, the file is on Herr Hauser – his friends, where he goes, etc. You know, all the stuff the secret police gather on people these days.' He gave a sarcastic laugh. 'No one is immune. Sometimes I think they do it to blackmail people. My uncle said you can't imagine the dirt they dig up on people.'

Fischer could see Christina was deeply affected by this news and apologised. 'I'm sorry, *gnae'* Fräulein, I didn't mean to upset you. After what you did for Gretel, I am indebted to you and I thought you should know.'

'Thank you. You did the right thing. Did your uncle say who gave him that file?'

'A man called Dieter Klein. He works for Ernst Kaltenbrunner. Do you know him?'

Christina reached out and grabbed the rail of the open-air cabin. It tilted and rocked precariously at her sudden movement, giving them a clear view of the people below through the immense structure of steel beams and struts.

Fischer moved quickly to catch her arm and make sure the iron grating was firmly locked. 'Careful! It's a long drop from here.'

'What else did the dossier contain?'

'He didn't say much more – oh yes, there was one other thing. It seems they checked the details of his parents. I forget where. A village near Graz, I believe.' Fischer pointed to a row of seats in the carriage. 'Please sit down, Fräulein. You're worrying me being so close to this open window. You might fall.'

Christina took his advice. 'I'm very grateful for this. There is one thing however that I feel you've left out. Something else your uncle must have seen in the folder.' Fischer found it hard to look her in the eye. 'Tell me. I need to know.'

Fischer lowered his eyes. 'The file is stamped with a red "J" – *Juden*.

I came to tell you the authorities are snooping around, that's all. I don't know your private life and I don't want to. It's not my business. My uncle told me this because you have been good to us.' He gave a smile to put her at ease. 'There are plenty of Jews in Vienna. It probably means nothing – just a routine check.'

Christina knew he wouldn't have arranged the meeting if it was simply a routine check. No, this was the news she'd dreaded. The Gestapo knew Max was a Jew. Worse still, Dieter Klein knew this. Max had been right when he said Dieter would be snooping around. She felt sick at the thought of it. The ride had almost ended and Christina reached into her purse and handed Fischer some money.

He shook his head. 'I don't want money. That's not why I did it.'

Christina thrust it into his hand. 'I know you didn't, but I want you to have it for your trouble. Take your uncle for a meal and buy Frau Fischer something nice.'

Fischer refused again but she quickly stuffed it into his pocket. 'Not another word.'

The giant Ferris wheel clanked to a halt and they parted ways at the ticket office where another long line of people waited eagerly for a ride.

CHAPTER 18

CHRISTINA CONFIDED IN Karin about the meeting. She knew she would have to tell Max immediately and was afraid of his reaction.

'It's the "J" that worries me the most,' she said. 'If that came out it could be the end of his career.'

'You cannot delay the inevitable. You *must* let him know as soon as possible.'

'I know, but he's been so strange these past few months. Sometimes he's his old self – loving and carefree – and at other times, he's moody and despondent. He has always had a mercurial personality, but there are times when I look into his eyes and feel he is hiding something from me. I never felt that before.'

'You're probably reading too much into it. We're all different these days.'

'You're right. I will tell him this evening.'

Max was working on a commission when Christina arrived. His friend Otto was just leaving.

'Will I see you both in Grinzing tonight?' Otto asked. 'I hear one of our favourite taverns is featuring a group of Hungarian musicians. I know how you like gypsy music.'

Max's face lit up. 'Sounds like a good idea. What do you think, Kiki darling?'

Christina nodded. After Otto left, Max returned to his painting. 'You could have sounded more cheerful,' he said, adding a little more linseed to a cerulean blue making it smoother and easier to mix with other colour pigments.

'Max, I need to speak with you. Something's come up which you

140

need to know about.' He applied the paint to the canvas in a bold stroke and then stood back a little, concentrating on the image of a street scene with a church in the distance. He added another few strokes, worked them in, and stood back again. 'Did you hear me?' Christina said, a little irritated at his seeming lack of interest. 'I have something important to discuss with you.'

'I heard you. Go on.'

'I met Herr Fischer in the Prater today. He left a message at Café Landtmann for me.'

'What did he want?'

'The news is not good. His uncle told him the Gestapo has a dossier on you, compiled by Dieter Klein.'

'Did he say what was in it?' His voice was cool.

'They've been looking into your background. The file is stamped with a "J". They know, Max – they know you're a Jew.'

Max wiped his brushes, swirled them in turpentine and then went into the kitchen to retrieve the letter from his father. 'This came from my father a few weeks ago. I wasn't going to tell you, but after what you've just told me, maybe it's time for me to be honest with you. What you've just said doesn't exactly come as a surprise.'

My dear son,

I hope this letter finds you well. I read about your success in the magazines and newspapers and I cannot be more proud of you. Your mother, my dearest Klara, God rest her soul, would also be proud. I never told you this, but her father was a great painter in Budapest. Maybe you take after that side of the family as I am sad to say, there is no creativity on my side. I also read of the success of your girlfriend. In all these years, you have never brought her to meet us. The door is always open and we will welcome her with open arms.

As you well know, I am not a letter-writer. I find it hard to write down my thoughts, but something has happened which I think you should know about. A close friend told me that two men were at the Town Hall and asked to see the registry on Births, Deaths, and Marriages of everyone in the area. They made notes of several and I believe we were among them. I thought you should know. Maybe they are looking into Klara's background. Many Jews in this area have been sent away. I am glad she didn't live to see what was taking place. All the same, your mother was a Jew, and in her heart, proud of it, but we changed everything legally to protect you.

God bless you and keep you safe.

Papa.

Christina read the letter with dismay. 'You do realise, don't you, that if they think you are a Jew, you will be in trouble for not registering and declaring your assets?'

'I don't consider myself a Jew. I was baptized and brought up a Catholic. I didn't even know my real mother. I don't even know the Jewish prayers.'

'The file puzzles me. I can't believe Dieter is behind this – after all this time. It doesn't make sense. What would he achieve by it? Once you thought he was jealous of you, but now he has Lina, so why would he want to bring you down? Surely he would know if anything happened to you, it would devastate me too.' Christina was not only frightened, she was confused. 'Maybe Dieter was given the file by someone else.'

'He's not a paper-pusher, Kiki. He's a big-wig. I don't like him and the feeling is mutual. He only puts up with me because of you.'

'We can't exactly go and ask him what he's up to, can we?' Christina said. 'I was told this in good faith.'

Max went to the cupboard to get a bottle of wine. Neither of them felt like going to Grinzing after this news.

'If Dieter knows and hasn't done anything, I'd say there's a possible chance he may be in doubt as to your Jewishness and as such is prepared to leave you alone,' Christina said, taking a sip of wine. She realised she was trying to put herself at ease as much as Max.

142

Max gave a sarcastic laugh. 'On the other hand, if he *does* come after me, it could be because Jews are forbidden to do business and have to liquidate their properties under the supervision of a governmental trustee. In my case, my business is my painting; it's hardly an enterprise, but I do own this apartment. He may be biding his time.'

Christina looked at him. 'What are you saying?'

'I have an idea. It's something I've been thinking about for a while now, especially since my father's letter. I want to transfer my assets to you.'

'What! Are you crazy?'

'Hear me out. If I sell my apartment and my car to you – an Aryan – for market value, it's a legal deal and there will be nothing he can get me for. Of course, I would never sell to you, it would be a gift.'

'Wouldn't that be seen as an admission that you *are* Jewish after all?'

Max didn't answer. He stood up and started pacing the room. Christina poured them more wine and lit them both cigarettes.

He took the cigarette from her outstretched hand and inhaled, while mulling the situation over in his mind. 'Think about it, Kiki. This way, if he does go after me because of my so-called Jewishness, he will no longer have legal grounds to do so. It's all about legalities in the eyes of the law. In fact, I should have done this before but, as you pointed out, it might have looked like an admission to being Jewish.'

'You have a point.'

Max sat down again. 'You are my life and if I can't trust you, I can't trust anyone. We'll see the lawyer tomorrow.'

Christina nodded in approval. She had never considered Max as Jewish, yet reluctantly, she was being drawn into this web of fear and confusion just as much as any other Jew in the Reich. 'When the Nazis are out of power, it reverts back to you – okay?'

Max lifted her chin and looked into her eyes. 'Let me tell you something else.'

'What?'

'When the bastards have gone and there's no more racial bigotry, I'm going to marry you, that's what.'

In her heart, she wondered if she would ever live to see them marry, but they had to be optimistic. Christina proposed a toast. 'That day can't come quickly enough.'

Christina contacted their trusted family friend, Judge von Nauckhoff, to transfer Max's assets to her, including his car. Von Nauckhoff also suggested they backdate the documents to April 1938. They were not surprised to hear that he'd done that sort of thing for quite a few people. He handed her two copies of the agreement and told her to keep them somewhere safe. Christina was now the legal owner of his apartment in Nussdorf. In the eyes of the law, Max was a tenant.

The downcast mood of the Gestapo file on Max was quickly replaced by one of joy. After several years of being unable to conceive, Karin discovered she was expecting a child. The family was euphoric. Apart from this, the other good news was that another Kindertransport train had safely reached England and most of the children had found placements. It had been hard work, but ultimately rewarding, and preparations were in place for another, due to leave in September. Knowing that the earlier transports had all gone well, the amount of parents now wanting to send their children away multiplied, and the Baroness was finding it hard to keep up. Lucien was back in Paris for a season with the Paris Opera and unable to support her. Fortunately, there were others eager to help. Max's painter friend, Otto, was one of them. He liaised with the various charities for the guarantee of funds, and with Anton and Johannes to have the photographs taken. In all, over a thousand children had left Vienna, and many more had emigrated from Germany and Czechoslovakia.

CHAPTER 19

CHRISTINA AND MAX were having breakfast in her apartment in Mariahilferstrasse when the telephone rang. It was Stephen Pembroke.

'Have you heard the news?' His voice was unusually calm and measured.

'No. What news?' She glanced over her shoulder at Max who was in the process of smearing apricot conserve on his *semmerl*.

'Germany has invaded Poland. It's on the radio.'

Christina almost dropped the telephone. 'Who is it?' Max asked.

'Stephen. He says Germany has just attacked Poland.' She ran to the radio and switched it on while Max took the receiver to speak with him.

Patriotic German music blared from the radio for a few minutes and then came the voice of Adolf Hitler declaring that Poland was planning, with its allies Great Britain and France, to encircle and dismember Germany. Because of this, Germany had no alternative but to retaliate. An advance force of more than 2,000 tanks supported by the Luftwaffe with 900 bombers and over 400 fighter planes have been deployed to the region.

'German forces have already attacked Warsaw,' Pembroke told Max. 'Britain and France said they would stand by their guarantee to defend Poland. If they do, there will be an immediate declaration of war.'

Max put down the receiver and grabbed his jacket. 'I have to go, Kiki. I will be back tonight.' He gave her a quick peck on the cheek, grabbed his apricot-slathered roll, and ran down the flight of stairs to his car in the courtyard.

Christina looked through the window and saw him talking to Beck. By the shocked look on Beck's face, she knew he'd just given him the news. She immediately got on the telephone to Karin and then to her mother, who was still in the country. There was little they could do but sit tight and wait for Britain and France's reaction. Whatever happened, it didn't look good. If they declared war, their lives would change for the worst. If they did nothing, Hitler would try to grab more territory in the name of the Reich, and that did not bode well for Jews, communists, and a host of others who disagreed with his policies.

Two days later, on September 3, the inevitable happened. Stephen Pembroke got wind of the impending announcement, and he, together with Max and Christina, were at the Baroness's villa when the announcement was made on the BBC.

"This is London. You will hear a statement by the Prime Minister. I am speaking from the cabinet room at 10 Downing Street. This morning the British Ambassador in Berlin handed the German government a final note stating that unless we heard from them by eleven o'clock that they were prepared, at once, to withdraw their troops from Poland, a state of war would exist between us. I have to tell you now that no such undertaking has been received and consequently this country is at war with Germany."

'That's it,' Max said matter-of-factly, after they'd digested the terrible news. 'As part of the Greater Reich, Austria is now at war.'

The telephone rang. It was Lucien, calling from Paris.

'*Ma chérie*, this is terrible,' the Baroness said in a quiet voice. The line went dead. 'I think the line's tapped,' she said to them. 'This has happened a few times recently; a few strange clicks and then nothing.' She took a cigarette and placed it in her cigarette holder. 'Lucien just read out the headlines from *Paris-soir* – "La guerre est déclarée".'

Stephen Pembroke brought up the subject of the Kindertransport.

'This means the borders will be closed. We won't be able to get any more children out.'

'We've done our best,' the Baroness replied, 'but it's not going to be easy for those who were due to leave in a few days' time. I'm dreading telling them.'

Although they'd hoped it wouldn't come to this, it wasn't entirely unexpected. There was so much to discuss. Lucien had been due to return for the Vienna Opera's winter season but that would now be impossible, and Stephen Pembroke, although he was an American, decided he should leave and go to London as the British legation in Vienna would be closed and foreign journalists targeted by the authorities.

'What are *you* going to do, Max?' Pembroke asked. His voice had a grim undertone. 'You know things are only going to get worse for the Jews. You should leave as soon as possible. Use the fake documents.'

Everyone stopped talking. 'What fake documents?' Christina asked.

The Baroness came to his rescue. 'Occasionally we had to resort to fake documents when we were processing the children for the Kindertransport. Knowing Max is a Jew we thought he should get a fake identity at the same time, in case things turned sour.'

Max saw the look of alarm on Christina's face. 'Kiki, we are among friends here. You know that. No one here would betray my secret.'

Christina wanted to know if anyone other than Karin knew of the Gestapo file on him and the fact that he had transferred his assets to her, but she declined to ask. She suddenly felt vulnerable and scared.

'Are you really thinking of leaving Austria?'

Max shook his head. 'I've thought about it, but I cannot leave you, Kiki. You know that.'

Stephen Pembroke gave a deep sigh and tried to smooth things over. 'We thought it best he had other documents in case he does need to leave. I have to admit, even though you are both my friends, I think Max should leave. The writing is on the wall for the Jews. The problem is, he should have left before the borders were closed.'

The Baroness agreed. No one said anything else and the subject was dropped while they concentrated on how to break the news to the parents of the Kindertransport children that there would be no more train departures. That evening, Christina and Max dined with Julia Lehmann who had just returned from Steinbrunnhof. They were joined by Karin and Walter. Karin had been feeling unwell due to the pregnancy and this news only made her feel worse. Christina decided to close down the salon for a few days until things settled.

Stephen Pembroke left Vienna a few days later. Christina gave him a small gift of fabric to send to Hannah so that she could make dresses for herself and Malka. It was difficult to see him go as they had no idea when they would see or hear from him now that communications with France and Britain had been cut, but he promised to stay in touch through the American Consulate. Before he left, he had one last meeting with Max who kept it a secret from Christina.

Within a few weeks, several thousands of Austrians were drafted into Germany's Wehrmacht, including a few of their friends and relatives. The ranks of the Waffen SS – the elite Nazi military unit – also swelled. Johannes was the first to receive his papers. Both he and Anton had found a doctor who proclaimed them unfit for the army, but they were also forced to visit one of the many doctors belonging to the Nazi Party. Unfortunately for Johannes, the new doctor declared him fit for service. A few days later, Anton was called up. This time, the doctor was in a hurry to get through his long list of patients and merely glanced at Anton's medical details, saying he was a chronic diabetic, and signed him off. Otto also received notification and went into hiding. As a chilling lesson to others who might be thinking of following his example, his family was rounded up and interrogated. After a harrowing few days of questioning, Otto's father was deported to Mauthausen labour camp where the conditions were said to be as bad as Dachau.

Christina was anxious that Max might be called up. The fact that there was a secret file on him proclaiming him a Jew threw them into confusion. How would the authorities act? This confusion was made

148

even worse when Max received a letter from his father saying that his stepbrother, Friedrich, an engineer from Graz University, had been called up and sent to work with a Panzer Division of the Wehrmacht in Poland, and his stepsister, Anita, and her husband, had been told an SS officer would be billeted on their farm.

In November, Walter also received his mobilization papers. He too was declared fit for action and sent away to an unknown destination. Karin, already suffering from a difficult pregnancy, was beside herself with worry. 'Look at him,' she cried through her tears, 'a gentle soul who wouldn't hurt a fly. How can those hands kill someone – or fire a gun? He's a musician.'

By Christmas the atmosphere was one of gloom, and even Christina's love for her work did little to relieve her constant bouts of nervous tension. She worried for herself, for her family and, most of all, for Max. He had neither been called up nor forced to declare himself a Jew. With Karin too ill to work in the salon, Max helped with the office work when he wasn't painting, and she hired another vendeuse, an Austrian woman, Hella, who had worked in Paris with Madeleine Vionnet. Hella was about the same age as Karin, an enthusiastic worker, creative, and good with the seamstresses in the workroom. Being used to the embroidery ateliers in Paris, she spent a lot of time helping the seamstresses with their embroidery techniques.

Two weeks before Christmas, the weather turned icy cold and Vienna was once again shrouded in a colourless thick fog. The people, walking about, hunched in their winter coats, boots, scarves, and warm hats, looked like sinister dark shadows – marionettes in a macabre puppet show. At night, this scene was even more pronounced, the soft yellow lamplight throwing eerie pools of light against the facades of grand buildings and long rows of leafless trees. Except for the soldiers and police, the odd gangs of hooligans, or those returning home from a wine bar, there were few people on the streets now. It was not only the thick fog of winter that kept people indoors, but the thick fog of uncertainty. The inhabitants of the proud, imperial city of the mighty Habsburgs preferred to remain locked in the safety of their homes rather than venture into the unknown from which they might never return. In the evenings, Max and Christina spent time together in her apartment in Mariahilferstrasse, listening to music or reading in front of the *Kachelofen*. At other times, they retreated to his apartment where he painted well into the early hours of the morning. Apart from the Baroness, they rarely entertained any longer.

Christina managed to put her emotions aside and created a winter collection that once again exceeded expectations and pleased her clientele. Lina ordered several items and told her she wanted them before Christmas as she was returning to Berlin. She arrived at the salon for one last fitting wearing a long sable coat with matching hat, black leather boots and gloves. People shopping in Mariahilferstrasse recognized her and crowded around, asking for her autograph. Hella took her hat and coat and offered her a glass of champagne while they prepared for the fitting. She showed her the evening dress they'd prepared for her to wear at a Christmas function in Berlin thrown by Dr Joseph Goebbels and his wife in honour of the Reich's most famous movie stars and directors. The dress was smoke grey chiffon with a bodice of silver spangles and a flowing train that draped from the narrow shoulders, exposing a daring amount of skin at the back. It was soft, yet dramatic, and Lina was delighted with it.

'I don't think it needs too much jewellery. Maybe I will wear a long rope of pearls,' Lina said, as she fingered the embroidery. 'What do you think?'

Christina remembered Mirka's bracelet and tried to hide her emotions. 'I think that will be perfect,' she replied, as she stood behind her and adjusted the dress in the mirror.

'I want to take this opportunity to thank you for all your hard work,' Lina added. 'I will miss Vienna.'

Christina looked surprised. 'Aren't you returning?' she asked, kneeling to make one final adjustment to the hemline.

'I'm afraid not. Helmut Käutner is making another film and both he and Dr Goebbels think I will be perfect for the part.'

'What about Dieter?' This revelation caused Christina to prick herself with a pin. She paused to wipe the spot of blood rising from her finger and at the same time realised she'd blurted it out too quickly. 'I mean, won't he miss you?'

Lina gave a little giggle. 'Oh, my dear, I doubt that. He will be far too busy to even notice I've gone.'

'Surely you can't mean that. You seemed so close.'

Lina looked at herself and touched the waves of her platinum hair. Not a strand was out of place. 'I thought so too, but he has wandering eyes. Two can play that game, but in the end it becomes tiresome.' She sighed.

'I'm sorry to hear that.'

'Don't be. Life goes on. Tell me, how is that lover of yours – Max the painter? I could tell from the moment I met him how much he adores you. Such expressive eyes; he should be in film.' Before Christina could answer, Lina made another astounding comment. 'Dieter told me your families are close and that you grew up together. He said he couldn't understand why someone like you could fall for a Jew. Is it true, Fräulein Christina? Is the dashing Max really a Jew?'

Lina couldn't help noticing the look on Christina's face. She realised she'd spoken out of turn. 'Don't worry, your secret is safe with me. I'm discreet.' She leaned over and whispered in a confidential voice. 'In fact I've had a few Jewish lovers myself.' She smiled. 'I almost married one until they brought in these ridiculous new laws.'

Christina felt a rising sense of anger tinged with shame and quickly changed the subject. When the fitting was over, Lina gave her a framed autographed photograph for the salon and wished her all the best, saying that even though she wouldn't be back in Vienna for a while, she would still be a loyal client. After she left, Christina asked Hella to take over for the rest of the afternoon as she wasn't feeling well and needed to lie down. She went upstairs to her apartment to be alone and think. Lina's revelations had shaken her. *What sort of game was Dieter playing?* Whatever it was, something in the pit of her stomach told her Max was in grave danger. She picked up the telephone to tell him, but then thought better of it and hastily put the receiver down. Such a discussion should be in private. If the Gestapo *had* tapped the Baroness's telephone, then it's possible, her line was also being tapped.

Max was due to return to Mariahilferstrasse that evening. They would discuss it then. By nine o'clock there was no sign of him and she started to panic. It wasn't like him to be late. She telephoned to see if he had left, but there was no answer. Straight away she called Beck who had just gone home for the evening.

'I'm sorry to bother you, Kurt, but Max hasn't returned and he's not answering his telephone. I'm worried something has happened. Can you take me to Nussdorf?'

The loyal Beck pushed his plate of food aside and grabbed his hat and coat, telling his wife he would finish the meal later. Fifteen minutes later, he pulled up outside the salon. The temperature had fallen below zero and it was now snowing. Christina wrapped her coat around her tightly, rushed outside and jumped into the back seat, almost slipping on the icy pavement. She apologized for calling him out in such terrible weather.

'Something's terribly wrong, I know it is. If he was going to be late, he would have called.'

Beck tried to calm her down, saying he was probably stuck somewhere due to the weather, but when the car turned into Max's street, his car was there and there were no lights on in his apartment. A middle-aged woman carrying a bundle of firewood on her back stood in the deep recess of a doorway talking to an old man clearing away the snow building up on the pavement. Christina recognized him as the caretaker from the next apartment.

When Beck pulled up outside Max's apartment, she got out and rang the doorbell.

'He's not in, *gnae'* Fräulein,' the man said, in the strong Viennese accent of the lower working classes. 'They came earlier and took him away.'

'Who – who came?'

Beck saw the look of distress on her face and got out of the car. 'What's going on?'

The man repeated himself. 'Two men – I think the *Geheime Staatspolizei*. They were discreet, but we don't miss much around here, you know.'

Christina fumbled in her bag for her key and frantically unlocked the door. In the blackness of the hallway, she groped along the wall until she found the light switch. Beck stayed outside talking to the man and woman. There was nothing in the apartment to indicate any force or search had taken place. In the studio, the paint on the picture he'd been working on was still wet and she noticed his brushes were not cleaned. Max was fastidious; he would never have gone out without cleaning his brushes, unless he was forced to. After a few more minutes of checking through his things, she went back outside.

'From what this man says, it must have taken place just before you called me,' Beck said in a low whisper, making sure the caretaker did not hear. 'He said Max went quietly.'

Christina noticed the slight movement of a curtain. 'Let's get away from here. We're attracting too much attention.'

The caretaker called after them. 'I hope there won't be any trouble. We're respectable people.'

Christina ignored him. When the car turned out of the street, she asked Beck to stop the car. He swerved to a standstill on the icy road. She got out, leaned against a tree doubled up and retched. Beck jumped out after her.

'Fräulein Christina, you'll catch your death of cold. Let me get you back home.' He put a fatherly arm around her and guided her back to the car.

CHAPTER 20

SS-Untersturmführer Szabó had been interrogating Max for over two hours, making copious notes in the file he had been given by his chief, *SS-Standartenführer* Dieter Klein. With him was a secretary sitting at a nearby desk typing the conversation between the two men. Szabó was no stranger to interrogation, having previously worked for *SS-Obergruppenführer* Reinhardt Heydrich's security service—the *Sicherheitsdienst* (SD) in Munich. In a short time, the counterintelligence service had grown into an effective machine of terror and intimidation.

The interrogation room was small and featureless, with a desk and chairs for the interrogators and another for the prisoner. It had one window and a small grid behind which someone could listen, unseen, to what was taking place. Since the Gestapo had taken over the hotel, this room at the back of the building had been refurbished specifically for the purposes of interrogation. The walls were stripped of the plush wallpaper and replaced with white tiles, making it easier to clean up after the increasingly heavy and bloody interrogations. Apart from the cubicle behind the grid, it was also soundproofed. In the basement below, the unfortunate prisoners awaited interrogation, shackled in chains in near darkness. This darker side of life in the shadows was in stark contrast to everything else taking place in the grandeur of one of Vienna's most luxurious hotels. During the day, the SS worked from their plush offices, overseeing minute details that were to have far-reaching consequences throughout Austria, and in the evenings they would relax in style at one of the many in-house concerts and orchestras.

Whether it was excellent wines, luxury cars, fine art, or beautiful women, Dieter Klein had always had a taste for the good things in life, and, since being promoted to work with Ernst Kaltenbrunner, he now had a well-appointed suite at the hotel overlooking Morzinplatz and the Danube. He was certainly glad he had joined the NSDAP in the early days. With the Anschluss, his work had been rewarded, both in rank and financially. Besides his suite at the Hotel Métropole, where he spent most of his time, he also had a fine apartment on the Ringstrasse. Positioning himself as comfortably as he could in the cramped room behind the grid, Dieter had a clear view of Max's face under the bright lights, and although Szabó's back was towards the grid, he could clearly hear his silky voice interrogating him. He had asked his subordinate to conduct the interrogation, as he wanted to remain hidden, behind the scenes.

Dieter stared at Max's face with cold hatred. He had always suspected he was a Jew. *How could a fine woman like Christina Lehmann fall for a man like that?* As much as he loved women, he could not work them out; they slept with Jews at the drop of a hat. Lina was like that too. When he discovered she'd had Jewish lovers, his fascination for her left him. The actress was beautiful, but she disgusted him and he was glad she was going back to Berlin. He'd experienced a rising anger when he saw her flirt with Max at Christina's fashion show. Her words cut him like a knife. *You must paint my portrait too, Max!* Damn the woman! If it had not been for their family connections, he would have pulled Max Hauser in after the Anschluss. But it was not only the family connections that stopped him. He still loved Christina. He had always loved her. She was his only weakness, and he hated himself for it.

Szabó's questioning continued. He was smooth, yet cold and calculating. 'I will ask you again, Herr Hauser. Why did you not register yourself as a Jew after the unification of Austria into the Reich? You knew you were Jewish.'

'I told you,' Max replied calmly. 'I was baptised a Catholic and brought up in the church. I know nothing about Judaism.'

'Your mother, Klara, was a Jew.'

'I have no idea about that. She died when I was a baby. I grew up in a Catholic family.'

'Herr Hauser, it states here that your father knew his first wife was a Jew. He met her family in Hungary on several occasions. Records here show her parents as being Eva and Miklos Farkas. He was a greengrocer. From what we know, he fancied himself as an artist too – rather like you. I would say that's evidence of you being a Jew, wouldn't you?'

'I told you. I have no idea about that. No one mentioned her after her death. I've never heard of Eva and Miklos Farkas.'

The smart-suited Szabó lit a cigarette and blew smoke in the direction of Max who could barely move, his hands being tied to the chair. 'Of course we could bring your father in for questioning. Do you think his health would hold up under interrogation? Your file states that, as a society painter, you own your apartment and car. You didn't declare this and that is a serious offence against the Reich, punishable by hard labour.' He paused for a moment. 'That wouldn't be good for a painter's hands, would it?' Max glared at him. 'You are aware of the Decree for the Reporting of Jewish-Owned Property – that all Jews in Austria, were required to register any property or assets valued at more than 5,000 Reichsmark from furniture and paintings to life insurance and stocks straight after unification. Nothing is immune from the registry.'

Max knew this was state-sanctioned theft masquerading as "Aryanization", but kept that to himself. He did, however give a little smirk when he realised they didn't know about the assets transfer.

'I am afraid if you were out to get me for that, you've made a mistake. I transferred my assets to my...' Max stopped himself saying fiancé knowing that was unacceptable according to Nazi racial ideology, 'to my friend, Christina Lehmann as a thank you for her help over the past few years.'

Dieter clenched his fist in anger when he heard this.

'So you really have no grounds to hold me here,' Max added.

Szabó was not to be deterred. 'According to the Nuremberg Laws, the Reich Citizenship Law requires that *all* citizens have German "blood." As a result, Jews and others lose their rights to citizenship. This will not only strip you of the right to vote, you will never get a valid passport or visa and, as a consequence, you will be stateless. The purity of German blood is the essential condition for the continued existence of the German people and the Reichstag has unanimously adopted the following law, which I will advise you of.

'Article 1: Marriages between Jews and citizens of German or related blood are forbidden. Marriages nevertheless concluded are invalid, even if concluded abroad to circumvent this law. Annulment proceedings can be initiated only by the state prosecutor. You see, Herr Hauser, your father's marriage to Klara was illegal.' Szabó looked pleased with himself. He ran his finger down the list of laws and continued.

'Article 2: Extramarital relations between Jews and citizens of Germany or related blood are forbidden. Article 5: Any person who violates the prohibition under Articles 1 and 2 will be punished with a prison sentence, and in Article 2, paragraph 2, the following applies: A Jew is also one who is the offspring of a marriage with a Jew.'

Clearly Szabó was enjoying this intimidation but Max kept his wits about him. Up until now, half-Jewish children of the male spouse and head of the household who had been baptised were *Mischlinge* and did not fit into these categories, so none of these laws applied to him. *What was the interrogator's game? Was he purposely bluffing in order to get him to admit to Jewish ancestry?*

Szabó showed Max a few photographs of him together with Christina at public functions at the theatre, opera, and coffeehouses. He tutted, as if he were chastising a naughty child. 'As a Jew, you have broken the law being in such public places.' He put the photographs back in the file and pressed his fingers together clicking the knuckles. 'So what do you have to say about that? There is no escaping us, Herr Hauser. I am going to leave you for a while to consider your fate. Lying is something we take seriously.' He walked over to the door and with his hand on the door handle, advised Max to think carefully about the position he faced.

Left alone, Max considered his options, which were few and far between. The Nuremberg Laws meant that Jews could no longer define their identities for themselves. Those Jewish friends who left straight after the Anschluss were right after all. He knew that whatever happened, he was a marked man and must consider his life with Christina over. If he walked out of here now and met her again, he would be followed by the Gestapo, waiting for a chance to haul them out of their lovers' bed. He had been right not to marry her, but he had not been right to let love rule his head. He should have gone when he had the chance. Strangely, even though he had no sleep, his mind was focused. If he did get out, he knew he could never see her again – for both their sakes.

Outside the interrogation room, Szabó conferred with Dieter. They had all the evidence needed to send him to a labour camp, but Dieter needed his superior to sign off on it. Szabó wondered what was so special about this Jew for Dieter to take such great interest in him. He appeared to procrastinate and Szabó couldn't understand why.

In the meantime, Max wondered why the Gestapo hadn't pulled him in before if they had so much evidence against him. He'd never trusted Dieter, but he couldn't be sure if he *was* behind all this. If he was, why hadn't he shown his face? Gloating was his style. And Christina? After Fischer told her about the file, she would suspect what had happened and try and find him. He wanted to stop her, to tell her to stay away, but even if he could, he knew she wouldn't listen. *Kiki, my love; our affair was doomed from the start.*

'Take him back to his cell,' Dieter said. 'Let him stew for a while.'

Szabó clicked his heels and saluted. 'Heil Hitler!' He went back inside with two guards who untied Max and pulled him to his feet. 'Don't think this is the last of it,' said Szabó, menacingly. 'Next time, I won't be such a gentleman.'

CHAPTER 21

BECK TOOK CHRISTINA back to Hietzing where she confided to her mother about the Gestapo. Knowing that she would need him, Beck refused to go home and waited downstairs in the kitchen. Irma and Gitta had gone to bed, but their keen ears told them something bad had taken place, and they went downstairs to see what was going on. He told them nothing and the women didn't pry. Gitta gave him a glass of hot milk and a few biscuits. She invited him to lie on the old couch near the pantry to get some sleep.

'What are you going to do?' Julia Lehmann asked Christina.

'Wait until daybreak and go to Landesgerichtesstrasse Criminal Court.'

'Is that wise after the last time? You don't even know if he's there.'

'Where else would he be?'

Julia Lehmann shrugged. 'I honestly don't know, my darling.' After a few minutes' silence, she suggested it might be better if Beck went. 'He will attract less attention, and if he has to give them a bribe, we can give him money.'

Beck had already offered to go, but Christina was reluctant to put him at risk because of his family. For the next few hours, they talked the situation through, wondering what could have led to this. Christina firmly believed that there was no reason for the Gestapo to haul him in.

'There is one other thing you could do,' Julia Lehmann said. 'Ask Dieter Klein. 'He's sure to know.'

Christina jumped up off the couch. 'How can you suggest such a thing? If the truth be known, it's probably him that's behind all this.'

159

Julia Lehmann put her hands out to calm her daughter down. 'I know, I know, but it is an option. He's a family friend. I can always mention it to his mother.'

'I cannot believe what you're saying. It's preposterous.'

'Don't let your dislike for him rule your head. If he knows where Max is, he could help. The sooner you get him away from the Gestapo, the better.'

Christina put her head in her hands. 'I don't want him to see me crawling to him for favours. He will gloat. Let's see what tomorrow brings first.'

At dawn, Beck and Christina made their way to Landesgerichtesstrasse. As usual, there were long queues of desolate people huddling together in an attempt to protect themselves against the cold wind that whipped against their faces. This time, Christina stayed in the car while Beck went into the building. At first, he was told to wait in line, but, after slipping money to the soldier, he was allowed to enter. Once inside, he patiently waited his turn until he was directed to an official.

'I'm looking for a man by the name of Max Hauser. I have reason to believe he may have been brought here last night.' Beck said.

The official consulted a ledger containing the last previous night's entries and shook his head. 'I'm sorry. There's no one of that name here.'

Beck thought the man might be after a bribe and tried to slip him some money. The man looked indignant. 'Take it back before I have you arrested. I told you, there is no one of that name here.' He flicked his hand towards the door as if flicking away a fly. 'Next please.'

Beck thanked him and left.

Christina looked dismayed when she saw his face. 'Let's go and see the Baroness. She might be able to help.'

The Baroness was in the middle of her singing lessons when Christina arrived. Seeing the distressed look on her face, she dismissed her tutor, telling him they would make up for it another day.

'It's Max,' Christina blurted out when they were alone. 'The Gestapo took him last night, but he's not at Landesgerichtesstrasse.'

After listening to what took place and the revelation that the Gestapo had a file on Max, the Baroness suggested the only other place she could think of was the Hotel Métropole.

'That's where I was told they had a file on him,' Christina said.

'Then you must try there.' She gave a deep sigh. 'I'm sorry to say this, but we advised Max to leave while there was still a chance. He only stayed because of you.'

'I've been selfish, haven't I?' Christina replied. 'I couldn't bear to think of him leaving and it was impossible for me to go with him. Only God knows what will happen to him, now.'

'Put your pride aside and go and see Dieter Klein. He's your only hope. I heard he spends most of his time there now that his actress friend has gone back to Germany.'

Reluctantly, Christina agreed.

ℂ

Christina entered the hotel lobby dressed in a calf-length sable coat with a matching pill-box hat with netting that partially covered her eyes. All eyes turned toward her. She had purposely dressed to make a grand entrance and carried it off with the adroitness of a consummate actress. Her body language conveyed a woman of importance, and she was received that way. She strode confidently across the lobby to the desk, took off her leather gloves, finger by finger, and asked to see Herr Dieter Klein. Judging by the initial reactions of the men in the lobby, they were favourably impressed.

The receptionist picked up the telephone. 'I have a Fräulein Lehmann here to see you,' he said, his eyes still fixed on the beautiful woman standing in front of him. A few words were exchanged and the man replaced the receiver.

'Herr Klein is in a meeting at the moment. He will be with you as soon as possible and asked if you could wait in the bar.' He asked Christina to follow him.

'I am to see that you have a drink,' the man said. 'What will you have?'

Christina sat down on a blue velvet chair. She opened her coat wide, allowing it to drape around her, and crossed her slender legs. 'A cognac will be fine, thank you.'

The bartender brought it over and placed it on the table along with a small silver tray of fine chocolates. Soft music played in the background. She picked up a magazine and looked through it while she waited, but nothing she read registered; her thoughts were only of Max. *What if he's not here? What if they sent him to a labour camp?* Wild thoughts spun around in her head, making her crazy. She had to remain cool.

Then she heard a voice behind her – deep, cultured, and self-assured. 'Hello, Christina, how delightful to see you. What can I do for you?'

Dieter's coolness caught her off guard. 'It's about Max. He was taken from his studio yesterday – sometime during the evening – and I have no idea where he is. I thought you may be able to help me.'

He looked around. 'Not here. Come to my office.'

She followed him through the lobby and into the lift, aware that all eyes were on them. Two uniformed Gestapo officers were waiting to take the lift with them. When they reached the third floor, where Dieter's office was, the men saluted him and gave Christina a polite bow. A uniformed officer sat at a desk at the end of the corridor. He too saluted Dieter and handed him a few documents as they entered his room.

Inside, Christina quickly scanned the large room with its opulent furniture, fine paintings and Persian rugs. The view from the balcony, overlooking Morzinplatz and the Danube, was magnificent.

'So this is your *office*?' Christina said, with a tinge of sarcasm. 'You have certainly done well for yourself.'

Dieter stepped behind her and took her coat. 'Come and sit down and tell me what it is I can do for you.' He ushered her to a couch strewn with gold and scarlet silk cushions edged in silken braids with fine tassels and offered to get her another drink. Wanting to keep her wits about her, she refused.

'I thought he might have been taken to Landesgerichtesstrasse, but it appears not.' As much as she wanted to, she couldn't mention the file Fischer had told her about.

Dieter's sharp eyes watched her every movement, the tense way she folded her hands, how she rubbed her thumb over the back of her hand nervously. She could see he was enjoying seeing her so vulnerable.

'Well,' she said, 'do you know anything about this? If so please tell me.'

He reached his hand towards hers, as if to comfort her, but she moved them to one side. His facial expression hardened.

'Yes, I can help you. He was being held at the nearby Liesl Prison but was brought here for questioning.'

'Why? What on earth has he done wrong?'

'Look Christina, it has come to our attention that Max Hauser is a Jew. Of course you already knew that.'

She felt her heart pound in her chest and her throat turned dry. 'What on earth are you talking about? He's a Catholic. You know that as well as I do.'

Dieter shook his head and gave a little sigh. 'I am afraid not, my dear. Either you are lying to me or he has taken you for a fool. We have irrefutable proof that he is a Jew, and he has committed a serious crime against the Reich for not declaring this fact – or his assets.'

'Don't be absurd.' She jumped up from the couch and stared down at him. 'There must have been some sort of mistake. As for his assets, he gifted them to me as a token of his... friendship a while back.' She started to panic. 'Dieter, you have to help him.'

Dieter stood up and put his hand on her shoulder. This time she didn't back away. 'Sit down. I will see what I can do.' He went into the adjoining room, pressed a button on his desk, and seconds later a man entered the room.

'Tell Herr *Untersturmführer* Szabó to bring the file on Prisoner 11218.'

The man clicked his heels and saluted. '*Jawohl, Herr Standartenführer!*'

Five minutes later, another man arrived. She could see that he realised Dieter was playing a game with her. He coughed slightly and listed the charges.

As he neared the end, Dieter put his hand up.

'Thank you, Herr Szabó. Now please tell me, what is likely to happen to the accused.'

Szabó made a show of pondering the question. 'The charges are most serious, sir. It is possible he could be given the death sentence, in which case he will be hanged or... guillotined.' Christina gasped. 'But on the other hand, he could be deported to Dachau or Mauthausen. There, he will endure hard labour.' Szabó was obviously enjoying playing part in Dieter's little game. 'There is another option, however.'

'What is that?' Dieter asked, as if he were somehow removed from the situation.

'He could be deported to Poland for resettlement.'

'Poland! What on earth does that mean?' Christina demanded.

Szabó opened his mouth to continue, but Dieter answered the question for him. 'Litzmannstadt –Lodz. The Reich is giving Jews an area of their own to live where they will not be disadvantaged. They will be able to find work and look after themselves.'

The atmosphere was charged with expectation. Christina wasn't sure what to say next. She had a feeling that her next utterance could decide Max's fate. She felt she might faint at any moment.

'It's what *you* want, not the people being forced to go there,' Christina gasped.

Dieter shrugged. 'The issue is out of my hands. The plan is already being implemented by Himmler and Heydrich. There is nothing I can do.' He thanked Szabó and dismissed him.

'Heil Hitler!' Szabó left the room.

Christina gathered her reserves. She got to her feet, drew herself up to her full height and glared at Dieter. 'This is all some sort of game to you. Our families have been close for years. Doesn't that mean anything to you?' She raised her voice. 'How dare you treat Max and me like this!'

Dieter held up his hands and shook his head in an attempt to calm her down, but she refused to be quiet. 'Damn you,' she shouted. 'I have known you all my life and yet you do this to me. You know these allegations are false. My God, I invite you and your mistress to my salon, treat you with respect, and you repay me like this. You are not an honourable man. You disgust me.'

Christina was shaking with rage and hurt. He simply smiled. Seeing this, she lashed out, beating her fist on his chest. He grabbed it and squeezed hard, twisting it around her back until she screamed out in pain.

'You're hurting me.'

He jerked her closer. 'I'm trying to help you. Can't you see? This man is no good for you? He's broken the law and the Reich doesn't take kindly to that.'

'The Reich. Is that all you think about?'

Dieter's face was only inches away from her face. She could smell his sickly Eau-de-cologne. The triumphant tremor in his voice told her the delight he was feeling, knowing he had her exactly where he wanted her.

'No, it's not all I think about.' His voice suddenly changed. It became mellow and warm. He moved his mouth closer to hers, let it linger for a few seconds, and then pulled back.

She stopped struggling. *So that's what this is all about*, she thought to herself. He wanted *her*, and to get her, he had to get rid of Max. Dieter let go of her arm.

She took a step back.

'It's really me you want, isn't it? Not Max. He's just a pawn in this whole game.' With trembling hands, she started to unbutton her blouse exposing her breasts, heaving up and down in her beautiful

165

lace-edged brassiere. 'Here!' She grabbed one of his hands and pressed it against her right breast 'Is this what you want?'

Dieter's eyes rested on the curves of her breasts for a few seconds and then he pushed her away. 'Make yourself decent,' he replied, coolly.

He turned sharply and walked toward the balcony. Stunned, Christina ran towards him and threw herself at his feet, clutching his legs. 'I'm begging you, take me. Do what you want with me...' her eyes looked up at him imploringly, 'but please let him go. He's done nothing wrong.'

Christina was puzzled. Why was Dieter hesitating? She was giving him what he wanted. He looked confused. Then she understood. He wanted her, but not like this, not under duress. He would wait until she came to him of her own free will.

'Please get up, Christina.' He stared out of the window, watching the traffic and the boats on the Danube. 'Go home.'

Christina pulled herself up, buttoned her blouse and smoothed her hair. 'I'm sorry. I don't know what came over me.' She walked across the room to get her coat and headed to the door, feeling ashamed of herself.

As she was about to leave, he turned around. 'I will do what I can.' He turned back to look out of the window.

Outside the room, she found the officer at his desk, staring at her, goggle-eyed. Taking a deep breath, she pulled herself together and headed to the lift.

From his vantage point on the balcony, Dieter watched her stride across Morzinplatz to where Beck waited with her car. After she'd driven away, he smiled at himself in the mirror, ran a comb through his hair, dabbed a little Eau-de-Cologne behind his ears, and left the room to join Szabó in the interrogation room.

CHAPTER 22

'What are we going to do with him?' Szabó asked Dieter. 'He denies his Jewishness even though he knows the evidence is against him. Furthermore, he declares he gifted his assets to Fräulein Lehmann.'

'Has he eaten?' Dieter asked, peering through the grid at Max tied up in the chair.

'He's been given only water.'

Dieter flexed his knuckles. 'Take him back to his cell and give him a meal.'

Two policemen bundled Max out of the room. He was so tired and exhausted, he could barely stand. As yet, Dieter had given no orders to beat him – more for Christina's sake than anything else. He told Szabó he would decide what to do with him by the morning.

'In the meantime,' he said, 'I will check out whether he really did transfer his assets. Even if he did, he's broken the law, and that's that.'

After leaving the Hotel Métropole, Christina cancelled her appointments and stayed in her apartment mulling over what to do next. She couldn't believe how she'd acted. It was inexcusable. All she could do was wait and see if Dieter showed some compassion. She was sure he wouldn't want his callousness to affect their family relationships. His mother would never forgive him. Beck refused to go home and hung around in the courtyard in case she needed him. She took a sleeping tablet and tried to get some rest. In the evening, the telephone rang. It was the Baroness asking how she got on, and aware that the telephone line was probably tapped, she asked if she would like to join her for supper.

As soon as she laid eyes on her, Christina burst into tears.

The Baroness knew immediately things were worse than she suspected. She put her arms around her. 'Come on, my darling. This will do you no good.'

The table was already laid for two and supper was served straight away. They began with a chicken broth, followed by pheasant in a red-wine sauce. It was delicious, but Christina couldn't eat.

The Baroness sighed. 'If you fade away, you will be no use to anyone. I know how much you miss Max. I'm in the same position. Goodness knows when I will see Lucien again.'

Christina apologized. 'I'm sorry. I wasn't thinking. I didn't mean to be insensitive.'

'That's all right. I understand, but please, don't let this excellent food go to waste.' She took a sip of her wine. 'How did it go at the Métropole?'

Christina told her half the story. The rest she would keep to herself. The Baroness listened attentively, aware that it wasn't the full story.

☾

Two days before Christmas, Christina told her mother it was highly likely that Max would not be joining them at Schloss Steinbrunnhof. They still had no idea whether he was in prison or had been sent away to a labour camp, and Julia Lehmann pressed Christina to let her ask Frau Klein. Christina was adamant she didn't want her involved.

The day before Christmas, Hella and Christina gave the seamstresses their usual Christmas party. This time the gift was a silk scarf, each one adorned with their initials embroidered in one corner. They were delighted. She wished them a merry Christmas and looked forward to working with them in the New Year. Afterwards, Beck drove them all home.

When they'd gone, she found herself alone with Hella.

'You don't look at all well, Fräulein Christina,' Hella said. 'Is it Herr Max? We haven't seen him for a few days. I hope he's all right.'

'You may as well know, the Gestapo took him away and I've heard nothing since. It's killing me.'

Hella put an affectionate arm around her. 'He'll be fine. I'm sure the Gestapo won't do anything to cause you undue distress. You're too well-known.'

'I wish I could believe that.' She reeled off important names of those they all knew who had been forced to emigrate at a moment's notice. 'I'm afraid they don't care who their victims are.'

A despondent Christina joined the family for Christmas at Stein-brunnhof without Max. His incarceration cast a dark cloud over their celebrations and, along with the fact that Walter was thought to be somewhere in Poland, they all felt miserable. Everything about the hunting lodge reminded her of Max – the walks, the large painting of the stag in the drawing room, the music they played. Added to this misery, were thoughts of Hannah and Malka, but at least they were safe.

Two days after Christmas, Christina and Karin were returning from a walk to the village when they spotted a black car turn into the driveway of the schloss. They stopped in their tracks and Christina reached for Karin's arm. 'My God, that's Max's car!'

She started to run and quickly realised the pregnant Karin could not keep up with her.

'Go on,' Karin urged her. 'Don't let me slow you down. I'll catch up with you later.'

The road was covered in snow and the ground was icy, but it didn't stop Christina running as fast as she could. At the gate, she slipped and fell heavily, but in the excitement of the moment, didn't feel any pain. She picked herself up and continued along the allée of beeches. At the point where it ended in front of the moat, Max appeared from the courtyard, ran over the stone bridge toward her, and clasped her tightly in his arms.

'My darling, I can't believe it,' Christina said, her voice trembling with emotion. She cupped his face with her gloved hands and kissed him, again and again. Then she pulled back. 'Let me look at you. Are you all right? Have they harmed you?'

Max's stubble-bearded face looked drawn and there were dark shadows under his eyes, yet for all that, there was still a sparkle in his dark eyes. 'No, they didn't harm me, but the threat of torture hung around like a bad smell. I was lucky.'

Karin caught up with them. 'You cannot know what a blessing this is to see you safe and sound.' She smiled and crossed herself. Both women looped an arm through his, and they continued to the schloss. In the courtyard, Julia Lehmann stood by the door with Irma, Albrecht and Hildegard. Irma had no idea what had happened to Max, but she knew it wasn't good. Now, she was just as relieved to see him as everyone else.

Julia Lehmann gave him an affectionate kiss on the cheek. 'My dear Max, let's get you a drink.' She turned to Irma and asked her to bring cake and biscuits and to prepare a hearty venison stew for dinner. 'I think Max needs fattening up, don't you?'

In front of a warm fire, Max tucked into the cake and biscuits with relish. Christina poured him a cognac. 'When did they release you?' she asked, sitting close to him and running her fingers through his curly and somewhat unkempt hair.

'In the early hours of the morning, I was taken from my cell, bundled into a car with three other men, and driven to Nussdorf. Outside my apartment, one of the men held the passenger door open and told me to get out. Then they drove away, leaving me standing on the pavement. I couldn't believe my luck. I expected to be deported to a camp. There was a man by the name of Szabó who kept questioning me. I told them I wasn't a Jew, but they've discovered my mother was.' He laughed sarcastically. 'In fact, they knew more about her than I did. You know, I was convinced Dieter was behind all this, yet I never set eyes on him once.'

Christina brushed the back of her hand softly against his cheek and told him he was right, that after finding out he wasn't at

Landesgerichtesstrasse, she had gone to see Dieter at the Hotel Métropole. She was careful not to mention his show of affection towards her.

'He told me they had you there and that as a Jew, you had flagrantly flouted the new laws. Naturally, I argued. The subject of your assets came up and I told him you'd gifted them to me a while ago. I begged him to release you.' Recalling the meeting was making her anxious again. 'All I could do was pray he'd let you go because of our family connection. When you didn't appear, I feared something bad would happen.'

Max polished off the plate of biscuits, and Julia asked Irma to bring more. 'Your meeting probably saved me,' he said. 'They tortured almost everyone, and I was waiting for them to set on me. I know some died as I could hear the guards dragging bodies away. Then out of the blue, I was told I was leaving. During the drive to Nussdorf, I half-expected them to stop the car and dispose of me. When they'd gone, I got straight into my car – which fortunately, they hadn't confiscated – and came here. As you can see, I didn't even shave.' He apologized for looking like a tramp.

'Darling, the beard suits you. It reminds me of when we first met. It gives you a rakish look – rather Bohemian I would say, wouldn't you, Karin?' Karin agreed. 'All the same, I'm going to run you a hot bath and find you some clean clothes as I presume you didn't bring any with you?'

'I didn't think about it. I just wanted to get to you as soon as possible.'

Karin said she'd lay out some of Walter's clothes. They were a similar size.

While he bathed, Julia Lehmann pulled Christina aside. 'There, I told you all would be well. Dieter came to his senses after all.'

Christina nodded. 'He has let him go now, but for how long? He'll look for another excuse.'

Over the next week, Max's health improved, but Christina could see his spirit was broken. The fact that he'd been targeted by the Gestapo had impacted him enormously. He had expected it, he told her. It was only a matter of time. When they were due to return to Vienna, they took one last walk through the woods and he told her he was thinking of "disappearing". His words did not exactly come as a shock. 'Whether *I* think I am a Jew or not is irrelevant, *they* think I am, they will take me in again if I flaunt their rules. As a painter, I am finished. Who will want a Jew to paint their portrait now?'

Christina was forced to conclude he was right and the fact that he was not sent away was probably due to the fact that he had transferred his assets to her.

'When do you plan on leaving?' She felt so numb she couldn't even cry.

'I'm not sure, and if I did know, I'm not even sure I would tell you. It would put you in danger too, and I couldn't bear that.' They stopped walking and he held her in his arms. 'There's a group of people who have formed a resistance network. I have links to it. Please don't ask any questions because that's all I will tell you.'

'Will you cross the border?'

Max shrugged. 'I don't know, but whatever happens, I want you to know I love you with all my heart and that when this nightmare is over, we will be married. I never want you to forget that.'

'I won't.' She could barely say the words.

'Now, my darling, let's go back. There's going to be another snowstorm.'

Knowing they wanted to be alone, Karin and their mother went to bed early that evening. Max and Christina played records and danced cheek to cheek until the early hours of the morning, savouring their love while they still could. The clock on the mantelpiece ticked away the minutes. Soon their lives would change in a way neither could have expected.

CHAPTER 23

MAY 10, 1940

ALMOST A MONTH after Germany occupied Denmark and Southern Norway, the invasion of the Netherlands, Belgium, Luxembourg, and France, took place. This was expected as, two months earlier, Max and the Baroness had confided to Christina that they had it on good advice that Germany's expansionist policy was about to be implemented. In fact, Stephen Pembroke and the Baroness had warned of this at the time of the Kindertransport. Around Christmas, they also received word that Polish Jews were being forced to wear an armband with the yellow Star of David. At the time, Max deliberately kept this fact from Christina, thinking she would worry about him. There was one thing that she was aware of however, the Lodz Ghetto had been sealed off and the fate of the Jews sent there from Vienna was in doubt. Word had it that there were at least 165,000 people there at the time. At the same time as the Germans invaded France, a new concentration camp at Auschwitz was set up.

The Baroness feared for Lucien, but word reached her through the American Embassy that he had been in contact with Stephen Pembroke and decided to stay in Paris. Like Max, Stephen Pembroke had urged both the Baroness and Lucien to leave for England or America while they could, but they had both refused. Now it was too late. It was getting harder to understand what was happening outside Austria – or Ostmark, as the officials called it – due to Dr Goebbels' extensive propaganda machine. If one listened to reports or read the Nazi controlled press, Britain would fall too, within weeks.

While thousands endured the German bombing raids and the waves of the mighty Wehrmacht machine that swept through Europe, Christina continued her work in the salon. Not to do so would have aroused a rebuke from her growing Nazi clientele. Away from the horrors of the German killing fields, the summer season was in full swing and the 1940 collections well-received. Most of her clientele were the wives and mistresses of high-ranking Nazis in the Reich. Hilda Bürckel, the wife of the Reich Governor of Reichsgau Vienna, was an enthusiastic patron. When Joseph Bürckel earned the displeasure of the Nazi hierarchy by embezzling confiscated money and property, he was replaced by Baldur von Schirach. Von Schirach's wife, Henrietta, a woman with strong anti-Semitic views, and whose father was Hitler's official photographer, soon became a patron of the fashion house, even more avid than her predecessor.

Henrietta – or Henny as her close friends called her – was an attractive woman with a taste for the good things in life. Like Lina Lindner, she was a follower of fashion and the arts, and sent Christina new customers, all of whom spared no expense when it came to their wardrobe. Ernst Kaltenbrunner was also there, this time with his wife, Elisabeth, and not his mistress. Christina could never understand what women saw in him. With his high-pitched voice, deep facial scar, bad teeth and foul breath, she thought him an odious character. Adolf Eichmann's wife, Veronika, was invited too. Christina found her to be quite shy and conservative; a woman more suited to wearing *Tracht* than couture. Amongst this who's who of the Austrian Nazi party, one man was noticeably absent – Dieter Klein. At first, she had no idea whether he was purposely avoiding her due to their confrontation over Max, or because he was no longer with Lina. It was neither. He had gone to Prague with Reinhard Heydrich.

The launch of the 1940 collections had certainly come at a difficult time. Her heart wasn't in it. Max stayed away, which made it even more unbearable for her. He had helped her with illustrations, but that was all. After what had happened, he rarely ventured out during the day and only came to her apartment in the evening when he was sure she was alone. Often, she would go to him and sit with him while he painted, listening to their favourite records.

Occasionally they went to a tavern in Grinzing, but he no longer accompanied her to the theatre, Café Landtmann, or for walks in the park – for fear of being pulled aside and questioned. He wanted to avoid giving them a pretext for taking him in again, or putting his beloved Kiki in danger. The only other place where they could be together in private was Schloss Steinbrunnhof. They went most weekends, and occasionally, Max stayed on while Christina returned to Vienna. Taking long walks, painting, or reading, were ways of shutting out a world quickly descending into chaos. Albrecht and Hildegard enjoyed his company and, being used to the simple things in life, Max often ate his evening meal with them in their kitchen, when Christina was in Vienna. Having no children of their own, Hildegard looked after him like a son, baking him cakes and making him hearty soups. He thought he was safe until a black Daimler swept into the courtyard one day and a man got out and looked around. It was Kemény.

'I wonder what he wants,' Max said, peering through the lace curtain.

'He's trouble, that one,' Albrecht replied. He put on his cap and told Max to leave the house via the vegetable garden.

Kemény was just about to walk towards the Schloss when Albrecht came out to greet him, shooing away the hens that had gathered near the doorway.

'The family is not in residence, *mein Herr*. Can I help you?'

'I was just passing and thought I would pay my respects.'

Albrecht asked if he would care to come inside for a glass of wine, but he refused.

'Have you had any visitors – what I mean is, have you seen any strangers around?' he asked.

'No one that I don't already know, *mein Herr*. Are you looking for someone?'

'I'm just carrying out my duties, making sure all is in order. You never can tell these days – lots of trouble-makers around, you know.'

Albrecht wanted to say he was looking at one, but held his tongue. Kemény saluted and returned to his car. Max watched him drive away before returning to the house. He wondered what would have happened if he'd been walking along the road. Would he have been picked up? He was becoming used to his life in the shadows.

There was also happy news during this time. Karin gave birth to a boy, but the happiness was short-lived when he developed breathing problems. The doctors couldn't find the cause of his illness and the child remained weak and sickly. When Julia Lehmann mentioned this to Frau Klein, she said she would have a word with her son, Sigmund. She informed her that he'd been in Berlin working with doctors, and since returning to Vienna, was furthering his research on infants and young children at Am Spiegelgrund, the new children's clinic that was now operating as part of the psychiatric hospital, Am Steinhof. Maybe he could help. Karin jumped at the chance and an appointment was soon arranged. She would take him in for tests.

Because she'd found it difficult to conceive, Karin was beside herself with worry. If anything happened to the child, who was named Karl after Walter's father, she feared she might never conceive again. She was no longer young and with a war on, she was terrified Walter could be killed. He had returned to Vienna for a few days at the end of March, but was called away again before the birth. She worried about him constantly; he'd lost weight and looked drawn, but when she pressed him about what he'd been doing, he refused to talk about it. After he left, her nerves got the better of her and she took to her bed until the child was born.

It was a beautiful warm summer's day when Karin, accompanied by Christina, entered the extensive grounds of Am Steinhof, heading in the direction of what was now known as *Am Spiegelgrund* – the Playground – after the street nearby. They were to take the child to Pavilion 17, just a stone's throw from the famous Kirche am Steinhof landmark at the very top of the hill. Beyond the complex, with its modernist buildings surrounded by beautiful manicured gardens, stretched the picturesque *Wienerwald*.

Inside the building, a pretty young nurse greeted them and asked them to wait while she located the Herr Doctor. Several small children sat with their mothers, one clutching a doll which reminded Christina of Malka and Hannah, and another, a boy about three years old, playing with a wooden car. A tearful young woman held a listless small child not much older than two years in her arms, wiping spittle from her mouth and talking gently to her. Like the last time, the waiting room smelt of disinfectant. An anxious Karin held baby Karl closer to her. Christina assured her everything would be fine.

After about ten minutes, Sigmund Klein appeared, ushered them into his room, and asked them to take a seat.

'How have you both been? It's a while since I last saw you, particularly you, Frau Krassner.' The women were polite, saying they were well, given the circumstances. 'My mother told me the boy is sickly, is that right?'

'He was underweight when he was born and doesn't seem to be gaining weight,' Karin said. 'Now, he's having trouble breathing.'

Sigmund, dressed in a smart suit over which he wore a starched white coat, got up and came to inspect him. 'Let's take a look, shall we,' he said in a soft, kindly voice, as befits one who is used to dealing with children.

He took baby Karl from Karin's arms, lay him on a blanket on a table and started to undress him. Christina's eyes glanced around the room. Along one wall stood a bookshelf and a cabinet filled with medical instruments and glass bottles and jars of formaldehyde containing strange masses. Another wall was lined with certificates and photographs, one of which was Adolf Hitler. There was also a large eugenics poster from the exhibition *Wonders of Life* in Berlin in 1935. In this clinical atmosphere, the only warmth came from the sun streaming through the window.

Sigmund placed his stethoscope on Karl's tiny chest and listened.

He tapped and prodded and then scribbled down a few notes. 'I'm just going to weigh him,' he said, and left the room for a few minutes. When he returned, he asked Karin to dress him while he went back to his seat. Karin and Christina waited for him to say something.

'It's rather a puzzle. I will have to conduct a few more tests.' He took off his glasses, sat back in his chair. 'Tell me, Karin, are there any hereditary problems in the family – maybe on Walter's side?'

Karin shook her head. 'Not that I am aware of.'

'It might be a good thing if you left him here with us for a few days and we'll keep him under observation. I'm sure we can diagnose the problem by then.' He paused. 'Of course, it's completely up to you, but I'm afraid if we don't act, he could deteriorate.' Sigmund pressed his fingers together and waited for her reply.

Karin looked at Christina who told her she must do what she thought best. Reluctantly, she agreed, and Sigmund gave her a paper to sign.

'The right decision,' he said. He pressed a button on his desk and the pretty nurse came in. 'Fräulein Ursula, take baby Karl to section 15, please.' He turned to Karin. 'My dear, are you able to express milk?' A tearful Karin said she would try. 'In that case, go with Nurse Ursula. She will take you to a cubicle and give you a bottle.'

Ursula picked up Karl and asked Karin to follow her.

When they were alone, Sigmund asked Christina how the salon was doing and mentioned that his mother was always proud to wear her designs. Sigmund had always lived in his elder brother's shadow. Like Dieter, he was not married, but unlike Dieter, who enjoyed the company and attention of beautiful women, Sigmund never seemed interested in women. In fact, growing up with him as a child, she'd been acutely aware of his shyness and somewhat anti-social personality; a person who seemed far happier with his books than with girls.

Christina hadn't seen Dieter since the meeting at the Hotel Métropole and she took this opportunity to ask after him.

'I rarely see my brother,' Sigmund replied. 'He goes to see Mama every now and again, and it's mostly from her that I hear what he's doing. I gather he's been spending time with Kaltenbrunner. My mother says he doesn't talk much about his work, except to say that he did tell her he was involved in implementing something big. It comes from the Führer and Himmler in Berlin.'

'I met his girlfriend,' Christina said, 'the actress, Lina Lindner. She's been a loyal customer since Dieter brought her to one of my collections.'

'I met her only once, so I can't say I know her.'

The conversation was cut short when Karin returned. She was distressed at having to leave her baby behind. Hans gave her a bottle of pills and told her they would help calm her nerves.

'Take one before you go to bed. It's a mild sedative and will do you the world of good. I will see you again tomorrow.'

When they left the consulting rooms, Karin said she wanted to go and pray in the church before going home. Since St Leopold's Church was built for the mentally ill patients of the complex, the construction was completely adapted for this purpose. It was the first time Christina had been inside, and she found it quite strange. The church's floor sloped from the south entrance towards the sanctuary. Not only did this allow for a better view from the back rows, but was also for hygienic reasons. An elderly woman was mopping up a section where a patient had obviously had an accident earlier. There was a first aid room where a doctor was present during the opening hours of the church, as well as a built-in toilet – a rarity for the time – and emergency exits built into the side walls in case a patient needed to be speedily removed. The benches had rounded edges and legs lined with copper plates to reduce the risk of an injury or tripping. Christina and Karin took a seat not far away from two restless patients and two nurses while the doctor in the first-aid room looked on. Karin was too pre-occupied with her prayers to really absorb the atmosphere, but Christina felt oddly uncomfortable and couldn't wait to leave. Not even the beautiful stained glass windows, designed in the Art Nouveau style, could make her stay any longer than necessary.

That evening, Christina went to Nussdorf to visit Max and told him about the meeting with Sigmund. They worried for Karin, fearing that if anything happened to Karl or Walter, she might not cope.

'I asked him about Dieter and he told me there's something important going on,' she said. 'Apparently he's been in high level talks in Berlin. He couldn't tell me what the meeting was about as he rarely sees his brother these days.'

Max had been working on another portrait of her wearing one of her antique silk kimonos, this one with a background of large wavy bands representing waves of the ocean with exquisitely embroidered brown, green, and gold pine trees. It was lined with gold silk which he arranged in such a way that it highlighted her mane of thick golden hair. Another day and it would be finished. He frowned when she told him about Berlin. 'That doesn't sound good. It probably means more trouble for the Jews.'

He stood back and after squinting at the painting on the easel for a few seconds, added a few more brushstrokes and asked her to switch on the radio. 'See if there's any good music on – something to cheer us up.'

Christina pulled the silken kimono around her shoulders and twiddled the knob on the radio until she found a station playing band music. She went into the kitchen to get a bottle of wine and two glasses while he cleaned his brushes and washed his hands.

'Have you seen Baroness Elisabeth?' Christina asked as she poured the wine. 'It's been a few weeks since I saw her.'

Max took a glass from her and they lay down on the bed together. The silk kimono fell open as she lay next to him, exposing her breasts and abdomen. His eyes fell on her body and after taking a sip of wine, he gently caressed her breasts.

'I saw her a few days ago. She's busy with the upcoming opera and sends her regards.'

'Has she heard from Lucien?'

'Yes. Apparently he has denounced Pétain's treason and wants to do everything in his power to help General de Gaulle in exile, although he has to be careful or he'll find himself deported to a labour camp. The British Cabinet is behind the General, but from what I gather, de Gaulle has a long way to go to get people on his side, as most of the French don't admire him for fleeing. Only time will tell.' He took the glass from her hand and put it on the floor along with his own. 'Enough of this tiresome talk. I want to make love to you.'

Christina smiled. There had been many times since he was taken to the Hotel Métropole when making love was far from his mind; now she was only too happy to see him back to his old self. Max had always been a good lover, sensuous, instinctive, and spontaneous. He knew what aroused her, and she him. They were like one, caressing each other's bodies in the most intimate of places. She laughed when he said discovering her body was like discovering a fine sculpture in the Louvre or the Uffizi for the very first time – a living masterpiece, which he painted over and over again, and which he was never totally happy with because he couldn't quite capture her perfection. Yet in those dark times when she thought she'd lost him, he reminded her that true love was eternal. Tonight, he was his old self and she surrendered herself to love once more. When it was over, she made a comment about her senses being alive again.

Max covered the lower part of her body with the kimono. After a while, she asked him the question that had been on her mind since Christmas at Steinbrunnhof.

'You know,' she said, twirling a lock of his hair between her fingers, 'you told me a while ago that you might "disappear" one day. Do you still have those thoughts?'

Max got up and lit a cigarette for them both. 'It's not easy living in the shadows, as you put it.' He took a long drag and exhaled slowly, watching the smoke curl upwards in the soft lamplight. 'So far I've been lucky, but the fact remains that I haven't been called up to fight as my stepbrother, or Otto and Walter. That means they still must have me down as a Jew. While things are worsening for the Jews, I will never be safe.'

'You didn't answer my question.'

'I can't.' Christina wasn't expecting him to say this. She was expecting an answer – yes or no. 'Please don't bring it up again.' His answer was terse and she apologized for ruining the moment.

He kissed her on the lips to stop her questions, and then stroked her face tenderly while looking into her eyes. 'My darling, Kiki, I live only for you. *You* are what sustains me. Let's leave at that.'

Christina was left in no doubt that one day soon he would be gone, but she was not the sort of person to make those she loved suffer needlessly or to burden them with her own feelings of insecurity. *What will be, will be*, she thought to herself. For now she needed to savour every moment they had together and resolved never to mention it again.

CHAPTER 24

OVER THE NEXT few days, Karin went to see Karl at Am Spiegelgrund and for a while it seemed he was getting better. She was never allowed into the ward. Nurse Ursula fetched him for her to hold in the visitor's room, often in the presence of other women and their children in the same situation. On the fifth day, his condition inexplicably worsened and she was told she wouldn't be able to see him. On the sixth day, baby Karl died. Christina and Julia Lehmann accompanied Karin to the clinic and were taken directly to Sigmund Klein's office. He tried to console the distraught Karin, assuring her they had done everything in their power to save the child, but he was a weak and fragile baby, and in the end his death was most likely due to the fact that he was born prematurely, combined with an underlying hereditary defect.

Julia Lehmann was incensed at the insinuation that there were genetic problems in the family. It was the first time anyone had ever made such a suggestion. Sigmund issued a death certificate stating the cause of death as pneumonia. They were not even allowed to take Karl's body home and give him a proper burial. When Karin protested, Sigmund reminded her of the document she'd signed. In it was a clause saying that, in the event of a death, the body was not to be removed from the premises and any burial would be taken care of by the clinic authorities. Karin had been so consumed with worry at the time that she'd neglected to read it through. Sigmund put a caring arm around her shoulder and said he would be given a Christian burial and prayers said for him in the church. Everyone was in such a state that no one bothered to argue.

Karin's loss affected them all, none more so than Julia Lehmann who had looked forward to the sound of a small child's laughter in the house again. Added to their despair was the fact that they couldn't contact Walter, as they had no idea where he was. It was a terrible period for the Lehmann family, and Christina worried that their days of good fortune were drawing to a close.

Christmas that year at Schloss Steinbrunnhof was another dismal time. Max was with them, but the cloud of despondency deepened. Walter hadn't been home since before the birth of Karl, but the fact that they'd heard nothing meant that he was most likely still alive and gave a glimmer of hope, although it didn't stop Karin from sinking further into depression. She suffered from nightmares, had sudden bouts of uncontrollable crying, and hardly ate. Her mother feared that if she didn't get help soon, she would lose her mind.

At the same time, the news for anyone opposed to the Nazis was disheartening and Max started to disappear for several days at a time. At first, she thought he really had "disappeared" for good, but he told her he'd been away visiting friends. He would never say where and who these friends were, and she didn't ask. If he wanted her to know, he would tell her.

Throughout March 1941, Christina spent most of her time in the sewing room with Hella and the seamstresses discussing the best way to conserve fabric while not diminishing the beauty of a design. She made good use of as much silk and wool as she could get her hands on, fearing that it would soon be rationed. With the fall of France, the first edition of *Die Mode*, published in January 1941, stated that "*The German victory over France has an incisive meaning for fashion.*" Other articles continued this theme. The trade publication, *Manufaktur*, wrote that "*The fashion of the past was Paris – the fashion of the future lies with Greater Germany*", and the foreign press reported:

"*VIENNA'S FASHIONS FEATURE FEATHERS; Spangles Are Also Stressed in Evening Models at Spring and Summer Exhibition. PUBLIC IS NOT ADMITTED. Four-Day Show Is Primarily for Buyers From Germany or Those Friendly to Nazis.*"

The Nazis' plan, which they'd attempted to put into operation in 1940, was to merge the French and German couture industries by relocating its ateliers and workers to Berlin and Vienna. The plan was stalling, thanks to couturier Lucien Lelong, who pointed out that it was unworkable because French fashion was dependent on thousands of skilled artisans in tiny ateliers, each specialized in skills, such as embroidery, which would be hard to retain if they relocated. The Nazis backed down.

One afternoon, Christina received a telephone call from Baroness Elisabeth. Would she join her for supper that evening at Hotel Sacher?

The Baroness, who rarely went out without being dressed in her finery – something she believed was expected of a famous soprano – was wearing a simple black suit with a mink collar. She looked as stylish as ever. She was signing autographs for a group of uniformed officers when Christina arrived, and excused herself from her admirers to join her at the table. After they'd ordered, the Baroness apologized for the short notice, but she had some information to impart.

'I thought you should know, my dear Christina,' she said in hushed tones, 'I was in Berlin last week, where I met Herr Eichmann. He is now head of the department for Jewish Affairs of the Reich Security Main Office, Section IV B4 of the Gestapo. I think you'll agree that this is a big promotion from running the Office of Jewish Emigration.' The Baroness stopped talking while the waiter poured them each a glass of champagne, placing the bottle in the ice bucket next to their table. 'I was there with a member of the Swedish Red Cross checking on a group of orphans who had left Austria when the war started. I never told you, but they were taken off the trains and put in a holding camp in Belgium. Just before Christmas they were about to be sent somewhere east, but the Swedish Red Cross intervened, and we managed to get them safely to Sweden. Eichmann made no bones about telling me not to bother him again about orphans and Kindertransport. He was angry and said he had better things to do than help Jews. Those days are over.'

'Are you telling me all this because of Max?' Christina asked.

'Yes. He's not safe. In the end, even lying low won't help him. You know the authorities have systematically been sending trains of deportees east. They say for resettlement, but we don't believe that. There are darker forces at play, and you must realise the only reason he hasn't been called up for mobilization is because they have him down as a Jew, even though he hasn't registered himself as one.'

Christina thought back to Max's conversation a few weeks back. He'd said that very same thing. She sensed Baroness Elisabeth's words were underscored by some hidden meaning. Both she and Max's deliberate evasiveness meant they might be involved in some sort of underground work. She wondered how much they collaborated together. Both kept things close to their chest. By the time the waiter brought the main course, the Baroness came straight to the point.

'You are probably not going to agree with me, but I believe the only reason Max doesn't leave is because of you. He knows how much it will devastate you, particularly with your sister being the way she is. He doesn't want to add to your woes.'

'Of course it would break my heart if anything happened to him, but it's not up to me. I don't know what I can do.'

'My dear, you must actively persuade him to go away. He has access to false identity papers and should be able to leave the country. You can manage without him – until this is over. Besides, non-Jews who harbour Jews will also be punished. From what I know, Polish Catholics who aid Jews are being rounded up too. If this happens, you will be denounced and lose your couture house.'

Christina tried to put on a brave face, but she knew the Baroness was right.

The following evening, Max brought the finished portrait to Mariahilferstrasse and hung it up in the salon for her. It complemented the first one he'd painted when the salon was first opened.

'Now I have something else to remind me of you,' she said with a smile. 'I miss your presence here, particularly at my showings.'

'I miss them too,' Max replied, 'but your descriptions are so alive, I feel as if I've been a fly on the wall. You know that whatever happens, I am here with you in spirit. Now show me what you've been working on.'

She picked up a folder of drawings and they retired to her apartment.

'I like this one,' he said, pulling out a midnight-blue satin dress with a lace top and a low back, 'and this.' He pointed to another, this time a Grecian-inspired evening dress in a choice of four colours – cream, mint, pale blue, and copper. 'It would suit you, especially the copper colour. It complements your hair and complexion.' The last one he pulled out was an ivory paper taffeta blouse. 'These are my favourites.'

She noticed he took a great interest in the collection, and put it down to the fact that he was in a better mood. The rest of the evening they talked about art, design, films and music, and reignited their plans to travel when the war was over. Italy, Greece, maybe North Africa; there was so much to see. Cocooned in their love of art and each other, they managed to block out politics and the war. After such a beautiful evening, they retired to bed, made love and fell asleep in each other's arms. The world could fall apart, but in that moment, they had each other.

Max left the next day before Hella and the seamstresses arrived. He gave Christina a particularly long, passionate kiss. 'Kiki, I love you very much my darling.'

'And I you.'

Two days later, when he failed to arrive at Mariahilferstrasse or answer his telephone, Christina asked Beck to take her to Max's apartment. It was mid-afternoon. Beck waited in the car while Christina rang the bell. There was no reply. The caretaker from the next apartment looked out of his window, opened it, and told her that Herr Hauser had left.

'What do you mean – left?' Christina asked, thinking the Gestapo had taken him away again.

'He left yesterday – around lunchtime. He was carrying a backpack. I cannot tell you anymore.'

'And he was alone?'

'Yes, *gnae'* Fräulein – alone. When he saw me, he waved.'

Christina felt a tightness in her chest. Beck got out of the car to see if she was all right. She unlocked the apartment and went inside while Beck conversed with the caretaker to glean a little more information. Her heart was pounding. Everything was tidy, especially his art materials, and there was a large folio on the bed with her name on it. It was the moment she'd dreaded. He had gone, and this time she knew it was for good.

After a few minutes, she heard Beck's approaching footsteps. He found her sitting on the bed in tears. 'Oh God, Kurt, he's gone,' she groaned aloud, barely able to utter the words. 'I expected it, but I was not ready for it.'

She set about searching the apartment just in case he'd left a message for her. There was nothing. The folio said it all; he'd left her all his sketches. She checked his drawers to see if there was anything of a personal nature he might have left, but only found a few photographs which she placed in the folio. She took one last look at the place where they'd shared so much, a place filled with happy memories, and with a heavy heart walked away, knowing she would now have to face the tyranny of Nazi rule alone. After a short while, her thoughts changed from fear to a kind of understanding. Max had prepared her for this moment, and deep down, a part of her was glad he'd gone into hiding. If he was taken in by the Gestapo again, he wouldn't be so lucky.

CHAPTER 25

By September, all the Jews in the Reich were required to wear the yellow Star of David with the word *"Jude"* on it. The first time Christina saw this, she was walking along Mariahilferstrasse and felt an acute sense of disgust. Jews had been barred from all Aryan shops, cafés, parks, and institutions as early as 1938, but there were some who had ignored it. Having to display the Star of David meant it was not only the authorities who were now able to identify them, but the citizens as well. This caused more problems as those kind-hearted Austrians who'd previously been trying to help them feared for themselves; they could be sent to a labour camp. The sweetness of Viennese life dissipated and an invisible darkness seeped through the population, dulling the senses and soaking the soul in melancholia. No one could do anything without thinking of the consequences.

Christina had just left Café Central with her mother when they heard screams followed by gunshots coming from the Volksgarten. They turned to look and saw a group of policemen standing over two bodies – a man and a woman. Neither wore the Star of David. The woman had been shot in the head and was lying in a pool of blood. The man had been shot in the chest; a bright red stain appeared though his coat as he lay groaning. Other policemen rounded up another couple with a screaming child, holding them back at gunpoint. This couple wore the yellow star. The man in charge lifted his revolver and shot the dying man in the head.

Julia Lehmann let out a muffled scream and tugged at her daughter's sleeve. 'Please let's get away from here.'

An open-backed truck appeared and the crowd made way for

soldiers who roughly escorted the couple with the crying child away, forcing them to climb into the back of the vehicle. The dead bodies were thrown in with them and two soldiers with rifles sat alongside them. The truck drove off and the policemen angrily told everyone to move on. People looked on, some shocked, others indifferent.

'What happened?' Christina asked an on-looker, a well-dressed, middle-aged woman with a dog.

She shrugged. 'They were sitting in the park when the policemen spotted them and told them to go away. One of the policemen discovered one couple wasn't wearing the Star of David and asked to see their papers. The man refused and abused them. The policeman dragged him off the seat and set upon him, kicking him and hitting him with his baton. The woman came to his rescue. That's when the police fired.' The woman recounting the story shook her head and added, in her refined Viennese accent, 'They shouldn't have been there. They got what was coming to them.'

Christina stared at her, ashamed to be Viennese. 'Thank God Max isn't here to see this,' she said to her mother in disgust as they moved away.

'Still nothing from him?' Julia asked. 'It's been a while now.'

'No. Not a day goes by when I don't think about him. I pray he crossed the border and is safely away in Switzerland by now.'

'I hear they've established a camp in Poland – an extermination camp,' Julia said. 'Frau Klein mentioned it.'

'News travels fast, although there are many who deny it. Baroness Elisabeth told me she has it on good authority they're going to exterminate Jews, Poles, Gypsies, and now Soviets, as we are at war with the Soviet Union. Let's change the subject. How's Karin?'

'She's not much better, I'm afraid. Since hearing that Walter accompanied the Panzer Group 2, led by General Heinz Guderian, into the Soviet Union she's worsened. The army has taken Minsk, Smolensk, and captured Kiev. Frau Klein told me several Russian armies have either been trapped or destroyed, and over 300,000 troops taken prisoner, so at least there's a good possibility he's still alive. We live from day to day.'

'Can we get her some sort of treatment?' Christina asked.

'Frau Klein suggested she should go and see Sigmund. Apparently he's had a lot of success with new treatments for the mentally ill. She says he's always away at conferences in Berlin where they think highly of him. He's treating Gudrun at the moment. I mentioned it to Karin but she refused.' Julia sight deeply. 'She was always so calm, so self-assured, I never would have imagined she'd turn out like this. If anything, you were the sensitive, highly-strung one, and here you are, accepting your fate with Max in a way I never could have imagined.'

Christina didn't want to tell her mother there were nights when she cried herself to sleep, took sleeping tablets, or forced herself on a regular basis to put one foot in front of the other to carry on. What would be the point? It wouldn't bring Max back.

Julia asked about Christmas. 'Are you coming to Steinbrunnhof?'

'Of course. The Baroness asked if I wanted to spend Christmas with her and Lucien in Salzburg, but I declined. The authorities are still allowing both of them to travel and perform at various opera houses in the Reich, which gives them a chance to see each other.'

'How is Baroness Elisabeth?'

'She takes performing for the Nazi hierarchy in her stride, and as much as she hates it, she says she gleans information from them.'

'What sort of information?'

'I don't know, and I didn't ask.'

They parted ways and Julia took a taxi home while Christina walked to clear her head. When she arrived at the salon, Hella was preparing to leave.

'This came for you,' she said and handed her an envelope with the official stamp of the Hofburg Palace on it.

Christina opened it and was surprised to find it was an invitation from Baldur von Schirach and his wife to the Silvesterball – the New Year's Ball – to be held in the Hofburg Hall of Ceremonies. There was no mention of a partner.

Hella made a comment about clients ordering new dresses for the occasion. 'They will all be vying with each other to look their most glamorous,' she said, with a smile.

'Maybe some think it an honour, but I can't say that being among the Nazi elite is quite how I envisioned spending the New Year,' Christina replied, sarcastically. 'After all, we have little in common.' She thought of the Baroness and decided to take a leaf out of her book; she would keep her eyes and ears open in case she learnt anything useful, although what she would do with it, she wasn't quite sure.

The following two months leading up to Christmas grew worse by the week. The Japanese attacked Pearl Harbour and the United States declared war with Japan. On December 12 the United States was at war with Germany too. Christina hoped that bringing the Americans into the war would shorten it. One of the consequences of this was that the Americans had to leave Vienna and, because of that, their contact with Stephen Pembroke was severed.

Prior to Christmas, Christina went to Grinzing to visit the tavern owner who'd employed Nathan. The news wasn't good there either. When it was announced that all Jews had to wear the Star of David, he said he'd had to let them go or he'd be in trouble himself. He had five Jews working the vineyards and they all left at the same time.

'I was sorry to see them go,' he said. 'They were hard workers.' He had no idea where Nathan went.

The tavern owner never asked her where Max was either, and she had a sneaking suspicion he knew he'd gone into hiding.

CHAPTER 26

CHRISTINA COULD NOT pass through Heldenplatz without thinking back to that fateful moment of the Anschluss. Hitler, brimming with success, stood on the balcony of the Hofburg and addressed the cheering crowds. Hundreds of thousands of Austrians bridged the gap of the square, some even climbing on the two famous monuments of Prinz Eugen and Archduke Karl. How could she ever forget that moment? It had changed her life forever. Now the crowds were gone and the Heldenplatz, surrounded by grey imperial buildings bedecked in Nazi flags, was covered in a layer of thick white snow that glistened in the lamplight.

Beck drove through the Swiss Gate and drew up outside a grand entrance. There, Christina was met by officials and ushered into the building while Beck parked the car alongside those of other visiting dignitaries. As she was alone, on entering the Palace she was immediately joined by a handsome man with light-brown hair, deep blue eyes and well-defined features. He introduced himself as Tibor Bajusz, and stated that he was honoured to be assigned as her escort for the evening. She judged Tibor to be a similar age and although he spoke perfect German, there was a trace of a Hungarian accent. His warm, friendly smile made her think she might actually enjoy the evening far more than she'd imagined. He offered her his arm, and they made their way along the marble hallway toward the Hall of Festivities, to the welcoming strains of the *Emperor Waltz*. They were greeted by von Schirach and Henny, who looked most glamorous in a figure-hugging pale blue satin dress with a U-shaped bodice and V-shaped back panels, designed by Christina.

The hall was decked out to perfection. With its high, coffered ceiling and 26 crystal chandeliers, it was indeed grand. The 24 Corinthian columns – painted to resemble marble – looked magnificent, surrounded by ornate ceiling paintings dedicated to the greater glory of the Habsburgs. Now the Habsburgs had gone and the Nazis were reaping their successes in grandiose style. The Vienna Symphony Orchestra was playing on a stage decked out in flowers and couples were dancing across the floor. Tibor took a glass of champagne from one of the many tables lining the walls, and handed it to her.

'I hope you have an enjoyable evening, Fräulein Lehmann.'

Christina smiled. 'Thank you. I'm enjoying myself already, but please, do call me Christina. Fräulein Lehmann is far too formal.'

Tibor's eyes flashed. The orchestra began to play music from Offenbach and he asked if she would care to dance. It had been a while since she'd been to a ball and she happily accepted. The waltz started slow, and then accelerated . . . three steps per second, two seconds for one whole turn: one, two, three, four, five, six. Tibor never put a foot wrong.

'You're an excellent dancer,' Christina said.

He thanked her and complimented her on her dancing too. The perfect companion, she thought to herself – handsome and attentive. When the music finished, they left the dance floor and it was then that she noticed Dieter. He was standing with Ernst Kaltenbrunner and his wife, Elisabeth. A dark-haired woman with a flawless olive complexion was with them whom she presumed to be Dieter's partner.

'You look as beautiful as ever, Fräulein Lehmann,' Dieter said.

Kaltenbrunner and Elisabeth also bid her a good evening. The dark-haired woman was introduced as the wife of the Italian Ambassador. Elisabeth asked if she was enjoying herself and then commented on her couture house. 'I am sure you must have designed some of these wonderful dresses yourself,' she said.

'Fräulein Lehmann is the Reich's finest couturier,' Dieter informed the Italian Ambassador's wife, 'and I am privileged to say I've known her since she was a small girl. Even then she had talent.'

Elisabeth Kaltenbrunner smiled. 'Is that so? Well, well. Both of you have come a long way since childhood. Isn't that so, Ernst?'

Ernst Kaltenbrunner agreed. The orchestra started to play the waltz from The Merry Widow and Dieter asked Tibor if he would mind if he asked Christina to dance. She had the feeling they knew each other. He took her elbow, led her back on to the dance floor, and in a confidant move, took her into his arms, leading her with his elbows held away from the body, up high. His left hand held her right and his right hand sat firmly on her left shoulder blade, and their pelvises touched, right side to right side, like magnets. His hold was tight. Tibor was an excellent dancer, but Dieter was even better. The tempo picked up and they twirled around the floor with deft, poetic movements. When the music stopped, those around them stopped and clapped. Christina was overcome with a surge of emotions, most of all because she and Max had often danced to the music of Lehár and she realised how much she still missed him, and now here she was, dancing with the man who had caused her so much unhappiness. She felt light-headed.

'I must sit down,' she said in a whisper. 'I don't feel well.'

Dieter took her aside, and Tibor, who had been watching them, saw she looked pale and asked if she needed a little air.

'Thank you, Tibor,' Dieter replied, hastily. 'I will take care of Fräulein Lehmann.'

So they did know each other. Outside the hall, Dieter indicated for her to sit on one of the couches. He asked a waiter to bring her an orange juice and sat beside her until he was sure she was fine.

'Christina, I want to apologise for my behaviour the last time we met. It's been bothering me. What I did was not the act of a gentleman. Will you forgive me?'

His eyebrows knitted together in a frown. She wished she could believe him, but she couldn't. He was part of everything she hated.

His apology was followed by a compliment. 'Allow me to say how wonderful you look tonight. The dress is beautiful and it suits you perfectly.'

She was wearing the midnight-blue satin dress with the lace top that Max had picked out from the last collection of sketches she'd shown him. Wearing it reminded her of him. At that moment, a group of people headed towards them and Christina recognised their faces. The first was SS-*Obergruppenführer* Reinhard Heydrich, chief of the Reich Security Main Office or RSHA, and Deputy Protector of Bohemia and Moravia. Officially a deputy to Konstantin von Neurath, in reality he was the supreme authority over the entire state apparatus of the Protectorate. He was also the Chief of Security Police and SD – a very powerful man. The second man was even more powerful – *Reichsführer-SS* Heinrich Himmler. The two were reportedly very close. Both men were accompanied by their wives.

Dieter stood up to greet the two men.

'Who is this delightful lady, you've been hiding from us?' Heydrich said, with a smile.

Heydrich's wife immediately knew who Christina was and complimented her on her designs. It was evident that Frau Himmler wasn't as familiar with her work, so Lina Heydrich proceeded to tell her. Christina couldn't warm to either woman, finding them both cold and aloof. Thankfully, they were there less than a couple of minutes before they moved on. Christina felt a cold chill run down her spine. It had been a bad idea to accept the invitation, yet not to do so would have been a slight, and she'd already learnt the Nazis had long memories.

Henny von Schirach and Tibor came over together, concerned to see Christina fanning herself and looking pale. Henny fussed over her but Christina assured her she was fine. After a few minutes, she stood up and informed Tibor she was feeling much better and would like to dance again. He was delighted. This time the orchestra was playing *Vienna Blood*. Tibor glanced at Dieter for a second to judge his reaction. Dieter gave an almost imperceptible nod. *Was he really asking his permission?* She had the distinct impression Dieter wasn't too pleased.

Once on the dance floor, she asked Tibor how he knew Dieter, to which he replied he worked at the Hotel Métropole with him. Dieter was his superior. Christina swallowed hard.

'Was it he who asked you to accompany me?'

Tibor looked a little flustered. 'It was. Is that a problem?'

She didn't answer. Instead she dived straight into the next question. 'How did he know I would be on the guest list – and unaccompanied?'

'Von Schirach showed him the list and asked if there was anyone else they should invite. I was in the room at the time. I'd just been appointed his secretary.'

On hearing this, it all made sense. Fearing he had said something wrong, Tibor said he was glad he'd accompanied her as he found her company most charming. Throughout the rest of the evening, Christina had the unfortunate pleasure of dancing with Heydrich, Himmler, and Kaltenbrunner, but it was Heydrich who surprised her the most. Although she found him unattractive, she also found him extremely cultured, something that belied the work he was doing. Just before midnight, the orchestra played the *Blue Danube* and 1942 was heralded in with a rousing speech from Baldur von Schirach followed by an even louder Heil Hitler to the Führer. It was time to leave.

As Christina thanked her hosts, she glanced over at Dieter who was watching her. He bowed his head in a courteous farewell. Tibor walked her to her waiting car. 'It's been an honour,' he said. 'I hope you have not found me too boring, because I have certainly enjoyed your company.'

'If the truth be known, I was grateful for your company.' She gave a little laugh. 'And you are an excellent dancer.'

He stood in the courtyard and watched her drive away. As soon as she'd driven through the gate, he turned on his heels and went back inside.

During the drive home, Beck asked how the evening went.

'An exquisite hall decked out to perfection, enchanting music, fine wine – and the most despicable men you could wish to meet all together under one roof.'

Beck laughed.

CHAPTER 27

By the middle of 1942, the men she'd met at the Silvesterball had set about implementing some of their worst crimes to date. The Baroness told her she had it on good authority that a couple of weeks after the Ball, most of those same men had met at an industrialist's house on the shores of Berlin's Lake Wannsee.

Baroness Elisabeth was often in the habit of imparting a little news which was always accompanied by the words "I have it on good authority". After hearing this several times, Christina now came to the conclusion she was involved in something clandestine. There were constant rumours of resistance groups in the Reich, many of them thwarted and the perpetrators sent to concentration camps or executed, so one day when they were taking a walk, Christina asked her outright.

At first the Baroness laughed, but it was too late. Christina caught a flicker of hesitation and pressed the issue.

'Well, let's say, I know friends of friends.'

Christina smiled. 'Don't worry, your secret is safe with me. In fact I'm glad you're able to impart news every now and again that doesn't reek of Nazi propaganda.'

'There's something I want to tell you,' the Baroness said. 'There's a Catholic priest here in Vienna who has contacts outside Austria. I was given his name by Stephen Pembroke. He's been involved in resistance work for a couple of years now.' She paused for a moment to see how Christina took this news. 'In a way it's a relief to tell you this. Now I suppose you want to ask me if Max is involved too.' Christina nodded. 'Yes, he's aware of the priest – and one or two others in the group. We got to know them around the time we needed to forge documents for the Kindertransport.'

'What about Otto? He disappeared too didn't he? Is he part of the group? He's Max's best friend. Surely they'd look out for each other.'

The Baroness put her hand out to quieten her. 'Shhh! Not so loud. Maybe.'

'Why didn't you tell me this before?' Christina asked.

'Max asked me not to. Believe me, I wanted to, but he thought the less you knew the better.' She sounded weary. 'He was afraid Dieter Klein might try to exert pressure on you.'

'Always thinking of others. It's one of the many reasons why I love him so much.'

They went to a Kaffeehaus near the Baroness's villa for cake and coffee and seated themselves at a table near the window. All day, they'd both noticed an unusual amount of army traffic, but as the day wore on it worsened. Long lines of trucks filled with soldiers continuously passed them by.

'I wonder what's happening,' Christina said. 'Have you heard anything?'

The Kaffeehaus owner came over to tell the Baroness there was a call for her. The look on his face and tone in his voice told them something was terribly wrong. She went to an enclosed booth next to the cloakroom and took the call. Within two minutes she was back.

'Come on, we must leave.' She left a few coins on the table and hurried out into the street. 'It's finally happened. They are rounding up all the Jews and taking them to the train station for deportation.'

'What! *All* of them?' Christina was aghast. She knew trains were constantly leaving for the east, but up to now it had been on an ad hoc basis. Never in her wildest thoughts had she expected this.

'This is what I was trying to tell you earlier when you asked if I belonged to a resistance group. That conference – the one that was held in Wannsee – it was then that they decided on what they have termed – "The Final Solution". They mean to get rid of every Jew in the Reich.

Reinhard Heydrich and his cohorts are behind it, and this evil task was sanctioned by Göring and the *Führer* himself.'

The Baroness advised Christina to go home. She herself was going to find out what was going on. Christina was adamant she would go with her. They made their way towards Aspang Railway Station where they were told the army trucks were heading, but it was not easy, as many of the roads were blocked off and they were constantly asked for their papers. Situated away from the larger stations and main railway routes, and hence less frequented, the Baroness said it was likely this particular railway station was deliberately chosen as it wasn't near the others and deportations could take place under the noses of the Viennese without raising suspicion.

When they arrived, a large crowd had gathered at the station entrance and soldiers barred entry to anyone who didn't hold a pass. Inside, more soldiers carrying machine guns, many with guard dogs straining on leashes, patrolled a packed platform filled with distraught men, women and children. People had already started to board the allocated freight cars of the "special train". Christina and the Baroness did their best to get a good look in case they recognised anyone, but the crowd was so thick it was difficult to see.

Within minutes the pair became separated. Christina looked around for the Baroness, but she'd disappeared. Through the sharp whistles, loudspeakers, barking dogs, and the never-ending wails and screams, she heard someone calling her name. 'Fräulein Lehmann! Fräulein Lehmann!'

It took a few seconds for the voice to register, but when she saw his face, she knew in an instance who it was – Joseph Fischer. He was waving his arm in the air and pushing himself through the crowd towards her.

'Thank God you're here.' He lowered his voice to a whisper. 'Have you come for the boy?'

'What boy!'

He lowered his voice. 'The one who lived at the premises you visited in Zirkusgasse, the one whose name was on that list you asked me to get. He's here.'

Christina put her hand to her mouth. 'Nathan! You mean Nathan Rosen?'

'That's him. I recognised the name on this new list.'

Without thinking, she said yes. 'He shouldn't be on this train. There's been a mistake. Can you get him for me? I want to take him away from here.'

Fischer looked worried. 'There's a problem, I don't know what he looks like.' He thought for a minute. 'Don't worry, I will call his name.'

He said something to a guard who opened the gate to let Christina pass through. Checking to see no one was watching, he hurriedly led her to an empty waiting room. 'It's not safe here, so please stay here out of the way. I will do what I can.'

He disappeared into the crowd leaving her nervously sitting on a wooden bench. After twenty minutes, which seemed like an eternity, the door opened and Nathan stumbled into the room, followed by Fischer. Christina let out a loud gasp. Nathan was bloodied and bruised and his clothes were dishevelled and torn.

'Good Lord, what have they done to you?'

'They found me hiding. I tried to make a run for it, but they cornered me – bastards.'

Fischer interrupted. 'Not now. You can talk later. Come on. The transport is due to leave just after midnight so let's get you out of here before someone asks what's going on.'

Christina reached into her purse, took out some money, and pressed it into his hand. 'Please take it, a token of my thanks.'

For a brief moment Fischer hesitated and then shoved it in his pocket. There was no time to argue. He led them out of the room and back to the gate. They had almost reached it when a loud voice bellowed out. 'Achtung! Halt or I shoot.' They ignored him and hurried on but the man shouted even louder, causing everyone to turn around and look. 'Stop or I shoot.' Within seconds, their path was blocked.

The man strode towards them and angrily asked what was going on. He looked at Christina and then at Nathan. The contrast between her elegant clothes and Nathan's dishevelled state couldn't have been more striking.

'This boy should not have been on the list, Herr *Hauptsturmführer* Brunner,' Fischer said, looking decidedly scared. 'There was a mistake.' Beads of sweat appeared on his brow.

Alois Brunner, dressed in his smart SS uniform, snatched the list from Fischer and ordered them to one side. By now they were joined by several other soldiers pointing machine guns at them. Christina realised it was she who had put them all in this situation and it was up to her to get them out of it. She started to explain about the mistake. She was in mid-sentence when Nathan made a run for the gate, darting through a family of Jews who'd just arrived. Without a moment's hesitation, the guards opened fire. Nathan went down in a hail of gunfire, along with five members of the Jewish family, who happened to be in the wrong place at the wrong time. Amid the wild shrieks, others were also injured. Brunner strode over to take a look. Nathan was dead. In utter disgust, Brunner put another bullet into his already bloodied body. The remaining members of the Jewish family wouldn't stop screaming and Brunner shot them without even a warning. Terrified onlookers backed away, almost crushing people in their haste. Suitcases peppered with bullet holes lay scattered among the bodies, and the bright yellow Star of David of the hapless victims were stained a dark red.

Fischer went deathly white, and Christina stared at the devastating scene in horror. Her head pounded, her vision started to blur and she passed out. Somewhere in the haze, she was conscious of more wailing and gunshots, and then a stern voice saying, 'I'll take care of her.'

When she woke, she found herself in a warm bed in an opulent room. Her vision was still blurred and her head throbbed, but she was aware of a man sitting on the side of the bed holding a syringe and watching her. When he saw her eyes flicker, he went out of the room and quickly reappeared with another man – Dieter. In her dreamlike state, Christina heard them talking, but their voices were muffled. She felt herself drifting into oblivion again until the doctor leaned over and slapped her on the cheek several times.

'Come along, Fräulein. You will be fine.' Christina's eyes opened again, but she couldn't find the words to speak. 'You fainted and hit your head,' the doctor said. 'I've given you an injection and you'll be fine. No lasting damage.'

He took out a small flashlight and shone it in her eyes. She was aware of his smell – a mixture of cologne, cognac, and cigars. He smiled, yet his eyes were chillingly cold. The men left the room and after a while, Dieter returned alone. He pulled up a chair and sat by the side of the bed looking at her for several minutes without uttering a word. She thought it was all a dream – a bad dream.

Then he smiled. 'My dear Christina, this is the second time I've come to your aid. It's beginning to be a habit.'

'What happened?' Her voice was barely a whisper. 'How did I get here? I'm presuming I'm at the Hotel Métropole.'

'You'd gone to the railway station,' Dieter replied, 'to rescue the Jew.' His smile faded. 'You really should have left well alone.'

'How did you find me?'

'As luck would have it, Tibor Bajusz was there. He saw what happened and when he realised it was you, he told *Hauptsturmführer* Brunner you were a friend and called me over straightaway. I brought you here.'

'The man I was with – what happened to him?'

Dieter gave her a look of contempt. 'Shot! He disobeyed orders.'

At his words, Christina felt herself becoming light-headed again. Dieter helped her sit up, propped a pillow behind her head, and handed her what tasted like a bitter milk drink which he assured her was medicine prescribed by the doctor.

'He didn't do anything wrong,' she said weakly. 'I asked him to look for Nathan.'

'That may be so, but how we deal with such people is our business.

It appears this isn't the first time this boy – Nathan Rosen – tried to escape. He disappeared sometime ago. Putting two and two together, I see that Fischer has an uncle who works here. Now that's what I would call a coincidence, wouldn't you?'

'I wouldn't know,' Christina replied.

Dieter sighed. 'Why were you trying to save the boy? You know that all Jews have to be relocated. I told you before. They can start a new life in the east, find work again and not be a burden to society. It's for their own good.'

Christina was too distressed to reason with him. 'Nathan was the son of my best seamstress. She was killed in Leopoldstadt on *Kristallnacht*. I felt responsible for him.'

'Didn't she have two other girls – the two you sent to England?'

'How do you know that?'

'Nothing escapes my office. Every name that was processed by the Central Office of Jewish Emigration came to my desk, along with their sponsors. How could I fail to notice when you are such good friends with Baroness Elisabeth.'

Even though her head was foggy, she was aware he hadn't mentioned Max, and she certainly wasn't going to bring his name up.

He got up and put the chair back in place. 'Get a little more sleep and I'll have my chauffeur drive you home.'

He walked out and closed the door, leaving her in semi-darkness. After the last time, she couldn't believe his behaviour. She turned her head away from the bedside light and closed her eyes. The drink with the sedative was taking affect.

CHAPTER 28

AFTER THE DEATH of Nathan, Christina's nerves finally caught up with her and, on the advice of her mother, she left the couture house in the capable hands of Hella and took a few weeks off to recuperate in the peace and solitude of Steinbrunnhof. After several days of taking long walks through the woods and cornfields flecked with colourful wildflowers, listening to the sound of birds, and breathing in the fresh country air, she slowly started to feel better.

She was returning from one of these walks when Albrecht came running out of his house toward her. 'Fräulein Christina, something terrible has happened. It's on the radio now. Quickly – come and listen.'

She ran toward the house, pulled off her walking boots and as she did, heard the solemn voice of the newsreader saying that at 10:30 that morning, there was an assassination attempt on Deputy Reich Protector of the Protectorate of Bohemia and Moravia, Reinhard Heydrich. *"It took place as he started his daily commute from his home in Panenské Břežany 14 km north of central Prague to his headquarters at Prague Castle. The Deputy Reich Protector was rushed to Bulovka Hospital and is undergoing surgery. A manhunt for the assassins is underway."* Martial music started to play and Albrecht turned off the radio.

The three stared at each other in disbelief. Heydrich's reputation for implementing terror was well known and they wondered what would happen next.

'I can't say I will pray for him at Mass,' Hildegard said, 'but I am fearful of what will happen now. I wonder if they'll get the perpetrators or take their anger out on innocent people.'

Over the next couple of days, they listened to the radio to see if he would live. At first the reports said the operation had been successful and the doctors were hoping he would recover, but that did not stop Baldur von Schirach declaring that by autumn, Vienna would be Jew-free. A week after the attempt on his life, Heydrich died and the Reich was thrown into mourning on a scale never seen before. Reaction to the attack was swift. Hitler immediately ordered the Gestapo and SS "to wade through blood" to find the assassins. Czechoslovakia went into lockdown, and hundreds of citizens were arrested and tortured as the Gestapo ramped up their manhunt.

Julia Lehmann arrived from Vienna with news that Dieter had left for Prague. His mother had called to give her the news. Apparently, she was most distressed as Dieter considered Heydrich a close friend and mentor. In fact, the majority of the Viennese Nazi bigwigs left with him.

'You would think it was Hitler himself who'd died,' Julia said to her daughter. 'All this because of one man who, from what I heard, was hated anyway.'

'But not by the powerbrokers of the Reich,' Christina replied. 'He was their golden boy, the perfect example of the Aryan man.'

The newspapers were filled with photographs of Heydrich's coffin in the courtyard of Prague Castle and its subsequent journey to the Mosaic room in the New Chancellery in Berlin. Thousands came to pay their respects in this carefully stage-managed spectacle of Nazi propaganda. To the strains of Wagner's *Funeral March* from "Twilight of the Gods", the leadership of the Third Reich paid their final farewell in a state funeral to a man they portrayed as a martyr who died for the cause. Julia Lehmann picked up a newspaper in the village, proclaiming: *"Heydrich was a member of the new racial aristocracy who has fallen victim to those dark forces that flourish in the twilight of the ambush"*, and throughout the Reich, newsreels covered the funeral service. Also paying tribute, sitting alongside Himmler, Kaltenbrunner and von Schirach, was Dieter Klein.

On 9 June, Heydrich's body was laid to rest and the massacres and mass arrests began in earnest. When the radio reported the destruction of Lidice, Christina decided to return to work. She'd had enough. Losing herself in her work was far better than listening to vitriolic speeches by the Führer, Himmler or Goebbels about sub-humans and the noble, decent character of the man who had almost attained sainthood.

Hella and the seamstresses were delighted to see her. The women had been occupied working on new ideas and trying out different embroidery techniques, albeit on off-cuts, as fabric was becoming scarcer by the month. Summer in Vienna that year was quiet, mainly due to the dark cloud cast by Heydrich's assassination, and Christina spent a lot more time with her mother and sister in Hietzing, taking walks through the Vienna Woods and visiting friends.

Karin was still unwell. She'd received a letter from Walter saying that he was in Russia. It said very little else but at least she knew he was alive. Her bouts of depression from the loss of baby Karl fluctuated. Some days she was fine, and at other times she sat in the garden talking aloud to herself – imaginary conversations and endearments with Karl as if he were still alive. Julia Lehmann tried never to leave her alone. The nights were always the worst as she suffered nightmares and her screams could be heard throughout the house.

Hella was replacing a dress on the mannequin in the salon window when she saw a large black car bearing the Nazi flag pull up outside the couture house. She called Christina over quickly.

'It's Dieter Klein's car,' Christina said. 'I wonder what he wants.' She was even more shocked when she saw Tibor get out.

'To what do I owe this honour?' Christina asked.

He handed her an embossed envelope. 'It's from Herr Klein. He asked me to see that you got it personally.'

She took out the contents and saw that it was an invitation to a soiree in which there would be music by the Reich's leading opera singers and musicians. Baroness Elisabeth's name was among the line-up.

Surprisingly, it was going to be held at his apartment on the Ringstrasse and not at the Hotel Métropole. Tibor noticed the curious look on her face and said it was to celebrate his promotion. Kaltenbrunner was stepping into Reinhard Heydrich's shoes, which meant Dieter was in line for a promotion to work alongside Gestapo chief Heinrich Müller. Christina looked at the invitation and mulled it over for a few minutes. There really was no polite way to refuse this, and he *had* saved her from a fate for which she could have found herself imprisoned, and possibly tortured.

Tibor waited patiently. 'Please tell him I accept,' she said.

He saluted and bid her good day.

Hella gave her a sad smile. She too knew it was impossible to refuse. 'What will you wear?' she asked.

Christina brought out the folder with the sketches she'd shown Max. 'I think this one.' It was the Grecian-inspired evening dress, which he'd admired. 'Perhaps in copper; Max always thought copper shades suited me.' She added that this was the last time she'd probably make such a beautiful dress for herself as good fabrics were harder to get. They had to conserve and design to suit the times. Fortunately, they had experienced cutters who never wasted fabric.

Dieter Klein's apartment was in a grandiose building designed in the Neo-Baroque style, which, prior to the Anschluss, had belonged to a prominent Jewish family. Dieter had moved in a short time after they left, appropriating most of the previous owner's belongings, including valuable paintings, furniture, and carpets. He rarely spent time here as he preferred the company of his like-minded acquaintances at the Hotel Métropole. Now that he had attained a certain stature in the Nazi hierarchy, he decided to use it more often, more for show than any other reason. Christina thought the apartment ostentatious and cold– the faded grandeur of the Habsburg era.

There were about fifty guests at the recital, among them many new faces. Dieter greeted her warmly, introduced her to several acquaintances and, after an hour, they took their seats in the music room, an elegant room with a decoratively painted and gilded ceiling, and walls covered in fine paintings. After making a speech – which he proudly stated was in honour of the late Reinhard Heydrich – the recital began. The first part was music played by a fine chamber orchestra, a piano recital by Franz Liszt, followed by an aria sung by an Italian tenor. During the break, the guests refilled their glasses and mingled.

Christina happened to glance in the direction of Dieter. He was with Tibor and, after whispering something in his ear and handing him what appeared to be a key, Tibor nodded and left the room. Something in the way they communicated with each other intrigued her and she decided to follow him. The room opened into a long corridor along which were placed statues and vases on pedestals. To one side there were windows overlooking the courtyard below. She spotted Tibor disappearing around a corner. Three men in SS uniform were standing nearby, engrossed in conversation, and barely noticed her follow him. She managed to get to the end of the corridor in time to see him unlock a door, when two waiters came out of another door carrying trays of canapés. One of them asked if she was lost. She said she was looking for the ladies room and the man pointed to a door opposite.

There was no one else in there and she stood by the door keeping it slightly ajar to check on Tibor. She looked at her watch nervously. If he didn't return in five minutes, she would have to get back to her seat before the second half of the recital started. Fortunately, she heard him close the door and he walked past the restroom carrying a large tray of small, beautifully wrapped gifts. She followed him back to the recital hall without being seen. The tray of gifts was deposited on a table near the stage and the key handed back to Dieter. Christina managed to take her seat only moments before the recital resumed.

During the second half, Baroness Elisabeth sang an aria from "Tosca" – *Vissi d'arte*. The music and the words reminded her of Max and she fought hard not to burst into tears. *I lived for my art, I lived for love. I never did harm to a living soul! With a secret hand I relieved as many misfortunes as I knew of. Always with true faith my prayer rose to the holy shrines. Always with true faith I gave flowers to the altar. In the hour of grief why, why, O Lord, why do you reward me thus?* She wondered where he was, if he was still alive and if he still thought of her every minute of the day as she did him. She turned her head slightly and caught sight of Tibor in the row behind watching her. He averted his eyes when she noticed him.

When the recital ended, the musicians and singers took a bow and everyone stood up and clapped for several minutes in a show of appreciation. Bouquets of flowers were presented to Baroness Elisabeth and several female musicians. Dieter then proceeded to personally give each one a gift from the tray Tibor had been carrying.

Afterwards Dieter gave every other lady present a gift. He was certainly sparing no expense to impress. She took a sip of champagne as the Baroness came over to join her. Christina started to tell her how much she enjoyed the music but the Baroness wasn't interested in compliments.

'I need to talk to you,' she whispered, and pulled her to one side 'It will only take a minute. Something has come up and I'm going away tomorrow. I can't tell you any more except to say it's out of Vienna.' Christina tried not to look concerned as people were looking at them. 'Do you recall when you asked me if I was involved with a resistance group, that I mentioned a priest? I just want to say that if anything happens to me, contact him. He is in the parish of Gersthof, St. Leopold in Währing. His name is Heinrich Menzel. Should you feel the need to discuss anything with him, you can be assured of absolute privacy. Sit in the third row on the left at the far side of the aisle and wait. Don't ask for him by name. Someone will come to you.'

Christina tried her best not to look alarmed. 'What would I have to tell him? I keep myself to myself. Is everything all right? You're not in any trouble are you?'

The Baroness shifted her gaze towards Dieter making his way towards them. 'I'm fine. I can't say anything more.'

'Baroness, you were wonderful tonight,' Dieter said, 'and such a moving aria.'

After exchanging a few polite words, she apologised for not being able to stay longer, saying that she had a few busy days ahead. When she left, Dieter handed Christina her gift.

'I hope you like it. It's something special I picked out myself.'

Christina thanked him and commented on his beautiful apartment. 'So you won't be spending as much time at the Hotel Métropole, then?' she asked with a touch of sarcasm.

'Ah, Christina, you really have got the wrong impression of me, you know.' She didn't reply. 'My guests are leaving now. Would you like to see the rest of the apartment? I'd be honoured to show you around.'

The less time she spent there the better, but taking a leaf out the Baroness's book, she said she'd be delighted. Dieter was pleasantly surprised. The apartment was even bigger than she'd imagined, and every room was lavishly decorated, albeit not to Christina's taste. She preferred the modernist lines of the *Wiener-Werkstätte-Stil* to the grandeur of the Habsburgs. She did, however, appreciate the paintings and was able to recognize the artists: Titian, Rubens, Franz Hals. Three Rembrandt portraits and a landscape were among them. Dieter made a caustic remark about such works of art being far superior to the decadent art the Führer had rightly banned. He took her into his private salon, a smaller room with a fine view overlooking the Ringstrasse. She noted the beautiful Persian medallion carpet, which set the tone for the rest of the décor.

'You asked me if I spent much time here,' he said. 'I would love to, but as much as I love it, it's a place of emptiness.' He moved closer. 'If, on the other hand, I had a family…' He didn't finish the sentence because Christina had a feeling she knew where this was leading. She turned to walk out, but he caught her arm. 'You know what I'm trying to say.' His voice took on an urgent tone. 'You know full well what I think of you. I am in love with you.'

She shook herself free of him and looked into the eyes. 'Have you forgotten about Max – the man I love? Have you forgotten how cruel you have been to me?'

211

'If I have been cruel, it is because of my love for you. Max! Max! Max! You cannot possibly love a Jew. It's impossible. He's no good for you.' Christina took a step back, but he reached out to her again, his temper rising. 'There are plenty of women in the Reich who I could have – Lina for instance – but I don't love them. Forget this Jew. Where is he now? He left you didn't he? What kind of man would do that to the woman he loved?'

Christina's frustration and anger rose to match his and she slapped him hard on the face. 'You bastard – you and your Jew-hating is what drove him away. If he hadn't left he would be in a concentration camp by now.'

Dieter tightened his grip and put his face closer to hers. 'And how do you know he isn't?'

His words were like a knife in her heart. *What is he saying?*

'Do you know where he is?' Her eyes pleaded with him. 'If you do, *please* tell me.'

'No, I don't know where he is, but I hope for his sake he is not in the Reich, because soon there will be no Jews left. And again, I remind you, *I* let him go when I could have sent him away.' His voice softened and he stooped to kiss her.

She tried to wriggle away and in doing so, almost fell over the edge of a chair. This time he was not going to back away. With one hand holding her tightly, he grabbed her chin with his free hand and pressed his lips to hers. Her wide eyes stared at him with a mixture of fear and hatred. He pulled away slowly. Christina understood he was volatile – capable of killing at the drop of a hat – and that frightened her more than anything else.

'I want to leave,' she said coldly. 'Please escort me out.' She put his gift on a table, but he picked it up and thrust it back in her hand.

'Let us put this behind us,' he said, reverting to his softer side.

On the way out, they walked along the corridor and passed the room Tibor had entered. 'You didn't show me this room,' she said in a light-hearted voice that hinted she had probably forgiven him.

'Oh, that one – it's private. No one enters that room. I keep my personal things there – away from the servants.'

Outside the building, Beck waited patiently. He could tell by the look on her face something bad had happened again, but refrained from asking her. As the car drove away, she caught a glimpse of Tibor's face at one of the windows. *What is he doing here? Why hasn't he left with the other guests?* At first, she had thought him a charming gentleman, even though he did work for the Dieter. Now she wondered exactly where he fitted into his life.

Back at her apartment, she opened his gift. Like most of the gifts that night, it was small and delicately wrapped, tied with a gold ribbon. To her surprise, it was a pair of Art Deco sapphire and diamond earrings. They were exquisite, yet she felt a chill run down her spine looking at them. Were these also plundered as was Mirka's bracelet that he had given Lina? Were *all* the gifts he had so graciously given, plundered? It was highly likely. She put them in a drawer, vowing never to wear them. Too many questions swirled through her head and she resolved never to accept another invitation from him. He was far too unpredictable. With unpredictability came danger.

During this time, she saw Baroness Elisabeth twice, once at Café Central where she told her about Dieter's declaration of love, and another time when they went for a walk together before she left for another concert tour. Apart from urging caution with Dieter, the Baroness said nothing about what had now become her frequent performances throughout occupied Europe, which Christina suspected she was combining with work for the Resistance. Worst of all, there was no news from Max. He had literally vanished.

By the end of the year, a cloud of despair and hopelessness had settled over the family. This worsened when they received news from the Russian Front that Walter had been killed by partisans while returning to Vienna on leave. Karin, already in a fragile state, suffered a nervous breakdown, and on the instigation of her mother – after conferring with Frau Klein and Sigmund – was placed into care at the Am

213

Steinhof Mental Hospital. There, she was given sedatives and would undergo a course of shock therapy. Christina was not happy about it, as the place reminded her sister of Karl.

CHAPTER 29

IT WASN'T LONG before news reached Christina of the deportation of Jews from other occupied Nazi countries, including Greece and Norway – always under the guise of resettlement. She despaired that no one was able to stop them, but found heart in the fact that the Allies had stepped up their bombing campaigns, particularly in France, Germany, and the shipyards of Rotterdam. In September, a Soviet air raid was conducted on Vienna and the air defences were strengthened. She gathered most of her information from the BBC World Service at great risk, but it was a risk she was prepared to take, as Goebbels's propaganda machine about heroic battles still dominated the Reich radio stations.

In January 1943, The German 6th Army surrendered at Stalingrad. It was a major blow to the German psyche and, once again the Reich's anger was directed the remaining Jews in the conquered territories, along with other groups considered undesirable, such as gypsies, homosexuals, communists, and anyone else who didn't agree with their doctrine.

The strain of recent weeks had taken its toll on Christina and, as much as she enjoyed her work, she decided to scale down her couture house. With a scarcity of quality fabric, she could no longer create glamorous seasonal collections, and switched to designing on a smaller scale. This meant letting go half of her seamstresses, because she could no longer guarantee them work. Hella was kept on as manageress as she was loyal and indispensable – just as Karin had been. It was a relief to have fewer responsibilities.

She was sitting in the salon, pinning the hem of a dress on a mannequin when Beck came in. His face looked grave.

'Fräulein Christina, I have some bad news. I've just seen the Baroness's chauffeur. She's been taken into custody by the Gestapo on allegations of spying.'

Christina's heart missed a beat and she dropped the pins onto the rug. Beck bent down to help her pick them up. 'They've not put her in the Liesl Prison yet. She's being held in a cell at the Métropole. He couldn't tell me anymore except that it happened while she was in Linz. Her lawyers are working to free her as we speak. Do you want me to see what I can find out?'

He went into the office to get her a glass of water and Hella came out to see what was going on. Her face dropped when she heard the news. 'Baroness Elisabeth! There must be some mistake.'

Christina had difficulty taking it in. Knowing what she did, maybe she had been spying after all. She felt powerless to help. She could hardly go to see Dieter after what had happened, and besides, he knew the Baroness well, so what was the use of her interfering. Yet she couldn't sit and do nothing.

'Come on,' she said to Beck. 'I know where her lawyer's office is. Take me there and I'll see what I can find out.'

The offices were in the next street to the Liesl – the prison in Elisabeth-Promenade, within walking distance of the Hotel Métropole. When she reached the lawyer's suite of offices and made enquiries about the Baroness, a blonde secretary with a pleasant smile picked up the telephone and announced her presence. Almost immediately a man came over and directed them to a private office, where several other men were sitting around a table scribbling notes. The man introduced himself as her lawyer, a small, dignified man with a shock of silver hair, wearing gold-rimmed glasses. After introducing the other members of his legal team to Christina, he told her the situation wasn't good.

'They're charging her with espionage, which brings the death penalty,' he said.

'What happened?' Christina asked.

216

'I'm afraid Baroness Elisabeth is saying very little, except that the Gestapo arrived at her room in Linz a few hours after she'd had supper with friends. She had given a performance at the theatre earlier in the evening. They searched the room and took her away. She spent the night at Gestapo Headquarters in Linz and arrived here today. It will be headlines in the newspapers tomorrow.' The man threw his hands in the air. 'She denies doing anything wrong, and of course the Gestapo are keeping things close to their chest. I suppose they don't want a backlash – such an international star. We'll have to wait to see what evidence they produce.'

Christina gave a sarcastic laugh. 'What's to stop them concocting something?'

The man shrugged. 'I could only see her for thirty minutes. How can I prepare a case when I don't have access to my client? Her husband has been notified and will be here tomorrow.' He paused for a moment. 'Look, why don't you go home? There's nothing you can do here. I will tell her you called and if I have news, I'll let you know.'

Reluctantly, Christina left, wondering what to do next. There was one other thing she could try – the Church of Gersthof, St. Leopold, in Währing. She asked Beck to drop her off a few streets away from the church so as not to attract attention, and told him to come and look for her if she was not back in two hours. It was late-afternoon when she arrived at the red-bricked church that dominated Bischof-Faber-Platz. There was only one other person in the church. She seated herself in the third row as she had been told and, enveloped in the fragrance of candles and incense, knelt to pray. The other person left the church soon afterwards.

After a few minutes, a priest wearing a simple cassock came out of the sacristy and walked over to her. He introduced himself as Heinrich Menzel and asked if she would like to make a confession. His face bore a serious, yet kindly look, his eyes were dark and penetrating, his black hair oiled and combed neatly back. She judged him to be in his early to mid-thirties. When they'd settled themselves in the confessional box, the priest said he recognised her from her photographs and asked what he could do for her.

'I am a friend of Baroness Elisabeth von Fürstenberg. She told me I could trust you.'

'What is it you want?'

'I've just been to see her lawyer, but he can't tell me anything except that she was taken in by the Gestapo and charged with spying. Do you know anything about this?'

Father Menzel said he knew and couldn't tell her much more, except that he'd heard the Gestapo had rounded up others too, but they were not in Vienna. Christina had the distinct impression he knew far more than he was letting on.

'Father, there is someone else I am worried about. I need to know if you know him and if he's safe.'

'Who is this person?'

'Max Hauser. He's my fiancé. He's a Jew. He went into hiding almost a year ago and I believe he may be living under a false name.'

There was a moment of silence, and Christina wondered if he would terminate the conversation.

'This man that you are concerned about, I can tell you that he is safe, but you will understand that's all I can say.'

Christina wanted to shout out with happiness. 'God bless you, Father. You have put my mind at ease.'

The conversation drew to a close and Father Menzel warned her that, even if he couldn't always impart any information, it was advisable for her to come to the church to pray as the Gestapo kept a watch on all the churches. 'If they think you are a regular to this parish, it won't attract attention – and of course, should I be in a position to help, I will.'

Christina said she was more than grateful. She walked the two blocks back to where Beck was waiting. She decided not to tell him what Menzel had said about Max. She was learning fast; the less people knew, the better it was for them.

The Baroness was held for almost a week before her trial. From what her lawyer said, there was still no evidence, yet the more Christina thought about it, the more she thought it highly likely the Baroness *had* been up to something. The good news was that she had not been tortured or ill-treated, which was a good sign. In the meantime, Christina visited the church to pray as Father Menzel suggested, but he didn't call her into the confessional box again.

During the next few days, Christina paid another visit to Karin at Am Steinhof. In the beginning, Karin was considered a suicide risk and kept sedated and under constant twenty-four-hour watch. After the electric shock treatment therapy, she was more subdued and sat in a window seat staring out into the garden. She was a shell of her former self and both Christina and her mother found this immensely distressing. Sigmund Klein imparted very little information except to say Karin was getting the best medical treatment possible.

On the day of the Baroness's trial, which was held at Landesgerichtesstrasse, Christina sat in the packed courtroom with several of the Baroness's other friends. She noticed Father Menzel slip into the room at the last minute and take a seat in the back row. The Baroness's husband, Baron von Fürstenberg, was also there, seated near her lawyer. His mistress, a dark-haired Italian Marchesa, sat in the same row as Christina. Fifteen minutes before the trial began, Dieter entered, followed by the man Christina recognized as the one who had been called to bring the file on Max to his room at the Hotel Métropole. They were accompanied by several other uniformed SS men.

The Baroness was led into the courtroom flanked by armed guards. Her face looked drawn, yet she carried herself with a regal dignity. The judge entered, armed with a mountain of files, and the prosecution presented their case.

When it came to the turn of the defence, Christina feared by the look on the judge's face that he'd already made up his mind. After the lawyer finished his speech, the Baroness was asked if she had anything she wanted to say, to which she replied, no. The court adjourned to consider its verdict, and Christina went into the foyer to get some air. Amid the throng of people, she noticed the Baroness's husband in an animated conversation with Dieter and wondered what they were saying. A few hours later, the court resumed and the judge delivered his verdict. The atmosphere in the courtroom was highly charged as the verdict was read out. The Baroness was found not guilty of subversive action against the Reich and was free to go. It was all over.

Her lawyer looked very happy. 'We won!'

Christina was relieved, but she felt mentally exhausted. 'I saw her husband with Herr Klein earlier,' she said.

'He knows Klein is one of the most powerful Gestapo men in Vienna and I believe he pleaded for him to intervene. They must have done some sort of deal. It happens all the time. Von Fürstenberg is a member of the Party.'

As much as Christina despised Dieter, if he had been influential in the Baroness's acquittal, she was grateful to him.

Christina caught up with the Baroness at her villa later that evening, where a few friends had gathered to celebrate her release. She mentioned that she'd been in contact with Father Menzel who had told her Max was still alive.

The Baroness flashed her dark eyes. 'The fact that Father Menzel has seen fit to tell you this means he trusts you. It's a good sign. Stay close to him.'

'You mean you knew Max was alive?

'Yes, I wanted to tell you, my dear, but I was bound to secrecy. Please understand.'

'I understand. It all makes sense now – all the times Max used to disappear for a day or two at a time. Whatever he's doing now, I am sure it's for the best. I'm just happy he's alive. That alone has given me a reason to carry on.'

The Baroness touched her arm tenderly. 'Everyone has secrets these days, Christina.'

Christina nodded and leaned closer. 'Tell me, were you *really* spying?' she asked, in a whisper.

The Baroness threw her head back and laughed, and her eyes flashed playfully. 'I was acquitted. Let's leave it at that.'

Christina felt rather silly for asking such a question and apologized. These were not the times to be naïve or gullible.

'I have to go away again next week. I have a concert in Zurich. Lucien will be there too. In the meantime, I think you should keep in touch with Father Menzel.'

Her words struck a chord with Christina– that and the events of the past couple of years – and she realised just how consumed with her own life she'd been to see what was taking place around her – Max, the Baroness, probably Otto too – they were all risking their lives in some sort of capacity to help rid Austria of the Nazis, and she'd been too blind to see it.

'It's not too late for me to do my bit to help, is it?' she asked the Baroness.

The Baroness squeezed her hand and smiled. 'It's *never* too late, but be careful.'

CHAPTER 30

FATHER MENZEL WAS in the sacristy when he saw Christina take a seat in the third row. He picked up his prayer book and walked towards her.

'Would you like to confess?' he asked in a soft voice.

Christina said she had something to discuss with him that would take longer than a confession.

'In that case, we'll go to the rectory. Meet me outside.'

Fifteen minutes later, they were sitting at the kitchen table in the rectory. Over ersatz coffee and biscuits, Christina told him the reason for her visit.

'I want to help my fellow Austrians claim their freedom back,' she said. 'I cannot live like this. Please tell me what I can do to help.'

Father Menzel sat back in his chair and studied her. 'The war is slowly beginning to turn in favour of the Allies,' he replied. 'Unfortunately we still have a long road ahead and we are surrounded by a network of informers. They lurk in every shadow and around every corner. Knowing this, are you still prepared to put your life in danger?'

'If my friends can risk their lives, so can I.' She was referring to the Baroness, and possibly to Max, although she still had no idea where he was or what he was doing.

Unknown to Christina, Menzel had already run background checks on her, especially in light of her being closely associated with Baroness Elisabeth, and he already knew about her involvement with the Kindertransport. To become a member of his network, he wanted someone who was loyal, dedicated, motivated for the good of the cause rather than for their own ego, and with the right disposition. It also helped if they were well-connected. Christina Lehmann fitted the bill perfectly. The priest was good at reading faces; it was in his nature, and he saw in her a truthful and passionate woman who was able to take risks. She didn't strike him as an impulsive person either, and as such, she was ideally suited to work effectively with them.

'Your chauffeur,' Menzel asked, 'do you trust him?'

'Yes, of course. He's loyal. Why do you ask?'

'I am presuming he's familiar with your comings and goings, because if you are to work with us, we must take into account all your associates. I will leave you to go through them all. If there is the slightest doubt about any of them, get rid of them immediately.'

Father Menzel thanked her for her frank discussion and asked her to come to the rectory for another chat in a week's time. It was all very nebulous and she still wasn't sure if she'd been accepted into the group or not. Maybe that was how it was – people said very little. As far as her couture house went, she was a successful business woman, but when it came to clandestine work, she still had a lot to learn.

After the meeting, she went through all her family, friends, and business associates, to see if there was anyone at all she didn't trust. Apart from the obvious known Nazis and Nazi sympathizers, some of whom were her customers, and the others she kept at a distance, she couldn't think of anyone. In fact, her personal friends and social life had shrunk considerably since the Anschluss. Knowing that she had now committed herself to working with Father Menzel, Christina felt as if someone or something had breathed life into her again. The melancholia that had clouded her mind over the past few months dissipated and by the time she arrived for her next meeting, she felt she had a reason to live again.

Father Menzel began their next discussion by saying that because of her contacts, many of whom he knew were the wives and mistresses of Nazis, he wanted her to make a note of anything they said concerning the activities of their husbands – anything at all, however insignificant she though it was.

'I want you to keep your eyes and ears open at all times,' he told her.

'I try to avoid mixing with them,' Christina replied.

'You may have to put your distaste aside for the moment. Obtaining information of their activities is helpful to us. There is something else I'd like you to do though. There's a village about thirty kilometres away from your hunting lodge, Schloss Steinbrunnhof. The village has been cleared of its inhabitants and is used for military training purposes, but there's a labour camp in the area. From what we know, it holds several thousand prisoners-of-war, mainly French, although there are a few Poles too. Occasionally they move out of the camp to work in the surrounding area. There's a French officer in the labour camp who leaves messages for us at the side of the road. We call this a *dead drop*. I want you to pick up the next message and bring it to us. The *dead drop* is timed, which means you will have no more than twenty-four hours to retrieve this.' Menzel paused for a moment to judge her reaction. She was quite cool. He liked that.

'The message is always left on Saturday. Sunday is the day the men never leave the camp. On that day they are assigned other jobs.'

'How will I know where to pick it up?'

'It will be left in a tin under a rock by a wooden signpost which points to the village – three kilometres away. Because of your standing in the community, I know you have an Ausweis. It's one reason I'm asking you to do this.'

'And the other reason?'

'You reside in the schloss not far away. Moving around the area is not so difficult for you. Make some excuse as to why you are there.'

'When I have retrieved it, what do I do then? Do I bring it straight back to you?'

'As soon as possible.'

'All undercover work is far more dangerous than it seems, please remember that, especially with regards to the pick-up near the village. Can you trust your chauffeur or will you drive the car yourself?'

'I trust Beck with my life, Father,' Christina replied. 'He will look out for me as he has in the past.'

'Then you will be fine.'

'One other question, Father, why do you want me to pick this up? Don't you already have someone else who does it?'

'It's simple. The agent before you was compromised. We've moved him away from Vienna. Does that answer your question?'

Christina felt her heart skip a beat and her mouth went dry. She took a few sips of water before replying, 'Thank you for your honesty.'

Father Menzel shook her hand. 'Good luck. God be with you.'

She walked away from the rectory feeling a mixture of dread and excitement. Excitement because she was now working with people who were trying to rid her beloved country of the Nazis, and dread because she couldn't afford to put one step wrong.

The following weekend, Christina went to Schloss Steinbrunnhof. Most of the time she spent taking long walks through the countryside or reading books in the drawing room. Beck stayed at the schloss with her, helping Albrecht work on odd jobs around the estate or shooting game. It made a change for him to be in the country, and he was always rewarded with a rabbit or a brace of pheasants to take back to his family. When the time came to pick up the message, Christina told him they were going to pick up wine for the cellar from a winegrower fifteen kilometres past the village near the pick-up point.

It was a beautiful crisp day and the drive was pleasant. On the way, they passed several oxcarts and very few cars. Obtaining a travel pass was getting more difficult as the war went on and petrol was rationed. When they neared the pick-up point, Christina scanned the area for any soldiers or army vehicles. It was all clear. The rolling countryside was as peaceful and beautiful as ever and the only sign of habitation was a church spire peeking out from a copse in the distance. After a sharp turn in the road, she spotted the wooden signpost and asked Beck to stop the car while she went to retrieve the message.

'Keep a watch out for me, will you?' she said to him. 'If you see anyone coming, let me know.'

Beck knew Christina well, and it wasn't hard for him to guess that she was up to something untoward.

The signpost stood near a stone wall amid clumps of purple and white wildflowers. Behind the wall was a freshly ploughed field. She crouched down to search for the container and found it underneath a pile of stones. It was an old biscuit tin. Inside was a small package wrapped in cloth and tied with a string. As Beck watched her anxiously from the car, she stuffed the package in her pocket and placed the tin back under the stones. Just as she got into the car, two armoured motorcycles came round the bend, almost crashing into the back of their car. They halted abruptly, and one of the soldiers angrily jumped from the sidecar demanding to know what they were doing.

'You are not allowed in this area,' he declared, checking their papers. 'This is a military zone. It's out of bounds.'

'We are going to pick up wine and took a wrong turn.'

'Where is this vineyard?'

Thankfully, Christina had checked it out prior to leaving and the men accepted her explanation.

'Whatever you are up to Fräulein Christina,' Beck said as they drove away, 'be careful. We were lucky this time. Maybe next time they will shoot first and ask questions later.'

In case the soldier made enquiries, they continued to the vineyard and purchased several dozen bottles of wine to take back to Steinbrunnhof.

Father Menzel congratulated her on her first successful assignment. 'Do you know what would have happened to you if you had been searched?' he asked.

'I have a pretty good idea.'

'What you picked up is vital for the Allies. Some of the prisoners work in the Heinkel Factory at Schwechat – slave labour. You were carrying important details about the manufacturing plant.'

'I'm glad I was able to help. Let me know if you need me to do anything else.'

'I may have something else for you soon. Again, it needs a person with an Ausweis. Let's leave things as they are for the moment. Just keep your eyes and ears open.'

Christina knew Father Menzel had tested her out with the first assignment and was disappointed not to be given another straight away, but she trusted him. He would make a move when he was ready.

She returned to Mariahilferstrasse. There was the Winter Collection to get on with and she was already behind. This year she would have to be particularly creative, due to the lack of certain fabrics. One of the seamstresses was discussing a sample of appliqué to adorn the shoulders of a jacket when Hella popped her head around the door.

'Your mother is on the telephone. It's urgent.'

When Christina took the call, the colour drained from her face.

Hella knew it was serious as Frau Lehmann was in such a state when she answered the call, she could barely understand what she was saying. 'What's wrong?' she asked, anxiously.

Christina replaced the receiver and took a deep breath. 'I can't believe it. Karin's dead.'

Hella stared at her wide-eyed, not knowing what to say.

'My mother just received a call from Am Steinhof. Apparently she caught a chill last night and passed away a few hours ago.' She paused for a few minutes trying to take it all in. 'Please call Kurt. Tell him to get the car ready. I have to go home.'

Hella ran outside into the courtyard where she found Beck sitting in the shade of a tree reading a newspaper. 'What's happened?' he asked.

'Fräulein Christina has just received terrible news. She wants you to take her to Hietzing.'

Minutes later, Christina appeared and gave Beck the sad news. Karin was like family to him and he was visibly distressed. They drove to Hietzing to pick up Julia Lehmann before continuing on to Am Steinhof. The same nurse that had taken baby Karl from Karin greeted them and took them straight to Sigmund Klein's office. Christina noticed she could barely look them in the eyes.

Sigmund was sitting at his desk reading a book when they entered

– Die Freigabe der Vernichtung lebensunwerten Lebens – Permitting the Destruction of Life Unworthy of Living. He snapped it shut and asked them to take a seat. Several bottles, labelled morphine, sat in a tray on his desk next to a folder stamped "Aktion T4". He indicated to the nurse to take the tray with the bottles away.

'My sincere condolences,' he said. 'We found the window in her room open this morning. She must have opened it during the night and caught a chill. I am afraid she was very weak. Her heart simply couldn't take any more.' He put on his glasses and pulled a death certificate out of the drawer and signed it. The cause of death was stated as "natural causes". 'We did our best,' he added.

Julia Lehmann could not stop sobbing and Sigmund pushed a small container of pills towards her. 'Sedatives,' he said. 'They'll help to calm you.'

She slipped them into her bag and asked if they could bury Karin in the family plot. Sigmund seemed hesitant and suggested she be buried in the grounds of Am Steinhof.

'We were not able to bury Karl,' Christina said angrily. 'At least let us bury Karin. It's important – especially for my mother.'

'Yes, yes, I understand.' Sigmund's demeanour was clinical and detached. Christina wondered if he really did understand. 'I tell you what, because we have known each other a long time, why don't you let me arrange the coffin and the burial. Karin was a special person, a family friend, and she deserves the best.'

Julia Lehmann was too distressed to even think about funeral arrangements. Christina took her mother's hand and asked her softly if this was all right. She nodded and thanked him. Sigmund assured them he would make the arrangements that very day. Christina put the death certificate in her bag and they left.

'I hate this place,' she said to Beck as they drove away. 'Something's not right. First little Karl and now Karin, and that nurse did her best to avoid us.'

Sigmund Klein was true to his word and arranged an elaborate funeral for Karin. Her body was removed from Am Steinhof and lay on view in the family villa in Hietzing before being taken to the cemetery. No expense had been spared. The gleaming mahogany coffin was lined with silk and Karin was dressed in her favourite cream dress; the one she had worn in happier times with Walter.

Christina bent over the open coffin and kissed her sister's forehead one last time. She looked serene; the months of worry and despair erased in death. The coffin was closed, covered with the Reich flag, and placed on the hearse surrounded by wreaths of fresh flowers. Friends and family all came to pay their respects, including Sigmund and a tearful Frau Klein. With them was Gudrun, accompanied by a nurse. It had been several years since they'd seen her and she didn't look at all well. Skinny, an introvert who stared at the ground most of the time, and prone to fits of laughter at other times, she was clearly descending into madness. While the mourners gathered around the grave, Christina observed Sigmund speak with Gudrun's nurse. Moments later she left, taking Gudrun with her.

After the funeral, people were invited back to the house for refreshments. The mood was sombre, but everyone remembered Karin with fondness. Throughout it all, Christina felt oddly disconnected, as if in a dream. In a matter of a few short years, she had lost those she loved and trusted; first Mirka, and now her beloved Karin, Walter and Karl. Added to this growing list was Nathan, and the man who had helped her try to save him –Joseph Fischer – who was shot for his part in the debacle at Aspang Railway Station. How many more would die before this war was over? And then there was Max, but according to Father Menzel, Max was alive. That alone kept her sane.

CHAPTER 31

AFTER KARIN'S DEATH, Julia Lehmann left the house in Hietzing to spend a period of mourning amid the peace and tranquillity of Steinbrunnhof. She took Irma and Gitta with her. Christina needed to be strong for both herself and her mother and she threw herself into her work. Her priority now was to obtain available fabrics and accessories. Most of her old contacts were Jewish whose businesses had been Aryanised after the Anschluss. Unfortunately, having bought the businesses at a bargain price, the majority of new owners simply did not have the contacts or know-how to run the businesses as the previous Jewish owners had. Many of those businesses had been in the family for several generations. It was hard to replace that sort of knowledge.

A message arrived from Father Menzel. Could she come to the rectory as soon as possible? Christina felt a rush of adrenaline. *Did he have another assignment for her?*

Father Menzel was waiting for her and this time there was no smile on his face. 'I have something important to tell you.' The look in his eyes frightened her. *Dear God. Please don't let it be bad news.* 'I will come straight to the point. It's about the man you know as Max. The news is not good. The Gestapo raided several apartments in Linz and arrested six people. He was one of them.' Christina slumped back in the seat. This was the moment she'd dreaded. Now it was a reality and she couldn't speak. 'He was taken to Gestapo headquarters there and is being transferred to Mauthausen today. I haven't got the full details yet. When he left Vienna, we gave him a new identity. To us, he is known as Stefan Baumann, a carpenter. His papers say he is Austrian – Aryan of course – and he has medical papers signed by a doctor stating that he suffers from epilepsy and is unsuitable for military service. He was also given a bottle of tablets for the epilepsy which he was to keep on him at all times in case he was pulled in and questioned.'

Father Menzel reached for a bottle of wine and poured out a drink. 'Here, drink this. It will do you good.'

She took a long sip, staring into the glass for a few minutes to collect herself. 'If they realise who he is, I dread to think what will happen.'

'His new identity is from a dead man, so it's highly unlikely.'

'I'm not too sure about that. The Gestapo have his photo on file.'

'Then we must pray that they don't send him back here.'

These were not words that reassured her. Father Menzel promised to call her when he had more information. All she could do was wait and hope that the Gestapo would not charge him.

Two weeks passed before Christina received more news. Her worst fears came true. The authorities at Mauthausen sent the files of the prisoners from Linz through to Gestapo Headquarters in Vienna, and Max's true identity was quickly discovered. This news didn't come from Father Menzel, who was out of Vienna at the time; it came when she received a surprise visit from Tibor Bajusz. He arrived at the salon one day, attracting the attention of passers-by with his black car flying the Reich flag. Hella shivered with fright when he entered the premises.

'Good afternoon, Fräulein Christina.' He clicked his heels and gave a salute. This time he was rather more formal. 'I must ask you to accompany me to Gestapo Headquarters.'

Christina had that sinking feeling of what it was about, but Tibor said he was not at liberty to discuss the situation. She would find out soon enough.

A terrified Hella watched her leave. 'Look after everything while I've gone,' Christina said to her. 'Don't worry, I'll be back soon.'

'The first time I met you, I thought you were a good man,' she said to Tibor in a low voice, 'but the company you keep makes me doubt that.' The driver of the car heard her and looked at them both through the rear view mirror. She knew it had been an unwise thing to say, but she couldn't resist it. Tibor turned away to look out of the window.

Walking through the ornate portico of the Hotel Métropole filled Christina with dread. Inside the lobby, Tibor asked her to wait while he went to a desk and made an internal telephone call. From where she stood, she had a clear view of the inner courtyard with the late afternoon sun streaming through the glass roof. SS officers dined and took coffee to the strains of a small orchestra. It looked so elegant, belying the evil of the place, and she was reminded of happier days when she too had done the same thing. Tibor asked her to follow him. She knew where they were going – Dieter's suite.

They exited the lift and the same man as before was there, sitting at the desk writing notes. Tibor quickly showed him his badge before knocking on the door. A voice inside called out – 'Herein'.

Dieter was sitting at his desk dictating to a dark-haired secretary. He stood up to greet Christina and at the same time dismissed the secretary. 'Thank you Fräulein Kessler. That will be all for now.'

The secretary saluted and left, as did Tibor.

For a brief few seconds there was an awkward silence. The tension between the two was palpable. Dieter was the first to speak.

'You know why I've called you, don't you?' he said.

'Should I?' Christina was careful not to give any hint that she knew about Max. It would put Father Menzel in danger.

'Do you know a man called Stefan Baumann?'

'No.'

Dieter put his hands behind his back and casually walked up and down in front of her. He reached for a folder on his desk, pulled out an identity card, and showed it to her. In it was a photo of Max. This time her emotion showed on her face.

Dieter gave a little half-smile. 'It seems that Stefan Baumann is none other than Max Hauser, wouldn't you agree?'

Christina feigned surprise. 'I had no idea.' But seeing Max's face unleashed emotions she had fought so hard to keep in check. 'How did you get this? Where is he?' There was a tremble in her voice.

'Let's go for a little walk shall we? There's something I think you should see.'

Dieter took her to the mezzanine where the cells were kept. This part of the hotel was strictly barred to all but a few and was patrolled by armed guards. At the far end was a small cubicle, and in it were two seats. He asked her to sit down, opened a peephole in the wall, and indicated for her to take a look. She cautiously edged closer, peering into one of the cells. A man paced the room with a large stick. Christina recognized him as *Untersturmführer* Szabó, the man who had brought the file on Max to Dieter's apartment the first time he was brought in for questioning. Dieter pressed a buzzer near the peephole which alerted the man to send for the prisoner. The door opened and two men dragged a broken and bloodied man into the room, sat him on a chair, and tied his hands to the armrests. The barely conscious man slumped forward. Szabó grabbed his hair to pull his head back so that the Dieter and Christina could get a good look at his face.

Christina jumped out of her chair and pummelled on the wall. 'Max! Max! Dear God, what have they done to you?' She turned sharply to Dieter. 'You bastard!'

When he ignored her, she continued to pummel on the wall. After a few minutes, Szabó started to beat Max with his stick. With every beating, Max jerked forwards and sideways like a rag doll. Christina continued screaming.

'It will do you no good,' Dieter said. 'He can't hear you. The cell is padded.'

The beatings continued for ten minutes before Szabó ordered the men to give him a drenching. He was dragged to a bathtub and his head plunged into ice-cold water. Christina watched in horror as his legs jerked desperately. When he was about to lose consciousness, his head was pulled out of the water. A minute later, it was thrust back in the water again. This went on several times until he passed out. The guards let his body drop on the floor, awaiting orders from Szabó.

Dieter pressed the button on the wall again, and Szabó ordered the men to take Max away.

By this stage, Christina was in such a state, she could barely stand. Unable to control herself any longer, she doubled over and vomited. Dieter casually handed her a handkerchief to wipe her mouth.

'Why have you done this?' she roared. 'Do you get pleasure out of seeing me suffer?'

Dieter laughed. 'On the contrary, I want you to see what happens to people who do the wrong thing.'

In sheer frustration, the tears started to flow. She was trapped. Dieter led her out of the room and back to his suite. The man at the desk averted his eyes when he saw Christina wiping away her tears. In his suite, Dieter led Christina towards the desk and asked her to take a seat. He took his gun out of his holster and placed it on the desk.

'It distresses me more than you know to see you like this,' he said. 'You deserve better.' He opened the file on Max and told her what had happened.

'We've had our eyes on this group of people for a while. They are accused of disseminating leaflets against the Reich. One of them was found with a printing press in his cellar. Under interrogation, he divulged the names of the others. *Herr Baumann* was one of them. They were taken to Mauthausen and would have languished there had it not been for people here who paid a visit to the camp. When they looked through the files, someone thought he recognized Max's photo from our files here. It was sent to me and of course I knew immediately it was Max.'

'Have you told anyone else?' Christina asked.

'I cannot hide it. Not only does *Untersturmführer* Szabó know, but Franz Huber too. The fact that I was the one who let him go when he was questioned before does not look good for me.' He paused for a moment. 'You see what I am trying to say, Christina?'

She didn't answer.

'We knew he was a Jew and not an Aryan. If he truly believed he was an Aryan, he would have come forward and signed up for military service. He didn't do that because he knew he was half-Jewish and would be found out sooner or later. Therefore he should have been deported for lying – for being a Jew. Not only that, but I made sure his father was not brought in for questioning. I am sure he would have willingly told us what we wanted to know, if only to protect his second wife and family.' Dieter picked up a packet of cigarettes and gave one to Christina before taking one himself. Her hand shook as he gave her a light. 'And people wonder why we can't trust Jews. If I'd sent him away in the first place, I would not have this distasteful situation to deal with now.' He took a long drag on his cigarette and flicked through the papers in the file. 'As far as I can ascertain, he was not caught with any leaflets on him, but being associated with the perpetrators doesn't look good.' He closed the file and looked at her. 'What do *you* think I should do?'

Christina stared at him in bewilderment. He was playing mind games again.

'If you have no evidence, why can't you let him go?' she asked.

'There's no evidence for distributing leaflets – although my colleagues can be very persuasive with the People's Tribunal about that sort of thing, and that would mean certain death – by guillotine. But what about using false identity papers?' He waved it in the air.

Christina stubbed the cigarette out in the glass ashtray. 'Why are you doing this? Why do you hate him so much? Don't you have everything you want without persecuting a man who has done no harm to anyone?'

Dieter pulled up a chair and sat next to her. He leaned over and took one of her hands. She didn't pull away. 'I saved him once – for you. Remember that.'

His voice was soft, yet stern, and it gave her goosebumps. 'What are you saying?'

'You know how I feel about you. You and I could have everything. This Jew – he cannot give you what you want any longer. Those days have gone.' He squeezed her hand tighter. 'His life is now in your hands, Christina.'

He let go of her hand and asked if she would like a cognac. Stalling for time to think, she said yes. She watched him as he poured the drinks. He was the sort of man most women would fall for: tall, blonde with steely-grey eyes, and a good physique – the perfect Aryan male. Maybe most women wouldn't care if he was a dedicated Nazi. He was powerful, and power was an aphrodisiac. She thought how different he was to his brother, Sigmund – a small, bookish type who was uncomfortable in a woman's presence. Her eyes fell on the gun. She could pick it up and fire – or could she? She didn't even know how to shoot. Maybe she would miss. Either way, the noise would attract attention. No, he had her where he wanted her, and he knew it. Christina could not recall another time in her life when she felt so powerless.

There was a mirror next to the drinks cabinet and he watched her as he poured their drinks. 'Let's sit over here,' he said, indicating the couch.

She did as she was told. Dieter changed the subject. He told her he was saddened to hear about Karin. 'I was always fond of her, a good woman and a loyal wife – true Aryan qualities. If more women were like her, the Reich would be a better place.'

His conversation touched on other subjects of a more artistic nature – the plays he'd seen at the Burgtheater, the concerts he'd enjoyed, the latest acquisition to his art collection – another Rembrandt. He asked how her next collection was coming along. Was she happy with it? He talked of everything except the reason she was there. None of this fooled her. Dieter Klein was a chameleon. Unfortunately she knew that to save Max, she too must learn to be a chameleon.

She handed him her empty glass. 'May I have another?'

He fetched the bottle and poured them both another drop. 'Do you mind if I use your bathroom?' she asked.

He pointed to a door and watched her closely as she crossed the room.

She closed the bathroom door and steadied herself against the washbasin to regain her composure. She studied herself in the mirror. Outwardly, she looked the same; inwardly she had turned to ice. It was the only way she could cope. She took a comb out of her bag and ran it through her hair.

After five minutes, Dieter called out. 'Is everything all right?'

She finished tidying herself up and returned to the sitting room.

'I thought perhaps you were feeling ill again.' His tone was caring. 'Sit down and finish your drink.'

Christina looked at him for a few moments. It was now or never – before she had second thoughts and crumbled under the strain. Placing herself in front of him, she slowly lifted her skirt. His eyes widened. 'Christina...'

'Shhh. Don't speak.' She put a foot on his knee. His eyes rested on her dark red leather shoe with the gold buckle – beautiful shoes – elegant, like its wearer. She brought her foot higher until it was on his chest, and gave a little push, forcing him to lean back in the couch. She moved her foot away and reached under skirt, slowly pulling down her silk knickers. Dieter's face reddened a little, but the gleam in his eyes told her how much he wanted her. Her smile was coquettish, her attitude seductive. *For Max*, she told herself over and over again. For Max she would do anything.

She stepped out of the knickers, cast them aside, and sat on the coffee table, provocatively pulling her skirt up around her thighs and opening her legs wide. Dieter's eyes rested on the blonde pubic hair and his heart raced with desire. He sat up to reach out to her, but she pushed him back again with her foot. He wanted to play games; she could play games too. One by one she undid the buttons of her blouse and slipped it from her shoulders until her breasts were bare. At this point she reached for his hands and placed them on her breasts.

Dieter could take this teasing no more and pulled her to him. 'You are the most beautiful creature I've ever laid eyes on,' he said, devouring her with kisses. 'If only you knew how much I've dreamt of this moment.'

He pushed her down on the couch, his hands and mouth exploring her body like a hungry wild animal. Christina closed her eyes, her brain numb to what came next. She could smell him, hear the sounds of his love-making, feel him thrusting himself inside her, yet strangely, she had detached herself. All she could think of was Max.

CHAPTER 32

THE SALON WAS in darkness when Christina arrived back. Hella had left a note hoping all had gone well and to call her if she needed anything. Hella was a bright light in her quickly disintegrating life; she was thankful to have found her. She switched on the light and sat for a while in the salon staring at her portrait that Max had painted in happier times. Tears rolled down her cheeks when she thought of what she'd done. She'd made a pact with the devil and prayed Max would understand – if he survived.

She looked at her watch. It was almost midnight. She badly needed to sleep but instead, she put on the radio and turned the dial to the BBC. Apart from the usual coded messages, there was an announcement about the Battle of Berlin. The British were deploying long-range bombers which were highly effective at night. There was also mention of the Allies in Italy, and the war in the Pacific where the Japanese and the Americans were battling it out for the islands. The good news was that the Soviets were pushing back the Germans in Russia. This was in stark contrast to Goebbels' speeches proclaiming the Wehrmacht were still in control. She wondered if anyone really believed that now. The truth was, Germans and Austrians were dying in their thousands.

After the broadcast, the BBC played music by Artie Shaw and Glenn Miller. She thought of the times she and Max had danced to it, and felt a momentary surge of happiness – treasured memories which at the time, neither of them had realised would keep them going. Yet not even the music and memories could erase the disgust she felt for herself. She had given herself to a man she despised. Worse still, there was no one to turn to for help – except Father Menzel. How could she tell him that?

Christina couldn't stop thinking about what she'd done. She had lain with Dieter for several hours before leaving the Hotel Métropole and only at the last minute did the subject of Max come up.

'I know you did this for him,' Dieter said, matter-of-factly, as he dressed himself, 'but I would like to think there's a part of you that *does* have some feeling for me.' He sat next to her, tracing her naked body with his fingers. 'After all, you appeared to enjoy it.' He cupped his hand over her breast and squeezed until she let out a soft moan. He smiled.

He put on his jacket and checked himself in the mirror, smoothing back his blonde hair. 'I tell you what, why don't you come to see me tomorrow evening, and we'll discuss the issue of the Jew again. Perhaps we can come to some sort of arrangement.' He turned to face her. 'What do you say?'

'On one condition,' she replied, covering herself.

'What's that?'

'That you don't refer to him as "the Jew".'

Dieter grinned. 'I agree.'

He picked up her clothes from the carpet and handed them to her. 'Get dressed. Tibor will take you back to your apartment.'

Tibor was waiting for her in the lobby. Neither of them spoke during the journey home and she avoided looking at him, but he must have noticed the tears rolling down her cheeks.

Feeling dirty and wretched, she switched off the radio, went upstairs to her apartment, ran a long hot bath and soaked herself for a while before taking a sleeping pill and retiring to bed. Thankfully, sleep came easily that night.

In the morning she made a call to the rectory on the off chance that Father Menzel had returned. The housekeeper asked her to hold the line while she fetched him. She breathed a sigh of relief.

'Hello! Father Menzel speaking…'

Christina barely let him finish before she blurted out that she needed to see him urgently. He asked her to come over straightaway.

Father Menzel had already heard about Max being transported to Vienna. 'It's not good news,' he said, 'but at least he's still alive. I'm sorry to say the others were executed – gassed.'

His words rocked her. She had been so concerned with Max, she'd forgotten about his companions. It made her realise how Max's life hung by a thread. She began to wring her hands together nervously.

'I've sinned, Father. I've done things I shouldn't,' she said, ashamed of herself.

'Your conscience is your own, Christina. It is between you and God. I am not here to judge you, only to guide you.' His voice was calm and reassuring. 'But there is one thing I do know – you'll get through this. The Lord has given you more strength than you know. Use that strength wisely.'

'I am not sure what to do any more. My love for Max is clouding my judgment.'

'I haven't known you long, but I am a good judge of character. If you have a chance to save him, do so. You know, there is a saying: you must dance with the devil to know the devil. By getting close to your enemy, it may not only be Max that you may save, but others too. Have you thought about that?'

Christina's meeting with Father Menzel had the desired effect. It had given her a renewed strength and the determination to carry on regardless. She would put her own emotions to one side and concentrate on the bigger picture. By the time she left Mariahilferstrasse to see Dieter again, she was a different person.

Tibor picked her up again and noticed a change in her demeanour. He informed her that this time they would be going to Herr Klein's apartment on the Ringstrasse. Immediately, she knew Dieter was intending to impress her. She was correct.

Dieter greeted her with a kiss to the hand, commenting on how ravishing she looked. She removed her sable coat and her fine leather gloves, finger by finger, and handed them to a maid. She had purposely worn the copper-coloured dress so favoured by Max, as a slap in the face to Dieter, but she also wore the earrings he had given her – a small attempt to impress him. His sharp eyes noticed and it pleased him. Tonight, Dieter had exchanged his SS uniform for a Tuxedo, and despite her revulsion for him, she thought he looked particularly dashing.

'Come, my dear, I thought we would have cocktails before dinner. I hope you're hungry. My chef has prepared a fine meal in your honour.' She sat in one of the magnificent couches, taking in the opulence of the décor, while he mixed the drinks. He offered her a cigarette and asked if she would like to see his new Rembrandt acquisition. It was a self-portrait, already framed, and no bigger than fifty centimetres square.

'Quite a rare one I would say, probably painted shortly before his death.' Dieter touched it with reverence as a believer touches an icon.

Christina resisted asking where he got it from, knowing he'd never tell her the truth, anyway.

Dinner that evening was a grand affair, even though there was only the two of them. The walls of the dining room were decorated with finely woven tapestries of hunting scenes and under the shimmering chandeliers and flickering candles the animals and figures appeared to come alive. Dieter had spared no expense in his effort to impress her. The finest French wines were brought up from the cellar and paired thoughtfully with the menu – an entrée of sole purée in pastry shells, followed by braised pork with onion sauce, a variety of charcuterie and vegetables, and a dessert of *oeufs à la neige*.

He waited until the dessert was served before bringing up the subject of why they were there.

'Max is in the Liesl at the moment. He has not admitted any guilt with regard to helping his friends, who unfortunately were executed for crimes against the Reich.' Christina didn't tell him she already knew about their deaths. 'However, there is pressure on me to put him on trial. The Public Prosecutor is known to go hard on anyone who appears before him these days. He is not a very sympathetic man. The only other option is for him to be deported to Poland with the other Jews.'

Christina had already heard that the ghettos in Poland had been liquidated and that there had been an armed revolt in Sobibor where it was said Jews were being systematically executed. She doubted Max would survive there. She came straight to the point.

'Dieter, please don't insult me with more foolish talk. You have declared your love for me. You know it's not what I wanted, but yesterday I gave myself to you to show that I too am open to being – how shall I put it – accommodating.'

Her forthrightness took him by surprise. 'You mistake my motive, Christina. I love you and I want what's right for you. A Jew has no future here and I am offering you a future; riches and a place in society that you deserve. For that I am prepared to strike a deal for the sake of this man.'

'What is the deal you propose? Can you help him to cross the border into Switzerland? Maybe get him a visa for Palestine?'

'I cannot let Max go free, but I can make sure he gets preferential treatment in a labour camp.' There was a pause. He cast his eyes over her face, noting her calm expression. 'In return, I want you to share your life with me.'

A clock chimed nine-thirty and the sound of soft music could be heard coming from the radio.

Christina's throat swelled and she felt a surge of panic. She waited a moment before she felt confident enough to ask the next question. 'Are you asking for my hand in marriage?'

'That is exactly what I am asking.' His manner was gracious, at odds with the fact that he was blatantly blackmailing her.

'I need time...'

He cut her short. 'Max doesn't have time.' His voice had sharpness to it, the changeability in his temperament showing again.

She muttered something under her breath.

'What did you say?'

'Marriage is not something I was prepared for, but I will make a pledge to you. If you let him live, I will be your mistress. Maybe in time I will say yes to marriage – but only on one condition – that Max remains alive. There – I've committed myself. Now it's up to you to commit yourself.'

A big grin crossed his face. 'I will keep my end of the bargain.' He got up and pulled her away from the table, wrapping her in his arms and kissing her neck. He looked into her eyes. 'My darling, one day, you will have the same feelings for me as I have for you.'

'There's something else,' she said. 'Every few months, I want evidence that Max is still alive.'

He looked at her, his eyes cold and secretive. 'You don't trust me, do you?'

'It's simply to put my mind at rest.' The atmosphere was charged with expectation.

'All right, you have my word.' He took her hand and led her to his bedroom. 'Now, if you are going to be mistress of the house, this is where you will have my undivided attention.' He smiled playfully. 'Not even the Reich will come between us there.'

Wanting to keep his spirits high, Christina joined in his playfulness. 'Not even Herr Hitler!'

He pulled her into his arms. 'Not even the Führer, my darling.'

❦

By committing herself to Dieter, what sweetness there was left in life completely disappeared from Christina's life. Times had changed, but she was a survivor. She pulled Beck and Hella into the office and calmly informed them that from now on, she would be seeing more of Dieter and didn't want them to worry if any of his associates came to the salon more often. She didn't explain herself to them; she didn't need to. Both accepted what she said without question. They knew full well why she was doing it. The only thing they said was that they respected her judgment and would be there for her.

Christina was with a client when Tibor arrived unexpectedly. She excused herself to see what he wanted. Hella discreetly left the room.

'Herr Klein asked me to give you this.' It was a brown envelope. 'He also said he would be going to Prague for a few days and asked that you accompany him.' He paused for a moment and added that Dieter was a lucky man.

His comment took her by surprise. She had long suspected he held feelings for her, even though he kept them to himself.

'Tell Herr Klein I accept,' she replied, her cheeks flushed with embarrassment.

After he'd gone she waited until her client left before opening the envelope. In it was a photograph of Max sitting in the back of a truck with what looked like four other prisoners. The photo appeared to be taken outside the entrance to the Liesl Prison. Armed guards with guns and dogs stood nearby. On the back was written – Destination Mauthausen. From what she could see, Max's face was covered in cuts and bruises, but he was alive and out of prison. That was the most important thing. She brought it to her lips and kissed it.

CHAPTER 33

In late autumn 1943, Christina and Dieter travelled by train to Prague. They were to be guests of Ernst Kaltenbrunner, Dieter's mentor, who had replaced Heydrich as Chief of the Security Police and the SD in January 1943. His mistress, Countess Gisela was also with him. Gisela was delighted to see Christina again and welcomed her warmly, telling her that she had friends who were interested in having her design something for them. During the journey, Christina thanked Dieter for sparing Max from the People's Tribunal and hoped he wouldn't suffer at Mauthausen as she'd heard terrible things about the camp. Dieter said he'd arranged for him to be put in the carpentry section where his creative skills could be put to use. He didn't want to ruin the journey with talk about Max and quickly changed the subject. Hitler had rewarded Kaltenbrunner for his work with the Knight's Cross of the War Merit, Cross with Swords, a rare award and a sign of what Hitler thought of the man. Dieter added that perhaps he, too, might receive one someday soon.

Heinrich Himmler also joined them, along with an entourage of other SS dignitaries. When they were in the company of the women, the men only spoke about the war in general terms, although they did mention that American bombers had struck a hydro-electric power facility and heavy water factory in German-controlled Vemork, Norway which they considered a serious blow to the war effort. After dinner, the men retired to another room to talk business and the women socialised separately. One of the wives of a Slovak SS man informed her, in confidence, that the meeting had been called to discuss the acceleration of deportations throughout the Reich and the fate of the

246

Gypsies and "part-Gypsies" who were to be put on the same level as Jews and placed in concentration camps. Gisela didn't want to talk politics; she wanted to talk about fashion. What were the latest trends? When Christina told her good fabric was hard to come by because all her Jewish suppliers were no longer in business, she said she might be able to help.

'There are warehouses in Prague where they store bundles of cloth – very good cloth I might add. Ernst said they are auctioned off and the proceeds go to the Reich. The rest is distributed to our people.' She laughed. 'I'm surprised you didn't know about this. These warehouses are everywhere. How remiss of Dieter not to mention it.' She picked up a Czech newspaper to show her. 'Look, advertisements for upcoming auctions.'

Christina *had* heard of similar warehouses in Vienna, but had never thought to visit them. To her it seemed like adding further insult to the deportees. Another woman said she'd been there and had her own dressmaker make something with them.

'You can't imagine what wonderful things you can get,' she said.

When Christina was alone with Dieter later that night – the first night she had been with him in public since agreeing to become his mistress – he was particularly warm towards her, and to all intents and purposes, genuinely interested in her welfare.

'I hope you enjoyed yourself tonight. You looked enchanting and I was proud of you. Ernst commented on how well you looked too and said he was glad to see us together.'

'Gisela said the same thing,' she added.

'There you are. I told you we made a fine couple.' He laughed, as if the real reason they were together was attraction, and not Max.

'Dieter, can I ask you something?' She smiled sweetly at him. 'You may not realise, but it's been very difficult for me to lay my hands on good quality fabric lately. Many of the fabric and accessory suppliers were Jewish and, with a war on, fine cloth is not easy to find. I have some put aside, but after the next collection it will all be gone. Tonight the women told me they get good supplies from warehouses. Apparently there are some near here. Do you know anything about them? If so, maybe I could take a look.'

Dieter looked at her thoughtfully. 'Yes, I know about them. I'm not sure it's a good idea to visit them though.' His tone was subdued.

'Why ever not! If it's good enough for Gisela and her friends, it's good enough for me. Besides, they know what I design and wouldn't have suggested it if the fabric wasn't suitable.'

'All right. I will take you myself. I have a meeting in the morning. We'll go after lunch. Do you think you could occupy yourself until then?'

'I'd like to check out the designs here – visit a few stores, and then perhaps I'll have coffee and Honey Cake at the Café Imperial.' She gave him a seductive smile. 'Now come to bed and hold me tightly.'

The main reason Christina was looking forward to being alone for a few hours, was that Father Menzel had asked her to meet a member of the Czech Resistance in Prague who passed information to them. The assignment was to meet a woman in the Café Imperial who would give her a package to take back to Vienna. She would recognise her by her red hat with a trim of netting partially covering her face. The Gestapo were everywhere in Prague and it was a highly dangerous mission, but she reasoned that if she could give herself to Dieter, she could help her country.

The German occupation in the Protectorate of Bohemia and Moravia had divided the citizens, especially after Heydrich's assassination, and Dieter cautioned her about straying too far from the main thoroughfare. The fact that hundreds of Czechs had been rounded up, deported and executed, and the village of Lidice razed to the ground, meant the Resistance was still active. Christina was pleased to hear that, but as she didn't speak Czech, was afraid someone might mistake her for a German. The next day the weather was cold and bleak and she was glad to have brought warm clothes. She donned her fur coat and hat and set out to explore the shops for a while. Despite the melancholic atmosphere, Prague was still a wonderful place to visit. There were plenty of things in the shops and the cafés were full. After visiting a few shops – in particular, a shoe shop where she purchased a pair of crocodile shoes – she headed to the Café Imperial. It too was doing a brisk business.

The woman with the red hat was not there, but Christina was early. She took off her coat, sat at a table near the window and ordered Honey Cake and coffee and picked up a Viennese newspaper. At the allotted time, a young blonde woman wearing a red hat and carrying a magazine and a bag walked in, looked around, and spotted her. She walked over and asked if the seat next to her was taken. Christina indicated it was free. The waiter came over with Christina's cake and coffee and asked if the woman with the red hat was ready to order. She ordered coffee and a slice of *Bublanina*.

The woman opened her magazine and flicked through it. After the waiter brought her order, she said in a low voice that she recognised Christina from her picture in the magazine she was carrying. She showed her the photograph. It was of Christina with a model wearing a coat from her Winter Collection. 'I didn't think they'd send someone quite so famous,' she said with a little smile.

The two ate their cake in silence. When she'd almost finished eating, the woman opened her bag, cautiously took out a package, and slid it across the seat towards Christina. Without looking in her direction, she told her to pick it up after she'd left. A few minutes later, the woman wiped her mouth with the serviette, got up and bid Christina good day. 'Be careful,' she cautioned in a whisper. 'The Gestapo have eyes everywhere.'

Christina slipped the package into her bag and finished eating her cake. How she would have liked to ask the woman a few questions, but that was impossible. When she left the café, it had started to snow. She was just about to hail a taxi, when a black Mercedes arrived. It was Dieter. He called to her to get inside. Kaltenbrunner had lent him his car and driver for the trip to the warehouse.

'How was your shopping?' he asked.

'Prague has the most elegant women, and there are some particularly good shoe shops. I couldn't resist a pair.' She patted the bag. Proof that she really had been shopping.

The warehouse turned out to be a ten minute drive away. It was a heavily guarded, large, red-brick building on the outskirts of the city. The SS officer in charge welcomed them.

'We received several truckloads of goods this week. I'm sure you will find something to your liking,' he said, obviously proud of the work he was doing.

Once inside, Christina got the shock of her life. Bales of textiles lined the walls from floor to ceiling. They were divided into sections by the cloth category; silks, cottons, woollens, etc. Clothing was divided too; underwear, blouses, dresses – day and evening wear – coats, jackets, cardigans. There was also an area for notions such as ribbons, buttons and zippers, another for feathers, and an even larger area for fur goods. Most poignant of all was a section for baby and children's clothes. She was horrified.

'Are you telling me these are all from Jews who were deported?' she asked.

'They were left behind,' Dieter said sharply. He looked at his watch. 'I haven't got much time. Tell me if there's anything you want and I'll see what I can do. In the meantime, I will be in the office.'

He clicked his fingers and called to a middle-aged, thick-set woman with light brown hair swept towards the back in a tight roll. 'Come and help Fräulein Lehmann. She will advise you what she wants.'

The woman hurried over, her wooden-heeled shoes clattering on the stone floor.

Christina told her that she was a couturier and would like to see the finest cloths available, preferably in meterage, rather than clothing. The woman in turn called other women over and after a discussion in Czech, they disappeared between the aisles, returning with bundles of stuff which they laid out on a large table for her to look at. She noticed the girls all wore the same course blue dresses and headscarves. All of them, except the overseer wore a yellow star, and none of them made eye contact with her – except one.

'Fräulein Lehmann,' the woman said, her voice barely audible. 'How good it is to see you.'

Christina stared at her for a few seconds, trying desperately to place the face. It was Ruth Zweig – one of the Jewish seamstresses who used to work for her. She barely recognised her, she was so thin and gaunt.

'Ruth! Thank God you're still alive!' She lowered her voice. 'What on earth are you doing here?'

'I was rounded up and sent to Theresienstadt when the deportations started. Ella is there too. I have no idea what happened to the others.'

The overseer noticed Ruth talking, hurried over and whacked her heavily on the back with her stick. 'No talking!'

Christina put her hand out. 'Stop! I know this woman. Leave her alone.'

The other girls stared at the ground as the overseer's face reddened. It was evident she didn't like being made a fool of in front of the girls.

'I have my orders, *gnädige* Fräulein. They are not to talk.'

'This girl used to work for me. I would like to speak with her. Now, if you don't mind, please continue with what you have been asked to do – before I report you to Herr Klein.'

The woman hissed at two girls to help her and moved away.

'What's going on, Ruth? Tell me quickly.'

Ruth informed her that everything was stolen from the Jews and other deportees. 'The Nazi hierarchy come here with their wives and fancy women and they take what they want. The rest is sold.' She wiped the tears from her eyes. 'Ella and I are in the camp. They say it's a model camp, but that's a lie. What they show to the world is false. Those of us able to work, do so as slave labour. Ella and I have been sewing. They wanted someone to help sort through the fabrics here and I was chosen because of my background. I've been lucky. I get an extra ration of food for this.'

Before she could say any more, the women returned with fabrics.

'I'll see what I can do, Ruth. Don't lose hope.'

Christina began to look through the fabrics and chose quite a few. 'Wrap them up for me, please,' she said to the woman. 'Is there anything else you should show me before I go? What about embroidery threads?'

The woman bellowed to one of the girls to fetch a few boxes from a certain aisle.

'There are sewing machines too,' Ruth whispered, when the woman's back was turned.

After an hour, Dieter appeared. 'Have you found anything suitable?'

'I have. I'm very glad you brought me here.' She pointed to the mound of parcels ready for collection. 'I'm taking those.'

Dieter asked that the parcels be loaded into the car and for the woman to give her list to the man in charge of the warehouse.

'One more thing,' Christina said, turning to the woman in charge. 'Do you have any sewing machines?'

The woman threw Ruth a sour look. 'We do. Would the *gnädige* Fräulein like to see them?'

'Are they in good working order?'

'They most certainly are.' The woman reeled off a few makes.

'Then I will have six. Add them to the list.' She thanked the women for their time. As she walked away, she threw a quick glance at Ruth and winked at her. Outside, another truck pulled up and soldiers pulled more bundles out of the back for the women to sort out. It was never-ending.

Driving back, Christina thanked Dieter for taking her and told him that it had given her an idea. Tactfully, she wouldn't tell him while the chauffeur was listening. As soon as they returned to the villa, Christina waited until she was alone in the room to check the contents of the package the woman in the cafe had given her. It was a large amount of money. The Resistance in Vienna would put that to good use. She hid it in the side of her suitcase, taking care to cover it in such a way that if anyone searched it, she would know.

After the previous evening, dinner that night was a quiet affair, with just two couples, Dieter, Christina, Kaltenbrunner and Gisela. Gisela was happy to hear that her visit to the warehouse had been fruitful.

'It's such a pity to let all those beautiful fabrics go to waste,' she said, with no regard to where they had come from.

Alone in their room, Christina approached Dieter with another request. She wondered how he would react, but it was something she had to do and it had to be done before they left Prague.

She sat at the dressing table removing her make-up with cold cream, while he lay on the bed smoking a cigarette and watching her. 'I've been thinking,' she said, in a soft but deliberate manner. 'The visit to the warehouse today has solved my problem of fabric supply, but I have another problem, an even bigger one.'

'What's that?'

She put the lid back on the cold cream jar, ran a brush through her hair, and sprayed herself lightly with perfume. She could tell by the tone in his voice, he was wary of her. She swung herself round to face him and crossed her legs, provocatively.

'I haven't enough seamstresses.'

'Is that all?' He laughed. 'Hire some more.'

'I wish I could, but it's not as easy as that. I've tried. I don't just want someone who can sew, I want someone who is skilled, and they are hard to come by. I had several excellent ones before, but I had to let them go when you introduced your new laws.' His smile faded but she persevered; she had nothing to lose. 'Today, I saw one of them. She was at the warehouse. Like the others, she was there for the day from Theresienstadt. She told me another of my seamstresses is there too.'

He looked at her angrily. 'What do you want me to do about that? I am not responsible for where these Jews end up. Do you think I can save every Jew?'

'I know there are many labour camps in the Reich, and that many detainees have found work in them. I am asking if you could help me get some of these experienced women to help me with my own business.' She was careful not to use the term "slave labour". 'It would help me enormously.'

Dieter's eyes narrowed. 'Don't push me too far, Christina. I've helped you once.'

She threw her hands up in the air and gave a sigh of resignation. 'Fine. I won't mention it again.' She went over to him and touched his arm gently. 'Please don't be angry with me. It was just an idea.'

'Let me think about it.' He pushed her back on the bed and lifted her nightdress, kissing her belly, his mouth searching for more. She moaned with delight. Her charm had the desired effect.

Dieter was not by her side when she woke up in the morning. It crossed her mind that maybe she *had* pushed him too far. She found him in the breakfast room with Kaltenbrunner.

'Ah, there you are, my darling,' he said. 'I've been discussing your proposal with Ernst, and he agrees it's an excellent idea.'

Christina couldn't quite believe what she was hearing, but she was relieved to see him in a good mood.

'Indeed,' replied Kaltenbrunner. 'Why not make the most of their skills.'

Dieter looked pleased with himself. He'd not only made Christina happy, but the man he admired too. 'This is what we propose,' he said to her. 'It's not possible for any of these women to go back to the Ostmark, especially Vienna. After declaring it to be Jew-free, we cannot allow them back. You must understand that.'

'Then how can I operate? It will be difficult for me to keep coming here,' Christina replied.

Kaltenbrunner interrupted. 'Prague, yes, but there is another solution. There's a labour camp just over the border in Slovakia. They can work from there.'

'Where is this place?'

'Sered, an internment camp set up a couple of years ago by the Slovak Ministry of the Interior. The camp already has several manufacturing workshops producing joinery products, toys, clothing, and other goods. I am sure they can add another workshop for your seamstresses. It's well guarded and quite secure. I know Alexander Mach well. He's the person in charge of the Slovak camps. I'll have a word with him. Leave it with me.'

Dieter told her it was less than an hour and a half drive from Vienna. 'I think you'll agree, that's easy enough for frequent visits.'

Christina hadn't envisioned this. In her mind, she wanted to get the girls back to Vienna. Now she understood that was impossible, her only option was to go along with their suggestion. At least this way she would be able to save Ruth and Ella from possible deportation. She was careful not to show too much happiness. To all intents and purposes, this was intended to be purely business.

'That's an excellent suggestion, but I would like to choose the seamstresses. I demand a high quality.'

'Naturally,' Kaltenbrunner said. 'Dieter told me you met one of them yesterday.'

'That's right. She and another of my seamstresses are in Theresienstadt.'

Over breakfast, it was decided that, rather than Christina go to Theresienstadt herself, she should return to the warehouse and discuss the matter with the seamstress in question. If she was trustworthy, she would find other seamstresses and they would be relocated as soon as possible. Fearing the proposal could fall through if she didn't act quickly, Christina didn't hesitate to agree. After hearing Kaltenbrunner mention there was a joinery workshop at Sered, it crossed her mind to ask Dieter if there was a possibility of Max being transferred there, but she decided against it. She knew he would never agree to them being anywhere near each other.

The same women were busily sorting new bundles of clothing when they arrived. The SS officer in charge called the overseer to his office.

'Bring the woman...' he looked at the slip of paper Dieter had given him, 'the woman called Ruth Zweig here.' He also read out Ruth's prisoner number, which the overseer was more familiar with. She gave a Hitler salute and left the room. When she returned, Christina hid her shock behind a mask of indifference. Ruth stood shaking in front of the overseer, her head lowered in fright, fresh bruises on her face.

The SS officer did not ask her to sit down. He was brusque and to the point. 'This good lady, Fräulein Lehmann, whom I believe you are already acquainted with, has requested you work for her as a seamstress. She speaks highly of your skills.' He paused to see her reaction, but Ruth continued to look at the floor, afraid to speak in case she received another beating. 'She also says there is another woman at Theresienstadt, Ella Edelstein, who is also a seamstress.' After more silence, the SS officer started to lose patience. 'Speak woman!'

The overseer prodded Ruth in the back with her stick.

'Yes sir, that's correct,' Ruth stammered.

The man gave a surly smile. 'You see, they can speak when they want to,' he said to Dieter. He turned his attention back to Ruth. 'You will return to Theresienstadt, pack your things, and together with Frau Edelstein, be moved to another camp where you will work for Fräulein Lehmann.'

'May I speak, sir?' Christina said. The man nodded. 'Ruth, I will need more seamstresses. Do you know of any others that are as good as you and Ella?' She saw Ruth's eyes were moist with tears and desperately wanted to tell her everything was going to be fine.

'There are quite a few, Fräulein Lehmann.'

'The *gnae'* Fräulein does not need all of you,' Dieter said, irritably. 'She needs eight. You must choose six more.'

'You know my work and my standards, Ruth.' Christina added. 'Can you find me another six?'

'Certainly, Fräulein Lehmann.'

The SS officer stood up. 'Good. Then it's settled.' He turned to Christina. 'When you have your eight, they will be relocated. Are there any other requests?'

'Yes. Yesterday, I purchased a few sewing machines. I would like some more for the new workshop. If you don't mind, I have drawn up a list of all that I will need.' She handed it to the SS officer. He glanced through it, signed and stamped it, and handed it to the overseer, telling her to see this was acted upon. Ruth was led away.

When they were alone, Dieter gave her one of his charming smiles. 'Maybe now, you will not think so badly of us.'

All Christina could think of at that moment was Ruth. She desperately hoped she wouldn't receive another beating.

CHAPTER 34

FATHER MENZEL WAS pleased with Christina's visit to Prague. He knew it had been an emotional ordeal, but she had sacrificed herself for the sake of the Resistance *and* saved eight Jewish seamstresses from future deportation. She also gave him the names of the men Dieter associated with in Prague. The last few months had taken its toll on her and, with Christmas nearing, and the new workshop at Sered, he told her to take it easy; she was taking on too much. Christina told him it was the only way she could cope.

She left the rectory and caught a tram to Café Central. It had been a while since she'd been there and inevitably, her mind wandered back to happier times with Max. The manager welcomed her and, making sure no one overheard, lamented the life they now lived.

'I heard about that man who came here to leave you a message,' he whispered. 'Is it true he was shot at the train station for helping you?' Christina nodded. 'I also heard Herr Hauser is in Mauthausen. I pray he survives, especially through the winter. The weather forecast is not good – the worst winter in ages.' Christina wondered how he knew all this, but he was well connected – and far too discreet to divulge his contacts. She wondered if he knew about her relationship with Dieter, but if he did, he didn't show it. He brought her a slice of apricot strudel and a glass of wine, compliments of the house.

She glanced around, looking at the customers reading their newspapers or chatting with friends. Like Prague, there was a noticeably melancholic atmosphere. Only the SS men and Wehrmacht officers appeared cheerful. The manager made a caustic remark. 'Let them have their moment of glory while they can.'

Christina recalled happier, carefree days there. She saw Max everywhere, smiling and calling her his darling 'Kiki', telling her about his latest exhibition and the portrait he was painting of her. She missed him dreadfully and hoped he would understand her relationship with Dieter and forgive her. She wasn't sure.

She dreaded Christmas. The family was torn apart and not in the mood for celebrations. Julia Lehmann was still in mourning after Karin's death and wasn't really up to entertaining, and the thought of spending it with Dieter was not at all appealing. He hinted at being invited to Steinbrunnhof and she desperately looked for an excuse to put him off. She'd already told her mother she was seeing him, and why, and the response was cold and unemotional. 'Find happiness wherever you can,' was all her mother could say. 'Happiness is fleeting.' In the end she invited him over, if only to thank him for helping her.

A few days before Christmas, Beck drove her to Sered. It was the second time she'd been since the authorities allocated her a workshop. They had been swift to act on her behalf and gave her a building previously used by toymakers who had been shifted to another area of the camp. The women would be housed and working in a long, rudimentary brick building divided into two: a small, cramped section with bunk-beds for sleeping quarters, and a larger area for the atelier. The camp carpenters had put up a wooden sign over the door: "Textile Workshop".

Ruth had no trouble finding six more seamstresses besides herself and Ella. In fact, it distressed her that she had to turn so many away, especially when they pleaded with her. She and Ella couldn't believe their luck at seeing Christina again. Their prayers had been answered. All the women had terrible stories to tell her. Four were from Vienna, two from Prague, and two were Slovaks from Bratislava. All had lost friends and members of their family, including their husbands, and had no idea where they were. They told her that Theresienstadt was not the model labour camp it showed to the world, but compared to what they'd heard about other places, they were grateful to be there. 'It's all a lie,' one of the women said, referring to Theresienstadt. 'When they deem people useless, they send them away.'

All the women were photographed and given a number as soon as they arrived. The rules were that they report for roll call at the beginning and end of each day, work a twelve-hour day, eat their meals with the rest of the camp inmates, and use the shower facilities daily. There were male and female dormitories, but Christina managed to get permission for her seamstresses to sleep in the workshop. Because of her connections, that was granted. If they got sick, they were to report to the camp medical centre straightaway. Sickness brought with it epidemics, and that was to be avoided at all costs.

Christina said she would do her best to look after them, but warned that they must adhere to the strict camp rules. Most of the guards were recruited from the Hlinka Guards and were known to be notoriously harsh if anyone put a step out of place. She checked their beds. The mattresses were made out of straw, but at least they had blankets. There was also a wood stove which heated the whole of the building. She told them she would bring them extra food when she could and they could cook it on the stove.

The camp was situated in the countryside surrounded by farmland. Women could be seen working the fields. Worst of all, it was exposed to the elements. Howling ice-cold winds swept across the countryside in winter, and temperatures soared in summer. A high barbed-wire fence with a guardhouse at the entrance encircled the camp. In the centre was an area for roll call and public announcements. During the day, music was played through a loudspeaker – often opera – a great favourite of the camp Kommandant. Kapos monitored the factory workers at all times, and if the workers were courteous and hard-working, there would be no trouble. Dangerous items, such as scissors, had to be shown and ticked off at the end of each day.

Ruth had done an excellent job of getting everything Christina had asked for, and a supply of fabric and clothes would be sent to them every week. She'd made sure two women whose families had been in the textile trade, sorted out quality items for them in Theresienstadt. After choosing what they needed, the rest would be bundled up and auctioned off elsewhere.

Christina still had no idea what she was going to do with the clothes the seamstresses made at Sered, so she gave them a folio of drawings and several fashion magazines and asked them to run up a few designs. Two of the women were given the task of unravelling knitwear and knitting them into something more fashionable. The whole situation was appalling to her, but she told herself that she was saving eight good people. The women assured her it was luxury compared to what they'd been through. In adversity, their hard times had given them a sense of humour to survive and they nicknamed the workshop, *Le Bon Marché* after the famous Parisian department store. It didn't make her feel any better, though.

It was a quick drive from Vienna to Sered and on her last visit before Christmas, she took them extra food and a couple of gifts. Due to several roadblocks and heavy snow, the last drive took longer, but they made it in time for afternoon tea – unheard of in labour camps – but which Christina managed to get away with by bribing the Kommandant with a cake from Sacher's.

The women were delighted to see her. They had been busy producing an array of beautiful clothes – simple and elegant. Valeska, the Slovak girl, and Jana from Prague, added fine embroidery, and Madlenka and Miriam unravelled old-fashioned woollen jumpers to knit something more fashionable. Beck placed the items in the car and joined them for cake and a drink of tea. Always wanting to make himself useful, he asked if there was anything he could do for them. Madlenka said her bed had collapsed, and he fixed it. Next was the stove which kept belching out smoke. He fixed that too. They were in desperate need of more fuel too, and Christina made a note to ask the Kommandant.

When she asked if they were treated well, they replied yes, but they had to be careful using the toilets, especially at night, as certain guards loitered around waiting to take advantage of them. As a consequence, they went in twos. After they'd eaten, Christina gave them a gift of food – sausages, rye bread, jam, eggs, tinned food. There was also toothpaste, and soap. When she handed them each their small gift, consisting of a handkerchief, a small bottle of Eau-de-Cologne, a hairbrush and comb, Madlenka burst out crying. Such a small act of kindness meant so much to them.

Before leaving the camp, Christina reported the women's excellent work to the camp Kommandant as she was required to do. When she asked how many workers were in the other workshops, he replied up to one hundred.

'We have workshops for everything from leather manufacturers to electricians, carpenters, watchmakers. Even feather dusters are made here.' It was clear he was proud of his work and seemed to have conveniently forgotten it was slave labour.

'Then I must double my workers,' she replied.

'What am I going to do with all these clothes?' Christina asked Beck as they drove back to Vienna. 'The idea of adding them to my collection appals me. I will have to think of something.'

❧

Dieter informed Christina that, unfortunately, he wouldn't be able to join her at Schloss Steinbrunnhof as he had to go to Berlin. Her happiness was short-lived when he said he'd be back in time for the Silvesterball.

'This time I will have the pleasure of accompanying you myself, rather than Tibor,' he told her. 'I have to admit to feeling a pang of jealousy at seeing you dance with him.'

Secretly Christina would have preferred Tibor accompanied her. There was something attractive, yet unfathomably frightening, about the mysterious Tibor, something she couldn't quite put her finger on. He was often present when she saw Dieter, hovering in the background, watching her. After his remark in the salon, she was sure he found her attractive and was a little envious of Dieter, yet at the same time, she wondered if he was waiting for her to put a step out of line.

The winter was particularly cold that year. Even the pond on the estate froze over, bringing back childhood memories of the times she and Karin had enjoyed skating on it. Heavy snowfalls made driving hazardous and, for almost a week, Steinbrunnhof and the surrounding countryside remained isolated from the outside world, blanketed in snow as far as the eye could see. Even the snow-laden branches of the birch trees lining the allée bent so low it seemed they would break under the weight. In the drawing room, the log fire was constantly replenished, thanks to the tireless work of Albrecht who'd chopped wood throughout the year. Once the place was full of life, now it was occupied, yet devoid of happiness, devoid of soul; a museum of memories.

There was only the four of them, Christina and her mother, and Albrecht and Hildegard. Gitta and Irma had returned to Vienna a week earlier. It was Hildegard who cooked and looked after the schloss, but she was getting old and suffered from arthritis. Julia Lehmann spent her time embroidering or reading, retiring early to bed. Alone in the evenings, Christina read by the fireside or listened to music, trying to find peace within herself.

Before Dieter left for Berlin, he called to give her a Christmas present – another piece of jewellery. This time it was a diamond necklace. With it was a second photograph of Max. It was taken in Mauthausen itself and he was photographed working in the carpentry area alongside other inmates. He looked thinner than before, but there were no signs of bruising – at least not on his face. She thanked Dieter, pleased that he was still keeping his end of the bargain.

It was around this time that Christina started to feel ill. Her body ached and she couldn't keep her food down. She would visit the doctor as soon as she returned to Vienna. Perhaps he could prescribe something. Julia Lehmann gave a heavy sigh. 'The doctor won't tell you anything you don't already know, my dear. You're pregnant.'

The words cut like a knife, but her mother was right. She had suspected she might be pregnant; she'd already missed a period.

'If I am, I certainly can't keep it. The idea of carrying Dieter's child fills me with horror.'

'Think carefully. You are not young any more. If you terminate the pregnancy, you may never have a child again. With Karin gone, who would inherit all this?' Julia waved her arm around the room.

Christina didn't care. She couldn't face the thought of being tied to a man she despised because of his child.

CHAPTER 35

BECAUSE OF THE heavy snow, Christina couldn't get back to Vienna until the day of the Silvesterball, which meant she would have to visit the doctor the day after. She tried to put it to the back of her mind as she dressed for the ball. What would she wear? It had to be something that Max would have liked to see her in. This time she chose a pale rose chiffon dress with a bodice of delicate beading and embroidery. Dieter was enchanted. He took her hand and led her onto the dance floor, pulling her close to him as they swirled to the *Blue Danube*.

'You are the most beautiful woman in the room,' he said. 'I am the envy of everyone here.'

The dancing was starting to make her dizzy. It was not a good idea to come. She should have cancelled it.

'Dieter, do you mind if we sit this one out? I don't feel well.'

He took her outside the ballroom into the hall. She sat down and started to fan herself.

'Your face is flushed. I hope you haven't caught a cold.' He seemed genuinely concerned. 'Let me get you a drink.'

Everything suddenly appeared blurred and when he handed her the glass, she dropped it.

'Christina!'

His voice sounded as if he was in a tunnel. 'I'm sorry...' At that point, she fainted.

When she came round, she found herself in Dieter's bed in his apartment in the Ringstrasse, surrounded by a nurse in a white outfit, a doctor she didn't recognise, and Sigmund Klein. The nurse was preparing an injection.

'What happened?' Christina asked, weakly. 'How did I get here?'

The doctor came over to check her pulse while Sigmund went to fetch Dieter. 'You'll be fine,' he said. 'Nothing to worry about, but for now you must rest.'

Panic started to set in and she tried to get up. 'I have to go home.'

The nurse held her down firmly and administered the injection. 'Shhh – no need to panic.'

Dieter came into the room, followed by Sigmund. She tried to speak but the words wouldn't come out. Dieter sat on the side of the bed, brought her limp hand to his mouth and kissed it gently.

'My darling, you gave us a scare, but you're fine. In fact this is cause for celebration. You're going to have a baby.' His eyes shone with happiness. 'But you are tired and need rest, that's all.'

Sigmund and the doctor congratulated them. Christina felt trapped. How could she terminate the pregnancy now?

'We're going to take you to Am Steinhof to rest for a few days,' Sigmund said. 'You'll get the best care there.'

Whatever she had been sedated with worked fast. She drifted in and out of consciousness for a few minutes, and then fell asleep. It was almost evening the following day when she recovered enough to get up. The nurse was still with her, sitting in a chair and watching her like a hawk.

'Get me my clothes, please,' Christina ordered.

The nurse ignored her plea and instead fetched Dieter.

'I cannot stay here,' she said. 'I have work to do, dresses on order – not to mention the work in Sered.'

'That's impossible. If you don't rest, you will lose the baby. I cannot allow it.'

'You cannot stop me!' Christina was so angry and frustrated, she started to beat his chest with her clenched fists. The nurse moved to take her but Dieter told her he would take care of it. 'Get my mother,' she screamed.

At that moment, Julia Lehmann entered the room. Her face showed little emotion.

'Mama, help me!'

'Dieter called me this morning and gave me the news. He asked that I come back to Vienna and keep an eye on you.' Christina flopped back on the bed. Her mother too had been dragged into this sordid nightmare.

'Will you leave us for a minute,' Julia Lehmann said to Dieter. 'I need to speak with my daughter alone.'

After Dieter had left the room with the nurse, Christina burst into tears. 'You know I can't keep it, Mama,' she said in a whisper.

Julia stroked her daughter's wet cheeks. 'You have to, my darling; it's too late for that sort of talk now. If you lose it, he will blame you. Accept it. What will be, will be.'

Christina wiped her tears. 'I cannot go to Am Steinhof; it holds too many bad memories. I need to work.'

'You must rest for your own good. I've already spoken with Hella. I will go to the salon and help out. Dieter has promised an Ausweis for Hella to go to Slovakia to pick up the clothes from the workshop, so you don't have to worry. She can go with Beck. He even said Tibor could take her.'

'You seem to have it all sorted, don't you – all of you.'

Julia Lehmann didn't reply.

'All right, I'll do as everyone asks. The sooner I get stronger, the quicker I can get my life back together again.'

Christina was taken to Am Steinhof that evening and given a well-appointed room of her own, overlooking the gardens and the church.

'If there's anything you want, Christina, ring the bell,' Sigmund said. 'There's always someone on call.'

'How long do you intend to keep me here?' she asked, irritably.

'That depends on you. When you make a full recovery, you can go home.'

Christina vowed to herself to be out of the place within a week. To the outside world, it was a modern facility, the finest sanatorium in

Vienna, but after what happened to baby Karl and Karin, she didn't feel safe there. Twice a day she was given pills, but when she was alone she flushed them down the toilet. The afternoons were spent sitting by the window, looking through magazines which her mother brought her or strolling through the grounds. One day she noticed a group of people being led to a large grey bus parked behind a cluster of bushes. She'd seen this same bus before on two other occasions and wondered why it never pulled up outside the main entrance. This time she saw Sigmund and several other doctors accompanying the people.

As she watched the scene unfold, she decided she was well enough to leave. She'd been there five days already. She went to his office to wait for him to return. Thankfully, there was no one in the corridor to order her back to her room. Finding the door unlocked, she entered, seated herself by his desk, and waited. After ten minutes, he still hadn't returned. She went over to the window and looked in the direction of the grey bus, but it was impossible to see it from the office. She turned to sit down again and noticed the same folder marked *Aktion T4* that she'd seen on her first visit. *Aktion T4* – what on earth did that mean? Curiosity got the better of her and she took a peek. What she saw sent shock waves through her body. Surely this couldn't be right! Yet the more she looked through the papers, the more she realised what was taking place around her. *Aktion T4* was a euthanasia program being implemented at Am Steinhof.

She picked up the first sheet and read it with horror. *"Reich Leader Bouhler and Dr. Brandt are entrusted with the responsibility of extending the authority of physicians, to be designated by name, so that patients who, after a most critical diagnosis, on the basis of human judgment, are considered incurable, can be granted mercy death"* It was signed A. Hitler, and dated September, 1939.

Other words jumped out at her – eugenics, racial hygiene, and forced sterilization. There were copies of death certificates and a list of the ways to bring about death naturally, like open windows and gradual starvation. She thought of baby Karl. Sigmund had issued a death certificate stating the cause of death was pneumonia. *Was he left by an open window to die? How would they ever know?* Karin had not been allowed to take Karl's body home to give him a proper burial. And Karin – did they kill her too? *Was she given a lethal injection?* Only the medical staff would know.

Along with the file, was a ledger listing the names of patients sent away to Hartheim Castle near Linz. There were several thousand names. It made for chilling reading. She looked at the Eugenics poster on the wall and wondered why she'd never questioned it before. She clutched her chest, trying to breathe. It was incomprehensible, inhumane, but there it was, in black and white – the Reich Euthanasia program – and the man in charge – Dr Sigmund Klein. At that moment, she turned to look out of the window and saw him walking along the path toward the entrance. She closed the file quickly, making sure it looked untouched, and fled the room.

Outside, a nurse was approaching. 'What are you doing here? You have no right to be in that room.'

Terrified, Christina hurried away with the nurse calling after her. She had to get away as soon as possible. She ran to her room, grabbed her coat and bag, and fled the premises by a side-exit. In the street, she hailed a taxi and gave the driver the address of the rectory in Gersthof. Father Menzel was just leaving the church when the taxi drove up.

'What's happened?' He invited her into the rectory. 'You've lost weight, Christina. I advised you to take it easy.'

'Father, I'm pregnant.' She had never meant to blurt it out in such a manner. 'About six weeks. I was suffering from sickness and couldn't keep my food down. As a consequence I passed out at the Silvesterball. Dieter sent me to rest at Am Steinhof under the care of his brother.'

At the mention of Am Steinhof he looked concerned. 'I wish I'd known; I would have warned you against the place. It has a bad reputation.'

'That's exactly why I'm here.'

She went on to tell him about what happened to Karl and Karin, and about the file marked *Aktion T4*.

Father Menzel told her that all the people sent to Hartheim, were gassed on arrival. 'There was a huge outcry about it,' he added, 'especially in Berlin, and the program was supposed to have stopped. I'm surprised you didn't know. The thing is, what you saw is vital for us. We need to let the Allies know about this. I always suspected it was still going on. One day, when this war ends and the Allies are victorious, they will have destroyed the evidence. Everyone concerned will deny it. But you, Christina, *you* saw the file. *You* can testify.' He paused, allowing her time to come to terms with the enormity of the euthanasia program which she still found hard to believe. 'I don't have to tell you that you must not mention this to anyone, especially not Dieter or his brother.'

He saw her put her hand on her belly. 'The child – can you cope?' he asked. His voice took on a fatherly, compassionate tone.

'I intended to abort it. I was going to see the doctor the day after the Ball, but because I fainted, Dieter called his own doctor. Now he knows, and that makes it impossible for me.'

Father Menzel looked at her sadly. 'A child does not always grow up to be like his father, you know.'

'The idea of bearing his child sickens me. I hate him.'

'Hate is a strong word. He is more to be pitied. Anyway, I don't think of you as someone who hates. It's not in your nature.'

'I wish I had your faith, Father,' she replied.

He smiled. 'It's there – you just don't recognize it at the moment.'

When Christina returned to Mariahilferstrasse, the black Mercedes was already there. Tibor was standing outside. 'He's inside,' he said. 'You had everyone worried.'

She pushed past him. Hella was in the salon answering Dieter's questions. 'There you are,' Dieter said, relieved to see her. 'What on earth happened that you should walk out of the building without saying a word?'

'I had to leave. I'm fine. Don't keep treating me like a sick child. I'm pregnant, not ill.' There was a fire in her voice. She intended to take back her life, whether he liked it or not. Hella's eyes widened at the mention of a pregnancy. She picked up a mound of cloth and told them if they needed her she would be in the sewing room. 'I appreciate your concern, Dieter, but I can't stay cooped up in a hospital room. I have things to do here. There's a collection to get on with, and seamstresses to oversee.'

Somewhere in this bravado, she feared he and Sigmund might have discovered she had seen the file, but logic told her they had no reason to suspect that. The nurse who saw her didn't even know how long she'd been in the room. Dieter backed down.

'Have it your own way.' He'd already seen the stubborn side of her before and it wasn't what he wanted.

'Come here.' He pulled her to him. 'Move in with me – today, my darling. Let me take care of you,' he stroked her belly, 'and our son.'

Christina burst out laughing. 'A son! How can you be so sure? Besides, I'm needed here. There's too much to do.'

His eyes narrowed. He didn't like being made a fool of. He picked up his gloves and turned to leave, saying he would see her again when she was in a better mood.

'Wait,' she said as he headed towards the door. 'There's something I want to discuss with you. It's about the workshop in Sered. I need to double the seamstresses. Can you help me?'

'So I have my uses after all,' he replied, sarcastically.

She backed down and gave him a sweet smile. She was learning to be as manipulative as him and was determined to stay one step ahead. 'I'm sorry. It's just that there's so much to do. I've decided that I will keep a selection of the finest clothes to show my customers and the rest I'll give to the war widows. I want to do my bit for the Reich and these women must surely be suffering. Tell me where I must take them, and I'll get Beck and Hella to help out. Of course, none of those made in the workshop will bear the name of the salon. That wouldn't be right. I'll think of something else.'

Christina was rather proud of her idea, and Dieter was only too pleased to accommodate her request. Such was his arrogance that her loyalty to the Reich meant he too would be appreciated, both by his superiors and the woman he loved. Little by little he meant to erase Max from her mind.

By spring, the workshop in Sered had doubled. One of the new seamstresses was French. Chloe had worked with Hella in Paris and knew her well. Between them all, they decided to call the new label *"Wiener Modehaus"*– Vienna Fashion House. The clothes were brought back to the salon in Vienna, and after existing clients were given the opportunity to purchase from the new collection, the rest of the clothes were given away to the war widows. By doing this, Christina was able to live with herself for using slave labour. The seamstresses in *"Le Bon Marché"* were grateful to her for everything she did and worked hard for her. Compared to other labourers, they had it good. Even the Kommandant and Kapos treated them well.

CHAPTER 36

IN MARCH THE first American air raid on Vienna targeted the Floridsdorf refinery just north of the city. Thick black clouds of acrid smoke hung in the air when Christina approached the rectory and she was forced to cover her mouth and nose to avoid the choking smell of burnt-out buildings and gasoline fumes.

'The Nazi's are losing the war,' Father Menzel said, 'but it will be a while until they admit it. It will be a fight to the death.'

Christina asked if the air raid had anything to do with information the Resistance had passed on to the Americans.

'If they heed everything we sent them, then we will have done our bit in shortening the war. Let's hope the bombing remains targeted to industrial sites. We must limit the deaths of innocent Austrians.'

Christina told him the reason for her visit was that she was going to Prague again with Dieter. There was to be another important meeting of the Nazi hierarchy. Bombing raids in Germany were causing disruptions to the flow of armaments, and, fearing Hungary's intention to leave the Axis partnership, the Germans had occupied Hungary. Father Menzel wanted her to meet the same woman and pick up another package for them, but as she was now four months pregnant, he was concerned she might think it too dangerous. Thankfully, the sickness had passed and she had regained her strength, so she was happy to be asked.

On the day of the meeting at the Café Imperial, she walked around the shops beforehand, in case anyone was following her. Spotting nothing out of the ordinary, she headed to her rendezvous. Father Menzel cautioned her against being late as the woman would not wait longer than ten minutes; it was too dangerous. She arrived at exactly one minute past the allotted time and was just about to enter when two black cars pulled up. Four men got out and headed to the café. Terrified, she thought the men were there for her, but that appeared not to be the case. Her heart racing, she stood aside to let them pass. Through the glass door, she saw them make their way to the woman with the red hat. While the other customers watched, the woman stood up and calmly allowed them to lead her away. Flanked by the Gestapo, she threw Christina a quick glance before being bundled in the car. Horrified, Christina bit her lip to stop herself from crying out. The scene unfolded as if in slow motion and she felt utterly powerless to help her. Before the cars had even turned the corner, she hurried away, found another café, and ordered a glass of wine. After what had taken place, she hardly felt like drinking, but she knew Dieter would check her whereabouts. She was right. When she returned, he questioned her.

'I went to the shops and then to a café.' She feigned innocence, but her heart was thumping wildly. 'Why do you ask?'

'I believe we've just had a major breakthrough with the Resistance. We've been following several leads for a while. Today a woman was caught and is helping us with our enquiries.'

'What has that got to do with me?' Her reply was sharper than she intended.

'I wondered if you saw it. She was arrested in the Café Imperial. Isn't that where you went last time?'

Christina tried not to look alarmed. 'That's right, but today I went to Café Slavia. It has excellent views of the town.'

Dieter was in no mood for small talk and told her she would have to occupy herself for the next two days. He had important things to discuss with Kaltenbrunner.

'In that case, why did you bring me here?' she asked. 'I've hardly seen you as it is.'

He stormed out of the room. Minutes later, she saw him get in the car with Kaltenbrunner. When he returned, he told her to pack her things. They would be leaving that evening. It was what she wanted, but throughout the return journey, he was cold and detached and Christina worried she might be under suspicion. Worst still, she wondered if the arrest of the Czech woman meant the network was blown. The consequences didn't bear thinking about.

He dropped her off at Mariahilferstrasse, saying he would see her in a few days' time. Her first thoughts were to alert Father Menzel, but she knew that was far too dangerous for both of them. She called Beck and asked him to come round straightaway.

'Can you go to the Rectory and give a message to Father Menzel? It's urgent.' She gave him a coded message. 'If there's anyone hanging around, drive on.'

She said nothing to him about her activities in Prague. She didn't have to. He knew her too well and understood what she was doing.

It was still early in the morning. She made herself a drink and ate a few hard biscuits to settle her stomach. Every now and again she looked outside. At the back of her mind was the niggling worry that the Gestapo would turn up at any moment. Then she spotted Beck returning and ran downstairs into the salon.

'Well, did you...?'

Beck stopped her mid conversation. 'I have bad news. The Gestapo have taken him away for questioning. The place is surrounded. Even the church is being guarded. There are soldiers and police everywhere.'

Christina could barely breathe. She slumped down on the couch, clutching her belly. Maternal instinct made her want to protect her unborn child. Beck cautioned her not to do anything she would regret. She must stay calm. The telephone rang and he answered it for her.

'I see. Thank you.' He put the receiver down and stared at her.

'What is it?' she asked.

'That was the Baroness Elisabeth's butler. She's just been taken in for questioning.'

Christina felt as if the world was closing in around her. The hopelessness she'd tried so hard to fend off was back again. This was the reality of war. There was never any certainty. Beck wanted to fetch her mother, but Christina was adamant she didn't want to worry her any more.

It didn't take long for news to circulate through Vienna about the arrests. Not only were the Baroness and Father Menzel important figures in the community, there were others too, equally important, who were rounded up at the same time – industrialists, engineers, university professors. Because of this, it was several days before Dieter contacted her again. When he did, he asked her to meet him at his apartment on the Ringstrasse.

After everything that had taken place, Christina expected a frosty reception and was surprised when he appeared cheerful, but then, he had a lot to be cheerful about.

'I've neglected you because I've had a lot on my mind,' he said. 'For that, I apologise. I know you've heard about the raids – about the Baroness – and I am just as saddened as you.'

'Dieter, you know her well. She's an international opera singer, what on earth has she got to do with all this? It can't be right.'

'She's your friend, and I understand your concern, but I'm afraid this time the charges against her are watertight. She was part of the Catholic priest's network. They passed on information to the enemy.'

Christina feigned shock. 'I don't believe it. She would never do that.'

'I didn't want to believe it when she was brought in before. Like you, I hoped there'd been a mix-up. Now I regret letting her go.' Seeing she was afraid to look into his eyes, he reached out and forced her to look at him. 'Are you quite sure you knew nothing of this?'

He scrutinized her carefully. It was as if he could read what was in her mind, but she called his bluff. 'Are you mad? I've got enough to think about without all this.'

'That's what I wanted to hear. I just needed to hear you say it.'

'She burst out laughing. 'If it makes you feel any better, I will say it again.'

276

'I believe you. We won't talk about it again.' He paused for a moment. 'Now, tell me, how are you feeling?' He placed his hand on her belly. 'Is he kicking?'

She nodded. 'Yes, it's going to be strong and healthy.'

'A strong, healthy boy for the Reich.' He smiled as he bent over and kissed her belly, at the same time pulling up her skirt to remove her knickers.

'Don't!' she said softly, running her hands through his hair. 'It's not safe.'

'Nonsense.' He wouldn't take no for an answer and she felt powerless to fight him off.

When it was over, he told her he had something for her. She thought it was another piece of jewellery, but was wrong. It was another photograph of Max in the workroom at Mauthausen. He watched her face as she looked at it. She fought back the tears. *How could he make love to me and minutes later, casually show me a photograph of the only man I have ever loved?* He was cruel, manipulative, and dangerous – incapable of real love. Her hatred of him only intensified.

The arrest of important members of the Resistance and the worsening situation in the Reich kept Dieter busy. He spent more time in Berlin, updating Hitler and the Nazi hierarchy on the situation in the Ostmark. They put pressure on him to leave no stone unturned in arresting every suspect of the Resistance, no matter how insignificant. Those arrested suffered hours of interrogation at the Hotel Métropole, but from the little Christina gleaned, they refused to name other members. When she thought of the gentle Father Menzel enduring torture, her heart sank. The only person who did not appear to suffer the same treatment was the Baroness. Dieter personally made sure of that.

With the child growing inside her, he took particular interest in Christina's welfare and showed his devotion by constantly sending her flowers accompanied by little notes – expressions of his love for her. Hella joked that the salon was starting to look like a florist's. Knowing that she now had to maintain the workshop at Sered and could produce couture at "special prices", he also sent more customers to her. There were almost a thousand SS men working at Gestapo Headquarters in Morzinplatz, and as Dieter was a man who gave favours in return for those who served him loyally, he did his best to promote her fashion house. The wives and mistresses of the SS flocked to Mariahilferstrasse so often she barely had time to work on a new collection. Among this new clientele were women who had never before had access to couture. Now, they were making the most of it. Not that she minded. Her heart wasn't in new collections any longer; her focus was on keeping her seamstresses safe.

On the early morning of June 6, Christina, Hella and Beck tuned the radio to the BBC and heard about the Normandy Landings. It was such a momentous moment that Christina opened a bottle of champagne Dieter had given her. After that, events moved so quickly, it was hard to know what to believe. The BBC would broadcast positive news and the Reich propaganda something else. On the evening of June 16, Christina had just returned to Vienna from Sered when there was another air raid. That night, the city suffered the first heavy bombing raid of the war. Hundreds of heavy bombers took off from bases in Italy to attack oil refineries around Vienna and Bratislava. The oil refinery at Floridsdorf, which had been targeted almost three months earlier, was attacked again, along with the nearby Kagran and Lobau oil refineries. The Heinkel firm's *Heinkel-Süd* Schwechat aircraft factory, and the Schwechat oil refinery were also bombed. The Viennese now had to face the horrors other cities had endured.

Ten days later the bombers revisited Floridsdorf, Lobau, and Schwechat. It was during this time Christina went into labour. She and Hella were discussing the latest shipment of clothes when her waters broke. Her mother was the first person to receive a call, and then Dieter. Fearing another air raid, she decided not to go to hospital, but to give birth at home in Hietzing. Dieter sent over the same doctor and nurse who'd attended her after the Silvesterball. On the morning of August1, Christina gave birth to a healthy girl. Throughout the pregnancy, she feared she might reject it, but when it was put in her arms, she felt an overpowering surge of love that reduced her to tears. She named her Karina after Karin. Dieter was in Berlin at the time. For him, the birth of his longed-for child couldn't have come at a worse time. The latest assassination attempt on Hitler had put immense pressure on those in charge in Morzinplatz.

A few weeks later, the bombers arrived again, this time bombing Axis petroleum facilities so badly that, for the first time in ages, Christina felt optimistic that the tide was turning and it wouldn't be long before Germany was forced to surrender. Recalling the information she'd passed on to Father Menzel about the Heinkel plant a while back, she hoped the strategic bombing of the plant had been as a result of the information his network had passed on to the Allies. No doubt he would get to hear of it in prison, and that alone would make him feel his efforts had been worthwhile.

CHAPTER 37

It was several weeks before Christina could return to work, but, with Hella in charge, the salon was in good hands. During her last few visits to Sered, she'd noticed another section of the camp filling up with deportees, and it worried her. The deportations worsened after the Germans took over both Slovakia and Hungary. One of the seamstresses, Jana, had become friendly with a Slovak guard who occasionally smuggled in food for her. Jana, a Slovak herself, was very attractive and the man was besotted with her. It was forbidden for guards and inmates to mix, but the two successfully managed to hide their liaison and meet behind the latrines or when collecting water from the communal tap. During one of these meetings, the man told her the new arrivals were being deported to Poland. He also added that when they'd gone, the rest of the camp would be closed down.

'Your privileged life in the Textile Workshop will not save you,' he said. 'They mean to close all the camps down, including the workshops – orders from Himmler.'

When Jana told the rest of the women, they began to panic. She asked if he could help, to which he replied he would do what he could. He had "friends" on the outside. By this she understood he was connected to the partisans. The women told Christina, but she was hesitant to speak to Dieter or the Kommandant in case the man got into trouble.

While Christina was convalescing after the birth of Karina, she asked Hella to check out what was happening. There was a separate part of the camp where imprisoned soldiers of the Slovak insurrectionist army, partisans, and others accused of supporting earlier uprisings were housed. Interrogations, rape, and torture continued throughout the day and night, and although it was in a separate area, it became so bad the women feared going outside alone. Under Himmler's new orders, deportations were now taking place at a frightening rate. At this time, *Hauptsturmführer* Alois Brunner, another of Dieter's SS men from Austria, and the same man who had been responsible for the deportation from Aspang Railway Station the night Nathan was killed, was placed in charge of the camp. Jana's Slovak friend warned her that, having been in charge of deporting Jews from France and Greece, Brunner had a fearsome reputation and was not to be trusted. On hearing this, Christina realised she had to get the girls out of there as soon as possible. This time she brought the subject up with Dieter, omitting any mention of the Slovak guard.

'The seamstresses mentioned there's a lot of activity at Sered,' she said to him casually one day. 'They hear screams and cannot concentrate. I fear their work will suffer.'

Dieter was holding Karina and looking into her eyes adoringly. 'If they cannot sew, they are no use,' he replied coldly.

It wasn't the answer she was expecting and she was outraged. 'These women are irreplaceable!'

'Come now. Surely you can find others?'

'I've spent months working with them. They understand what I want, and yes, they *are* irreplaceable. Not to mention the fact that the wives of your friends will be most disappointed if the stock dries up.'

Dieter backed down. 'All right, if it makes you feel better, I will put a word in to Alois that these women are not to be included in any further transports.'

Since the bombing and the arrests of members of the Austrian Resistance, there had been a noticeable change in Dieter. He no longer talked about marriage, but, because of the bombing, he did want her to spend more time away from Mariahilferstrasse and Hietzing, and return to Steinbrunnhof – for Karina's sake – as he put it. Even though he wouldn't admit it, she could sense he was preparing for the worst.

That made him even more unpredictable and she was careful not to antagonise him. He stayed for dinner that night and gave her another photograph of Max. It was dated September 7, 1944. She added it to the others at the side of her bed in Mariahilferstrasse. While there was a photograph, there was hope.

At the end of September, Christina received news that the Secret People's Tribunal at Landesgerichtesstrasse had imposed a total of eight death sentences on the "traitors". They were indicted on "preparation for treason" – transmission of information to the Allies about arms and industrial plants in the Reich along with several other charges. They refused to name other resistants. The following month, Father Menzel and other important members of the group were transferred to Mauthausen to await execution. For a second time, the Baroness had been spared; none of the other members had spoken out against her. In the end, the Tribunal thought there simply wasn't enough evidence against her, and being an international figure, decided against execution. However, she was not freed. Instead she was to remain in the Liesl Prison for an unspecified period of time. Dieter wanted to take credit for the Baroness's fate. Whether he did have a hand in it remained unclear.

The bombing was now relentless and although it was mostly confined to industrial sites, the air defences of Vienna set up around the city were inadequate, due to increasing lack of fuel and artillery. All this put pressure on the civilians themselves. What good were ration cards when there was no food to be had? The SS took whatever they could, and if it hadn't been for Dieter and the fact that Steinbrunnhof had agricultural farmland, Christina, too, would have been starving. Even so, she was careful not to flaunt her supply of food, and always shared what she did have with Hella, Beck, and the seamstresses.

It was the women at Sered that worried her the most. They needed to keep up their strength to fight off illnesses like dysentery, which was rife, particularly when the camp was filled with deportees. A few apples, lemons, eggs, bread and jam, went a long way in a place like Sered.

As soon as she was well enough to travel again, Christina paid another visit to Sered with Beck. The women told her they'd heard more rumours that over the next several months, all Jews would be relocated to Theresienstadt and Auschwitz. Whenever she went to Sered, she always paid a visit to Kommandant Brunner to thank him for looking after the women, but this time, she wanted to see if she could get any information from him regarding the deportations.

'Herr Kommandant, I was thinking about expanding the workshop. I simply have too many orders and not enough women. Can you help me out?'

Brunner laughed. 'Fräulein Lehmann, I am afraid that is impossible. Six months ago maybe, but not now.'

'Why is that?' she asked, innocently.

'I would have thought Herr Klein would have told you. All the camps are to be emptied. The Reich must defend itself from the Allies, and these,' he moved his arm through the air towards a crowd of people shivering to attention outside his window; 'they take up too much of our valuable resources. A few will be sent to Germany, the others...' He paused for a moment, '...the others will go to Poland.'

'Then who will do the work? That will leave me in a difficult situation.'

Brunner shrugged. 'I cannot help you. I am just following orders.'

'Of course, but will my women be among those sent to Germany? I would appreciate if you could look after them.' At that point, Christina handed him a small parcel. 'A little gift for Frau Brunner. I hope she likes it.'

Brunner smirked. He would miss this work; it always brought rewards. He was aware her seamstresses produced fine clothes and her gifts always came in useful. 'I will do my best,' he replied. 'But I cannot promise anything.'

Christina would not tell the women what transpired in the Kommandant's office. Instead she pulled Jana aside and asked if her Slovakian friend might be open to doing them a favour.

'What did you have in mind?' Jana asked.

'You said you believe he is in some way connected with the Underground. If we give him enough money, could he get you all forged documents and help you escape?'

Jana's eyes widened. 'You mean you would go that far for us, Fräulein Christina?'

'Of course. Surely you don't think I would desert you?'

❨

By winter the situation in the Reich worsened considerably. Heavy bombing of the refineries meant there was hardly any fuel available for civilian use. Dieter was able to get fuel for Christina in Mariahilferstrasse, but there was none available for Hietzing. The villa was so cold that Julia Lehmann decided to move back to Steinbrunnhof where at least there were logs to burn. She took Karina with her. Dieter tried again to persuade Christina to go with her mother, but she refused.

Jana's Slovakian friend agreed to get forged documents for the women, but it would cost thousands of Reichsmark. Christina didn't care and almost emptied the safe to pay for them. Careful note was made to get documents to suit the women. Not all spoke Slovak, four spoke Czech, and the rest spoke German. In the middle of December, Jana's friend managed to smuggle in the precious documents, which the women hid under the floorboards.

Making the journey to Sered had become harder. There was barely enough gasoline to go round and what little Christina was allowed was not enough to get them far out of Vienna. Even with her connections, it was now impossible to get more. To conserve what little fuel they did have, Beck left the car at Steinbrunnhof and he and Christina made the rest of the journey to Sered by horse and cart. A combination of roadblocks and bleak weather meant the journey took three times as long. They were well wrapped in their heaviest winter clothes, but travelling such a distance was not sustainable. At one point, they passed long lines of people trudging silently along the road guarded by the SS.

Dishevelled and with a look of hopelessness on their faces, they snaked their way through the countryside. All of them wore the Star of David. Shots rang out frequently and bodies lay at the side of the road, some as a result of starvation or exposure to the bitter cold. It was a scene from hell and the first time Christina was confronted with scenes she'd heard so much about. Beck wanted to turn back but Christina wouldn't hear of it.

When they approached Sered, the buildings lay shrouded in an eerie grey mist and the camp was unusually quiet. From the far side of the workhouses, long slivers of black smoke coiled in the air, blocking out the winter sun that struggled to pierce the grey clouds, and the smell of burning paper filled their nostrils.

They showed their passes to the guard at the gate. He looked at them in surprise.

'You're too late. Everyone's gone. There's no one left except the Kommandant and his staff.'

Christina was horrified and demanded to see him. At that moment another guard recognised her and hurried over. The first guard returned to his post leaving them alone with the man who introduced himself as Jana's Slovakian friend.

'I'm afraid what the guard told you is true,' he said in a low voice. 'The camp *has* been cleared.'

'What about the women?' Christina asked.

'Don't worry, Fräulein. I made sure they were put into one of the trucks going to Theresienstadt. The others went straight to waiting cattle trucks at the railway station in Sered. They were the unfortunate ones, but your girls will be fine. The Slovak Underground have been notified to watch out for the truck with the women. There will be an ambush at a point along the route. That's all I can say, but rest assured, they will be in safe hands. The partisans will look after them.'

The man could not stay any longer in case he attracted suspicion. He bid them goodbye.

'Wait!' Christina said. 'All those people we passed on the way here. Where are they from?'

His answer was quick and sharp. 'They are Hungarian Jews.'

Christina and Beck exchanged looks as the guard walked away. 'Let's hope he is a man of his word,' Beck said.

They found Brunner clearing out his office. Secretaries were scurrying about, taking files outside and burning them. He apologised that she'd had a long trip for nothing.

'You promised to look after them.' Despite trying to keep her composure, Christina was so distressed she could barely get the words out. 'You lied to me. I doubt Herr Klein or Herr Kaltenbrunner will look favourably on this.'

Brunner ignored her threats. 'I'm afraid you will have to go to the Labour Exchange office in Vienna and find new seamstresses. There are plenty of workers to be distributed out to employers, but the employers will be responsible for their housing, food, and detention, not the Reich. Herr Eichmann is in charge. I believe you know him.'

'What about the textiles in the workroom? Are there any clothes left?'

'You may go and check for yourself. Take what is yours, Fräulein Lehmann, but make it quick.'

As she left, Brunner called out after her. 'I'm afraid you'll find it a bit of a mess.'

The door to the workshop was wide open. Brunner was right. The place had been ransacked. Bits of fabric covered the floor and there wasn't a sewing machine or a pair of scissors to be found anywhere.

'It must have been the Hlinka Guards,' Beck said. 'The women certainly wouldn't have done this.'

Christina hastily checked the floorboards where the women had hidden their forged papers. Thankfully, they were gone. She stared through the barred windows at the empty workshops and gave a deep sigh. 'Let's pray the Underground does rescue them.'

The ride back to Steinbrunnhof was even worse than before. The roads were so clogged with more Hungarian Jews they could barely pass. Adding to their discomfort, it began to snow. By the time they arrived at the schloss, they were exhausted and soaked to the bone. Julia Lehmann had a roaring fire in the drawing room and they warmed themselves in front of it, eating a bowl of Hildegard's broth and drinking *Glühwein*. Karina was wide awake in her cot. Wood was too scarce to use now and the rest of the rooms were far too cold to use.

Christina picked Karina up and cuddled her. The child looked at her, making little gurgling sounds and kicking her legs playfully. How she hated being away from her. She kissed her and put her back in the cot. The child had given not only her a reason to live, but Julia Lehmann too. She was not sure why, but when she looked at Karina, she saw only love – there was nothing of Dieter in her. Something in her had blocked off the fact that he was her father.

Christina told her mother what had taken place at Sered, and about the guard.

'Maybe when this war has ended, we will find out if they survived,' Julia Lehmann replied. '*If* we survive.'

Her mother already knew about the Hungarian Jews from Albrecht and Hildegard who learned of the exodus to Vienna through the other villagers.

'Mama, this latest situation with Sered, the bombing, and the scarcity of almost everything that in the past we took for granted, has forced me to look at my business. I can no longer carry on. I've done my best but I'm going to have to close it down.'

Julia Lehmann looked at her daughter with sadness. She had lost weight and looked tired. 'How will you manage?' she asked.

'I've put a little money aside; enough to see us through the next six months if I'm careful. I gave thousands of Reichsmark to Jana to give to her Slovakian friends to get new documents.'

'My poor daughter, all those years of hard work.'

'I have to count myself among the lucky ones. We still had clients when others had nothing. It's the last few months working with the women at Sered that really took its toll on me. Saving those women was all that mattered.' She paused to watch the flames dance in the fire as she drank her mulled wine. 'I can't say I'll miss Dieter's Nazi friends' women flocking to the salon to get dresses at bargain prices. If I had my way, I would rather have gone door to door giving everything to the war widows.' She gave a little laugh. 'But I had to make him happy. Without him, the women wouldn't have survived. He may be a bastard, but I owe him that much.'

Karina made happy sounds in her cot and Christina reached out to touch her. Unleashing her emotions, the tears rolled down her cheeks. Julia Lehmann held her in her arms.

Christina looked at the painting of the stag. 'Mama, what is to become of us? I miss Max so much, there are times when I think my heart will break.'

Julia Lehmann stroked her daughter's golden hair. 'I know my darling, but you must be strong – for her.'

That night there were more bombing raids. Even from Schloss Steinbrunnhof, floodlights and tracer bullets could be seen streaking the night sky. In the morning, Beck and Christina prepared to return to Vienna. They had barely enough fuel to make the return journey and prayed they wouldn't get stranded. Julia Lehmann was standing at the window and called her over. In the distance they saw long lines of Hungarian Jews trudging past the gate – like scarecrows in the glistening white snow.

The drive back to Vienna was even worse than the day before. More screams, more bodies, more gunshots. It was never-ending. At several points on the outskirts of the city, those who'd made it were herded into camps surrounded by high fences with barbed wire. The others went straight to the military barracks. During the drive, Christina broke the news to Beck about the salon. He wasn't surprised at all. He was aware of the difficulties, including the lack of fuel.

'That means I won't need your services any longer,' she said. 'You do realise that, don't you?'

He laughed. 'Well as this is a morning for sharing our thoughts, I have something to tell you also. I received notice to report for duty – defence of the homeland, they called it. I have to report tomorrow.'

Christina looked astonished. 'Do you want me to have a word with Dieter – see if he can't ...?'

Beck stopped her. 'No, Fräulein Christina. I expected this day would come. I'm surprised it took them so long. I must do my duty by my fellow Austrians. Thanks to you, my wife and I have been fortunate.' He turned to look at her. 'It's now time to go.'

The news was distressing. Beck was like a father to her. They'd been through a lot together. 'I shall miss you, Kurt,' she said. 'More than you will ever know.'

Beck forced a laugh. 'Now, now, Fräulein Christina, that's enough of the sentimentality, you can drive the car yourself if you have to, and when the war is over, I will be back, you'll see.'

Hella was next to be given the news, and then the seamstresses. Lots of tears were shed that morning, but all thanked her for doing the best she could. She gave everyone a gift of fabric and the choice of any clothes they wanted, plus an envelope of cash. Beck parked the car in the courtyard, saying he would be back again after the war. They wanted desperately to believe him. Hella lived in an apartment a few blocks away with her elderly parents, and they promised to catch up. By evening everyone had gone home and the salon was empty and silent. Christina had never felt so lonely in her life. She sat for a while in contemplation and soon fell asleep. When she awoke, it was pitch black and cold. The electricity had been cut off. She lit an oil lamp and began to pack away the remaining contents of the salon into boxes to be stored in the basement until after the war.

She'd just finished packing three cartons, when the air raid sirens started. Floridsdorf oil refinery was being targeted again. Since the first air raids in June, everyone was now ordered to report to air raid shelters or remain in their basements. There was no time to go to the shelter and she went into the basement. With no heating, it was freezing. She sat through the air raid looking out of the small grated window at street level. The snow was falling, piling up against the window ledge. Beautiful crystals started to form on the glass, creating elaborate stellar dendrites with leafy, fern-like patterns on their branches; such fleeting beauty in a night of death and destruction.

CHAPTER 38

CHRISTINA WAS SURPRISED by Dieter's reaction to the closure of her business. He had always prided himself on his association with her couture house, now he seemed completely disinterested. When she asked him why he hadn't said anything about the closure of Sered, he said he had more important things to think about. He began to lecture her about motherhood. Why wasn't she spending more time looking after their daughter as Aryan women of the Reich were supposed to do? He told her his own mother had given up a promising career as a concert pianist to raise her children.

'Women should sacrifice themselves for their family,' he said.

Christina wanted to tell him she'd sacrificed enough as it was, but held her tongue. He was too temperamental and likely to take his frustrations out on her. She noticed he'd started to take an alarming amount of pills and when she questioned him about it, he said it was to relieve a back pain. For all her dislike of him, she did agree to bring Karina from Steinbrunnhof so that they could spend Christmas and the New Year together at his apartment on the Ringstrasse. Unlike most homes in Vienna, his apartment was warm. Elsewhere in Vienna, people were freezing and starving, but here, every single room was heated, the pantry was stocked with food, and the wine cellar with wine and cognac – the result of belonging to the upper echelons of the Nazi Party.

One evening after she had put Karina to bed, they sat together listening to classical music and Christina brought up the subject of Am Steinhof. She mentioned that she'd heard about the *Aktion T4* program and asked him directly if his brother was involved with it. His reply was evasive, but he did say the program was beneficial for everyone concerned. When she told him it was inhumane, he laughed at her.

'Christina, you must understand that those people who were euthanized were a burden on society – too many mouths to feed when we need to feed those most useful to us. Food spent on keeping such people alive means less food for our soldiers fighting for the Fatherland. It was for the best – a mercy death. No one suffered.'

'Karin and her son died there,' Christina said angrily, her eyes moist with tears at the thought of them. 'Did Sigmund purposely sign their death warrant also?'

'My darling, you've got it all wrong. You're confused. Sigmund wouldn't hurt a fly. He respected your sister.' He took her hand and brought it to his lips. 'Let's change the subject shall we, and enjoy our time together.'

But Christina wouldn't let it go. 'If what you say is correct, then tell me, where does your sister fit into all this? Why didn't Gudrun suffer the same fate as others? After all, she *is* a mentally sick girl – maybe there's a genetic trait in your family too. Maybe Karina will inherit it. Have you thought about that?'

Dieter lost control and struck her hard across the face. 'Enough!'

'When it's your own family you don't want to confront it, do you?'

He jumped up and was about to hit her again, but stopped himself. 'Gudrun is dead. She died soon after Karin was buried.'

Christina stared at him in disbelief. 'I don't believe you. Why did your mother never tell us? She and my mother were always close. Why was there no funeral?' The questions tumbled out.

Dieter started to pace the room. 'My mother couldn't bring herself to tell anyone. Even now, she still imagines Gudrun will return home.'

'Are you telling me *she* died at Am Steinhof too?'

Dieter reached for the cognac bottle, and poured them both a long drink. 'Do you remember she was acting strange at Karin's funeral? Well, Sigmund persuaded my mother to let him take her back to the sanatorium. He said they had a new treatment. She died a few days

292

later. Sigmund said her heart gave out.'

Christina was too stunned to reply. It seemed that this was a common cause of death at Am Steinhof – they all had weak hearts! He gulped down his drink and for the first time, she saw tears in his eyes. Her anger subsided, replaced by pity and loathing.

❦

Sirens wailed day and night. The bombing was now closer to the inner city and a decision was made to evacuate the Lipizzan horses of the Spanish Riding School. Without the salon, Christina had time on her hands and moved between her apartment in Mariahilferstrasse and Steinbrunnhof to spend time with Karina. She rarely saw Dieter at all. Worst of all, he hadn't given her any more photographs of Max and she reluctantly began to accept he was no longer alive. Reports about Mauthausen horrified her. Whenever possible, she listened to the BBC. The Allies were closing in, but the ones they feared the most were the Russians. Reports trickled back of atrocities committed on the civilian population as the Red Army marched westward, striking fear in the hearts of the Viennese. They wanted revenge for what the Wehrmacht had done to their people.

Travelling to and from Steinbrunnhof brought new difficulties. The long lines of Hungarian Jews were now replaced by supporters of the Reich fleeing the Russian onslaught in Slovakia and Hungary. In the chaos, Viennese citizens fleeing the latest assault on the city joined the exodus, without the slightest idea where they were going. Fear spread like a disease. They took with them whatever they could carry – push-carts, wheel-barrows, prams, wheelchairs, all piled high with a curious array of worldly goods – mattresses, crockery, saucepans. One of the carts even carried a grandfather clock. The roads were so clogged they were almost impassable.

That night bombs fell on the city again. Someone said there'd been over seven hundred bombers accompanied by hundreds of fighter planes. The city's defences simply couldn't cope. When Christina came out of her basement cellar the next morning, the city was in flames. The opera house, the Burgtheatre, the Albertina, the Heinrichshof, and the Kunsthistorisches Museum, were just a few of the fine buildings hit. The city reeked of oil, fire, and charred bodies.

Sometime during the morning, Hella arrived at the salon. She was dishevelled, dirty, and in tears. A bomb had fallen near her apartment and the building had collapsed. Luckily, she and her parents were in the basement at the time, but they were now homeless. She asked if they could stay with Christina. Having lost all their belongings, they moved in that day. Two other families moved in with them. There was hardly any food, but at least they were safe.

Except for the wall mirrors and chandeliers, the salon was now empty. Christina put all her belongings in the basement – the elegant couches, the Japanese screen, and the beautiful portrait that Max had painted – even the signed photograph Lina Lindner had given her. All were carefully stored away, waiting for the day when the nightmare ended.

Night after night, the bombs continued to fall, and every morning struggling groups of smoke-blackened people emerged from bombed-out buildings to walk the streets they no longer recognised. The smoke was so bad, it was hard to breathe, and to make matters worse, the water and electricity were cut off for long stretches at a time. Women wailed, children screamed; everyone was tired and disillusioned. Christina found it hard to turn people away, and by the end of the week more people took refuge in her basement.

Someone banged on the door, shouting out her name. It was Beck. He wanted to warn her there was an unexploded bomb further along Mariahilferstrasse and she should remain indoors. At the same time, he gave her the bad news about Father Menzel. He had been executed. His associates condemned with him, had also been executed. Only the Baroness was still in prison. Christina felt numb.

'I can't stop. I have work to do.' Beck said. 'Just make sure you stay safe.'

He headed away towards the unexploded bomb.

Thirty minutes later, there was a loud explosion. The windows in the salon shattered and a cloud of dust filled the rooms. She ran outside in the direction Beck had taken. Smoke and dust stung her eyes and amid the debris of glass and bricks, was a large gaping hole in the middle of the road. Next to a pile of rubble she saw several fire attendants tending to a man. It was Beck. She rushed over, but the men refused to let her see him. Christina felt so light-headed she thought she would faint, but one of the men grabbed her just in time. He asked if she knew him.

Christina nodded. 'A dear friend.'

Tears mingled with the dust and smoke, stinging her eyes so much she could barely see. Dazed and disoriented, she made her way back to the salon to give Hella the bad news. Together they shed tears in each other's arms.

Sometime during the night, they felt a blast so strong they were thrown against each other in the basement. Boxes and containers toppled from shelves, and debris flew through the small window, choking everyone. The building had been hit, but thankfully everyone was unhurt. Within minutes, the fire department arrived and pulled everyone to safety. From the street, Christina could see the extent of the blast. The top floor, where the sewing room had been, had completely vanished, as had her apartment, and the salon was filled with blocks of masonry and wooden beams. All around them lay mountains of rubble.

The firemen were kept busy again that night. It was then that rumours quickly went round that the Hotel Métropole had been badly hit, with many fatalities. Christina felt a lump rise in her throat. *Had Dieter survived?* She had to know.

It was almost dawn when Christina found herself in the Ringstrasse where the opera house was blackened by fire and the remnants of buildings jutted out in distorted angles from the debris. Cluttered, tangled ruins lay everywhere, and people walked by as if hypnotised, many of them in filthy and blood-stained clothing. Here and there deserters hung from ornate lampposts. In the half-light of a new day, it resembled a macabre scene from hell. The gay Vienna of her youth had disappeared – vanished as utterly as if it had never existed.

Outside Dieter's apartment, were mounds of rubble, put there after municipal workers, largely consisting of labourers from the Hungarian deportees, cleared the road night after night. Nearing the entrance, she spotted Tibor in the distance, loading boxes into an army truck next to Dieter's black Mercedes. The hefty door to the apartment was ajar and she strode purposely inside. More boxes lay in the hallway. She called out Dieter's name but no one answered. The place appeared to be deserted.

She ran upstairs and searched each room – the drawing room, the music room, his bedroom – all were empty. Noticeably, the walls, once adorned with great paintings, were now blank spaces. Straightaway she realised what was happening. He was fleeing the city and taking his priceless stolen artefacts with him. She called out his name again but there was still no answer. Then she remembered the locked room. Maybe he was there. She ran along the corridor, and turned down the hallway until she located the room. She tried the handle. The door was unlocked. Cautiously, she pushed it open, not knowing what she would find, and got the shock of her life. It was a small room, filled with boxes of crystal, silver and gold ware, and diamonds and jewellery – rings, bracelets, earrings, tiaras. There was so much that it resembled Aladdin's cave, sparkling in the dim light.

The sight of all these stolen goods shocked and sickened her. She picked up a few exquisite pieces thinking of the plight of the people from whom they'd been stolen. She recalled the beautiful bracelet she'd had made for Mirka, stolen when they killed her, and then given to Lina. She thought of her earrings and all the other gifts Dieter had given people. Her head was bursting. *How could he? How could anyone be a party to this?*

By the side of one tray of jewels was a folder. She opened it and found a series of photographs – Max! Her hand started to tremble as she leafed through them. In all there were fifteen. Accompanying them was a brief letter from the Kommandant at Mauthausen stating that, as requested, here were the following photographs of Prisoner 11218. She clutched them in anger and disbelief. All this time he had been double-crossing her, giving her photographs all taken at the same time, but which he claimed to be recent. Now she had no idea if Max really was alive or dead.

Christina didn't hear the approaching footsteps until it was too late. She swung around to find Dieter standing in the doorway pointing a semi-automatic pistol at her.

'What are you doing here?' His voice was cold and detached and she knew then he was capable of killing her.

'You cold-hearted bastard!' She threw the photographs in his face. 'You disgust me.'

He burst out laughing – a demonic laugh that frightened her. 'It was worth it to see you suffer as I suffered. I offered you everything, but still you could never love me.' His eyes narrowed. 'All you cared about was that Jew!' He kicked at the photographs on the floor with his shoe. 'I hope he suffered as I suffered.'

'You are not even fit to stand in his shadow,' Christina said, scornfully. 'Thousands have suffered because of you and your tyrannical friends.' She waved her hands around the room. 'All this – stolen from people you sent to the gas chambers; you're the most hateful person I know – you deserve to suffer.'

'You shouldn't have come here. You know I can't let you go after what you've seen.'

She moved a step closer to him, as if daring him to shoot her. He steadied the gun on her, aiming at her heart. In that moment a shot rang out. His eyes widened. Christina let out a scream as he buckled to the floor, landing in front of her. The point where the bullet entered his back was clearly visible. She picked up his gun and ran outside, but whoever had shot Dieter had vanished. One by one, she thrust open the doors along the corridor. Minutes later she heard someone running down the stairs and ran to the landing, just in time to catch a glimpse of a man leaving the apartment – Tibor! She rushed after him, but it was too late. There was no sign of Tibor, the truck, or the Mercedes.

It all happened so fast that it was hard to comprehend. Tibor had killed him. Tibor – the man she'd always felt there was something odd about – the man she suspected harboured a secret love for her. Now she would never know for sure. She closed the door and ran back upstairs to Dieter. He lay in a pool of blood; blood that seeped onto the photographs of Max. In a moment of clarity, she searched his pockets and found the key to the room. She dragged his body out into the hallway, went back inside the room and started to pile the stolen goods into empty boxes lying around. When she'd finished, she taped them up, looked for a pen, and scrawled across the largest one "I, Dieter Klein, used my position in the Reich, to steal these goods from the people I sent to die."

After making sure the room was securely locked, she slipped out of the building and hurriedly walked away.

CHAPTER 39

CHRISTINA BARELY REMEMBERED making her way back to Steinbrunnhof. The events of the last week had left her dazed and disconnected. All she remembered was that she managed to get to Himberg on a truck and from there she walked the rest of the way, passing civilians fleeing the Russian forces sweeping towards the city. They all told her she was crazy. She didn't care. Uppermost in her mind was her mother and Karina. She must save Karina, the innocent victim of this horror. After Himberg, the chaotic lines of stragglers became a trickle. Soon, she was alone. It was almost spring, and the trees were about to bloom. Here and there a hare scampered across the deserted fields and the intermittent chorus of birdsong sounded like the finest music in the world. Sorrow seemed to have dulled her emotions, yet amid such beauty, she sat at the side of the road and wept. She had longed for it all to end. Now it was drawing to a close, she feared for the future.

Nearing the schloss, she heard the booming of heavy artillery. Soon the Russians would be here and it would all be over. That night, the four of them – Albrecht and Hildegard, Julia and Christina – shared a hearty stew and several bottles of good Burgenland wine that Albrecht had hidden away. Living on adrenaline for the past few weeks, Christina had not realised how hungry she was.

'When this war ends,' she remarked to Hildegard, 'I am going to see that you get a job as Head Chef at the Hotel Sacher.'

They all laughed. The first laugh in a long time.

'You are lucky to have this,' Hildegard replied. 'The Wehrmacht have stolen all our produce. If we hadn't managed to hide a few things, we'd be starving.'

Over the next few days, the sound of artillery fire grew louder. Mortar shells churned up the countryside and at times it seemed as if the house would fall down, it shook so much. Christina sat in the drawing room with Karina at her side. All her life, her daughter would serve to remind her of a union she desperately wanted to forget, yet she couldn't help loving her so much. Father Menzel would have been proud of her for finding love amid so much hatred.

When the Red Army finally turned up, Christina and Julia went out to greet them. Albrecht had the foresight to remove the swastikas and burn them. If they had expected vengeance, there was none. The commander, a man in his mid-forties who spoke fluent German, introduced himself as Dmitry Andreyev and told them they were taking over the schloss.

Julia Lehmann was gracious. 'If you need anything, my daughter and I will be staying in the lodge with our gamekeeper.'

Andreyev thanked them. That night, what seemed like a small army of Russian soldiers moved into the schloss and set up tents on the estate. Their carousing and drinking could be heard throughout the night.

On April 13 the Russians captured Vienna after a fierce eight-day battle. Three weeks later, Adolf Hitler committed suicide. With the Führer's death, his much vaunted "Thousand-Year Reich," came to an abrupt end. It had lasted less than twelve years. The situation of the city was one of utter devastation. The population was nearing starvation and, with housing partly or completely destroyed and thousands of apartments uninhabitable, thousands of Viennese were left homeless. The Allied Occupation Forces refused to accept the Nazis' territorial expansion and the country was divided into four Allied zones. The inner-city district was administered by all four powers known as the "Inter-allied Zone", and the Lower Austrian communities, which had been merged with Vienna after the Anschluss, came under Soviet control. Schloss Steinbrunnhof was included in this.

With these new boundaries, Christina's life changed again. She now needed a pass and a very good reason to travel to Vienna and as the bureaucracy became too difficult to navigate, she rarely bothered. After the boundaries were established, the Russian commander moved out of the house, leaving behind a few soldiers. Christina was sorry to see him go. He'd treated her with respect and when he heard she was a couturier, had asked her to make a dress for his wife back in Moscow. With nothing else to do, she happily obliged. One evening before he left, over a bottle of Burgenland wine, she told him about Max, Dieter and the stolen jewellery, and the *Aktion T4* program at Am Steinhof. He thanked her and said he'd look into it with his superiors.

A few weeks after he'd gone, a Russian jeep turned into the gate and drove down the allée of birches towards the house. An officer got out and introduced himself to Christina as Lieutenant Shevchenko.

He handed her an envelope. 'Commander Andreyev instructed me to give you this.'

The man waited by the jeep while she opened it. Inside was a photograph of three emaciated men lying on beds in what appeared to be a hospital tent. A young nurse was sitting on one of the beds, tending a patient. She looked straight at the camera and smiled.

There was a letter with the photograph.

Dear Fraulein Lehmann,

It is with joy that I write this letter. This photograph was taken by an American journalist, Stephen Pembroke, at an American Field Hospital near Mauthausen. The man in the picture with the nurse is Prisoner 11218 – Max Hauser. When the camp was liberated, they found him near the quarry. He had been left for dead. He is still weak and unable to walk, but I have been told he will make a full recovery.

Comrade Shevchenko has been instructed to take you to him.

Yours,

Dmitry Andreyev

Commander of the Soviet 46th Army

'Stephen Pembroke!'Christina brought the photograph closer to her eyes, struggling to take it all in. The more she looked, the more she saw beyond the distressingly skeletal figure with the hollow eyes. It really was Max! There was no doubt in her mind. For the first time in years, the dull ache that had seeped into her soul disappeared, replaced by a surge of happiness so great she thought her heart would burst. In that moment life took on a whole new meaning. The war had scarred them all, but in time those scars would fade.

By now Julia Lehmann, Albrecht and Hildegard had gathered in the courtyard.

'Mama,' she called out. 'He's alive. Max is alive – and Stephen Pembroke's with him. What joy!'

Hildegard let out a large gasp, crossed herself and thanked God. Albrecht joyfully threw his hat in air, and Julia shed tears of happiness.

Presently, Lieutenant Shevchenko called out, 'Well, Fräulein, are you coming?'

'Yes,' she cried out. 'Please give me five minutes.'

She ran inside and quickly changed into a fresh set of clothes, picked up Karina from her cot and wrapped her in a shawl.

'Come on, my darling,' she said, tenderly caressing her rosy cheeks. 'There's someone special I want you to meet.'

POSTSCRIPT

THE VIENNESE DRESSMAKER is a fictional story based on real events which took place between 1938 and 1945. In the early 1970's, I worked as a carpet designer in Vienna. The factory, Karl Eybl, was situated in the village of Ebergassing, 30 kilometres outside Vienna. It was there that I first learned of some of the events that took place in Vienna during WWII. In the immediate aftermath of the war, Austria was divided into four occupation zones, jointly occupied by the United States, the Soviet Union, the United Kingdom, and France. The central district of Vienna was collectively administered by the Allied Control Council. Ebergassing was in the Russian sector. Austria was still under Allied occupation until 1955.

Being the only factory in the area, many of the villagers worked there in some capacity or another and it was a close-knit society. Most of the villagers and my fellow designers remembered the war well, especially the assistant Head Designer, who fought at Stalingrad, but it wasn't until I got to know them better that they started to open up to me. I discovered quite a few still held on to the values of the Reich, although to what extent, I was never quite sure, but I did believe there were secret meetings of like-minded friends who once belonged to the Nazi Party, even though it was banned.

Next to the factory, divided by a long avenue of trees, stands Schloss Ebergassing, a former hunting lodge, which at that time, was unoccupied and in a state of disrepair. I was told that immediately after the war, it was occupied by the Russians who burnt many of the books in the library. Schloss Ebergassing is typical of many small hunting lodges which dot the countryside of Austria, in particular, Lower Austria. Schloss Steinbrunnhof is based on Schloss Ebergassing.

A thirty-minute drive away is Schwechat, known for the Vienna International airport and large oil refineries. During the war, heavy armaments factories were located there such as the Heinkel factory, which is why it suffered multiple bombing raids. Further east of Vienna, towards Hungary, is the beautiful wine-growing area of Burgenland. Prior to the Anschluss in 1938, there was a huge groundswell in this region for the unification of Austria into the Reich and as such, anti-Jewish activity was swift and targeted.

The storyline follows the timeline of actual events which took place. This is important as it gives the reader a glimpse into the machinations of Reich laws and their effect on the population as the war intensified. It is a fact that immediately after the confiscation of Jewish goods, they were auctioned off in warehouses and the proceeds used by the Reich for the war effort. Advertisements were placed in newspapers about upcoming auctions on a regular basis.

As the labour camps became more streamlined, slave labour was used throughout the Reich for everything from factory work in munitions factories, tailoring workshops, agricultural work, road building, etc. Indeed, it can be argued that the Reich would never have operated as efficiently as it did without slave labour. The camp at Sered was one of three labour camps in Slovakia run by the notorious Militia – the Hlinka Guard. It was not an extermination camp but consisted of workshops. Sered became a labour camp in the spring and summer of 1942, and the idea came from the Slovakian Jews themselves calling it a "working group" to save the Jews from being deported to forced labour and extermination camps. During the August 1944 Slovak National Uprising, many prisoners fled Sered to participate in the revolt and the Germans immediately took over the camp and placed it under the command of Alois Brunner. Between October 1944 and March 1945, it was used as a transit camp and 13,500 Jews were deported to Theresienstadt and Auschwitz. Sered was liberated by the Red Army on April 1, just days before the Vienna offensive. In 2016, the Slovak National Museum, in conjunction with the Museum of Jewish Culture, set up The Sered Holocaust Museum on the site.

Christina's gradual involvement with the Austrian Resistance was inspired by the Cassia Network – otherwise known as the Maier-Messner group. The network revolved around the Catholic priest, Heinrich Maier who operated from the parish of Gersthof-St. Leopold in Vienna Währing. Together with other members of the group, including Franz Joseph Messner, director of the Semperit Works, and Walter Caldonazzi, they supplied Allen Dulles, head of the US OSS in Switzerland with invaluable information about the V1 and V2 rockets, oil refineries, armaments factories, including the production of the Tiger Tank and Messerschmitt Bf109. Their aim was to provide accurate information for strategic bombing in order to save Austrian towns and innocent civilians. Messner, in his capacity as a director of an international company, often travelled to Switzerland accompanied by the concert pianist, Barbara Issakides, who was also involved in the group. A double agent infiltrated the network on the Budapest-Vienna-Istanbul route. Istanbul was used to transfer money. An agent was arrested in Budapest delivering 100,000 Reichsmark and a radio transmitter; others were arrested in Vienna. Heinrich Maier was arrested on 28 March 1944. A total of eight death sentences were imposed by the People's Tribunal. Barbara Issakides was spared, but imprisoned. Heinrich Maier was beheaded by the Vienna Regional Court in March 1945 and Messner was gassed at Mauthausen in April 1945. Maier was the last victim of Hitler's Reich to be executed in Vienna.

Baroness Elisabeth and Father Menzel are based on Barbara Issakides and Father Maier, as are the scenes set in the café in Prague and Christina's retrieval of information about the Heinkel factory at Schwechat.

The events which took place at the Vienna Central Court, the Liesl Prison, and the Hotel Métropole, became notorious during this period.

The Hotel Métropole was bombed just prior to the Battle for Vienna. The ruins can be seen in the film *The Third Man*. The "Liesl" Prison, at Rossauer Lände, a fifteen-minute walk from the hotel, gained its nickname because of the original Police building on the former Elisabeth-Promenade on the Danube Canal. (Liesl being a shortened name for Elisabeth).

The Kindertransport from Czechoslovakia, Germany, Austria, and Poland, was one of the most important rescue acts to take place in the few months prior to the outbreak of WWII. Between December 1938-August 1939, a total of 2337 children left Vienna for London with a few going to France, Belgium, and the Netherlands. It was administered by welfare groups in the Reich and in London. The task of trying to save children grew harder with each passing month. The sum of £50 had to be paid by each guarantor, and medical checkups were required stating they had no illnesses and diseases and were of sound mind. The slightest anomaly could mean the child was rejected. Suitable photographs were deemed essential: the Refugee Committee wanted four passport-style photographs, banning family and personal photographs. Photographs were essential because potential guarantors often picked a prospective child from their photograph. Having a guarantor meant priority. Some local associations demanded certain types of children. Hampstead Garden Suburb requested orphans and the Manchester hostel expressed a preference for non-orthodox Jewish boys aged between eight and twelve years. All exit visas were obtained from the Central Agency for Jewish Emigration in Vienna run by Adolf Eichmann.

Am Spiegelgrund was a children's clinic in Vienna during World War II, where 789 patients were murdered under the child euthanasia policy in Nazi Germany. Between 1940 and 1945, the clinic operated as part of the psychiatric hospital, Am Steinhof, later known as the Otto Wagner Clinic within the Baumgartner Medical Centre located in Penzing, the 14th district of Vienna. Am Spiegelgrund was divided into a Reform School and a Children's Ward, where sick and disabled adolescents were unwitting subjects of medical experiments and victims of nutritional and psychological abuse. Some died by lethal injection and gas poisoning, others by disease, starvation, exposure to the elements, and "accidents" relating to their conditions. The brains of up to 800 victims were preserved in jars and housed in the hospital for decades. The Children's Ward at the Am Steinhof facility was made possible due to the implementation of Aktion T4 which called for the relocation of approximately 3,200 patients to the Hartheim Euthanasia Centre, near Linz, where they were gassed.

Many of the characters mentioned in the book all played an important role in shaping the Third Reich, and in particular that of Austria: Heinrich Himmler, Reinhard Heydrich, Ernst Kaltenbrunner, Adolf Eichmann, Odilo Globočnik, Franz Josef Huber, chief of the *Sicherheitspolizei* and Gestapo for Vienna, and Alois Brunner, known as "Eichmann's right hand" who later organized deportations of Jews from Berlin, France, Slovakia and Greece to ghettos and camps in eastern Europe. Where they appear in story, I have used them only to shape the narrative.

Lastly, the creation of Christina Lehmann and her Couture House in Mariahilferstrasse, came about because of my background as a textile designer and love of fashion. After 1900, Mariahilferstrasse was the most well-known shopping street of Vienna with large department stores and exclusive fashion houses. Emilie Flöge, muse of Gustav Klimt, opened a boutique there with her two sisters, aptly named Schwestern Flöge (Flöge Sisters). While Schwestern Flöge thrived for 34 years, the Nazi invasion in 1938 caused much of the store's clientele to flee and the shop was forced to close. Emilie continued to work from her home, but the business was never the same.

The idea of Christina setting up the textile workshop at Sered as an extension of her couture house, evolved after I became aware of the many and varied workshops set up throughout the Reich to utilize slave labour. In the 1930's, fashion houses in all the major European cities in Europe employed hundreds of highly skilled seamstresses

– Paris, Berlin, Vienna, Prague, Bratislava, Budapest, and Warsaw. These women were not only skilled, but aware of international trends through a plethora of style magazines. Their wealthy clientele demanded the best. From the moment the war began, the situation changed; women needed ration cards to purchase clothes or fabric and, in no time at all, fabrics and notions were hard to come by. Most of the elite Nazi women valued clothing and adored couture and it wasn't long before these women used their privileged positions to obtain plundered goods.

With several thousand skilled Jewish seamstresses deported to labour and extermination camps, tailoring and clothing manufacturing were among the first workshops to be set up. When the plundering of Jewish goods occurred, most of these women felt no compunction at wearing stolen goods and as time went on, those goods were altered, ripped apart, and reworked into stunning couture clothes that many could only aspire to before the war. Wherever there were vast numbers of women passing through the gates – Ravensbrook, Theresienstadt, and Auschwitz – their sewing skills were quickly put to work. The Upper Tailoring Workshop at Auschwitz was one of them. It was run by Hedwig Höss, wife of the Kommandant of Auschwitz, Rudolf Höss. With such a treasure house of plundered goods, Hedwig not only took advantage of the workshop herself, but allowed her high-ranking friends to benefit from the skilled slave labour too: Magda Goebbels – a fashionista herself – and Emmy Göring, to name but two. While the conditions were still harsh, in many cases, such work saved the seamstresses' lives, and they considered themselves the fortunate ones in a sea of misery and deprivation.

ALSO BY THE AUTHOR

The Secret of the Grand Hôtel du Lac

Conspiracy of Lies

The Poseidon Network

Code Name Camille

The Blue Dolphin: A WWII Novel

The Embroiderer

The Carpet Weaver of Uşak

Seraphina's Song

WEBSITE:
https://www.kathryngauci.com/

To sign up to my newsletter,
please visit my website and fill out the form.

The Secret of the Grand Hôtel du Lac

Amazon Best Seller in German

and French Literature (Kindle Store)

From USA TODAY Bestselling Author, Kathryn Gauci, comes an unforgettable story of love, hope and betrayal, and of the power of human endurance during history's darkest days.

Inspired by true events, *The Secret of the Grand Hôtel du Lac* is a gripping and emotional portrait of wartime France... a true-page-turner.

"Dripping with suspense on every page" — JJ Toner

"Sometime during the early hours of the morning, he awoke again, this time with a start. He was sure he heard a noise outside. It sounded like a twig snapping. Under normal circumstances it would have meant nothing, but in the silence of the forest every sound was magnified. There it was again. This time it was closer and his instinct told him it wasn't the wolves. He reached for his gun and quietly looked out through the window. The moon was on the wane, wrapped in the soft gauze of snowfall and it wasn't easy to see. Maybe it was a fox, or even a deer. Then he heard it again, right outside the door. He cocked his gun, pressed his body flat against the wall next to the door, and waited. The room was in total darkness and his senses were heightened. After a few minutes, he heard the soft click of the door latch."

February 1944. Preparations for the D-Day invasion are well advanced. When contact with Belvedere, one of the Resistance networks in the Jura region of Eastern France, is lost, Elizabeth Maxwell, is sent back to the region to find the head of the network, her husband Guy Maxwell.

It soon becomes clear that the network has been betrayed. An RAF airdrop of supplies was ambushed by the Gestapo, and many members of the Resistance have been killed.

Surrounded on all sides by the brutal Gestapo and the French Milice, and under constant danger of betrayal, Elizabeth must unmask the traitor in their midst, find her husband, and help him to rebuild Belvedere in time for SOE operations in support of D-Day.

Amazon Reviews

"Enthralling. This is a page-turner." Marina Osipova

"A historical fiction masterpiece." Amazon Top 100 Customer Review

"Incredible book." Turgay Cevikogullari

"Author paints wonderful pictures with her words." Avidreader

"Great storytelling of important historical time." Luv2read

"Complex characters and a compelling storyline." Pamela Allegretto

"An SOE mission to German occupied France fraught with danger" Induna

Conspiracy of Lies

A powerful account of one woman's struggle to balance her duty to her country and a love she knows will ultimately end in tragedy. *Which would you choose?*

1940. The Germans are about to enter Paris, Claire Bouchard flees for England. Two years later she is sent back to work alongside the Resistance.

Working undercover as a teacher in Brittany, Claire accidentally befriends the wife of the German Commandant of Rennes and the blossoming friendship is about to become a dangerous mission.

Knowing thousands of lives depend on her actions, Claire begins a double life as a Gestapo Commandant's mistress in order to retrieve vital information for the Allies, but ghosts from her past make the deception more painful than she could have imagined.

A time of horror, yet amongst so much strength and love Conspiracy of Lies takes us on a journey through occupied France, from the picturesque villages of rural Brittany to the glittering dinner parties of the Nazi elite.

Amazon Reviews

"My heart! What a fabulous story." Amazon Top Customer

"Gripping and Charismatic." B. Gaskell-Denvil

"This novel should be made into a movie." Wendy J. Dunn

"Beware, this story will grip you." Helen Hollick for *A Discovered Diamond*

"Well-written and emotional." Pauline for *A Chill with a Book Readers' Award*

The Poseidon Network

A mesmerising, emotional espionage thriller that no fan of WWII fiction will want to miss.

"One never knows where fate will take us. Cairo taught me that. Expect the unexpected. Little did I realise when I left London that I would walk out of one nightmare into another."

1943. SOE agent Larry Hadley leaves Cairo for German and Italian occupied Greece. His mission is to liaise with the Poseidon network under the leadership of the White Rose.

It's not long before he finds himself involved with a beautiful and intriguing woman whose past is shrouded in mystery. In a country where hardship, destruction and political instability threaten to split the Resistance, and terror and moral ambiguity live side by side, Larry's instincts tell him something is wrong.

After the devastating massacre in a small mountain village by the Wehrmacht, combined with new intelligence concerning the escape networks, he is forced to confront the likelihood of a traitor in their midst. But who is it?

Time is running out and he must act before the network is blown. The stakes are high.

From the shadowy souks and cocktail parties of Cairo's elite to the mountains of Greece, Athens, the Aegean Islands, and Turkey, The Poseidon Network, is an unforgettable cat-and-mouse portrait of wartime that you will not want to put down.

The Embroiderer

A richly woven saga set against the mosques and minarets of Asia Minor and the ruins of ancient Athens. Extravagant, inventive, emotionally sweeping, The Embroiderer is a tale that travellers and those who seek culture and oriental history will love

1822: During one of the bloodiest massacres of The Greek War of Independence, a child is born to a woman of legendary beauty in the Byzantine monastery of Nea Moni on the Greek island of Chios. The subsequent decades of bitter struggle between Greeks and Turks simmer to a head when the Greek army invades Turkey in 1919. During this time, Dimitra Lamartine arrives in Smyrna and gains fame and fortune as an embroiderer to the elite of Ottoman society. However it is her grand-daughter Sophia, who takes the business to great heights only to see their world come crashing down with the outbreak of The Balkan Wars, 1912-13. In 1922, Sophia begins a new life in Athens but when the Germans invade Greece during WWII, the memory of a dire prophecy once told to her grandmother about a girl with flaming red hair begins to haunt her with devastating consequences.

1972: Eleni Stephenson is called to the bedside of her dying aunt in Athens. In a story that rips her world apart, Eleni discovers the chilling truth behind her family's dark past plunging her into the shadowy world of political intrigue, secret societies and espionage where families and friends are torn apart and where a belief in superstition simmers just below the surface.

The Embroiderer is not only a vivid, cinematic tale of romance, glamour, and political turmoil, it is also a gripping saga of love and loss, hope and despair, and of the extraordinary courage of women in the face of adversity.

Amazon Reviews

"The Embroiderer is a beautifully embroidered book." Jel Cel

"Stunning." Abzorba the Greek

"Remarkable... even through the tears." Marva

"A lyrical, enthralling journey in Greek history." Effrosyne Moschoudi

"A great book and addictive page-turner." Lena

"The needle and the pen create a masterpiece." Alan Hamilton

"The Embroiderer reveals the futility of way and the resilience of the human spirit." Pamporos

"A towering achievement" Marjory McGinn

The Blue Dolphin: A WWII Novel

From Amazon Bestselling author of *The Secret of the Grand Hôtel du Lac*, Kathryn Gauci, comes a powerful and unforgettable portrayal one woman's struggle to balance a love she knows will ultimately end in tragedy, and of the hardships of war combined with the darker forces of village life. A real page-turner.

'I saw him everywhere: in the brightest star, in the birds that came to my window — he was there. After a love like that, you can endure anything life throws at you.'

Set on a Greek island during the German Occupation of Greece, *The Blue Dolphin* reads like a Greek tragedy. Rich with loyalties and betrayals, it is a harrowing, yet ultimately uplifting story of endurance and love.

1944 Greece: After Nefeli loses her husband during the Italian invasion of Greece in 1940, she ekes out a meager living from her Blue Dolphin taverna with the help of her eight-year-old-daughter, Georgia, their small garden, and Agamemnon the mule.

Four of Nefeli's close friends, who belong to the Greek Resistance, ask her to hide a cache of weapons, placing her in mortal danger from the enemy. When the Resistance blows up a German naval vessel filled with troops, three of them are killed, and the Germans start to make regular visits to the island.

With the loss of her friends, Nefeli's dire circumstances force her to accept a marriage proposal arranged by the village-matchmakers, but what happens next throws everyone on the island into turmoil and changes the course of Nefeli's and Georgia's lives forever.

"Kathryn Gauci is a storyteller who possesses a phenomenal ability to make her readers fall in love with her characters."

Extravagant, inventive, and emotionally sweeping, this is a novel that lovers of Nikos Kazantzakis, Louis de Bernieres and Victoria Hislop will not want to miss.

Amazon Reviews

"It doesn't matter in which country or century they take place, all of them are impossible to put down. Five stars for this masterpiece for sure!" Amazon reviewer

"Set on a tiny quiet Greek Island, this incredible and credible WWII drama by Kathryn Gauci has beautiful descriptions of the landscape and lifestyle to feed and calm all the senses." Pamporos

"Kathryn Gauci is a storyteller who possesses a phenomenal ability to make her readers fall in love with her characters, equally real and rounded, whether sympathetic or abominable. In this story, I rooted the most for Nefeli and Martin." Marina Osipova

"The ability to write sympathetically, with impressive details in atmosphere and fact, rising to a crescendo as the story develops is all part of Gauci's style." Suzi Stembridge

The Carpet Weaver of Uşak

A haunting story of a deep friendship between two women, one Greek, one Turk. A friendship that transcends an era of mistrust, and fear, long after the wars have ended.

"Springtime and early summer are always beautiful in Anatolia. Hardy winter crocuses, blooming in their thousands, are followed by blue muscari which adorn the meadows like glorious sapphires on a silk carpet."
Aspasia and Saniye are friends from childhood. They share their secrets and joy, helping each other in times of trouble.

When WWI breaks, the news travels to the village, but the locals have no idea how it will affect their lives.

When the war ends the Greeks come to the village, causing havoc, burning houses and shooting Turks. The residents regard each other with suspicion. Their world has turned upside down, but some of the old friendships survive, despite the odds.

But the Greeks are finally defeated, and the situation changes once more, forcing the Greeks to leave the country. Yet, the friendship between the villagers still continues.

Many years later, in Athens, Christophorus tells his grandson, and his daughter, Elpida, the missing parts of the story, and what he had to leave behind in Asia Minor.

A story of love, friendship, and loss; a tragedy that affects the lives of many on both sides of the Aegean, and their struggle to survive under new circumstances, as casualties of a war beyond their control.

If you enjoyed Louis de Berniers' *Birds Without Wings* then you will love Kathryn Gauci's *The Carpet Weaver of Usak*. "As she weaves her poignant story and characters with the expert hands of a carpet weaver."

Amazon Reviews

"An unforgettable atmospheric read." Amazon Top Reviewer

"So beautifully written." Elizabeth Moore

"Broken homes, broken lives, and lasting friendships." Sebnem Sanders

"Hooked from page one!" Francis Broun

Seraphina's Song

"If I knew then, dear reader, what I know now, I should have turned on my heels and left. But I stood transfixed on the beautiful image of Seraphina. In that moment my fate was sealed."

Dionysos Mavroulis is a man without a future: a man who embraces destiny and risks everything for love.

A refugee from Asia Minor, he escapes Smyrna in 1922 disguised as an old woman. Alienated and plagued by feelings of remorse, he spirals into poverty and seeks solace in the hashish dens around Piraeus.

Hitting rock bottom, he meets Aleko, an accomplished bouzouki player. Recognising in the impoverished refugee a rare musical talent, Aleko offers to teach him the bouzouki.

Dionysos' hope for the future is further fuelled when he meets Seraphina — the singer with the voice of a nightingale — at Papazoglou's Taverna. From the moment he lays eyes on her, his fate is sealed.

Set in Piraeus in the 1920's and 30's, Seraphina's Song is a haunting and compelling story of hope and despair, and of a love stronger than death.

A haunting and compelling story of hope and despair, and of a love stronger than death.

Amazon Reviews

"Cine noir meets Greek tragedy, played out with a Depression era realism. Gauci creates in this novel the smoke, songs and music of Papazoglou's tavern so convincingly one can almost hear the strings through the tobacco-fuelled murk. " Helen Hollick *A Discovered Diamond*

"A very beautiful novel, I couldn't put it down." Pauline *A Chill with a Book Award*

"A book like no other." Jo-Anne Himmelman

"Dark and emotionally charged." David Baird

"The Passion That Ignited Greek History." Viviane Chrystal

"Where there is love, there is hope." Janet Ellis

Code Name Camille

Originally part of the USA Today runaway bestseller, The Darkest Hour Anthology: WWII Tales of Resistance. Code Name Camille, now a standalone novella.

1940: Paris under Nazi occupation. A gripping tale of resistance, suspense and love.

When the Germans invade France, twenty-one-year-old Nathalie Fontaine is living a quiet life in rural South-West France. Within months, she heads for Paris and joins the Resistance as a courier helping to organise escape routes. But Paris is fraught with danger. When several escapes are foiled by the Gestapo, the network suspects they are compromised.

Nathalie suspects one person, but after a chance encounter with a stranger who provides her with an opportunity to make a little extra money by working as a model for a couturier known to be sympathetic to the Nazi cause, her suspicions are thrown into doubt.

Using her work in the fashionable rue du Faubourg Saint-Honoré, she uncovers information vital to the network, but at the same time steps into a world of treachery and betrayal which threatens to bring them all undone.

Time is running out and the Gestapo is closing in.

Code Name Camille is a story of courage and resilience that fans of *The Nightingale* **and** *The Alice Network* **will love.**

AUTHOR BIOGRAPHY

Kathryn Gauci is a critically acclaimed international, bestselling, author who produces strong, colourful, characters and riveting storylines. She is the recipient of numerous major international awards for her works of historical fiction.

Kathryn was born in Leicestershire, England, and studied textile design at Loughborough College of Art and later at Kidderminster College of Art and Design where she specialised in carpet design and technology. After graduating, she spent a year in Vienna, Austria, before moving to Greece to work as carpet designer in Athens for six years. There followed another brief period in New Zealand before eventually settling in Melbourne, Australia.

Before turning to writing full-time, Kathryn ran her own textile design studio in Melbourne for over fifteen years, work which she enjoyed tremendously as it allowed her the luxury of travelling worldwide, often taking her off the beaten track and exploring other cultures. *The Embroiderer* is her first novel; a culmination of those wonderful years of design and travel, and especially of those glorious years in her youth living and working in Greece. It has since been followed by more novels, set in both Greece and Turkey. *Seraphina's Song, The Carpet Weaver of Uşak, The Poseidon Network,* and *The Blue Dolphin: A WWII Novel.*

Code Name Camille, written as part of *The Darkest Hour Anthology: WWII Tales of Resistance,* became a *USA TODAY* Bestseller in the first week of publication. *The Secret of the Grand Hôtel du Lac* became an **Amazon Best Seller** in both **German Literature** and **French Literature,** and *The Poseidon Network* received **The Hemingway Award 2021 – 1st Place Best in Category – Chanticleer International Book Awards (CIBA)**

CPSIA information can be obtained
at www.ICGtesting.com
Printed in the USA
LVHW020717191122
733280LV00021B/1325